AiR's FaiRy tALeS

PrEAmBLe

Before we begin reading the tales let me tell you that I believe in joy of kids. Do you?

Now, let us understand the meaning of fairy tales. So what do fairy tales stand for? Fairy tales should stand for what they mean. Just to let you know what they mean, I have put down the meaning below. Read them carefully below

FAIRY - F-forever A-awesome I-innately R-readable Y-yummies
TALES   T-together A-all L-leading E-endless S-smiles

FAIRY - F-facts A-awesomely I-intuitively R-redeem's Y-young
TALES   T-tactically A-allowing L-lessons E-ecstatic S-superbness

FAIRY - F-forests A-are I-infinitely R-releasing Y-years
TALES   T-tackling A-all L-loads E-endlessly S-superlatively

FAIRY - F-fantasies A-are I-innate R-running Y-y'all
TALES   T-tackle A-awfulness L-lucratively E-eyeing S-sadness

FAIRY - F-forever A-all I-in R-rolling Y-years
TALES   T-talk A-and L-laugh E-enabling S-satisfaction

FAIRY - F-fool A-aims I-in R-rogue Y-yucks
TALES   T-true A-and L-lucrative E-exists S-smartly

FAIRY - F-factual A-aura I-is R-realizing Y-yesess
TALES   T-to A-allow L-leadership E-eradicate S-sorrows

FAIRY - F-fairness A-allows I-iconic R-ruling Y-yearly
TALES   T-teaching A-all L-looting E-endless S-sorrow

FAIRY - F-fair A-and I-intelligent R-rules Y-years
TALES   T-to A-awesome L-laughing E-endless S-softness

FAIRY - F-far A-away I-in R-rolling Y-years
TALES T-the A-awfulness L-leaves E-endlessly S-softly

TaLe 1 : ThE uNbReAkAbLe BuBbLeS

There was a beautiful village in a very dense forest where trees were more than 50 metres tall. In that town lived a boy called Breffi who was a very nice and a decent guy. He was born in the same village. He was born to parents who had died when he was too young. He had no siblings. He was always very polite to others and talked very respectfully and nicely with them. But the people of that village were not very nice to him. He was always scolded and talked to at rudely. He never minded that, but sometimes he used to feel hurt and lonely and miss his parents. But he couldn't do anything about it so he carried on with his life as usual with daily scoldings and mocked at behaviour by others.

His usual work was doing hard labour jobs which was tiring.

One day he was going to his work and saw that there was a job opening at a magic potion shop which was more paying than his labour job. So he went to the shop and asked if he could work there. The magical potion shop owner who was a rude lady asked him if he knew anything about making potions? Breffi replied politely "No miss I am just a labourer. I just saw the poster that said you needed a boy as a helper in this shop, so I came". She then told him "Strict rules have to be followed if you want to work here, no messing around with the magical potions as they can be dangerous you know". He politely said ok. She told Breffi that he could start the work next day and " Don't be late!" She said.

Breffi went back home that day a little happy that he got a better job.

The next day he went to the magical potion shop and reached there right on time. But the lady was late. The lady came 15 minutes late but then opened the shop with a key and they started working. The lady was rude and selfish. She first started giving Breffi a work of simply moving the magical potions here and there and measuring them and selling them to the customers. Breffi became good at it.

Now, sometimes the potion lady had to go out of village to other far away villages to give potions. So the potions that used be in the shop used to empty out and thus supply used to finish out and customers never stopped demanding. So she started teaching Breffi how to make potions so that in her absence he could make a few common ones. She taught him what plant or fruit or flower to put to make potions and where to get them from in the forest. Breffi became good at it and started making potions without any help. So when the potion lady was away Breffi used to make potions for the shop.

But Breffi was not very happy on how he was treated. Not only by the people but also by the potion lady who used to never let him sit while working and always made him work uselessly hard without any soft words coming out of her mouth.

So one day he was sitting in his small shanty and was thinking that "I have a good paying job but people are rude and mean to me. All I need is love from them and they keep on hating me", so he thought of a plan and thought of teaching people a lesson.

When he used to work he used to see that iron was a very strong substance and made very powerful potions. The potions made of iron never decayed and also things made of iron were pretty strong and nobody could break it. Secondly he used to observe that rubber potion that was formed of rubber from trees and other materials was very malleable and could be bended in whichever way you want.

So he thought let's make bubbles that don't break and distribute it in the market. So the next day after finishing work he bought iron and rubber potions from the shop and took them home. He set some proportions for the two items and heated them and cooled rapidly 2-3 times until he formed a soap like liquid that when blown through air could form unbreakable bubbles. He made first bubble and tried breaking the first bubble with all his might but did not succeed, then he blew air to form one more bubble. He tried breaking that bubble too but he did not succeed. So he was happy that he made unbreakable bubbles.

So after work he started selling the bubble forming liquid to people who were very impressed to see the bubbles that never break so people started buying in large quantities and what they did not realize was that the bubbles sticked around as they were made of iron and were heavy. Even the wind could not carry them away.

By that time Breffi had left his job and the town and went away into another forest and started living there alone.

Also by that time people had realized that bubbles actually had become a mess as they started suffocating them because more and more bubbles had accumulated and become heavy below blocking sunlight and air. Even plants in the village had started dying and the forest was so dense that the bubbles could not be dragged away. People became scared and didn't know what to do. Even the potion lady could not make a potion to burst the bubbles and thus she gave up too.

People started realizing that they were very rude to Breffi and thought that it was the result of their bad deeds against Breffi. So they thought that if they could say sorry to Breffi they would and never ever be mean and rude to him again.

By this time Breffi was hiding behind trees to see what was happening there. A boy saw Breffi hiding. The boy immediately shouted "Look there is Breffi". Breffi got scared and tried to run but people did not let him go and to his shock and surprise people instead of beating him started saying sorry to him and apologizing for being rude to him. Breffi understood that people there had changed along with him to being better and asked what he could do to help? They asked him if he could get rid of the bubble problem. Since Breffi had made that potion, he only knew how to break the bubbles. So he told everybody that the only way to break bubbles is to put mouth saliva itself on the bubbles that will weaken their outer walls and make them shrink because outer walls of bubbles would then become organic combining with some inner saliva already on inner bubble walls through minute pours in them. But to break them they had to be eaten once a day which will also help people to revive the lost nutrients in their body because of lack of air and sunlight. Secondly what he did was added various flavours of taste to the bubbles through a magic. This made bubbles tastier than they actually were and when people ate the bubbles it seemed as if they were eating ice-creams. Thus they disposed off bubbles happily and merrily while having abundance in flavours and their wonderful fragrance all around.

Later, Breffi apologized too for being too vicious in his thinking and deed.

The bubbles disappeared in one year and people became happy and fit.

Breffi never had to face harsh words again from anybody and every body lived happily ever after.

IMPORTANT: Now to understand that why the initial saliva that was being added to the bubbles while forming them by blowing air was not breaking them because the potion he had given people to blow bubbles with was forming a chemical bond instantaneously with one's mouth's saliva and thus there was no saliva left on bubbles to break them at that instant and moment. Only some saliva on inner walls was left which caused its non breaking properties at that time. All the saliva formed a chemical bond. That is why new saliva had to be added while eating them to break them which took at least 15 minutes to get broken and dissolved.

tALE 2 : tHe ShIp WoOd MoDeL mAkEr

There was once an area in the seas where there were many islands. One of the island was biggest of all islands and had 50 villages in it. Other islands alongside it had one or two villages each.

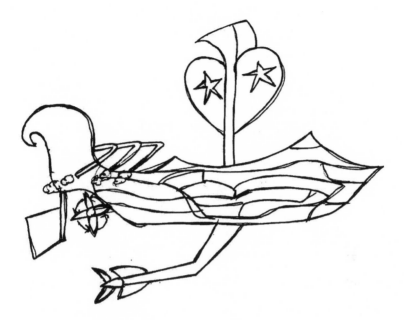

In the biggest island there was one village where lived the ship wood model maker who earned modestly through his work of making wood models of ships.

Ships used to come there from mainland and dock to their island to trade goods. Most of the goods consisted of grocery items.

Since unloading grocery items took time as it was all done manually through hand or wheelbarrow The ship wood model maker used to take advantage of this and used to enter ships with paper and pencil. He used to draw the interior and the exterior of the docked ships to perfection on his paper. It used to take him some time to do that but he had all the time in the world as ships used to be docked there for more than 12 hours usually docking there for whole night. So in the night he used to draw sketches of different ships and in the day he used to work on making their wood models. He used to sleep only for sometime and that too during the day.
His model making work was hard but he used to like doing it.

He used to love kids.

Once he puzzled the kids by showing that ship model was inside a glass bottle whose mouth was too small to fit in the ship. So the kids were dumbstruck! seeing this. He enjoyed seeing the weird and funny faces that kids were making while trying to understand how this happened. After having fun with this he told them secret of it that he did not put model of the ship in the bottle but first made the model ship and then asked a glass blower to make a bottle of glass around the ship. Children then understood the magic trick and felt happy.

He was a lover of kids. He used to receive great praises from the parents that their kids were very fond of him and liked him a lot. He used to be happy hearing that and carried on with his work.

The other reason why kids used to be happy with him was because he used to send kids special treats.

What these treats were is yet to know.

He used to also love the kids of the villages on neighbouring islands. To show this, what he used to do was make ship models having small coal engines in them. Now since there was no driver in the model ships he used to put the measured amount of coal in the coal tank which through gravity fell slowly into the burning chamber causing it to produce steam and run the engine thereby moving the ship model forward. In these models he attached candies, chocolates and some toy presents and sent to the kids of neighbouring islands. The kids knew that during Christmas they got presents from the ship wood model maker so they used to wait on the shores near their houses and used to see the model ships coming. They used to pick them up, take them, play with them and relish them.

The ship wood model maker was the talk of the town.
Wherever he went kids used to surround him and ask him to play with them which most of the times he did and enjoyed a lot.

So, sometimes there used to be storm in the seas but no harm used to happen.

It so happened once that 20 children had gone on a boat in the sea to just enjoy the sea. By that time the storm was building which they were unaware of.

This storm was something that nobody had seen before. Winds were gusting more than 100 miles an hour and no small boat could survive that so it was looking dangerous for the kids that had went on a ride on a small boat in the sea.

The wood ship model maker knew that today things can get out of hand so he started preparing for it. He picked up 50 wooden model ships and filled their in-built steam engines with coal.

Now he was worried that the kids had not returned to the island and it was time for them to be back. Also it was getting dark.

Then parents who were waiting alongside the shore for their kids, saw the boat on the horizon which was about 10 miles from the shore. All were hoping that the kids will make it back on their boat but suddenly in the storm there was a lightning bolt so strong that it hit the boat on which the children were coming back home. The boat suffered a crack. Parents got frightened! They did not know what to do. Some parents wanted to take boats themselves and get to their kids but it was too risky.

Suddenly the wood ship model maker came from behind. He shouted and said "I need help picking up my model ships to bring children back home safely" and people listened to him and helped.

What he did was this time he had overpowered the engines with more but tolerable amounts of coal to speed them up. He put calculated amount of coal in the model ships just enough to reach the kids who had got their boat sinking.

Since the model ships did not have cavity in them so they were just like logs of wood that would not sink even in the storm. Then he attached big orange flags on both sides of y axis of the model ships which were easily visible from distance.

He then started the engines up and put them in sea towards the children's sinking boat direction. 50 ship models that he had got were put in the sea and directed towards the sinking boat direction hoping that at-least 20 would reach their destination and save kids.

Meanwhile the storm was loosing its strength. The rain had stopped but the winds were still very strong. Too dangerous still to go in water.

He then told the people to bring lots of wood from their home. The people did what they were told to do and brought lots of wood from their homes.

He then put a big fire alongside the shore with the woods he got, so that kids could see it. As it was night and it is difficult to navigate at night without a reference point.

So the kids that were on the sinking boat saw orange flags coming near them and when they came more closer they saw that they were model ships sent by the wooden ship model maker. They were rejoiced to see this. The boats were of sufficient length and buoyancy and that they could sit on them and float. Kids were overjoyed to see this and jumped quickly from their sinking lightning struck boat and sat on the model ships. Some model ships were far from their reach but all kids somehow managed to grab one each and sit on them.

But to row 10 miles through hand was difficult so the ship model maker who was smart had attached a water turbine to each of them and had attached a rotating crank arm to them which the kids had to rotate to propel ship forward. The kids found this out as they were meddling with the crank arm and they started turning it to propel their model ships. Then one of them saw the fire that the model maker had lit up and they all cranked the boat and steered it to the fire's direction and in an hour all of them reached the shore safe and sound.

Everybody including the kids thanked the wood ship model maker and became more cautious to go to the sea next time.

TaLe 3 : FaIrY, DoN't Go NeAr ThE fLaMe!

Kids are often warned not to go near the flame. So is the story of this little fairy who was warned not to go near any flame of any sort as it could be harmful. But she was little in age and as other fairies are small in size, so was she about 5 inches in height. But this is what the size of fairies is, which is about 50 times lesser than the size of normal human and with this height the fairies lived by.

As everybody knows fairies are nice creatures but humans are wicked and cunning and not anywhere close to nice as fairies. And this is how the world goes by.

Now this fairy named Starwork who was a girl of course was always attracted towards the flames. She liked going near the flames and admiring their fire. When she used to see a flame she

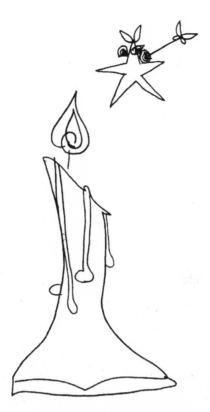

used to go near it and adore it for hours and hours together which sometimes she got scoldings for. But she did not pay heed to the scoldings and used to continue going near flames. She liked the colour and warmth and how the flame flickered and danced and lighted up the whole area around it.

Now there was this guy who used to trap insects by lighting up candles. As bugs are interested in light they used to come near it. He used to trap insects and keep them in a cage made of glass.

What he had was he had a candle light burning inside an enclosed glass chamber and when he used to see that sufficient amount of insects have flocked inside the enclosure, he closed the enclosure's door and the insects got trapped inside. Then he transferred the insects to another glass enclosure and saw them flying inside. The insects used to live for sometime and then die of suffocation inside the enclosure until a new supply of insects were brought in. This guy was evil.

Now so happened this fairy was passing by the trapper's house at night and saw this candle flame which looked very beautiful to her.

She went near to the flame in-spite of many warnings from other fairies who were flying with her and were telling her not to go near the flame. But she didn't listened and went to the flame.

At that time, the boy came and closed the door of enclosure in which the fairy also got trapped.

The trapper was sleepy and thus he slept after closing the door unaware that he had trapped a fairy.

The other fairies saw this and tried with all their might to rescue Starwork but they couldn't. They tried a lot lifting up the heavy iron lever which was locking the door but they couldn't . They thought they'll go to the Fairy-Land and bring some help but it was too far and until they'll come it will be too late. They, including Starwork all wept but nothing could be done at that time. So before sunrise, so that nobody else sees them the other fairies left for Fairy-Land and promised to help Starwork to rescue her

Now in the morning the boy trapper woke up and went near the trapping enclosure where he saw Starwork lying down who he thought was dead as her eyes were closed. He saw that and put his hand inside the enclosure and picked the fairy who suddenly woke up frightened. As fairies have a different tongue the boy couldn't understand what she was saying. Even if the boy knew what she was saying he wouldn't have payed a heed to it as the boy was evil.

The boy thought for a while and then at once decided to sell it to a guy who ran a fairy circus who will give him lots of money for the fairy.

The fairies couldn't escape Fairy-Circus because that was too inside a big cubical glass enclosures and the person who ran it was the wickedest person alive.

The Fairy-Circus was the worst possible thing for fairies. Fairies had heard great evil stories about the circus and that no fairy ever returned from that place and many fairies had died working there and trying to escape. It was like a very cruel prison for them. But so was the fate of Starwork.

When Starwork realized that she was going to Fairy-Circus she became pale of fear and did not know what to do. But she was not gonna give up easily. She said to herself that "I am not afraid of fire flames why should I be afraid of getting trapped in a circus". She also remembered that her friend fairies had promised to help her to escape. So she remained hopeful and strong.

This fairy circus used to be run in a forest near a small village where people used to flock in great numbers to see the fairies perform.

The owner of the Fairy-Circus had a freaky setup in the big glass enclosure. He used to fill a conductor gas and pass electric current through it if any fairy did not perform properly. So on passing electric current not only the fairy that was performing poorly suffered but all the fairies in the chamber suffered as the conductor gas was present everywhere in he aquarium and current goes throughout the conductor gas barely missing any spot or area. So this was hell for fairies.

Starwork was first taught to balance herself on wire with the support of balancing stick but she refused to do that, but continuous electric shocks made her give in so she started to learn balancing on the rope with help of balancing rod. It took her some time but she learnt to do it.

Then she was told to walk on sharp spikes with her bare feet which after lots of refusals and electric shocks she learnt walking barefooted on sharp spikes. She used to bleed first but then her feet skin became used to the sharpness of the spikes and she started doing it in the circus shows.

Thirdly she had to learn trapeze tricks like transferring from one horizontal bar to another while moving high up in the air.

The thing was that wings of the fairies were tied while performing trapeze acts so they couldn't fly to even protect themselves while falling down. It was not only difficult but also life threatening, as there were no nets below the trapeze act. If a fairy fell from trapeze while performing she could break her skull and kill herself. Some fairies had died doing that.

While Starwork was learning these acts she was planning how to escape from the prison circus. She saw that the circus enclosure was always closed except once a day when they were given food by opening the enclosure door. It was not easy to escape during that time too because the circus owner while feeding them kept hands on the switch that produced electric current just in case any fairy tried to escape.

But Starwork was adamant to escape so she devised a plan. She waited for the day when her fairy friends will find her and did not try to escape until then.

One day she saw one of her friend who had promised her to help her escape when she had got trapped in the flame enclosure.

What happened was Starwork had just finished performing in the circus and suddenly she saw her friend flying near the ceiling and waiving at her. Starwork was the happiest fairy at that time. She regained her strength and got hopeful again.

When the Circus owner put the Fairy-Circus glass enclosure in a room and left it alone there and went away Starwork and her friends talked and Starwork asked her fairy friend what took her so long. Her friend told Starwork that they had been looking for her from a very long time but couldn't find her. So they had a fairy spy on the trapper.

One day the fairy who was carefully following and listening to talks of the trapper while hiding heard trapper say to a friend that had sold the fairy whom he trapped by chance, to the Fairy-Circus owner. Then we knew where to find you. Then I flew faster than the other fairies and came here sooner. Starwork was delighted to hear that and told her friend her escape plan.

By that time other fairies who had promised to help Starwork escape had come there too and had heard the plan and agreed upon it. Also the circus fairies heard that and were happy to hear the escape plan.

Next day when the circus owner came there to give food to the fairies so that they don't starve and his circus keeps on generating him wealth he suddenly heard a noise coming from a fairy who was making faces at him. He got worried and thought that she was one of the circus fairy who had escaped. He suddenly got worried and took a net and went after that fairy. In a hurry he forgot to close the circus glass enclosure and left it open. The fairies inside the enclosure saw that and immediately started flying out of the circus enclosure. The circus enclosure owner who was chasing the other fairy heard voices and saw what was going on when he saw the circus fairies escaping he tried closing the enclosure door with the stick that he was holding but he hit the door along with the enclosure so hard with the stick that the enclosure glass shattered and broke the entire Fairy-Circus along with it which was the end of it.

Circus fairies thanked Starwork and her their friends and went back to their homes in Fairy-Land. There they were rejoiced to return back to their family and celebrated re-union.

TaLe 4 : ThE wItCh tHaT lOsT hEr FlYiNg BrOoMsTiCk

Do witches lose their flying broom stick on which they fly? Is it possible for that to happen?

I think so.

It so happened that in a small town named Witch-town lots of witches and humans lived together but witches had separate places to stay in.

This witch whose name was Kara lived with her fellow witches in a big building called Witch-Palace.

It so happened that the lady who used to come to clean Witch-Palace did not do a very good job. The cleaning lady used to clean very untidily and the witches living in the Witch-Palace didn't like that.

So one day all the witches had a meeting and decided to lodge a complaint against the cleaning lady. They gave this job to Kara.

So Kara went to the owner of janitorial services under whom the cleaning lady was working and lodged a written complaint against the cleaning lady. She also got mad at the owner.

The owner after facing all that, fired the cleaning lady whose name was Betty.

Betty felt very bad about that and thought of teaching Kara and witches a lesson.

What she did was the next day she sneaked into the Witch-Palace and went to Kara's room and hid at a place where nobody could suspect and waited for sometime. When she saw that Kara had returned after her daily flying activity and had gone to bed to sleep after keeping flying broomstick on the side wall, she immediately came out from her hiding place and took her flying broomstick and ran away. Nobody came to know about this until the next day when Kara screamed after realizing that her broomstick was missing.

It was not that the broomstick could be used by others to fly around . But it could be used to do other magical things.

Now it takes a year and a half to make the broomstick and after that witch's get used to it and can't live without it as they do all their magic and tricks with it.

So the Kara along with other witches of Witch-Palace was upset. The witches didn't realize that Betty could have done it. They went in all directions and tried looking for the broomstick while Kara waited in her room at the Witch-Palace.

The witches went far and wide and searched all around but could not find it. Actually Betty had stolen that broom and thrown it in the garbage burning site as she did not know how to use it for herself and thought that it was useless and risky for her to keep it. Also she wanted to see it get destroyed.

The witches couldn't have possibly thought that the broomstick could have been thrown in garbage as the broom was a precious object.

Kara's broom that was thrown in the garbage burning site was found by a garbage worker who was a young teenager and was poor. The garbage boy's name was Frank who lived in great poverty. The garbage boy saw the broom and it looked nicely crafted to him so he took the broom to his home without realizing that it was a witch's broom.

He did not needed the broom to clean or sweep but to use it to play with his pet dog .

Now to make the broomstick a plane stick and to start playing fetching game with his dog he had to clear the straw that was attached to it. So he decided to remove it. Now while removing he started singing "broom broom how big you are but can you be useful to me and make me some food?" The broom suddenly came into action and through magic from the broomstick came out a big cauldron and it then put some vegetables and water in the cauldron along with salt and pepper and in fraction of seconds made delicious soup and meals for both the dog and Frank.

The boy was very happy seeing this and he immediately realized that it must be a witch's broom but he tried to sit on it and fly but he couldn't so he doubted that. But still it was a good thing for him that it could make food for him and serve him when he returns home from work.

Now for a few days he ate good food and then one day he thought what else could it do. He wondered if it could make him a rich man.

But before asking for it he thought that he should change the way he looks because just in case the broomstick actually makes him rich and then people might think that he has stolen somebody's money.

So he asked the broom, "Broom Broom make me rich and change my appearance" and in an instant his face transformed to better looking face and his small cottage which was far away from town transformed in a big mansion with a chest inside the mansion filled with lots of gold pieces. Frank jumped in excitement seeing this and thought that this broom stick was the best thing that ever happened to him but he was careful to use it so that it does not come in the eyes of others.

But to know a witches broomstick derives magical power from the witch who owns it by draining witches life and energy. So the more magic you do from the broom stick and the bigger the magic is the more the witch's life and health reduces which takes time to replenish. That is why witches look thin and creepy and do tricks only when they think it is required by them and they really want it. So thy don't waste their magic and blood.

Now the boy didn't knew that and started doing magic daily with lots of demands everyday and there, Kara started getting weak day by day. Kara's friend witches saw this and became alarmed because Kara had lost all her strength and had difficulty even walking and had become just like an old helpless women.

Kara's friend witches realized that since Kara is becoming extremely weak day by day somebody must be doing lots of magic using broom stick which should be somehow visible. So they started search again in all directions and looked for clues.

One of the witch was flying over forest saw this big mansion which was never there before and looked newly built. She suspected something strange about that mansion and returned back to Witch-Palace and informed other witches about this. The witches suspected that it could be that Kara's broom is being used for magic there so all of them at once went to the Frank's mansion on their flying broomsticks and observed from the sky what was going on. They saw that a broom was being asked to do different things and broom was doing it. One of the witch took out a witch's binocular and saw that the broom that was being used for magic, was no other than Kara's broom.

So, immediately all the witches stormed Frank and the mansion and seized Kara's Flying Broomstick from Frank. All witches thought that Frank had stolen the broom but then they did magic on him and found out that he had got it from garbage burning site and broom told them that Betty had stolen it from Kara.

The witches left Frank's mansion just as it was and warned him to be careful with broomsticks next time. He promised and sweared that he will never use magic from any broomstick or anything ever.

If witches would have converted the Frank mansion back to small house then they would have required lots of magic and would have drained more life from witches and since Frank did not steal it and prevented it actually from burning in the garbage the mansion was like a present for him from the witches.

Kara got her broom stick back. It took a while for her to become young and energetic but she did got well and was back in her original witch energy.

And about Betty who stole the broom, she was thrown in a witch prison for many years to come and she still cries there for draining life blood off a witch.

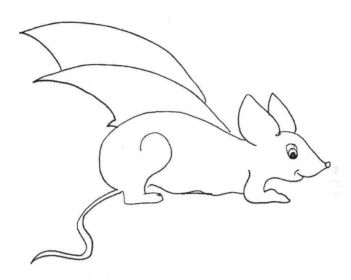

There was an age when dragons ruled. Dragons were trained by strong men and women and were used in many battles against each other. Many dragons were also killed during the battles.

So the dead dragon's meat was also eaten as food then.

It so happened that there was a crisis in one of the village. The king of one of the village who lived high up in the mountains wanted to empty that village and build a castle over there but people of the village did not wanted to leave their village and land.

They tried fighting the king with their dragons but could not win as king had a bigger army and more number of highly trained dragons which were very difficult to defeat.

So the people of the village went to the sorcerer of the village and asked for her help. Sorcerer knew that her people had tried everything to defeat the king but they had failed so she said only way to defeat the king is to have a mighty beast made, that can defeat all the kings dragons. And people wondered what could that be? She said since only diamond can cut a diamond, only a dragon can defeat a dragon and here the dragon on there side would be a magical dragon that will have the ability to disappear and reappear and defeat any number of dragons no matter how trained they would be. People were happy to know that and asked the sorcerer to proceed with the creation of such a dragon and she did. In nine days time she crafted a magical dragon who only listened to the village people to defeat king's dragons and had to win.

Then the village people declared battle against the king and fought again.

There was a big battle that was fought between the magical dragon and the king's dragons and his army. The magical dragon fought bravely but the king's dragons were too many and although he killed many dragons but since there were too many the magical dragon also got brutally injured and before killing all dragons he died and could not defeat the kings army of dragons. So the villagers had to give up and they surrendered.

All the people of village were taken as captives and thrown in a prison.

That day it so happened that a mouse was hungry and was trying to search for food. His dwelling was where the magical dragon that had fell during the fight and was lying dead on the ground.

As mouse eat meat sometimes the dragon's meat looked delicious to him and he went near it and chew and ate the meat.

He then went back to his dwelling and slept the whole night.

In the morning when he woke up he tried coming out his dwelling but he could not fit through the dwelling's opening as he realized that he had grown wings. He got astonished and didn't know what to do. So he made the exit of the dwelling a bit more wider and came out. Then he thought, could he fly with the wings or they are just flightless wings.

He tried flapping the wings and when he looked down he was in the air. He was happy and thrilled to see that he could fly so he kept on flapping the wings and practiced flying.

Now it so happened the day mouse had eaten the dragon and went back to its burrow to sleep, that night the sorcerer who had witch-crafted the dragon and had not surrendered as she had ran away came that night to bury the dragon so that its flesh could not be used to do more harm to the village by any other witch or person. So when she started digging a grave for the dragon she noticed that dragon's flesh was torn and some was lying besides it and it looked like it had been eaten by a little creature. She got a little scared as she did not knew what the outcome of that would be. She looked for something strange here and there but could not find anything unique and strange so she hid amongst the trees the whole night and waited for something different to occur.

By that time she had already buried the dragon.

In the morning she saw that a bird like creature came from beneath the ground and flew in the air and sometimes went back to the burrow. When she checked closely she saw that it was a mouse and at once knew that the mouse must have eaten the dragon's meat and because of that it grew wings.

She thought for a while and then thought that if a dragon couldn't defeat king than maybe a mouse can.

She then knew that the magical dragon's meat gave mouse wings. She dug out the mud from the magical dragon's grave who had still not decayed. She brought in as many mice as possible by luring them from jungle to eat meat of the magical dragon.
At least a million mice came from the jungle by her magic and each had a piece of dragon's meat. By the time they were eating she did some magic on that those mice so that they could understand the witch's talk and could get tamed by her to kill king's dragons and army to defeat the king.

And so it happened.

The mice started understanding what the witch was telling them and came to know that the king was cruel there and had put people of her village in captivity and stole their village land so they decided to avenge that by helping the witch to defeat the king and free people of his tyranny.

The witch then started to train the mice. The witch trained the mice to hit the eyes of king's men and dragons and make them go blind first and then attack them at the neck making them helpless and fall.

She knew that the mice were small and the king's men would not be able to aim at them by firing arrows . So she was happy about that.

So after the mice understood the tactics and knew how to defeat the king's army they attacked. Unaware, when the king's army saw a million bird like creatures attacking them they got a bit scared and tried attacking them back but they were too many and they were taking down dragons like flies and men did not know what to aim at and how to aim at the creatures. They tried but they failed.

The sorcerer's mice army won and took king and his remaining army captive. All dragons were killed so that they don't bother later.

The village people were made free from captivity and regained their village homes and lived happily ever after all thanks to flying mice and the witch.

The flying mice also lived happily because they now could escape the captivity of vultures or eagles if got caught by them.

TaLe 6 : ThE dRaGoN ThAt LoSt It'S FiRe

Dragons used to live in an isolated part of earth called Dragonsville. It was a very beautiful place which had everything a dragon wanted. It had lots of forests and fruits that dragons liked. It also had many wild animals to hunt and eat. There was nothing that was not there that a dragon wouldn't want.

But there was a dragon named Ficky who always wanted to see the whole world. He wanted to travel around the earth and see the different places on earth. But he was never allowed to leave Dragonsville. He tried many times arguing with his parents and elders but nobody allowed him and told that it was too dangerous for a dragon to leave Dragonsville but he never listened.

One day Ficky decided to leave the Dargonsville all by himself without letting anybody knew.

Dragonsville was located on the equator where it was warm and the dragons liked it.

So Ficky started his flight.
He flew alongside the equator first but he did not find it much different than Dragonsville.

Then he decided to fly to the south of the equator and discover something new.

He travelled over South America where he saw many two-footed creatures who were called humans that were afraid to see him and ran towards hiding on seeing him. He did not mind that and wondered why his fellow dragons said that it was dangerous to go out of Dragonsville.

But he continued his flight towards south pole.

On the way he used to stop and hunt animals , have some food and take some rest from flying.

But he continued his flight and at last he reached the south pole and saw that it was white everywhere which was nothing like he had ever seen before. He saw ice all around. He did not know what it was but he liked it so he went near it and tried touching it. It was cold when he touched it.

By that time he was tired and wanted a resting place to sleep.
He could not find trees so he just sat and laid on the ice which was pretty cold.

He started feeling thirsty by that time so he started looking for water but he did not find any. He did not know what to do. So he thought of flying back to Dragonsville but he couldn't, he was too tired. So he just laid down hoping to find some rest and peace. Suddenly it saw a creature with beak hitting the ice below it and after quite a lot of pocking and hitting on the ground it made a whole in it and then he saw drops of water splashed out.

He said to himself that there must be water beneath the icy ground so I should also break the ground to get some water to drink.

He used his tail to hit hard on the floor, being careful not to sink in the ground. He broke quite a lot of ice and found water beneath it. He was happy to see that and drank it in great quantity. It was cold but still he he did not stop drinking as he was thirsty for a long time.

Now he wanted some food. Since there were no trees for fruits he tried looking for some animals and found few bears and other creatures which he hunted and now he only ate cooked food so he tried burning the hunted animals with his mouth fire but there was no fire coming from his mouth. He was shocked to see that. Now how was he supposed to have his food. He tried eating raw food but could not get it below his throat so he just spit it out.

By that time he started feeling chilly too and wanted to burn some wood for fire but there was no wood and there was no fire. The dragon started falling ill and fell too ill. He could not move nor hunt which was useless anyways. He tried flying but had no energy left in him to fly and kept on falling as he tried.

He realized that there is no escaping from it and his end is here soon.

Suddenly he saw a group of dragons coming towards him. The dragons had been following him since day one. They had seen him leave and knew it was no use calling him back as he would not listen. So they followed him stealthily without him getting to know of it.

When they saw dragon not able to fly they came near him and asked what had happened. Then they came to know that the dragon had lost its fire power and was too ill. They knew that it was because of drinking icy water.

The dragons then decided to put fire in his mouth through their mouth. So one of the dragon opened his mouth and the other dragon breathed fire in his throat.

The dragon coughed a little bit but felt a bit better. He then kept on lying for a while and then he tried breathing fire, which he successfully did. He also starting feeling better after that and in a few days time he was ready to take flight back home and promised his fellow dragons and the elderly dragons to listen to them and pay heed to what they say as they had seen more life than him and knew more about the world than he did.

TaLe 7 : tHe TeLe-PoRtEr

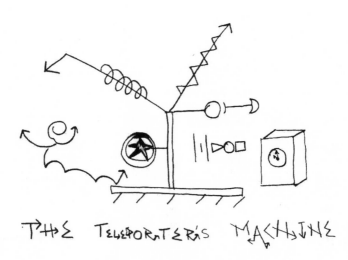

THE TELEPORTER'S MACHINE

There was a town named Bloomingsville. Just like the name the people who lived in the town were happy and blooming.

There was a man in Bloomingsville named Happysome. He was the favourite of all kids in the town. He loved kids and gave them presents, that were rare to find in the entire country. He brought them such different kinds of candies and cakes that were not easy to find. He was basically Santa Claus of the town.

He earned his livelihood by selling medicines. He earned quite a good amount of money with that but spent it all on buying presents for children during Christmas.

Now, how he arranged presents for the Christmas was a secret.

While studying science of making medicines he started making different kind of machines. He always wanted to make a teleporting machine so that he can go to whichever place on entire earth and whenever he wanted. He wanted to see different places on earth before he died and since there were no airplanes at that time it would had been very difficult for him to go and see each and every place on earth without that.

But after various tries he made a tele-porting machine.

He was happy about that and thought where to go first? He did not know at that time so he went to various different places on earth and saw different beautiful things on on earth. Even after seeing this he was not satisfied. He wanted to do something more. He said to himself "All that there is in the world is to see children smile. So I should do something for the kids in my town."

After being said that he started preparing for coming Christmas.

He went to different places of Earth by tele-porting through his tele-porting device and bought several difficult to find toys, candies and cakes and brought them home.

During the Christmas night he gave all the kids of Bloomingsville very beautiful toys and presents. The kids of the town were amazed to see such kind of presents and were very happy.

They thanked Happysome and wondered where he got the presents from. All he said was that he had machine that made all that presents. All the kids wanted to see the machine but he never allowed them to see it.

On one Christmas Happysome was coming from his last trip of buying presents from other countries when suddenly his machine failed. He somehow managed to teleport himself to Bloomingsville but that was the last trip of teleporting. When he checked the machine the machine had got rusted and could not be used again to teleport.

Now, the only way to teleport was to make a new machine which would take him more than a year's time and Christmas was less than a year so he did not know what to do. He was stuck. But he devised a plan to get Christmas presents for the next year also.

He told everybody that he would be going on vacation for a year and thus his medicine shop will remain closed for a year or so.

Now he had decided to travel the entire Earth to bring presents for kids without the teleporting machine. For this he had to travel on land and on water. But to travel on land and water at the current speed would take him longer than a year and therefore to collect all the rare and beautiful presents before Christmas would be impossible. So he devised a plan.

He bought a horse and attached 4 springs to each of the horses hoofs so that they could run faster.

Secondly, He built a big "O" shaped canvas air bag.

After doing that he departed Bloomingsville on the horse and took the big "O" shaped canvas airbag with him.

He reached the port where a medium size ship was docked and asked the captain of ship if he could make some adjustments to ship to cause it to have less drag. The captain was happy to hear that and allowed Happysome to do the adjustment.

Happysome went near the ship's base and attached the "O" shaped canvas air bag around it. He then filled air in it and because of that the ship got lifted above.

What he did was although the water friction was still there on the ship's movement but he reduced the direct water drag by attaching a big canvas bag filled with air to the base of the ship touching water. This made the ship more lighter and thus it moved faster.

Now on the ship he visited different ports from where he collected the presents and when he was sailing on the ship he built the teleporting machine in his room. The places which were not easily accessible by the ship he went there on the horse who had springs attached to its hoofs and made the trip faster.

Now, it was time for Christmas and he had collected all the presents by that time and had returned to Bloomingsville. By that time he had also built more than half of his teleporting machine and was able to complete it till next Christmas.

This time he made the machine with a better material so that it lasts a life time.

So the Christmas did not go in vain.

All the kids got their rare and awesome presents from Happysome and enjoyed the Christmas to the maximum.
Happysome also completed the teleporting machine before next Christmas and thereafter continued the use of teleporting machine for getting presents for the kids of Bloomingsville.

tAlE 8 : tHe FaIrY aNd "HECK"

Once there lived only fairies on planet Earth. The fairies were happy on the Earth. They used to play, dance, eat and enjoy on the planet. But one fairy named Earthfire always wanted to have houses on the clouds.

This fairy was a scientist.

Now, she had tried many things to form something as that could float in air and they could build houses on it. Helium balloons were useless because they could easily get punctured and fall on Earth. So, she always wanted to do something about that.

One day in her lab she was working. She mixed helium, epoxy and carbon fibre and heated them to a temperature of around 400 degree celsius. Suddenly there occurred a chemical reaction through which a big cloud formed.

She hadn't used much of chemicals to do that reaction. Approximately 1 gram of each of reactants was used but it formed a giant cloud of around 10 square meter. She checked the cloud and found it was pretty fluffy and also very strong and called it HECK(Helium Epoxy Carbon-fibre Kicking to form a cloud). The cloud floated in air. To check its strength she tried sitting on the cloud and found that it supported her completely and did not fall on ground. She was happy to see that and shouted "Awesome".

Upon further testing Earthfire saw that cloud she had made could fly in the atmosphere of Earth without ever getting crushed or without having to be rebuild again. HECK cloud could be made of different colours and could support heavy things on top of it i.e. houses and buildings could be built on top of it which would float in the air.

She was delighted to invent such kind of cloud.

Slowly the world of fairies starting using HECK as construction material to form buildings and houses on HECK clouds that floated in the air and until the turn of a decade all of the fairies started having houses built on HECK which were floating at approximately 3000 feet of altitude and fairies enjoyed that.

Sometimes the winds were strong and the houses got bumped into each other which was fun for them. They enjoyed it because it was like having bumpy car rides in the amusement parks in which upon pressing the accelerator the car goes into whichever direction one steers to and then gets bumped into another car.

Now, to generate electricity fairies had build windmills beside their houses on HECK . For drinkable water they did rain water harvesting. Some fairies got water from nearby stores but it was upon them to choose whatever type of water they wanted to drink.

The fun part with the HECK was that they could play in the air with balls that were made of HECK and floated in air. These balls could be hockey balls or hockey pucks, soccer balls, rugby balls, lacrosse balls, baseball balls or cricket balls.

Since the fairies had never played these sports in air even though they could fly it was difficult at first to hit the floating balls with hockey stick or baseball or cricket bat as they would miss the ball or slip and fall in air. But when they started doing that it was more fun for them to play these kind of sports as these sports became more challenging.

Now there was once a fairy born. She was born with no wings and named "Wingless". The fairy never minded that name instead she liked that name because she always interpreted it as Winner, Glorious and Sensible Surely.

Since HECK was already there she could still be floating in the air.

Now, because the fairy did not have wings she could not go from one HECK cloud to other so she had to be made special shoes made of HECK that supported her weight and so she could walk in the air without falling on ground, which was fun too.

Now since she did not have wings she could not fly as fast as other fairies, all of them who had wings.

She always wanted to prove that she could move as fast as the other fairies so she tried something different.

She went to an empty cloud made of HECK alone and tried running on HECK without her floating shoes she saw that she was a pretty good runner but she realized that running on ground and air walking/running was totally different so she figured that to fly faster in air one needs to swim through the fluid of air rather than run on it. To do that she needed a little bit more equipment than normal.

She then went to a HECK manufacturing shop and asked the fairy working there to make her wristbands made of HECK for both wrists of her arm that can support half her body weight. The shop fairy took her wrists sizes and made her wrist HECKs. When she wore them they fitted her perfectly and supported her weight completely. She was happy to see that.

Now instead of practicing running she started practicing swimming. She used to go to an artificial lake on HECK and practiced swimming there for hours everyday and became proficient in it.

Now, with the HECKs tied to her wrist and also wearing shoes of HECK started to practice to swim in air and realized that she was pretty fast to do that. After some time she realized that she was swimming in air with almost the same speed as with which other fairies were flying.

She then decided to challenge some of the fairies to beat them in a flight race. The other fairies did not wanted to say no to Wingless so they raced. Wingless could not win but she came second and that was pretty fast too. Other fairies were surprised to see that and hugged her rejoicing. She was happy for that and never felt bad even a little bit that she never had wings because she matched the pace of her fellow fairies without wings.

That day was the awesomest day ever for her and she never forgot it!

TaLe 9 : FaIrY gAvE bIrTh To A dRaGoN

Once there lived fairies and witches. Fairies were always nice but witches always tried to destroy fairies and their existence.
Fairies lived on separate land in a country called Fairy-Land and witches lived in a country called Witch-Land. Both the countries were on the same land mass so there were many fights amongst them but still fairies managed to survive.

Fairy-Land was beautiful. Fairies did many incredible things there and they were more advanced and better than witches in their way of working. Fairies grew fruits and vegetables in their farms. There was no shortage of food and fun for the fairies in Fairy-Land. Fairies also did many experiments using chemicals and their magic.

Now, there was this fairy whose name was Pansy. She did lots of experiments to form something new. Sometimes she formed a sandwich, sometimes a burger and sometimes muffin but nothing new. Even then she kept on trying.

One night she was experimenting and added many different chemicals to her test tube. What happened that time was that there was too much lightning in the sky going on and the fairy was experimenting outside. She suddenly got its test tube struck by lightning and that caused a small explosion. That caused a lot of smoke.

After the explosion's smoke cleared away she say that a small mammal like looking creature was sitting just in front of her in the broken test tube. At that time she did not know what to do. She picked up the mammal and took her home hiding it in her coats pocket so that nobody sees it. She reached home, put the creature in her room and shut the door. Now, she looked at the creature and wondered what it could be. She went to the kitchen and brought some grapes and tried feeding it to the mammal. The creature first was shy and tried running away and hiding in her closet but she picked it up and kept it on a table and tried feeding it again. This time the creature put its tongue out and licked the grapes. It liked it and then it put that grape piece in its mouth and felt happy and started jumping. It wanted more of the grapes. The fairy fed it quite a bit but then stopped as she did not know that if more fruit would do it harm or good. The creature started liking fairy and became its pet. The fairy made for it beautiful things. She made for it a running wheel, a small trampoline, a small swimming pool and many other playing things. The mammal also liked cakes and muffin and she fed them to him daily. She used to always keep it in her room so that nobody knows about it and does not consider it a witch's trick after seeing it.

One day the fairy came from her work and she tried to find the creature and couldn't find it. She tried looking in the closet or the drawers but could not find the mammal. Suddenly she saw that the creature flew across her face and when she saw she was surprised to see that the creature she was feeding food everyday was nobody other than a dragon with wings. She got very excited about that.

She now had realized that dragon whom she had named Ralph couldn't be kept in hiding. Afraid at first, she took the dragon from her room and put it into her pocket and went to a friend of her's.

When her friend saw that Pansy had a dragon in her hands she freaked out but when Pansy showed that it obeyed her and ate only fruits and cakes and candies and not fairies her friend fairy got relieved a little bit and started petting the dragon too. She too started liking the dragon. They then decided to show it to all the fairies in the village they lived called Greatsville.

The next day when the fairies of Greatsville saw the dragon they freaked out too but when Pansy told everybody that it was safe and Ralph did not hurt anybody. She told everybody that she had created it while working in her laboratory as an accident and that it was no witchcraft. After listening to the explanation the other fairies breathed a sigh of relief and although reluctant at first the fairies started petting it and became friendly to Ralph.

Now it so happened that there was a dam in Greatsville.

Fairies had repaired that dam many times but it used to leak sometimes. The dam was pretty big and if it would break it would flood the entire village of Greatsville so it was a risky.

It so happened that the witches knew about the dam and somehow wanted to break it so that they can flood the entire village of Greatsville.

They did that one day.

The witches flew with all their strength to Greatsville and started a fight. The fight was just a distraction but their main aim was to destroy the dam.

While some witches were fighting with the fairies of Greatsville some went to the dam to break it with their witch craft.

Now Pansy wanted to hide her dragon Ralph from the witches so that they can't get a hold of it and use it for any evil desire if their's.

She took the dragon put it in her pocket and started flying away from the Greatsville.

Her path of flying out of town led above the dam. So she was about to cross the dam when she saw that witches were trying to break the dam by doing some witchcraft. She immediately hid behind a tree and did not know what to do as the witches were too many.

Now, while she was hiding she suddenly felt movement in her pocket and realized that it was Ralph, who she had forgotten about in amidst of whatever was going on.

Now she realized that only way to stop the witches was too get help from other fairies and that was very difficult because the fairies of Greatsville were already fighting witches in their town.

The only way now was to call the help of army of fairies which was quite a flight from Greatsville. She thought that she would go but she did not wanted to leave the sight of evil witches so that just in case she could do something to stop the witches from breaking the dam. Now the only way to get help was to send Ralph for help.

She said to herself " If Ralph does not go all of he Greatsville will fall and the fairies of Greatsville will get captured and I don't want my friends to get into the hands of evil witches."

So she wrote a note, folded it and put it in the mouth of Ralph. The note contained emergency message from her and told that Greatsville was under attack by the witches.

She then aimed the dragon at a certain heading and told it to fly in the same heading until it sees somebody like her that was not engaged in battle with any witch. She then told Ralph to give the note to that fairy.

With tears in her eyes she made Ralph fly away towards the direction where she knew that he will find some army fairy personnel.

It was about two hours from the time Pansy had left the dragon in search of army, but there was no sign of him.
She was worried but she did not give up hope and decided to give Ralph more time. She went near the witches that were trying to break the dam and started distracting them.

The witches after seeing her became alarmed. They thought that there might be other fairies too nearby and they did not wanted to stop their evil plan of breaking the dam go into vain so some of them went after pansy and tried to look for other fairies too if any. Now doing that, the total witchcraft power to destroy the dam had decreased as some witches had gone after pansy.

Pansy kept on hiding behind the high trees and showing herself again and again to the witches and wasting their hunting time.

After sometime she saw Ralph coming towards her. She realized that Ralph had found out its way back. She was happy to see him but she did not see any army so she thought that Ralph couldn't get to any army personal. But as soon as Ralph escaping from sight of the witches landed on her hand she saw a huge flock of fairy army coming from the direction through which Ralph came.

She was happy to see that Ralph had accomplished its flight and had helped save the fairies of Greatsville.

The fairy army attacked the witches trying to destroy the dam and captured them. They also captured all the witches who were attacking Greatsville and threw them in a prison from where they could never return.

tALe 10 : tHe mOtHeR eLePhAnT tHaT LaiD aN EgG

There was a forest where lived many animals. Amongst them was a male elephant whose name was Refo. He had fallen in love with a female elephant. Her name was Girlie. They went on many dates.

Sometimes they went on dates in moonlight to the lake, sometimes they went in the evening to the river fall, sometimes they went to the tropical forest for enjoying tropical fruits, sometimes they went to the lake to take a dip and relax. They enjoyed many things in their forest and ultimately Refo asked the question to Girlie. Will you marry me? And Girlie replied "yes".

What was next? Their parents agreed and they got married.

They married with lots of pomp and show!

All the animals of forests including tiger, lion, fox and wolf came. Not only the biggest of animals but also the tiniest of insects including many crickets came to attend the wedding.

Now, the wedding was done.

Girlie was always found of kids. She loved them. So they wanted to have a baby for themselves too.

They tried to conceive a baby but couldn't.

Girlie always blamed Refo for that. They used to fight and quarrel with each other because of that

One day they became very gloomy. Girlie that day wished that if they couldn't get a baby at-least she could lay an egg!

Her wish became true one day.

One morning she woke up and had a great stomach-ache. They did not what to do. Out of pain Girlie sat down and screamed and suddenly a rock like thing came out of her stomach. It was white in colour was round but they couldn't figure out what it was. First, they thought it was a broken bone of Girlie but Girlie tried walking and checking herself and she felt okay.

They then thought maybe it is an egg. They thought that if it was an egg then they have to get it hatched. They knew that to get the egg hatched a mom has to sit on egg for hours. BUT SHE WAS AN ELEPHANT! HOW COULD SHE SIT ON AN EGG? IT WOULD BREAK!

Not knowing completely that it was an egg or something else. She picked up a scarf and put it around the egg.

They then thought even if it was not an egg let's try hatching it just in case if it was.

Now they thought, if Girlie could not sit on egg at-least a hen or duck or maybe on ostrich or any other animal that lays egg could sit or help them. But then they wondered, would one bird be sufficient to hatch an egg or they need more birds to hatch the egg or do they need a soft ass animal to sit on the egg.

So they made an announcement amongst the animals that they needed help in hatching Girlie's egg and the animals of the forest spread the word. When the parents of Girlie and other animals heard that Girlie had laid an egg they were amazed to hear that but they all wanted to help.

So all the animals who were not heavy including group of birds started taking turns in sitting on the egg and trying to hatch it. But there were 4 hours in the day when the animals took a break. At that time she used to put a sweater on the egg, pick it up, put it in a pram and took it out for a stroll. She told it stories and read many different fairy tales for it. But she used to think what if it was not an egg, then their all effort would go in vain and also she thought what if it was an egg and they were not able to hatch it her wish of having a baby would go in vain too. But she didn't give up hope and prayed to the Almighty everyday.

Secondly, in the 4 hour break she also used to light up some wood with fire and keep the egg besides it to give it warmth . Not only that, sometimes she also used to put the egg in Luke warm water and cover it with a blanket.

She did everything possible so that her egg if it was could hatch properly.

This went on for about 45 days.

Now, one day when a group of five birds were sitting on Girlie's egg suddenly they heard a cracking sound. A small baby elephant got out. He was a cutie.
When Refo and Girlie saw it they were in the most excited state ever. They went near the baby elephant and in excitement name it The-One! They then checked was it a boy or a girl and to their excitement it was a girl elephant. The-One looked fit and healthy.

They then thanked all the birds and animals that they helped hatch the The-One.

They then threw a grand party for all animals of the forest and thanked God!

TaLe 11 : tHe cHiLd ThAt NeVeR cRiEd

There are many children in the world but all do cry at one time or the other.

There was this kid named Franz who never cried or laughed. He was born to a family of rich people.

On the day he was born and took out of mother's womb, he just came out dumb although showing movement in body but was not crying or laughing, even if he could. His mom and dad were a little worried that the baby looked like a devil without any sad or happy emotions. Franz's mom and dad asked the doctor if there could be any medication so that he, if does not have any emotions can get some emotions. The doctor told them that there was no such medicine available and even if it was available he was too young for that. So they took the baby home although a bit sad about the emotional features of the baby but happy they at-least had a baby.

The baby was put in a cot. His parents tried to amuse him with toys and rattles but the baby lay dumb neither laughing nor crying. Franz's parents were afraid to show him to their relatives because of his non exhibition of human features. They used to keep him hidden from people. Even if anybody came to their house they would not show the baby to them and the baby was also silent as grave. He may make a bit of sound through his mouth but that was it.

Franz was going to be one year old. His parents thought that he has grown a little bit and maybe a party might help him feel happy and he might start showing some emotions seeing people around. They then decided to throw a birthday party for Franz. On his birthday came many rich people and wanted to see Franz and see him smile. But Franz never cried or laughed even in the party amongst so many people. He was like a ghost. So many people asked that if Franz was alright? Franz's parents were compelled to tell the guests that Franz had a problem exhibiting emotions and that he never smiled or cried. The guests somewhat freaked out knowing that and they started talking amongst themselves and saying that the baby was a devil. Franz's parents were disgraced in the party because of Franz's condition but they could not do anything about it. The party ended and guests went home some even taking their presents back as they were superstitious that Franz's parents had given birth to a devil and they don't want to do anything with the devil.

This was a true disgrace for Franz's parents.

Slowly Franz grew up and started going to school. His classmates called him a freak. He was never invited to any party or function. Even the school never let him come to any organized school fair or function. Even the transcripts and his graduation certificates were sent home without him attending any graduation ceremonies.

His teachers also called him a freak. They never cared about how he performed in his class. He was never allowed to compete in any competition in school or anywhere. His parents were never called to school to talk to teacher or principal, no matter how worst he was in his studies and even if he failed in certain subjects sometimes. The school did not care for Franz and was often called the devil.

Now, under these circumstances Franz was upset and used to talk to his parents about it but his parents told him that he shouldn't be upset and just try to do good and work hard in his studies. They told him that he shouldn't care what other people say to him. He should try to be happy.

But although Franz talked okay but he still couldn't exhibit emotions.

In his free time Franz used to go to the forest and sit all alone and saw animals running here and there. He used to see that even animals didn't cry or laugh and remained dumb but they were not called freak or devil. He felt sad about that and continued being tortured daily and coming in his spare time to the forest.

He prayed sometimes to God that he should get okay and be not called freak or devil.

One day he was sitting in the forest and saw a shooting star. That was the most beautiful thing that he had ever seen. It was like he had seen heaven through his mortal eyes.This caused him great mystery as it was the first time he had ever seen anything like that. Suddenly he saw a group of 5 shooting stars that followed that shooting star. That just filled water in his eyes and he cried a lot that day. He didn't know what he was doing while weeping but he kept on doing that for a while and when he stopped crying he laughed that actually tears came out of his eyes and he was not abnormal any more. He was very excited about that and went home.

When his parents saw him he was laughing and smiling they didn't know what to say and were astonished to se Franz. They asked him what had happened? He told him the complete story.

From that day onwards nobody ever called him a freak or devil.

He made new friends when he went to school next day and his teachers were surprised to see Franz now.

His parents then threw a grand party for their son's next birthday.

MORAL: You don't have to be on merit to be happy, just the quality of being human is enough merit forever.

TaLe 12 : HoW wItChEs BeCaMe GoOd

There was a witch named Sam. She was a witch but remained sad most of the times. If other witches asked her to come along with them and to do their witch stuff together or do some shopping together she used to refuse and remained gloomy. Her friend witches tried a lot but she remained sad and never went to any place with them and just stayed at her house.

Her house was also not too big. There was nothing much to do around in the house but she still sat in her tiny room and remained depressed and cried sometimes.

She never knew what she was missing.

One day, her friend witch forced her to leave her room and go with her to the market place. She did not wanted to go but she went.

In the market place she was still gloomy. Her friend tried to cheer her up by showing her different type of shops. She also took Sam to juice bar and ordered 10 different type of juices. She then asked Sam to try all of the juices and tell which one was the best. But she was still not amused or happy after trying all of them and did not find any juice sounding good to her taste buds.

Now she was sitting at the juice bar for a long time when she she heard a sound. She did not know what it was but felt very nice hearing the music. Sam asked her friend what it was. Her friend told her that that was called music. She asked her how does it work. Then she told Sam to go and check out herself.

They both went to the music shop from where the sound was coming.

There was a girl playing a piano. Sam asked the shop owner that what was that thing called from which the sound was being produced by the girl. The shop owner told Sam that, that thing was an instrument and was called a piano. Sam was excited and asked if anybody could play it. The shop owner replied with a yes. Then Sam asked the shop owner if she could buy it . The shop owner said smiling that the piano was good for sale and anybody who could afford it could buy it. Sam immediately payed the price of the piano to the shop owner and bought it.

Then Sam with her magic, lifted the piano up and flew along with the piano and her friend back to her house. Her room was tiny but she somehow made space for the piano.

She shrunk her bed's width to just the width so that she can snuck in and made her dressing table reduce to half the size with her magic.

Now, she somehow made the piano fit her room. She then put a stool besides piano, sat on it and struck a key.

She was wonderstruck hearing piano's sound when she struck a key on it. Then she used all her fingers and without any rhythm just moved her fingers up and down pressing the same piano keys at a high speed. Her expressions were super witchy at that time when she was pressing the keys very quickly. She enjoyed it a lot and was ecstasized at that time

Now she thought let's convert the piano into a witch piano.
She had 122 magic potions and same was the number of keys of the piano. So with magic she linked each key to a magic potion such that when she played a particular key the particular potion flew from the magic potion rack and came over her big witch cauldron. Then, for the amount of time she pressed the piano key till that time the potion fell in the cauldron drop by drop and when she lifted the same key up
the magic potion flew and went back to the rack.

Now, once her friend told her to make an evil potion as she wanted to do some evil magic using that potion against a man who had upset her in some way.

So when Sam started making the evil potion she got so much lost in the music that instead of matching set of potions to the keys she started to play a beautiful music and then instead of making an evil potion the keys matched potions in such a way that a good potion was made.

Sam gave that potion to her friend.

Now when Sam's friend used that potion against the man who had upset her before the potion instead of being negative turned out to be positive for him. Actually, Sam's friend had put the potion in the seeds of his to be grown crops and had thought that when the man plants the seeds his seeds will produce no crop and the entire harvest will leave him bankrupt. But the harvest yielded 50 times more crop than normal and the man was surprised to see that. He instead of becoming bankrupt payed of all his loans and saved money for his kids studies.

The man seeing such a bumper and impossible yield realized that it must be because of a witch's magic. He then realized that how cruel he was to a certain witch. Thinking that he felt bad. He then went to the witch's house who he had behaved badly to and apologized to her.

The witch at that time was already upset at Sam because instead of an evil potion Sam had made a good potion which turned positive for the man.

After hearing apologies from the man the evil witch cooled down a bit and thought why we have to do evil when we can get results from doing good.

She then went back to Sam and told her that instead of doing evil we should do good. Sam was confused at that time and asked why. Then Sam's friend told her the whole story. Sam after hearing the story also thought that being good is better than being evil.

They then went to their witch friends and told them what happened. They then discussed that if they could do good instead of doing evil. Some of their friends did not agree but then all of them agreed and they started doing good for the people from that day onwards.

People who used to be afraid of the witches started liking them and being thankful to them. The witches were benevolent from there on and never had hurt anybody ever from that time onwards.

All thanks to the piano!

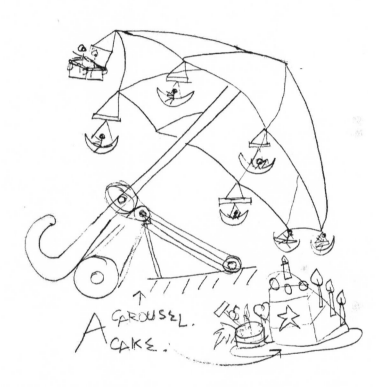

"Good morning Adrian. Rise and shine! Aren't you forgetting you have to go to your birthday party today". "What birthday party" asked Adrian. Adrian had hardly attended any birthday party in his life time but wanted to go to one. "Your birthday party" exclaimed Adrian's mom.

Adrian looked at his mom's face and asked "really"?

His mom told him not to mess with her and wished him happy birthday.

Adrian all confused, asked his mom "Is it my birthday party." She said "Of course, who else's birthday party could it be today? It's your birthday you naughty boy and your father and I are giving the party at a funfair. All the funfair is booked just for you and your friends."

Adrian jumped from the bed and said "Hurray! today is my birthday at we are having it at a funfair. All for me!"

He then went to the bathroom, brushed his teeth, took a shower and dressed up in his new clothes.

Now, at 5:00 pm he and his parents waited outside their house. A red coloured limousine specially painted for that day came in front of their doorway and stopped. A chauffeur came out and presented a bouquet of flowers to Adrian and then wished him " Happy Birthday!" Adrian took the flowers and said thank you to him.

The limousine was then driven out of town on highway. After one hour drive from out of town Adrian starting seeing a beautifully decorated Ferrous wheel and some roller coasters. When he came near he started seeing all the rides of the funfair magnificently decorated and ready to run.

The limo then came in front of the entry of the funfair and stopped. Adrian and his parents got off the vehicle.

At that time many of the guests had already arrived but were waiting for the birthday boy who was delighted to see his friends waiting for him to enter the party room.

As soon as they had got off the vehicle Adrian started hearing "Happy Birthday Adrian" in loud voices which were being said by his friends.

Adrian was delighted to hear that and rushed towards the crowd. His friends hugged him and gave him presents and cheered for him.

Now it was time to enter the all booked personnel funfair.

This time there were no tickets to be bought no standing in lines. All rides were open to Adrian and his friends and were free no matter how many times you take them.

Adrian took all the ground rides including Ferrous Wheel, Carousel and roller coaster, etc.

Now was the time to do water rides. Adrian and his friends rushed towards the water pool and to their surprise they saw something different.

The saw there was wave-pool and five other pools which had slides attached to them but there was no water in them. They were filled with juices of different colours and different kind including orange juice, blueberry juice, pomegranate juice, fruit punch, cranberry juice and grape juice.

All the kids run up the stairs of he slides and loo went on to the slides and splashed in the juice-pools.

The kids were thrilled to see all that and drink all the juices. They kept on doing it till they got tired.

Now, they were real hungry and to quench the hunger Adrian's parents had done something special this time too.

When Adrian asked his parents that where was the food as they were dying of hunger.

Adrian's parents took him to a big shed all decorated with flowers and opened its door.

When Adrian saw inside he was dumbstruck!

The shed was 10 metres tall and about 50 meters wide and was square in shape. Inside there was a whole house made of chocolate and candies. His parents told him that that was the birthday cake and wished him "Happy Birthday". They told him that he should cut the cake now and brought a knife. Adrian took the knife and everybody sang birthday song while he cut the cute big cake.

When Adrian starting cutting cake he saw that there was cavity in the house and Adrian asked his parents what that was? His parents told him to check it out himself. He then entered the cavity of the big cake house and saw sandwiches and candies all a metre long, more than his height placed on plates. They were real sandwiches. Parents told him that if he and his friends were still hungry they can chew the whole cake house and eat all the sandwiches in it which they said "were not gonna get finished by themselves."

All the kids including Adrian ate the cake house and candies and sandwiches but still couldn't finish them.

They all said that they were not tired of eating but they had eaten too much and couldn't eat more as they will get sugar induced coma!

It was time for everybody to go home.

Everybody went home wishing Adrian "Happy Birthday!" one more time.

Suddenly as Adrian was waving good bye he heard his mom shouting telling him to get up and get ready for school. Adrian got up suddenly and he saw that he was in his pyjamas and lying on his bed. Adrian asked his mom that where were his birthday presents. Mom scolded him and told him to stop dreaming and get ready as he was already late for the school bus. She also told him that there were 6 weeks still left for his birthday.

Adrian realized that it was all but a dream. But then he thought at-least he has memory of the dream and he was happy about that.

TaLe 14 : ThE sHoEmAkEr ThAt LoSt HiS OwN ShOeS

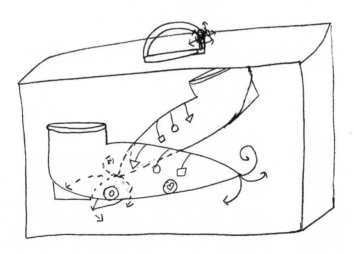

There are many shoemakers in the world but this shoemaker was unique.This shoemaker made so beautiful shoes that even the king wore his made shoes.

He made shoes on order and never hired any assistant to help him make shoes. So since he made shoes all by himself it would take time to complete them. For other shoemakers it took about a week's time to make a single shoe those days. But this shoemaker made a a pair of shoes in a single day. The secret to this was that he used to wear shoes that were gifted to him by an elf and were magical in nature.

His shoes were gifted to him because of his benevolent work. Once he was going through the woods and saw that an elf was upset and talking to himself that his feet skin gets scratched and hurt when he walks through the jungle and can't bear that anymore. The shoemaker approached the elf and told him and asked him that why does not he wear shoes? The elf told the shoemaker that he had never heard about anything like shoes. So the shoemaker explained the elf that shoes were a protective equipment that also gave comfort to feet when worn. So the elf was curious and asked how he could get one and where can he get it from. The shoemaker told the elf that he was a shoemaker himself and will make shoes for him. Then the elf asked the shoemaker that how much time it would take. The shoemaker told elf that it will take him a weeks time to make him good comfortable shoes. The elf was happy to hear that and told the shoemaker that he would be happy if he would make the shoes for him.

Then the shoemaker took out his measuring tape and measured the feet of elf and noted them down in his diary which he always carried. He also took out two big sheets of paper and told elf to keep each of his feet on the separate sheets of paper. The shoemaker then took a pencil moved it around the feet of the elf over the paper and marked them down. The shoemaker told the elf that in one week's time we will meet at this same place in the evening when sun is about to set and I will give you your pair of shoes. The elf agreed and went away thanking the shoemaker.

During that week the shoemaker got the best of the materials to make shoes and made elf's shoes with utmost carefulness and dexterity. The shoes were ready in the time frame and in that evening he went to the forest to give the shoes to its owner.

When the elf saw met him and saw the shoes he was delighted. He tried those shoes and felt very nice and comfortable. He thanked the shoemaker and thought what he could give to the shoemaker for giving him such a wonderful gift. He then decided that if shoemaker could give him such a nice gift then why can't he give him something nice like that. So he took out some magical powder from his pocket and said some magical words and threw the powder on the ground. Suddenly a pair of shoes appeared which were of perfect size of the shoemaker and the elf picked them up and gave it to the shoemaker. He told the shoemaker that those shoes were magical and when he will wear them they would help him in his work.

The shoemaker thanked him and by that time wondered how could those shoes help him in his work.

The next day he went to his shop taking the magical shoes along with him. He had one order of shoes pending which he decided to do wearing those magical shoes. It would had taken him a week to complete that order but he finished it in a day. The shoes that were made were like never he had made. They were so beautifully made that it looked like a machine had made them.

The buyer when came to get his shoes next week was ecstatic to see how finely his shoes were made. He not only thanked the shoemaker and gave him triple the price of the shoes.

Slowly his shoes became talk of the town and the shoemaker started receiving more orders than usual and he became a rich man. Even the king used to order one pair of shoes per week.

Now there was this carpet maker who was a friend of shoemaker. He used to come to shoemakers house quite often.
Although reluctant but once shoemaker told the carpet maker that all his wealth was because of the shoes he wore. The carpet maker wondered how that could be. He told the carpet maker that his shoes were gifted to him by an elf and were magical. When the carpet maker asked him that what was magical about them? The shoemaker told him that they helped him do his work and that instead of taking a week to make a pair of shoe he did that in a day and not only that they caused a workmanship on shoes that was incomparable.

It so happened that the carpet maker was jealous of his friend, the shoemaker and when he came to know of the secret to the shoemaker's success he then thought of using those shoes for himself.

That day the carpet maker went to another shoemaker and asked to him make a look alike shoe of his friend shoemaker who had already seen the shoes of his friend as they were of the famous shoe maker from whom the king got his shoes made. The shoemaker made look alike shoes and gave it to the carpet maker.

The next day the carpet maker went to his friend, the shoemaker's house and stealthily replaced the magical shoes of the shoemaker with the look alike shoes.

Now he went to his shop and wore the magical shoes. The shoes were a bit loose to him but he still decided to wear them and work on making a carpet. The carpet which took him a month's time to finish was completed in a day's time and the workmanship of the carpet was indeed the best of the best as was described by his friend the shoemaker. The carpet maker was surprised to see that and realized that those magical shoes were indeed magical and they really helped in work.

The next day the shoemaker went to work wearing the look alike shoes. He then started to work on his shoe orders but making shoe started taking a week as previously when he used to work without magic shoes.

In the mean time the carpet maker started making carpets that could fly. What he did was he attached wings to the carpet and sold them at a very high price which only rich people could afford.

The shoemaker was confused that he was unable to make shoes in less than a week and his friend the carpet maker had started making flying carpets. This caused him to suspect something fishy was going on so he went to see the carpet maker and when he met him in his shop he saw that the carpet maker was wearing the same shoes as his but were loosely fitted. Upon asking the carpet maker that where did he get the same type of shoe as him and why were they loose to him. The carpet maker replied that he liked the shoemaker's shoes and had asked a shoemaker to make similar kind of shoes as his but the shoemaker made a bit loose fitted shoes as he had lost his size while making.

The shoemaker realized that the carpet maker was lying. The shoemaker went away and did not know how to get back his magical gifted shoes.

The next day the shoemaker went to the king and told him the whole story. Now, the king ordered the carpet maker who had stolen the shoemaker's shoe to appear in front of him. The carpet maker appeared in front of the king. The king then told the carpet maker that he was accused of stealing the shoemaker's shoes but the carpet maker told that the shoemaker was lying and that he was a noble man and can't steal anybody's things. Then the king asked the shoemaker if he could prove that the shoes carpet maker had were shoemaker's shoes only. The shoemaker after thinking for a while told the king that one night he was working wearing those shoes and suddenly a candle felt on his shoes when he was trying to keep it on a table. So that caused some wax to fall on the shoes back. He had removed the wax but since the wax had fallen on his shoes back there must be a sign of oil at the back of the shoe. The carpet maker did not know that. Upon checking the carpet maker's shoe it was true what the shoemaker had told about his shoes. The carpet maker was then sentenced to prison and the shoemaker was returned his shoes.

Now the shoemaker went home thanking king for letting him get his shoes back.

Now that day he wondered that if the carpet maker made carpet that could fly by just adding wings to it why can't he add wings to the shoes he makes and then people can fly wearing them. He also thought the carpet maker was making flying carpets only for rich people but he will make flying shoes for poor people too and then they could enjoy flying too as other people would do.

From that day he started making flying shoes and was famous once again and this time not only in the town but the whole world.

TaLe 15 : tHe FiGhT bEtWeEn HoCkEy StIcK AnD pUcK

Hockey stick and puck usually never fight amongst themselves. It is always simple. Hockey stick tells the puck where to go and the puck goes where it is told to go. They always play along, but once there was a fight between a hockey stick and a puck.

This hockey stick was arrogant and told puck that puck was useless without it and there could be no play without hockey stick. It also told the puck that the hockey stick was so important that the entire game was named after it. Puck felt a little bad hearing that and told the hockey stick that whatever it was saying was not true and puck was important too in the game of hockey.

It told the hockey stick that what if there was no puck how could anybody score a goal. The hockey stick still in arrogance told that goal can be scored anyhow but hockey stick was the most important thing in a game of hockey.

So they challenged each other. Hockey stick told puck that no matter what the puck tries if a hockey player hits it hard using hockey stick it will have to go in that direction alone no matter what it tries and it would not be able to change direction because it won't be able to control itself at such a high speed. Puck disagreed to what the hockey stick said.

So next day at game time the hockey stick and puck were on the rink.

The game started and wherever the puck was forced to go by a hit the puck had to go and as challenged by the hockey stick puck couldn't control itself at that high speeds as it had never tried to do so in the past. It always was obedient and obeyed the push of the stick.

The time had to change and this time the puck talked to the hockey players when that hockey stick was not in sight. It told the players that instead of hitting it straight try hitting it so that it spins and skids at multiple angles. The players listened to the puck and agreed to what it was saying.

There was training match the next day and players did as they were told by the puck. They started hitting the puck so that it spins and skids at multiple angles. The hockey stick no matter how hard it tried to cause the puck to move in the linear direction of its hit but it was not happening as players were causing it to spin and it would go in quite different directions while moving. It would some times go in a circle sometimes in an ellipse shape and sometimes in other shape of motion. Seeing that hockey was a bit shocked and surprised to see what was going on. The hockey tried its level best for the puck to go straight but it failed almost everytime

At the end of the game the puck rarely had moved in any linear direction. The hockey stick realized that it itself was not the most important thing in the game but puck was equally or actually more important than it.

He apologized to the puck for being rude to him and asked for its forgiveness. The puck forgave him and they became friends forever.

TaLe 16 : tHe aLpInE tReE tHaT lOsT iT's ShAdE

There are many trees in this world but amongst them only alpine trees never lose their leaves. They are also known as Christmas trees and are ever green all year round. These trees have leaves like pines and bit of waxy coating that allow least amount of water loss thus making them evergreen all year round.

There was this neighbourhood where many alpine trees grew. Children there enjoyed climbing the trees and building tree houses. They enjoyed playing with the leaves of the alpine trees and sometimes used to break the branches of the trees too which they took along with them and fooled around. Breaking tree branches was not a big deal as they grew back again in some time so no harm was done to those trees.

Now, there was this tree in the same neighbourhood which was also an alpine tree but was a very ignorant and a rude one. He was not very nice to kids. Whenever kids tried to climb the tree it shook as if being blown by the wind and kids climbing the tree fell on the ground. If a kid wanted to break its branch or leaf it used to make them sharp and pricky so no kid could break it or play with it thus no kid ever went near that tree or played around it

The tree fairy saw that and was a bit upset as trees were meant to serve people and that tree was pretty rude and what to talk abut serving people it hardly let any kid enjoy it. After thinking for a long time she thought that if that tree is not pleasant for kids "I should punish it" so she cast a spell on the tree that, "that alpine tree would not grow leaves or branches anymore and also whatever leaves or branches it has they will shed off too". And so it happened.

After a year or so that alpine tree's all leaves were shedded and its branches became weak and started to shed off too which after sometimes were completely shed off.

The tree stood there all alone and cried and wept everyday but there was no turning back from it. The tree fairy watched all of it.

One day a group of men came and saw that the alpine tree was leafless and branchless and they thought that it could be cut down and used for wood. They thought the tree was diseased and it was better to truncate the tree so that the disease which that tree had does not spread to other trees and the other trees remain in good condition. So they decided to bring big saw the next day and bring down the tree.

It so happened that, that night a little girl came near the tree and started playing around it . It tried to look for its leaves but the tree did not have any. Then she tried looking for its branches but that also the tree did not had any. She felt sad seeing that.

The tree was watching all this and it started liking how the little girl was playing and did not wanted her to go so it applied its full effort to grow a small twig along its side when the girl was not looking and had back towards the tree. When the girl turned around and started moving in circles touching the periphery of the tree trunk with her fingers she noticed a small tiny twig (the tree had grown at that at that time without the girl getting to know of it) being felt by her fingers. She wondered that where it had come from. Then she plucked the twig and got excited and started playing around again and singing a song. The tree was delighted to see the little girl happy and enjoyed her company. She after playing got tired and lay her head on the tree's trunk near the ground and slept all night. The tree seeing her sleep on her, wished that if he had leaves he could have protected her form the wind and cold during the night. But as he had always been rude he had to face the punishment at that time.

The tree fairy watched everything and had realized that that alpine tree had suffered and has realized its mistake and has become a tree worthy of living. So when the tree was taking care of the sleeping girl she came near the tree took her spell away and wished that the tree be in its full bloom again.

In the morning when the girl woke up she saw that tree was blossoming with leaves now and also had many branches attached to it. The tree who was deeply sad hadn't realized that it had grown itself back again. When the girl started playing with its lower branches the tree felt a bit strange but when it saw that the girl plucked another twig off it then it realized that the fairy had gifted him good luck again by giving him leaves and branches and he was thrilled to see that.

He thanked the fairy and promised her that he will always be good to the people and kids around.

That day when the men who had decided to chop the tree down when came with the saw didn't find any branchless tree so they were confused but then they realized that it was evening that time when they had seen the lifeless tree and maybe it was a mirage in the cold thus that tree did not existed so they went back without cutting down any tree.

The tree was given a new life and was always making the kids enjoy itself.

TaLe 17 : A mOuSe ThAt gReW a MoUsTaChe

Long long time ago there lived vikings. Vikings were fond of eating and mice was a delicacy at those times which vikings would kill for.

Now mice who had families of their own were always afraid to go outside of their dwellings to gather or look for food as they were food themselves for the vikings who threw axe wherever they found a mouse and would roast them and eat them. The entire mouse population was in a catastrophical danger and if eating and killing of mice continued there would be no mouse left at all one day.Also there was no artificial breeding of them done by the vikings it was more of a game meat thing.

The mice once all gathered around and had a meeting. They decided that to stop themselves being killed by the hands of vikings they had to communicate with them and tell them that. But no mice could speak or write the language of vikings. So they asked for a volunteer who would learn language of the vikings and communicate with them, telling them to stop eating mice. All the mice were afraid to volunteer as everybody knew that no mouse remained alive when it was seen by any viking. The mouse who would volunteer for such a heroic act would have to be very careful and everyday would be a game of life and death for that mouse. Even after knowing all that there was one mouse who bravely stood up and said that he will volunteer for this task and would do his best to succeed. The name of the mouse was Bravo. All the mice cheered for him and hope once again was rising amongst mice.

Bravo started his work the next day. He started going to the school where kids of vikings went to study. He sometimes hid beneath the study desks, sometimes behind the chairs of classroom, sometimes in the broken ceiling but went everyday to the school and tried to learn the language of the vikings bit by bit. As classes advanced he advanced too and in a few years time Bravo not only learnt the verbal part of the language but also learnt how to write their language. Although sometimes Bravo was spotted by the kids who threw axes all around to catch him and eat him but Bravo was always agile and quick enough to run in a hole or hide somewhere where he could not be seen and thus remained safe.

After going to school for a while and learning the language of vikings Bravo was confident in communicating amongst them with their language.

That day all the mice were given notice for a meeting to be held. All the mice came there for meeting. In that meeting Bravo told every mouse that he had learnt the language of vikings and was ready to communicate with them in any form verbal or written. All the mice were happy to hear that and praised Bravo for his courageousness. They then made a plan on how will they communicate with vikings so they can stop killing mice as they were intelligent creatures too. That plan involved first of all to know who was the leader of vikings so that Bravo could talk directly to him.

To know that, mouse scouts were said to keep an eye on who was the viking that was praised the most and was always obeyed to. There were few vikings that were head of the viking chain but after much effort they found out the leader of all the vikings. He was a very powerful man and was always protected by viking soldiers and also was always obeyed to by other vikings.

Now Bravo had to talk to the leader of the vikings and tell him to stop killing mice as they had families too and had kids too who wanted to live their lives too.

Bravo had planned to go to table of leader of viking when he was eating with his family members and tell him straight away that he should tell his people to stop killing mice as they were intelligent creatures too and had families also.

So he did.

When the leader of vikings was sitting on his chair and enjoying meal with his family members sitting alongside the dining table Bravo stealthily snuck on the top of table and started saying hello and greeting them but there came an axe on the table which barely missed his tail sparing himself.

Bravo had to run away. He did not understand why did that happened. He said to himself that "I was talking to the vikings in a perfect viking tongue and in their accent and in a very respectful way, why did they not listen to me and threw an axe straight at me"? After much pondering he realized that he was too small and could not speak loud enough for vikings to hear. Then he decided that he would write a letter and give it to the head of the vikings and inform of his and other mice intentions and what they want from the leader of the vikings. But he realized that just writing a letter and leaving it for the leader of vikings to read would lead no result as they would never believe that that letter is from mice themselves. So that letter has to be written in front of the leader but how?

Bravo and other mice made a new plan they decided that a swarm of mice will run around the house of leader of vikings which would keep other family members busy and by that time Bravo will write the letter in front of the leader of vikings and would inform him of his intentions.

They followed the plan and a group of 100 mice swarmed the house of the leader of vikings and as they had thought all his family members roared FOOD! and got busy in killing the mice that were running around the house. Bravo wasted no time and went near the viking leader so that the leader could see him and started writing in big size letters on a paper while running for his life "Don't eat mice. We have families too. We will come again to know the answer." After he had written this he ran leaving the paper in the hands of viking leader who first of all freaked out that mice could write and understand their tongue too.

Then the viking leader had a meeting and discussed this with leaders of his army. They then decided that it was difficult to quit eating mice as it was part of their delicacy. So the viking leader thought that he could not say no to the request of mice of not eating them as they had families too so he waited until next day when mice would come and ask for his decision.

The next day mice came to the table of the leader and Bravo wrote asking that what was the decision of the viking leader. The viking leader told them that it would be difficult to stop eating mice because they liked them so much but he told that there was one way by which they could become of their class and that they would stop eating mice if any of the mice grew moustache. The viking leader thought that it was impossible for a mouse to grow a moustache so eating mice would never stop.

Bravo and mice left the table sad and depressed. But then they realized that they had a mouse sorcerer who could do some tricks on mouse so they went to her asking for her help. The mouse sorcerer said that it shouldn't be a problem to grow a moustache on a mouse so she did some spell casting and grew a moustache on Bravo which looked just as any other viking's moustache. All the mice rejoiced to see that.

Now they showed that to the viking leader who when saw that Bravo had grown a moustache had to keep his word otherwise he would have no honour left amongst his people.

From that day killing of mice stopped and mice lived happily ever after, not so true for the vikings who managed their taste buds somehow.

All because of Bravo, who grew a moustache!

TaLe 18 : tHe HoT aIr BaLLOoN tHaT eNtErEd SpAcE

Once there existed an era when there were only hot air balloons to fly in air. Airplanes had not been invented at that time. People only flew only hot air balloon if they wanted to fly in air.

But there was one boy whose name was Nick and he wanted to go to space and see for himself. At that time rockets had not been invented so it was impossible to enter space with only hot air balloons.

People might think that a person can go into space just by hot air balloon too if they keep the cylinders in the hot air balloon that makes the air in the hot air balloon hot burning but that's not true. Hot air balloons work on the principle of air pressure and density difference amongst the air mass in the hot air balloon and outside air. So as the air in the hot air balloon becomes hot it becomes less dense and less heavy and due to air buoyancy is lifted up. But that lifting up is to a certain point, after that if you keep on going higher the air inside the hot air balloon becomes so full of pressure that it will burst and the hot air balloon will fall down. Thus there is a limit up to which a hot air balloon can ascend too. The hot air balloon barely crosses the stratosphere and going beyond that is pretty impossible for hot air balloon, only a rocket could do that.

Nick grew up with a thought of entering space but did not know how. At that time there was a concept of space that it does not have air and if a body enters space would burst because of high internal body pressure but no outside pressure.

Nick realized that to enter space he has to go through atmosphere's air first as a point of crossing. So he started to learn to fly hot air balloon. While learning to fly hot air balloon he learnt that there was a limit to which a hot air ballon could fly to and come back because of the air pressure differences involved in it. He was always excited to fly hot air balloon. He studied hard and cleared all the papers required to pass the hot air balloon pilot exam and finally got hot air balloon licence. He was happy to get the hot air balloon pilot's licence and felt lucky that day. Now, he could own his own hot air balloon or fly other's hot air balloon without an instructor which always made him feel happy. His dream of going to space, finally started making some progress.

He thought of buying a hot air balloon for himself but for that he had to earn some money. So he worked full time at a hot air balloon manufacturing shop and studied those gaseous cylinders that emitted hot gases to make the air in the hot air balloon hot. While studying those hot air balloon cylinders he realized that going in space also demanded a support of his body blood pressure and at that altitude since there is no atmosphere there was also requirement of oxygen for breathing purposes. He thought about for a few days and decided that to support the body pressure and its functions he needed a pressurized suit that he called a space suite. The space suit should be fully closed and insulated so that nothing leaks from it. So he went to a shop and bought a thick nylon-cotton cloth and took it to his home. He measured the cloth and started cutting it to his size. He made three layers of the cloth and stitched them and insulated them. He then got a glass chamber big enough to fit his head. He then attached the glass chamber/helmet to the sewed three layer suit. To make it completely sealed after wearing it he attached a system through which air does not leak out. Now he had to attach oxygen cylinders along with it so that he can breath inside the space suit. It was then time to wear it and try its effectiveness. To do that he went to a nearby pond and took the suit along with it. He wore the suit, turned the oxygen cylinders on and jumped into the pond. When he was inside the pond he realized that the oxygen supply was good and there was no water coming inside the suit. To double check it's seal when he came out he put his hand all over inside the suit and realized that it was dry therefore the suit was good to go and test in space.

How to enter space was the next question. While working in the hot air balloon shop he also had studied that the cylinders that heat up the air not only do that but also exert a pressure when are fired up. So he saw that more the pressure was exerted down the more the pressure was caused upwards which was according to Newtons third law of motion that to every action there is equal and opposite reaction. To check that once he tilted the cylinder's exhaust downwards, when he did that the cylinder moved upwards with a great force which made him decide that he will use this system to go in space. He also noticed that the cylinder got depleted very soon when kept on maximum burning power so he had to use more cylinders for his flight towards space.

Now that was also the day when he had earned money to buy a hot air balloon and some he saved extra for a rainy day.

Next day he came to the shop and bought a hot air balloon and fifty cylinders along with it. He then attached one cylinder in the centre of the hot air balloon to heat up the air in hot air balloon in a normal upward exhaust releasing direction and remaining he attached inverted to the sides of the hot air balloon. He then waited for suitable atmospheric conditions to come. On the 5th day he saw that there was no cloud cover and the winds were calm too which was a perfect weather condition for his flight.

He went behind the backyard of his house and got geared up wearing the space suit and sat in the hot air balloon. He then turned on the supply of the one cylinder that was kept in the normal position in hot air balloon and lit it so that hot air balloon starts heating air in it and makes it fly. After an hour or so, hot air balloon started developing lift and rising up in the air. After two hours of flight the hot air balloon reached an altitude of approximately 80,000 feet. He then saw that hot air balloon was not going higher anywhere and this was the time he had been waiting for. At that time he turned the oxygen supply of his suit on and then opened the valves of the inverted cylinders and lit them with his pocket lighter. After doin that he immediately felt so much thrust that he sat tightly on his knees holding the hot air ballon basket. While going up he saw that the hot air balloon which initially caused the whole system to be lifted up to 70,000 feet burst and he was left with nothing but the basket of the hot air balloon being propelled upwards with a tremendous force. After some time he heard a big boom (which was the "sound barrier" breaking noise) and later realized that he was going faster than the escape velocity which is required to overcome the gravity of earth and started floating in space within another 3 hours of his flight. His basket was still thrusting up but then he turned off the supply of hot matter in the cylinders that was causing the thrust.

After reaching space tears came rolled down his eyes when he saw the earth. It was like nothing he had seen before and also he had accomplished something that nobody could ever accomplish at that time. After spending about 6 hours in space he wanted to go back and tell the people on earth that he went to space, but going back he did not know how to do that because he had never anticipated that to return it will be difficult. At that time he realized that going down would only be possible through the thrusters that brought him up. So by tilting the cylinders to upward thrust causing direction he entered the atmosphere and sometimes turning them upwards and downwards he slowed and speeded up and finally reached the ground of earth. At that time he immediately took off his space suit and jumped on the ground and ran on it. He was never more happy than he was at that time to see the ground as he had escaped death going in and out of space.

He then told this to his friends who never believed but he knew he had been in space and it was his dream come true!

tAle 19 : A bOy ThAt gReW A dOg'S tAiL

This is a story about a bully boy whose name was Bob. Bob ate the food of his fellow students and would let them go hungry during the entire school day. Bob could not be stopped as he was too smart to get caught. Every time any parent would complain about him he was never scolded or kept in detention because there was no proof of his wrong doing.

Bob was jealous of the intelligent ones in the class as he himself was not good in studies. He did not wanted any of his class fellows to score good marks in exam as he never did. What bob did was during class time he took note of whichever of his class fellow was giving too many correct answers to the questions the teacher was asking in the class and during each subject. At break time he went to that kid and told him to bring his food tray to Bob's food table and transfer all the food he had to his food tray. Bob then told the boy or girl that was bullied to sit besides him until he finished the both of their's food so that nobody notices and then told him to go away. His fellow students had to do that because if they didn't do what they were asked to do by Bob there were consequences. If someone did not give him food that day if he was asked to do so by Bob, then that kid was either made to sit on a to and fro swing and given great pushes until the kid goes higher and higher and until the time he can't control himself on the swing and falls. If not that the boy was made to sit in a miniature merry go around which was turned around till the time the boy sitting inside could not keep himself holding to the swing and fly's out, off the swing, falling to the ground. If that didn't work he made the kid do sit ups until the boy faints and remembers not to mess with Bob. This continued for a while, until there was a new admission of a kid named Sam.

Sam was a son of a witch. He was a nice guy and good in studies too. Sam got his admission in the same class as that of Bob who did not know that he was a witch's son.

So that day Sam came to the class and was introduced and greeted by all the students and teachers of the class except Bob who gave a rude look at him. Sam sat on his seat in the classroom and the class continued. Sam was an intelligent guy and good at answering questions. He answered many difficult   questions asked in the class. That day since Sam was answering too many questions asked by the teacher, during break time Bob did what he did with other kids who were smart in the class. He went to Sam and told him to give him his food but Sam refused at first but then his fellow classmates told him to do as Bob says, because Bob was a bully and he did very bad things to kids who did not listen to him. Sam after listening to his classmates gave food to Bob and went hungry that day. When Sam reached home he told his mom everything. His mom was furious over that. But his mom told Sam not to worry and gave him a magic pop can and told him if Bob does that again today, give him this pop can also, to drink. Sam did as he was told.

That day Sam answered questions put by teacher again and Bob was again mad at him and told him to give his food again to him. Sam did as he was told, he gave Bob the food from his food tray and also gave him the pop can that his mom had given to him. Bob ate the food and also drank the pop from the pop can. No sooner he had finished drinking the pop from the can he started feeling pain in his hip bone and in less than a minute a tail grew from there. It looked exactly like a dog's tail. Kids that were seeing this all started laughing at Bob and there was a great commotion around. Hearing the commotion the principal came there and saw that Bob had a tail attached to its back. She scolded Bob and told him that this was a school and not a costume party and put her hands on the tail, held it firmly and tried to take it out from Bob's back. To her surprise there was a huge cry from Bob who told her not to pull her tail as it cause a great deal of pain. She then noticed that the tail actually had grown from behind Bob's back and was no artificial one. She was shocked to see that and did not know what to do. All the kids were still mocking at Bob and were happy that Bob the boy who used to pick on others got himself picked at today.

Meanwhile, the principal called animal control and told them that there was a dog in his school who was causing great deal of panic amongst students. Animal control came and saw Bob who had a big dog's tail at that time and figured out that, that must be the dog the principal was talking about. Since Bob was screaming and running here and there the animal control had to fire a tranquilizer shot to calm him down. They took him away in a dog van to dogs facility.

Now, Sam was seeing all this. He figured out that it was because of the drink that his mom had given him for Bob to drink if he ate his food again. Sam felt a little bad at first but then at that day after school he went to where Bob was kept and told him that his mom was a witch and he had grown a tail because of the drink that he drank. He told Bob that it was a punishment given to him by his mom because he ate his food. Bob was in utmost shame and realized that he had been too mean and bad to the kids in his class so he apologized to Sam and told him that he would apologize to all the kids in the class and whoever he had bullied and would never do that again. Sam told him that since he had realized his mistakes and folly he would go to his mom and ask for an antidote of the magic pop which she had given to him for Bob.

The next day after school, Sam went to meet Bob taking another magic pop can and told him to drink it. Bob was first afraid but he then drank the pop and at the moment's instance his tail disappeared. Bob was then released of the animal control prison.

Next day Bob went to school and apologized to all the kids who he had bullied ever and told them that he would never bully again. Bob was a changed boy now.

He started being more attentive to what teachers were explaining and learnt more thus he himself became a good student and thus never had to be jealous of other students anymore. Sam and Bob became best friends forever.

TaLe 20 : GrAnDmA's GiFt Of TaLkInG mAgNeTiC dAnCiNg dOLLs

There are many kinds of dolls in this world but have you ever heard of dolls that are magnetic and dance too. These dolls were not only magnetic dancing dolls but they talked too. These were a gift by grandma to her granddaughter whose name was Alexandra. The gift was actually a big jewellery box which did not have any jewellery in it but in it lay 7 magnetic-base dolls. To make them dance these dolls where put on a small platform in upright position. The jewellery box also came with a key which was inserted to side of the jewellery box and rotated several times to start the mechanism which produced a song and also caused the dolls on the platform standing, to rotate and revolve causing it to look like that they were dancing.

What the turning key did was that when it was turned in its system it loaded up tension in the coil spring with further through a linkage system caused the platforms magnetic fields to change causing the dolls to rotate and revolve. These dolls fell too when the jewellery box was disturbed while they were dancing or the dolls were not kept properly to start with.

Now, Alexandra was very fond of these dolls. Everyday at-least five times she used to turn the key on that caused the dolls to dance. The song that was played along, matched their dancing steps and they looked very beautiful while dancing.

Alexandra grew up and as she grew up her fondness for the dancing dolls decreased and she stopped playing the dancing dolls. She kept the jewellery box in a locker and closed it and got busy in her work.

At those times people used to listen to news too but not by radio or television but through the word of mouth by messengers and it took several days, weeks and even months for people to hear news of the entire world.

One day Alexandra was walking near the locker in which she had locked her grandma's gifted jewellery box, thinking about something. She heard some noises coming from the locker. She thought that a rodent had entered the locker and to stop it from destroying things in the locker she opened the locker to get rid of the rodent. When she opened the locker she saw that the magnetic dolls were talking to each other. Alexandra got a bit afraid and did not know what to do. But the dolls seeing her get pale told her not to be afraid and that they were just dolls and won't eat or bite her. Hearing that Alexandra cooled down. She then asked the dolls that what in the world they were talking about. The dolls told her to make them dance on the jewellery box platform like she used to do when she was young and then they will tell her what they were talking about. Alexandra did as she was told to do. She took the key from jewellery box turned it in its system and placed the dolls on it. The music started playing and dolls started dancing. Now they told Alexandra that they were talking dolls and were telling each other about the news from the 7 different continents. They also told her that each of the dolls represented the 7 continents of the world and had the ability to know what was going on in those continents of the world without actually going there. One doll could tell the news about one continent only which it represented. Alexandra on hearing that, was excited and asked the dolls if they could tell the news to her if she wanted to know it. The dolls told her that since she was the owner of their house which was the jewellery box and had taken care of them they would happily tell her the news but they took a promise from her. They told her she wouldn't disclose their secret and neither will she exaggerate and neither will she lie the news if she had to tell it to anybody. She promised this to the dancing dolls. Now she wanted to check that those dolls gave the correct news and that they did not lie. So she asked a news from the country which she belonged to which was Africa and they told her that in a small town in Kenya an elephant had got mad and had attacked that town. In the attack it had killed a new born baby and then the Kenyan authorities had to kill the elephant as elephant had become too dangerous for the population there. Now to find out that if it was true or not she waited for a few days and then there was this same news heard by her and her fellow countrymen through a messenger. Now she was sure that the dancing dolls were not lying.

She thought that it was a good way to make money by telling news faster than any messenger. So she announced in her village that she can tell whats going on in the different continents of the world before any other messenger could deliver the news. She also told her countrymen that her authenticity can be checked any time before relying upon her. Now, she started playing her dolls on the dancing platform and started to listen to the news they had and told that news to her countrymen. Many times people checked if she was saying the truth and always found out that she gave the correct news. She started earning good money from that and became very famous. She also started becoming leader of the country. So she thought if she wanted to rule her country she has to do something wicked so that people choose her as their leader and overthrow the current leader. She was already famous but that was not enough for her. She wanted to lead her country and she had evil in her eyes. Now after giving news for such a long she was trusted as a news teller of the country and thus messengers from other countries had stopped coming.

She thought if she starts manipulating the news for her own good then she'll surely become the leader of the country. The first day she manipulated news about her country itself the doll who used to give her news about her country stopped talking at all and never spoke again. Even the other dolls stopped giving her news and did not talk. Those dolls never talked afterwards. Alexandra again got afraid and did not know what to do. So with nothing in her hand she thought that now she has to become the leader of her country any how because she couldn't give correct news to the people to earn money.

Once she faked a big news that the neighbouring country was about to attack them and before they could attack we should attack them and get them unaware and win the war. The leader of her country at that time listened to her and did what she said.

Doing that they won the war and she won the next election but caused lots of casualties in the neighbouring country. Many children and women had died in the war. That country had always been friendly to her country but just to rule she made her country an enemy of the that country. Now when she was leader her ministers wanted to hear the news of other countries from her so they could decide political matters with other countries and make their country better in all ways but the news telling dolls did not spoke and she did not know what to do and how to get news.

Then she remembered that when her grandma had gifted her that jewellery box with the dolls in she had told her that if dolls stop functioning tell the truth.

She at that time was too young to understand what her Grandma meant by that but she still remembered her words till that day.

In the evening that day she went to her jewellery box that was hid in her locker an opened it and twisted the key in the system and put the dolls on top of the platform. The dolls danced but did not talk. Then she whispered to one of the dolls that she had done wrong and falsified news. To her surprise she heard "Really. You should never do that again" and all the dolls started talking. Now she told them everything what she had done to be the leader. She told them how she caused war amongst two friendly nations and that how many children and women were killed. The dolls told that if she wants to hear them talk to her she has to tell that the news of attack was a fake news given by her to both the countries and as a leader she should surrender. She did as she was told. She although got arrested but got to keep her jewellery box with magnetic dancing dolls in it with her in the prison. She although died in the prison but the other countries became friends back again and they swore never to have a war. They demilitarized their defences and stood strong morally.
Until today they never ever had a war but still remember the folly of Alexandra and the results of fake news.

TaLe 21 : ThE mUsIc MaKeR

Long ago there lived a music maker in a world where everything was solved by his music. His name was Dremlin. People did not know what it was or how it was produced but they knew they liked it. To cure an illness or to cause rain when it was too dry Dremlin was called to play music. His music had cure for all the problems in the world. When there was a relationship problem or when there was flood Dremlin was called to play music. His music caused rain when it was too dry and also evaporated water when there was a flood. So his music was used to solve every problem.

Now nobody knew how this sound was caused or produced because Dremlin never showed it to anybody. Wherever he was called to cause music he just brought a big room size box moved by a horse on wheels. He then went inside the box and did something which produced the sound and solved the situation. He was most sought after, and even the king of used his services for national affairs.

The king always had undaunted success over his enemies in war as he never lost because of the music maker - Dremlin. Whenever there was a war against this king and country Dremlin was called to play music. The music Dremlin played screamed out the people of the attacking nation. The army of his Dremlin's country was not affected by the music because they wore ear plugs which were specially designed by Dremlin to prevent that pitch of music or squeaky noise from entering ears of ones who will be wearing them and were highly classifieds as secret weapons of Dremlin's country.

Dremlin was paid highly by the king for his music work.

Now, Dremlin was getting old but his music making should continue, to keep peace in the country and for good of people. He thought of keeping an apprentice. So he started looking for one. Many young people came to get the job of music making but he only found one who he saw some skills in hands that can be made to learn to play music. The young boy's name was Leemo.

Leemo was very enthusiastic to learn the music but he had never known how it was done. The first day Dremlin only made him listen to it which he played being hidden in the music box. He played an array of different kind of music which Leemo listened the whole day without interrupting. The next day he asked Leemo what he thought it could be, that produced the sound but Leemo had no idea. He did not know what caused those sounds. That day Dremlin took Leemo to his music room/box and showed him all the different instruments that he played to cause music. There were 5 string instruments including a piano and a guitar and the remaining were squeaky, drum instruments and different type of flutes. Next day Dremlin told Leemo to sit inside the music box and just play the instruments without worrying that if they were making any type of sound or not. Leemo listened to Dremlin and did what he said.

He went inside the box and touched the instruments one by one. First he pressed the keys of piano. When he pressed the keys he saw that all the keys had different sounds and they were not just meant for hammering your fingers for comfortable positions. Next he tried plucking the strings of the guitar. He found the same thing for the guitar too that all the guitar strings played different sounds. Same was true for violin, harp and the other string instrument that was called a cello. Next he tried playing the drums. He did not know how they worked so he tried knocking them. When he knocked on the drums' he heard boom noises which first freaked him out but later he understood that that was what they did. Now, it was time to know the flute instruments. First he touched the flutes and pressed their keys but no sound was produced. He did not understand how to cause sound from them. He then picked up a trumpet and started hitting it with the front flat face of his hand, now this caused sound but that was not much. After doing that for sometime he realized that air caused the sound in the trumpet so he blew air through the trumpet's mouth. When he blew air through the trumpet's mouth he realized that vaguely blowing air in the mouth of the trumpet did not work and there was a particular way of holding tongue between the lips and then blowing air which then caused the sounds through trumpet. This caused excitement in him and by that time he was done examining the instruments. He came out and told Dremlin that he tried all the instruments and played them one by one. Dremlin was happy to hear that.

Now Dremlin started taking Leemo to whichever place he was called for his services. Leemo and Dremlin both sat inside the music box, Dremlin played and Leemo saw how Dremlin played and tried to learn and remember how he played for his practice.

Leemo once asked Dremlin that why doesn't he show his wonderful music instruments to all, so that everybody could play them and solve their own problems. Dremlin told leemo that he had developed these instruments after a lot of hard work and also it was his bread earning source. Leemo argued back saying that even if he shows the musical instruments to people they wouldn't be able to make as much good music as him and he will still be able to earn his bread but Dremlin did not understand and agreed to it. He said that it was best if people did not know how to play it. Leemo listened to him and kept mum without arguing back again.

As years passed Dremlin became old and Leemo not only learned to play good music as Dremlin but also learnt how to make those instruments. Now, wherever Dremlin was called Leemo had to go as Dremlin was too old to travel even within the village. One day Dremlin died and only Leemo was left to do the music work.

Leemo continued the work. He became rich and prospered. He was respected everywhere.

In those days war got different. Before there was a war between a group of armies but this time there was a war between a group of enemies who came from outside got scattered and attacked civilians and their families including kids and women. This could not be tolerated by the people of the country and also it was not possible for Leemo to go everywhere to save people.

One day Leemo decided that even though he has earned a lot of money but that money was useless if people's lives could not be saved. So he remembered once he had thought of teaching music to the people of the country so that they would be able to hep themselves and especially in this time of war wherein people were defenseless as the attacking enemy army soldiers were too strong and well equipped which civilians weren't.

So he made an announcement in the entire kingdom that he will teach music to people so that they could defend themselves as gathering muscles for physical fight took longer and was not possible for all humans to become strong and learn to fight but music learning could be done by almost everybody so he started giving lessons.

People flocked from all over the kingdom to learn the music.
Leemo showed them all kinds of instruments he had and taught them how to make squeaky sounds through a single instrument which was small and was called a squeaker. People learnt that and they tested it while wearing the specially designed earplugs to protect themselves from the sound.

After learning to make squeaky sounds people were able to defend themselves from enemies. People always made themselves and their families wear the ear plugs which allowed hearing of normal conversations but prevented squeaky sounds to pass through their ears which kept their ears safe.

Whenever they saw the enemies attacking them they played the squeaky sound and the enemies freaked and screamed out and ran away and thus there existed peace in the kingdom forever. Later people also learnt to play other types of music and solved their own problems themselves.

Leemo became a minster in the kings court and became more rich but he always remained good at heart and always helped people.

TaLe 22 : tHe LaNd Of GlAsS tReEs

Once there were good dwarves and bad dwarves.

The bad dwarves lived in a forest which was so dark and black that even light did not enter there. The forest looked like as if it was made of trees that were burnt.

The good dwarves lived in a forest that was made of glass trees. It was the most amazing forest which was unimaginably beautiful.

The fascinating thing about the trees was that they were not non-living trees. These trees not only blossomed with fruits but also gave protection to the dwarves. The trick was that one could only devour the fruits that were fallen as only fallen fruits turned to organic eatable form. If fruit from trees was plucked it would first of all not break even if it broke from the trees stem it would become dust and disappear. So only fallen fruits were collected as only they were eatable. How the trees protected the dwarves was unique. As trees were made of glass it reflected images and thus multiplied them. So if one dwarf came near the trees it looked like 50-60 dwarves were there which was good as they looked more in numbers and thus in those days when strength was counted in numbers they seemed to be more in quantity thus more strong and powerful and any enemy including the bad dwarves were afraid to attack them or challenge them. This secret was only known to the good dwarves who never told it to anybody.

The good dwarves continued their life living and enjoying amongst the glass trees which were always loved and respected.

The bad dwarves always wanted to take over the glass trees forest and destroy the good dwarves. So they were always looking for a way to do that. In the previous battle they had always seen that the number of good dwarves far exceeded (due to reflection of trees) the number of bad dwarves. So whenever they had gone close to the attacking the good dwarves and had reached the border of the dark (which was dark and thus did not cause any reflection by the glass trees) and glass forests they would see that there were tens of thousand of good dwarves standing and defending their glass tree forest so they would have to return back to their dark forest without battling.

Now there was a meeting amongst the bad dwarves. They discussed the same agenda of taking over glass tree forest and capturing the good dwarves. They wondered that even though they were dwarves too but they could never had that much population as that of the good dwarves even though they tried their best. So they said that there must be a secret weapon which the good dwarves had that caused them to have so many of them of their kind. They then decided to send a scout and see how is it possible for them to be always so great in numbers.

The bad dwarf that was chosen to check out the cause of strength of good dwarves was called Wickedy. He was first reluctant and afraid to go to check out the secret of good dwarves but then he agreed.

He choose a day and prepared for it. He had to go near the border of dark and glass forest and enter it to check out the the secret of good dwarves. But he had to be very careful to do that because all along the border there were watch towers of the good dwarves which were always checking for any intruder trying to enter their forest. Wickedy slowly and wickedly hiding behind the dark forest trees reached near the border of forests. There he saw that there were watch towers all along the border and the good dwarves were in them keeping an eye for anybody who dared to enter their land. Wickedy did not know how to enter the highly protected glass tree forest so he stood behind a dark tree and just observed. While he stood behind a dark tree and observed he saw that the movements of a group of dwarves was always similar whatever they did. If one moved right the similar looking dwarves moved in the same direction, if they moved left the similar looking dwarves moved left and if one bended all the similar looking dwarves bended and all was very accurately being followed. First he got afraid to know how disciplined those dwarves were and thus how powerful their attack would be but still he did not leave that place and kept on observing. As he was looking something happened. He saw that a glass apple fell on the ground and turned into a real apple. He then saw a dwarf come down from his watch tower and eat that apple. Now when the dwarf came down to eat that apple he realized that how was it possible that only one apple fell and 50 dwarves are eating the same apple standing at different places he got scared and tried to run back to the bad dwarves. So he did. As he was walking back he realized that he had left the notebook in which he was taking notes of the positions and strength of the good dwarves behind the tree where he was standing. So he went back to get that notebook. He reached the tree and as he picked up the notebook the sun shined brightly at the notebook and since that tree was near glass trees the notebook had a reflection on the glass trees and it looked as if there were 50 of those. Wickedy freaked out again and thought how was it possible. He threw the notebook again on the ground behind the tree and tried picking it up again, he again saw 50 notebooks on the ground and when he picked up 50 hands picked it up and at same speed he started to understand that there is something with the light and the glass trees which were not only beautiful but caused some sort of reflection that caused one thing too look too many. He was rejoiced to know the secret. He immediately rushed back stealthily though and informed the bad dwarves about the secret of the good dwarves. The bad dwarves first mystified but gained mental strength to understand that and rejoiced after knowing this. Then they understood that the good dwarves must be almost same in numbers but only due to glass tree reflections they looked more. So they decided to attack in two months. They wrote a warning letter to good dwarves telling them that they now know the secret of their strength which was because of the reflection caused by trees and that they will attack them in two months. When the good dwarves read the received letter that was attached to an arrow shot towards their land and had landed on ground the good dwarves for the first time in their life had a nightmare. They did not know what to do.

They had to do something so to prevent themselves from getting captured and starved by the evil bad dwarves. They thought for a day and could not come to any conclusion. So they prayed to the fairy godmother to help them out. At that time came a voice "break the trees". The dwarves did not know what to make of it because breaking trees would mean destroying their own forest which they would never want but then they decided to listen to fairy godmother and tried breaking a tree. They had never broken a tree before so they first thought that breaking a glass tree would turn into a regular organic tree which will loose its reflective property just like a fallen fruit and leave them more vulnerable to enemies but even then they did and this was not the case. When they brought a axe and tried hitting and cutting the tree it took a lot of dwarves and strength but when they did the whole tree shattered into glass pieces which was strange because it should have turned into a normal tree but that did not happen. Now the tree got shattered into different small and big size glass pieces which looked beautiful. They took the glass pieces in their hand and checked them out. When they checked out the glass pieces, they found out that they were very pricky and when kept in front of sunlight caused the grass to burst up in flame i.e. it made the sunlight too hot causing it to burn wherever it was directed as sunlight passed through it. They were excited to see that and realized that it could be used as a weapon against the bad dwarves. They at that time thanked the fairy godmother and started preparing for war.

They broke few trees. Since the trees were very big, few trees were enough to accumulate so many glass pieces that could be scattered all across border. Then each good dwarf was told to carry one broken glass piece.

Two months ended and the bad dwarves came to attack. This time they were sure that they would win the war and capture the good dwarves and glass tree forest but they did not knew what lied ahead. The bad dwarves were warned before entering the glass tree forest but they did not paid heed to the warning and tried to run and cross the border. As they started crossing border and running over broken glass pieces their feet got brutally injured and started bleeding they screamed and yelled in pain and turned back. They then decided to shoot arrows towards the good dwarves who warned them again. The good dwarves had shields that defended themselves from attacking arrows. Now the good dwarves took out the glass pieces and aimed at the bad dwarves. Those glass pieces due to sunlight caused the dwarves clothes to lit up and burn with fire. The bad dwarves freaked out and got so scared that they ran back to their forest and swore to never attack again. They realized that good dwarves had many powerful weapons and that they could not win over the good dwarves ever.

Thereafter the good dwarves were never attacked and lived merrily and happily as usual forever after for many generations to come.

tALe 23 : It RaInEd OrAnGe JuIce ThAt DaY

Before Earth existed a planet called Ausmessy existed. That planet was one thousand time smaller than Earth. It was similar to Earth in a way that it also had a sun that was at appropriate distance from it and thus supported life on it. Ausmessy had only one island which was surrounded by water on all sides. The island's name was Peace. But it was not at all peaceful in that planet not because there was any war going on but because there was no peace in people's heart who lived there. It was all because of a king who ruled the land and the planet.

The king's name was Gred. He was the cruelest of all the kings ever existed and ever seen by mankind. He levied the taxes of highest order and of cruelest in nature. According to him man's eating was not good for the environment as more they ate the more they pooped so there were taxes on people's cooked food which was calculated by the amount of groceries they bought. Not only that, he did not spare the cattle and poultry also. There were food tax on poultry and cattle's food too. Also the regular tax on income was 90%.

People had no option but to live there and get agreed to circumstances which were upon them. They could not leave the planet nor could they die as there was death tax too which was imposed on family of the person who dies and was too much. People could not fight against the king because he had his soldiers who were far too strong and far well trained for battle if any and were mean like him.

In Ausmessy there were grown very delicious oranges that were very sweet and eating them was like eating sugar filled candies. The oranges were un-comparable to anything. But nobody had ever tasted them except the king. There was this rule in the kingdom that nobody was allowed to eat the oranges except the king and anybody who dared to eat it will face a very cruel tortuous death and a death tax equal to 100 times the normal death tax would be imposed on the family of person which would be carried out till his/her generations to come. Due to this nobody ever even dared to even smell the oranges except one.

This boy's name was Caouro. He was born to very poor family in Ausmessy. When he was just 3 years old he was taken to the market by his parents to get some things. At that time a cart full of oranges was passing through. That cart of oranges was meant for the king. As the cart was passing through there came a donkey in front of the cart and caused the cart driver to swivel the cart which further caused one of the orange to fell on ground. Now Caouro who was too young at that time. He left his mother's hand and crawled towards the shiny orange at picked it up and squeezed it lke a child does. Some juice from the orange squeezed out and got sprayed in his mouth. Caouro who was utmost delighted to have tasted the orange juice and tried to squeeze more but suddenly his mom came, picked him up and she along with Caouro's Dad swiftly walked away. The orange that was on the ground later was just squashed and squeezed by the traffic going on road and was not tasted by anybody.

That was the luckiest day for Caouro yet, who was the only person except the king who had tasted orange. Since orange was nothing like he had ever had before, he remembered it always.

Now, Caouro, when he grew up was a hard working lad. His father ran a candle shop. Since those were many candle shops they did not have much profit from their shop and also because the taxes were too high they could not save or start another business. Caouro helped his father in his work at the shop. But Caouro was a good hearted boy and he did not like the poverty that was all around Ausmessy so whatever he earned he distributed it to the poor beggars and saved very little for himself. His father knew that and used to tell him to save some for himself too but he used to say that "Better the needy than be in need." His father used to smile at him and used to thank God for a wonderful kid like him.

Not only his father but Caouro used to pray too. He used to pray that the orange juice that he had when he was a child while squeezing it on the road should be available to everybody in the kingdom and that no person should go hungry ever.

The king had a problem, he wasted all his food. The excessive food was given to his pet animals and the army he had. And about oranges because they came in millions to his palace and it was only he who ate them, tonnes of oranges went waste and were thrown in the sea and as there was nobody to question him he did that forever.

Now due to wasting of oranges and throwing them in the sea water started getting filled up with orange juice but since the sea is salty so orange juice never tasted sweet. The juice tasted sour. But it so happened that that year it was too hot and at those temperatures sugar including the orange juice started evaporating in the atmosphere and thus one day it was so hot that it rained orange juice. People when first saw the rain they got scared because it was orange in colour and people though it was another trick of the cruel king to kill them. So they ran to shelter themselves towards their houses but when someone tasted it when trying to gasp his breath while running he was overjoyed and yelled "It is sweet" and he tasted more and more of it. The someone who tasted it was no other than Caouro who had tasted it after a very long time, then realized that it was orange juice and he felt very excited after seeing that it was raining orange juice. So he went to his house and brought a big tub outside his house so that it can fill with the sweetest of drink that ever existed and show it to the people that it was something nice. Other people who saw that tried to taste the juice/rain water too and they felt delighted too because it was a bliss for them and everybody filled their tubs with the juice and thanked God! They later also thanked Caouro for telling them what it was.

From that day on there existed no food problem because it always rained orange juice after that day and the king could not do anything about it.

Tale 24 : tHe TrOuBLiNg iCe CrEaM mAChinE

Long ago in Antartica lived an ice cream maker. His name was Fred. He was the only ice cream maker in whole of Antartica. During those times there were no refrigerators so how did he make ice creams? He actually discovered the art of making ice cream by accident. Fred was actually a milkman who sold milk for living. What happened was once he had put the milk in a pot under the fire for heating and he did not have sufficient wood for heating but even then he continued to heat it up. At that time somebody called him and he had to go as it was an emergency. He forgot to turn off the fire and went away. He came back after 3 hours. When he came he saw that the milk was still being heated up with some fire still left. He quickly put the fire off and checked the milk. At that time the milk was too hot too taste so he kept it outside for it to get cold. After some time when the milk got a bit chilled he tried to taste it. The taste was a bit different and looked a bit curd like. Something came in his mind and he added lots of sugar to it. Then he tried tasting it again and this time when he tasted it, it was nothing like he had ever had before and as he was sitting outside to have the cold creamy milk he realized the more cold it got the tastier it was. He called it an ice cream.

Actually what had happened was the milk due to being heating in low heat setting because of less wood and then being heated for a prolonged time had caused the water in the milk to evaporate and only fat which is cream to be left in it and on adding sugar to it and cooling it further made it turn to ice cream.

Now, Fred realized that this was something that kids would love to eat and so if he starts making it and selling it to kids it would be more profitable as nobody ever made this kind of thing in their village. But he also realized that if he he makes it in front of people everybody will know how to make it and thus there will be competition in his business so he decided of making ice cream in a small closed container which he called as ice cream machine. He perfected the art of making ice cream in the container in such a way that when he poured condensed milk in the machine ice cream came out. What he did was he made propeller shaped fans and attached them to a small rotating handle. The wind passed at high velocity through the fans when the handle was rotated thus decreasing pressure and causing chilling effect thereby causing rapid cooling of the condensed milk and turning it into ice cream. The ice cream was then sold to the kids of the village.

The ice cream maker became so popular that even the prince of the village used to come to his place to eat his made ice cream.

It was so that Fred was a lover of kids. He used to distribute free ice creams during holidays and thus children loved him too. Not only that the money he earned, he spent some of it to buy gifts for the kids of the village for their birthdays. He knew every kid's birthday in his village and thus everyday was a party for him and all the kids.

Fred continued his ice cream business for many years. Since many years had passed using the ice cream machine the machine had gotten old and started giving him trouble. At that time he was too old the make the machine again so he continued with the machine.

One day he was making ice cream in the crowd surrounded by kids and the machine stopped working. He did not know what to do and also by that time his cream had got finished so he went back to his house to get more cream. By that time he had left the machine in the crowd amongst the kids. The kids had seen all that. They had seen that the machine had stopped working. They thought that Fred had gone to get some tools to fix it. The kids thought that let's do some mischief as what was the worst could happen? They started messing with the machine. What they did was they added orange juice, candies and cakes which were in their hands to the top of the machine where Fred used to add condensed milk and started rotating the handle. At that time what happened was that only orange juice passed through the mouth of the machine and the cakes and candies fell on the propeller fan blades. Now, when the kids rotated the handle the fan blades, something unique happened. The orange juice that was in the ice cream maker got condensed and the candies and cakes got crushed this caused the orange juice to force out causing it to snow of orange juice snow flakes and also form orange juice ice creams. What next? The crushed cakes and candies were also forced out and splattered all over the kids face and that made the kids have the happiest time of their lives. By that time Fred came and saw all that and he discovered that the troubling ice cream machine was not troublesome at all and it had endless possibilities. So after that day on he used the ice cream machines in birthday parties and many festivals and carnivals making it snow juices of all kinds and splattering cakes and candies to big crowds which everybody liked. Thus it was a machine but a little troublesome!

MORAL: Good things cause good things to happen but sometimes broken things cause wondrous things to happen too.

TaLe 25 : iT SnOwEd At EqUaToR oNcE!

Hi! How is everybody doing at the equator? I hope everybody is doing well here because its about to get really cold it is going to snow, maybe not outside but inside this book in this tale.

It's true that it snowed once at the equator. It so happened that long time ago there used to live flying fire breathing dragons on an island called Fireville which was at the equator. These dragons were very peaceful and lived together in families who cared about each other very much. They were so friendly they would lay down their lives to protect each other.

So, what was the use of the fire that came out of their mouth if they did not battle or kill each other. Nice question! First of all the dragons were made of fire-proof bodies. Second of all, fire was very useful for them as they played by breathing fire at each other and at dinner time they used to throw spit on food and burn it by flaming up the food with their mouth flames which not only cooked the food but made it tasty as well. Fire was actually fun for them as they played with it whenever they wanted and cooked food with them too. Now I told you that they used fire to cook their dinner but what about breakfast and lunch? Their breakfast was usually fruits and their lunch was juices. It was only at night that they ate warm food. They had everything they wanted and enjoyed every bit of it.

Now, amongst the male flying dragons there were female flying dragons too. Amongst them there were also old female dragons too. The oldest dragon amongst them was called Jen which was her name too. Jen was a very nice female dragon and was respected and cared for by all the dragons in Fireville. She was always the one whom dragon took advise from.

It so happened that, that day it was a birthday party of her great great great great great grandson and she was extremely excited about that so much so that she made a 50 tonne chocolate cake for all the dragons all by herself and prepared all the food, herself which included about 100 type of food items. Not only that she decorated the entire Fireville all by herself and took no help of anybody. The party was a blockbuster but something other than that also happened that night. After the party was over Jen got a fever. She could not get up from her tree house the next day. She felt so tired and sick that she thought that her death is approaching. That day nobody saw Jen, either at the bathing pool or during the morning prayers. So the dragons got worried and wanted to see that if Jen was okay so all of them went to see Jen at her tree house. They saw that Jen was moaning with pain and was unable to get off the bed. The female doctor dragon who had also come to see Jen amongst the dragon immediately checked Jen and she said that Jen had high fever and we need to cool down the fever by keeping her cold. So dragons flew and filled massive cauldrons with water and brought in her tree house. Then dragons kept on wetting rags with water and laying it on top of her forehead to cool down the fever. But a day passed away and there was no improvement to her health. Then the doctor dragon then told that they need something more cold . She then told the dragons that now the only way to cure Jen was lots of ice and which was only available at the north and south pole. First of all everybody wanted to know what ice was so they pondered. Doctor told them the ice was something white, very cold and was made from water. She also told the dragons that it was difficult to bring the ice here as it would melt completely until it reaches the equator. And the option of taking Jen to the poles was out of question as she would die with the exertion. The only way out was to bring so much ice that even with the high melting rate there should be enough ice left that would make Jen okay.

They then agreed to get the ice from both the poles, just in case ice from one of the poles melts. 500 dragons flew to the North pole and 500 of them went to the South pole it took them approximately 3 day to reach to the pole from equator. When they reached the poles they saw ice which was white and cold and was as described by their doctor. Now they knew if they picked up little ice and flew back it would melt the ice by the time they reach equator so they did something unique. All of them dived and went under water to the bottom. There, they breathed out lots of fire. It took them another 3 days to break the ice's foundation. By that time the dragons kept on coming up out of water to get air and then kept on diving back again to the bottom of water to cut the ice with fire. At at the end of third day the ice of both the poles was cut. It started floating on water. They then looked around for something to tie the ice with. They didn't find anything. They remembered that when they when they were diving to go to the bottom of sea they had seen lots of vines undersea of sea plants. They had found them very sturdy when they had checked them out so they decided to dive beneath and get the vines. The dragons immediately tied the ice at both the poles with vines and tugged the ends of the the vines to their mouths and started to fly back to Fireville. The ice was heavy and as told the ice started melting on he way but they reached their home Fireville in 5 days. The group of dragon that had gone to North pole reached an hour earlier than the group that had gone to the South pole. Since they had carried so much of ice quite a bit of ice was left even after melting so they put it in the ocean water around Fireville and tied it to the island. The doctor who as taking care of Jen immediately went to the ocean and broke some ice and brought it to keep it on Jen's forehead. Jen immediately started feeling better and relaxed.

Now, it so happened that that since the dragons had brought so much ice the climatic conditions changed at the equator. It started snowing the very next day. Dragon's freaked out because they did not know what was going on. Jen who was lying in her tree house also started to have snow fall all over her body which more than comforted her. The doctor calmed everybody. She told that it was nothing but snowfall and was not a cause of worry. This cooled down the dragons who started to enjoy it. They had seen nothing like it ever before. It was a beautiful view. It snowed for 10 days. By that time the kids of dragons also started to enjoy it. They made snowballs and played with it. This time instead of fire they threw snowballs at each other and made different objects from it on ground. Jen also get well by that time. She was also wonderstruck to see the snow. She then thanked the dragons for not only making her well but also for the wonderful snowfall.

tAle 26 : tHe bOoMeRaNg StAr

In olden times in Australia there used to be a boomerang throw competition. People from all around Australia who considered themselves good at it took part in this sports competition. But there was only one guy that won the competition and that was "Ace". He had been winning this boomerang throw competition from the past 5 years. He had been winning because of the special type of boomerang he had and not because of the strength he had in arms to throw the boomerang. He practiced a lot with the boomerang but there was also something unique about the boomerang which was a secret and was not known to anybody. This boomerang was made by his grandfather who was a very experienced boomerang maker. This boomerang was given to Ace when his grandfather was on death bed. His grandpa told him that this boomerang was carefully made by him with deep understanding on the behaviour of the air on the aerofoil shape of the boomerang and he had put all his experience to make it just for Ace so he can forever win the boomerang competition, which he always wanted. His grandpa was true and did not lie about the boomerang. His grandpa also told him to keep it safe and not let it fall into anybody's hand because once somebody takes it will be very difficult to make something like it again.

Because of winning the boomerang throw competition for the past 5 years he was talk of the town wherever he went. It so happened that because of being famous he had many friends but there was one friend that was his best friend and his name was Traf. Traf had become Ace's friend when he had started winning the boomerang games. Traf although showed that he was very helpful and caring about Ace but he was a deceit. He always had his eye on Ace's boomerang and wanted to steal it. Traf was always looking for a plan to steal the boomerang and be a star at the boomerang sports. But since Ace who was told by his grandpa to keep the boomerang safe, kept it safe and even his best friend Traf never knew where he kept it. Traf had tried asking many times but Ace never told him. Traf had seen him practice many times with it but after that it was always a hidden object.

Where Ace kept a boomerang was a secret. After practicing, he folded in a plastic bag, made it waterproof and then dipped in a river behind his house. He then went to the bottom of the flowing river 15 feet away from the bank, dug a 2 foot deep hole and put the boomerang in it. He then covered it back with mud. Then he took a small but sturdy flag made of five leaves glued horizontally in a symmetry and inserted it over the mud of burrowed boomerang and swam back to the bank of the river. This way he kept the boomerang safe and known only to him. But this secret got to be known by Traf when Ace was made to drink too much alcohol forcefully by Traf. Since Ace was a simple guy, Traf just had to ask him and this time since he was too intoxicated he got the answer. Traf was wickedly excited about it so he tried checking it out. When he did swam to the location that Ace told, he found Ace's boomerang. He took the boomerang and swam back. Just so that Ace doesn't come to know about it he got a similar boomerang made which was of same same weight and colour and went back in the river and kept it where the previous boomerang was kept by Ace. He then placed it similarly so that Ace does not come to know about it.Traf then painted the boomerang with a different light natural paint so that nobody comes to know that it was Ace's boomerang.

Now, next day Ace went to practice with boomerang but he felt something different about the boomerang and after throwing it for a while he realized that, that was not his boomerang and he had been deceived by his best friend. Since boomerang's are not registered under a name nor do they have any barcode he could not claim his boomerang.

This time winning the boomerang competition was not important but to avenge himself was more important. Ace wanted to teach a lesson to Traf but he did not know how. He then thought that if he could make a boomerang that was even a little better than the previous one and then if he could master the art of making boomerang he would never have to worry about his boomerangs getting stolen and then he would always be a winner. He then came upon a plan. He went to his house and checked out his grandfather's book shelf. In that book shelf his grandfather kept his work books. He started opening all his books and flipping through the pages to find something important that can help him in his quest to build a boomerang. Ace kept on flipping through the pages but he found only found few notes having some formulas written on them and nothing more. He then remembered that his grandfather had told him repeatedly that it would be difficult to make the boomerang again but Ace would not accept defeat. So he checked the notes out. In the notes he found a major combination of formulas that helped him understand how hollow a boomerang should be and where it should be shaved on the hollow area to get the best performance but he could not find any formula to make the outer shape of the boomerang. So he decided to do it by really throwing the boomerang in the air and then understanding the effect of air on their different aerofoil shapes. The next day he went to his usual practice area and took 50 wooden boomerangs with him. He started by throwing one boomerang in the air. Now to enhance its performance he started to chip it with a knife to make it have a better aerofoil shape and see how it went then. He kept on throwing the boomerangs and kept on modifying the shapes but that day was not a very successful day for him. The next day he did the same thing but still no success. After 6 months of doing it he started seeing some results. Before he used to shave quite thick chunks of boomerang and thus ultimately they got finished off as they got reduced to small pieces due to excessive chipping but after weeks of shaving he started shaving minutely and delicately and starting making high performance boomerangs. He spent another 3 months in practicing the art of making boomerangs and finally made a very high performance boomerang which was faster than his previous boomerang.

Now he was ready to put his mark on the ground.

There was about a month left for the next years competition and Ace felt like talking to Traf and just asking him for once that why he stole the boomerang. He went to Traf and told him that he knows that he has stolen his boomerang and if he wants he can return the boomerang and they can be friends again but Traf did not listen to Ace and told him that he had never stolen his boomerang and he does not know what he was talking about. He also told Ace that this time he will be competing too and he will definitely win and thus Ace will be a disgrace in front of people. Ace quietly listened to him and went away.

Ace never told Traf that he had mastered the art of making boomerangs and thus has a faster boomerang than his previous one. He just practiced with the new boomerang everyday.

The time came. Everybody was excited about the competition. There were 100 boomerang throwers and there were 3 rounds.

First round:
"SPEED TEST":The fastest boomerang to return wins the round. Everybody tried their best but at the end Ace won the round.

Second round:
"THE RADIUS OF CURVATURE":The boomerang that made the maximum radius and returned back to the hands of thrower without falling on ground won the round.

Traf thought that even though Ace somehow managed to get speed through a boomerang maybe because of application of more force but this round Ace won't be able to win. So he tried his best. To his surprise this round was also won by Ace.

Third round: "FASTEST OBSTACLE CLEARING". In this round the obstacles had to be cleared by boomerang without hitting and without falling on ground and the fastest one won. This time too Ace won

Thus Ace was this year's winner too. Ace not only avenged himself but his grandfather's work too by learning how to make boomerangs and winning the challenge.

MORAL: Never lose Hope!

TaLe 27 : tHe FaT mOnKeY tHaT wAs CuRsEd!

Can a monkey be cursed too? Yes. I believe so.

Once there lived a tribe of monkeys in the forests of Africa. The tribe was a very protective and a caring tribe. This tribe cared for each other a lot. Amongst the tribe existed a hierarchy. On the top was a king then there was the tribe religious leader and then were all the monkeys. The hierarchy was respected but it did not mean that friendship was a problem amongst the king, the religious leader and the monkeys. The monkeys were allowed to enjoy in whatever way they wanted. They were allowed to eat whatever fruits and vegetable they desired and as much as they wanted. The monkeys enjoyed all day to there heart's content. The monkeys did eat whatever they desired for but they all remained fit, except for one whose name was Watary. Except Watary all the monkeys did too much activity so they never coagulated fat on their bodies. All the monkeys used to swing around, run and play except Watary. Watary was very lazy. All he did was eat, eat and eat. He never played nor did he jump like the other monkeys did. He was the laziest of all.

In amidst of the monkeys enjoyment there was one fear that haunted them all. It was the fear of getting attacked and eaten by the tiger and tigresses of the jungle. So to keep that from happening one of the monkey was always on guard and it kept on changing from time to time.

Tigers did not attack the monkeys very often but when they did the monkey on guard used to make lots of racket that let the other monkeys know that there existed danger and so they should hide or run away from that area. The monkeys kept on changing guard duties one after the other as any monkey could do it because guard duty did not mean fighting with the danger but only to make a huge racket on time that was sufficient for monkeys to know about the danger and then hide from it. The monkeys did duty according to their schedules as designed by their king.

Watary was rarely given this duty because of his lazy nature. But since every monkey had to this duty at-least once a year that day came Watary's turn to do that duty. Watary was asked to keep on any eye on any danger that included tiger, forest fire, flood etc. He was asked to stay on a tree branch about 200 feet from the place where the other monkeys were playing and enjoying themselves. Watary thought that there was a rare chance that a tiger or any of the above mentioned dangerous events occur. So he took a bunch load of bananas and kept it where he was asked to do the duty. From the time duty began he started munching on the bananas.

Now those days were pretty dry and thus meat on the pastures was very less. Thus the Tigers and tigresses were looking for some delicious meat for themselves and their kids. From quite far they saw that a lot of monkeys were enjoying themselves near a lake on the ground. They thought of getting some of them for their supper. They planed to attack altogether and take them by storm and they did. They sprinted towards the monkeys. Now watary who was sitting on the tree branch was eating bananas and was stuffed with it. When he saw tigers and tigresses approaching the area he tried to cause a racket but due to too much stuffing of bananas in his mouth he could not cause any noise from his mouth and thus monkeys playing could not hear any racket of danger and continued playing.

That day was a horrible one for the monkeys and a day which they won't be able to forget. It was a massacre of monkeys that day. Many monkeys were killed and many lost their lives. The tigers and tigresses showed no mercy. Watary and few others monkeys including the king and their religious leader somehow managed to escape from the attack but they could not forget what had happened that day. The next day when the remaining monkeys were in hideout they all wanted to know why did not Watary raise the alarm and cause any racket. Watary did not know what to say. He was too ashamed on himself. He told them the truth that he was busy eating bananas and could not make a noise when was approached by the tigers as he was stuffed with them. All the monkeys and the king were furiously mad at him and decided to punish him. The religious leader was then asked to cast a spell on him that would turn him into a big fat ape. After he got turned into an ape he was banished from the tribe. Watary felt too bad and ashamed and tried asking for forgiveness but his crime was too great and thus was not forgiven. So he faced the consequences. He was turned into a huge big ape at an instant but his nature of being a glutten remained intact. He was then ordered by the king to leave them and find some other place to stay. Watary did not know what to do and left that place really ashamed.

He went to the far end of the forest to live his life all amongst himself. There he spent many years alone. Because of being turned into an ape his activity slowed way more and it looked like he had turned into a sloth who barely moved. It was difficult for him to move and it was a struggle for him to live his life like that. He could not move with speeds nor could he climb a tree to get food thus was very difficult for him to survive. But he somehow tried to make his ends meet by eating whatever fell on ground.

Now being at the far end of the forest he used to see many human activities occurring near his place of resting. As the end of the forest was mountainous and over a cliff he saw many humans come there and brought something called para-gliders attached to a wing with them. Then they used to jump off the cliff holding the bar of the wing with a set of looking device called binoculars till they reached the ground. When he saw that at first he was afraid of it but he realized that humans were not and it was actually a sport for them. How he came to know that the looking device called binoculars were meant to see long distances was that once some para gliding people had come to the cliff and the binocular through which one of the para glider was looking fell on the ground and one of its lens broke. The person who saw that his binocular is broken, left the binocular there on the ground and did not pick it up. In the evening when all the para-gliders went away and nobody was left he with difficulty moved towards the binocular picked it up and tried checking the binoculars out. He tried looking through the binoculars from both the sides. Although one lens was cracked but he still was Abe to see through the other lens and when he looked through the binoculars he saw one side made near look far and the other side made far look near. He was very intrigued by the thing so he took it for himself and went to his tree where he lived. He then kept the binocular hidden in his tree and sometimes during his free time when he was not looking for food he looked through the binoculars and enjoyed seeing the far end of the forest. This passed his time and it continued for quite some time. The humans kept on coming there and continued para gliding. All this continued for a while, until one day.

One day the day rose and he woke up. By that time he had developed a habit of looking through the binocular as soon as he got up in the morning. That day when he was checking out from the binoculars he saw that a group of baby monkeys came playing near a pond and were unadministered by an adult. He liked that view and kept on looking at them. But since there was no adult monkey around he was a little afraid seeing that and started to be more watchful. He looked through the binoculars all around and away from the baby monkeys so as to make sure that the baby monkeys were safe. That day was the same day when he was banished from the tribe and cursed to be an ape and therefore similar conditions in the forest existed that day. It was dry and meat for the tigers was scarce and there could be nothing more juicy than the meat of baby monkeys. So the tigers were ready to get a piece of it. Watary who was watching all this got alarmed and had to do whatever it took to save the baby monkeys. At first he did not know what he could do. But then he saw a group of para-gliders on the cliff who were ready to jump. He although afraid at first immediately with all his energy ran towards the para-gliders and roared. The para-gliders were taken aback by the ape and they left the equipment there and ran away except for one who was already tied up to para-glider and was too scared to get untied from it. Watary immediately pounced on the paraglider and suddenly they were off the cliff. Since the para glider was a wing and not a parachute type air-float it was faster to glide on. Now it took him less than a minute until he reached where the baby monkeys were playing and thus was less time than the time of tigers attack. He then jumped from the para-glider and stood in front of the baby monkeys . The tigers who came there too were about to attack when he roared in a very loud noise and the tigers got a bit scared because they thought that if one ape had come there maybe other apes coming there too and they went away. The loud noise caused the monkey parents who were looking for their kids to rush towards the noise. When they saw what had happened they thanked the ape and asked him if they could do anything in the world for him. Watary recognized that they were monkeys from his tribe so he asked them if they could accept him back to their tribe. He also told them that he has suffered a lot because of his mistakes and does not want to suffer more and was sorry for that day. The monkeys took him to their king and told the king what had happened. He was then forgiven. The religious leader took the spell away and he was then welcomed to his new life and his old tribe. He gave up his habit of being a glutten and lived his life happily and safely with the tribe.

tALe 28 : ThE mAgIcAL CoAL rOcK

This is a very old story about a magical rock that was black in colour and looked like a piece of coal.

Long ago somewhere in a town called Patrical a man whose name was Rilly was digging in a coal mine to get some coal out for his iron with which he used to iron people's clothes to earn money for his very poor living. This person used to dig a week's worth of coal for his iron and from the mine and take it home.   Therefore he came there every week be it rain or sunshine.

Now, he had a cart standing outside the coal mine. He was coming and going outside and inside and filling the cart with coal whenever he got some good quality coal. He was carrying all the coal from the coal mine to the cart that was parked outside with his hands. Most of the coal rocks he was picking were quit big in size but few ones he picked were so small that ten of them could fit in his one hand. He never picked up small coal rocks for his iron but these rocks looked very good as a fuel so he thought of using them out for ironing. Now since these coal pieces were small he put them on the top of the coal pieces that were already on the cart and started pulling the cart and moved slowly until he and the cart reached home.

Now, at home his kids were eagerly waiting for him. When the kids saw their father they got excited and came near him and hugged him and started moving in circles around him. They cheered that their father now had returned from a long day's work and that now he will spend time with them. Rilly got a little sad at that time and did not know what to give his kids out of love. So he checked his coal cart and saw a shiny piece of coal lying on the top of the cart. It was a bit dusty but he picked up the coal piece, rubbed the dust of it and gave it to his kids to play with it. Now the kids took it and started throwing it towards each other so as to play a game of "catch the rock".

Rilly was watching the kids play game and suddenly while playing the small black coal rock fell from one his kids hand and along with the sound of falling coal rock a metallic sound was heard. When Rilly heard the metallic sound he suddenly saw that a shiny copper coin appeared where the small coal piece had dropped. Rilly was dumb struck at the sight of copper coin falling on the ground. He did not know what to think of. He thought that when that piece of coal rock hit the ground a copper coin popped up (which he was somewhat right about). So he tried throwing the coal rock on the floor again but this time nothing happened. He got a little confused. He did not understand what was going on so he threw the coal rock on the floor again, this time with a little more force. But nothing happened this time too.

But he was intrigued with what had happened so he took the coal piece and kept it in a safe place. He then went to his coal cart took out another piece of coal which was also small but not as shiny as the previous coal piece. Although it was not the same piece but it was good enough for his kids, as they just wanted to throw it towards each other and play with it.

That night Rilly could not sleep he kept on thinking about what had happened. He realized that the coal rock was something special because most of the coal rocks will break when thrown on the floor but this rock didn't break and actually gave a copper coin on colliding to the floor but he was still thinking that why didn't it pop a copper coin the next time when he threw it on the ground. He did not lose hope in that rock. The next day as soon as he woke up he took out the rock from the secret place and thought of throwing the rock on the ground again. Just after thinking, in a wink of a eye he threw it on the ground and suddenly another copper coin popped up. Rilly yelled " yeah!". Now he understood that when the rock was dropped it popped up a copper coin but it did only once a day. So he came to know the secret of the coal rock. He came to know how and when the coal rock produced a copper coin.

Rilly was excited from that day on because although one copper coin a day was not that much money but was enough for them to come out of poverty. So he thought of a better days ahead and quit his ironing job. A whole year passed and Rilly kept on throwing the coal rock on the ground everyday and getting a copper coin out of it for his livelihood and savings. By that time he had built a better house and had started to live a better life maybe not a lifestyle.

After a year had passed something strange happened. The coal rock stopped popping up copper coins no matter how many times he threw the rock on the floor in day and no matter how many days he waited to throw the coin on the floor. Rilly felt somewhat bad about it. So he took it near the mirror and looked at it with a scorn. When he was looking at it he saw that the rock had faded its lustre and looked very dull. He did not understand why this had happened then he realized that maybe lustre in the coal rock was the cause of production of coins. He then thought of making it shine with damp cloth. He went to the kitchen and dampened lower part of his shirt with water and came back. He then tried rubbing the rock with the damp cloth so as to make it shine. After rubbing it a lot with the cloth he then tried throwing it on the ground again but no coin popped up still. In a rage he threw the rock in the mirror. It broke the mirror but something else happened. A small face made of wood and fabric resembling that of Rilly popped up. This astonished Rilly once again because his face was replicated in from of a toy puppet. He was shocked and surprised but felt somewhat happy about that. He realized that instead of copper coins this coal rock was yielding toys this time.

But he did not knew that if he had to break the mirror to produce toys or they just popped up by simply hitting the mirror. So he went to another mirror in the house removed it from the wall and took it to the carnival. Before entering carnival he had to buy a ticket to enter which although was a bit expensive but he still payed for it, trusting the coal rock. When he entered he took out the mirror put a big bag below the mirror so that whatever pops up falls in the bag and nobody comes to know about it. He then went near a ferrous wheel placing the mirror in such a way so that the image of that ferrous wheel gets formed on the glass. He then first tried, only hitting the mirror with the coal without breaking it. As soon as he did that a small ferrous wheel popped up and fell into the bag. Rilly checked the toy that was formed and it was the most beautiful toy that he had ever seen. It was the most intricate and delicately made toy and was worth a fortune. Rilly wasted no time and went to all different types of rides in the carnival. He went to the roller coaster placed it in front of the mirror so that the image of roller coaster is formed. He then took out the coal rock from his pocket and then threw it on the mirror. A model of roller coaster with a cart moving on it got formed which looked exactly like the real roller coaster but small in size and then got dropped in the bag attached to the mirror. Then he went to all the rides, put their image in front of the mirror and got the toys made, which fell into the attached bag.

He then went home happily and showed the toys to his kids. The kids got excited and asked if these toys were meant for them. Rilly smiled at them at told them that he will got more toys for them but first he has to earn some money by selling those toys and then he will make more beautiful toys for them.

That night Rilly slept peacefully. The next day he went to the market and sold each toy for 1000 copper coins and there were 10 types of models/toys which enabled him to make a lot of money. The prize he earned was more than what he had made ever in his entire lifetime. He then went back home. He had bought expensive toys, chocolates, candies, clothes and food for his kids that day and also popped up the same toys which his kids wanted by going to the carnival again that day. When he reached home the kids were overjoyed to see him and they had a celebration that day.

From that day on they never remained poor or hungry and had a lifestyle of their own. During his lifetime he earned enough money to last for his generations to come and the coal rock never stopped popping up toys!

tALe 29 : tHe FiReWoRkS-PLaY mAkEr

Once there lived a poor man. His name was Jelimny. He lived a very modest lifestyle and earned just sufficient to feed his belly. He had a small shanty which he called home. His parents had died long ago and therefore he lived alone. He never married because he earned very little and thus the thought of spending money extravagantly on his companion made him nervous. Although he was poor he thought of fame and wanted to be rich. He had thought of many ways of getting rich but did not have money to invest in them first of all. So he continued his life selling water which he used to bring after walking a distance of 15 miles daily. The fresh water he got was from was a river which he spent 5 hours daily reaching to and coming back. The wells in the town were always overcrowded so some people opted to get water from Jelimny who sold it for a very nominal price just so that he is able to earn his daily living. Now Jelimny being human and having nothing to help him to bring water had limitations on how much he could carry.

Now, that evening was a holiday and everybody was in a mood of festivity because that night a big business man had spent lots of money for exhibition of fireworks at the town centre as it was his daughter's first birthday. People from the entire town had come there to see the fireworks.

The fireworks started. They lasted for 4 hours and it was a very magnificent view until it lasted. People's neck got tired looking in the sky but the show did not stop. It was so magnificent that people kept on looking at them until it all ended. Even Jelimny kept on looking at the fireworks for the entire four hours and did not bend down his head. After the show ended he went home and realized that fireworks are something that everybody likes. He also realized that the fireworks that were bursting in the sky were from a fixed central point of "burst of rocket flares" and therefore were all "circular bursts" in nature. He kept on thinking about it for the whole night.

The next day he woke up and realized that a whole play could be formed out of fireworks but he thought that its gonna take some calculations to do that so he begun. Before making a whole play of fireworks he thought of just experimenting it and seeing how it would work. He went to the market and bought a pack of fireworks powder with whatever money he had. He knew that that day he would not be able to eat food because he had spent all his money to buy fireworks powder but he was still satisfied.

He then went home and cut 50 very small cardboard pieces and made a cavities which each of them. He then got a thread roll and calculated their length. Now what he did was he kept the cardboard pieces which he had made cavities in at separate calculated angles. Then he calculated the amount of powder to be put in each of the cardboard cavity and closed it. He then put one thread each in the cardboard cavity and then attached all the threads too a single thread connecting to the fireworks powder in the cardboard cavities. Then he arranged everything in a box in a calculated way and closed the cavities and the box. The box had a hole to see through and it was covered with a magnifying glass. Now he wanted to see what happens when he light's the thread and so he did. As soon as he lit the thread he immediately put his eye over the magnifying glass to see what happens.

What he saw was magnificent. It happened exactly as he had calculated. A play made of fireworks occurred inside the box and lasted for five minutes. The play consisted of a girl riding a bicycle whose entire face, body and clothes were made of bright colours of sparkles of fireworks rocket which were bursting in transition according to his calculations. As soon as the sparkle of first set of firework rockets faded the next set of rockets bursted which kept on forming different faces and motions of the girl's and bicycle's body and the bunny in this play of fireworks wherein the bunny falls from the bicycle while she is riding it. She then realizes that her bunny is missing from her pocket so she turns back and picks the bunny up and puts it on the basket attached to the front of her bicycle and rides away which ends the five minute firework play.

Jelimny was happy on his success of making a play of fireworks.

Next day he finished his work and again went to the fireworks shop and got some more fireworks powder. He knew that that day he would have to go hungry again but he thought within himself that it will not happen again, tomorrow.

He went home and did the same thing again. He made a box, calculated the amount of fireworks powder and measured the length of threads. He then checked the angles at which the very small cardboard cavity boxes had to be arranged and put them in the bigger box and covered it with a magnifying glass. Then he closed the box. It was night till he did that so he waited for the next day.

As the next day rose he picked up the box from under his bed and went to the market to sell the firework-play box. It took him some time to convince the buyers that the firework-play box was worthy of buying, until one of the buyer agreed to get it for his young son. Now since it was a unique product and was first time in the market Jelimny sold it only for double the amount of his daily wage. But Jelimny was sure that it would workout and he would be successful in his artful business and so it happened.

That night he had food after two days of starving and was very satisfied with what he had done. He was not worried at all for his future now because he knew the thing he has made is phenomenal and would make him rich which he always wanted. After having food he made another firework-play box and slept.

He did not actually know what he had done. Because it was way more ecstatic than he had imagined.

The next day he went to the market to sell his box it was nothing like he had ever thought of. People started bidding on his firework-play box and that box got sold for 50 times his regular daily wages.

It so had happened that the firework box he sold last night was shown to all the neighbours of the person who had bought it because the person wanted to show-off what he had bought. Since the firework-play lasted for five minutes, it was enough to be seen by at least 50 neighbours for about 5 seconds each and Jelimny's firework-play box had become talk of the town overnight.

Thus he started becoming rich. He then not only put the fireworks in the box but with the money he accumulated he started making big shows in the open grounds and sky. He earned way more money than by simply selling firework-play boxes.

He had accomplished his dream of getting rich. But it had a drawback he was so rich and famous that the he had lost the value of money and wherever he went he was greeted by fans who were overwhelmed to see him and meet him. He had lost his personnel life which daunted him.

Therefore after 15 years of business he started exhibiting the fireworks-play shows for free. He earned only through donations and stepped back to live modestly rather than richly and famously.

He had realized that richness does not matter but seeing smiles on people's faces matter and personnel life matters too. He did not marry his whole life but kept on putting a smile on many children's faces and that made him live happily and die peacefully.

TALe 30 : ThE RaCe Of ThE wItChEs On bRoOmStIcKs

Once the young witches living in Witch-Land decided that they wanted to see which witch could fly the fastest on their broomsticks and that which witch was more intelligent than the other. So they decided to have a race. They went to the witch's union and told them to arrange a race for them in which they can prove themselves and stand out in front of others. The head witch in the witch union who had to arrange for the race asked for 2 months time in which she would prepare the race for those witches. The young witches agreed to it and tried to wait that long.

Those witches were lazy. They did not want to practice also because they did not wanted to show other witches how fast they were and bring in more competition and thus cause themselves to exert themselves more.

Two months passed and those witches did nothing but fought and quarrelled amongst themselves, which was a part of their nature.

At the end of two months they went to the head of the witch's union and asked her if she was done preparing the race for them. The head witch said politely "yes". She said that the race will begin after 3 days when the sun is about to rise i.e. during dawn of the third day. She also warned the witches that the race will not be easy and all the young witches who want to take part in the race should come well prepared. Each of the witch boasted saying that she was better than the rest of them and that nobody could beat her.

Amongst all of them was a young witch whose name was Catastrophe. Although her name was deadly but she was very nice to the other witches and did not wanted to take part in the race as she did not agree to fact of racing and thus one being proven superior to others in her wit and activeness. But since she was young and docile she had to listen to other witches and therefore had to take part in the race. So when she was forced to do so she decided that if she takes part in the race she will definitely win it.

Now to do the wit part she said that time will tell but to do the racing part she did something unique. She got her broomstick and streamlined it. How she streamlined it was that she picked up a sharp blade and sharpened the blunt part of the front side of the broom in such a way that it looks like the sharp tip of front part of an arrow. He knew that this will decrease the drag on her flight when she flies during the race. Then she hid her broomstick so that nobody gets that idea.

Dawn of the third day approached therefore all the young witches lined up at the starting line before the sun rise before start of the race. Catastrophe also lined up there and waited for the race to start.

The rules of that race began as follows. In that race first they had to cross a circle made of smoke and that too in such a way so as to go around the circumference perpendicular to the circle's circumference so as to form a spring like loops or pattern around the circle's circumference. This had to be done 50 times. This was to be done to check that the witches had a fit brain and that they did not loose their concentration while flying.

Then they had to cross a star which was also made of magical smoke. The star had to be crossed in such a way that they fly over to the top of the star and jump down leaving the broomstick. The broomstick by that time had to follow the complete path of the star's circumference and meet the witch in the centre of the star thus catching her witch owner and making her sit on it. The witch who catches her broomstick and thus gets seated on it at the point nearest to the centre of the star scores the maximum point. This race was conducted to see that how well is a witch coordinated with her flying broomstick which she has to ride forever for her life.

The third part of the race was they had to fly over a triangle which was again made of smoke. While flying over the triangle they had to move over the triangle's perimeter cutting sharply through the corners. This test was conducted to see that how much control do witches have on their broomstick while turning. The witch who turns most sharply wins that round.

Fourth part of the race was to check the wit of the witches. In this part they had to go to the marked forest and pick up a green coloured flower. Now remember that the flower is green in colour i.e. it is difficult to find a green colour flower amongst green leaves because leaves are sometimes arranged in a flower like pattern too. Second thing that made it tough was that there was only one green coloured flower in that part of the forest thus it was difficult to find it.

Fifth part was also to check the wit of the young witches. In this part of the race they had to find a bonsai apple which was the size of the cherries amongst stack of cherries.

The sixth part of the race was to find a hail stone amongst ice in the icy mountains.

So the race began with the passing of a broomstick across the front of the starting line at the beginning of the sunrise. All witches yelled and squeaked and moved forward flying on their broomsticks. As they flew near the smoky circle all tried to go 50 times in a spring like pattern around the circumference but many of them fainted on their broomstick and many fell on the ground.

The remaining witches including Catastrophe who could complete it flew to the second round. In that round too, many witches fell on the ground away from their broomsticks as they were not well coordinated with their broomsticks.

Now the remaining witches tried completing the third round by doing steep and sharp turns on the corners of the triangle. Until now Catastrophe was leading the scores and thus she moved forward.

Now when the remaining witches reached the 4th round all witches looked confused except Catastrophe. Catastrophe had though about how to find flower that had colours of a leaf amongst leaves. She knew that that even though visibly it would be difficult to distinguish the green flower amongst green leaves but she knew that in that part of the forest there was only one flower of that kind so its smell should be different from the leaves. So she reached there early and started smelling the leaves. After a minute or so she found an arrangement of leaves that looked like a flower and also smelled like one so she realized that that was the green coloured flower that is required by the race rules. So she plucked it and kept it in her pocket as a proof and flew towards the next part.

In the next part there was a stack of 50,000 cherries in which she had to find a bonsai apple that was as small as the cherries were and was also red in colour, same as that of cherries. This time she did some magic. She waived her magic wand and with magic broke all the stems of the stack of the fruits in front of her in the pile and took them to a vacant land and with magic, planted them and made them grow in a blink of an eye. When the plants grew she flew across all the plants and saw that all the cherry plants had similar structure except one tree that was different than the cherry plants and then she knew which was the bonsai apple tree. Then she commanded her magic wand to tell her that from which stem did that bonsai apple tree grew from and that that belonged to which fruit. The wand told her immediately by pointing towards the fruit. She then picked the bonsai apple up and flew to the icy mountains for the next round. Since wands cannot decipher themselves she had to do that trick

To find a hail stone amongst ice was difficult but she did not lose hope. She though that since it was the last round it would be very difficult and since all rounds have to be won to win the race she had to win this round anyhow too.

When she reached the icy mountains all that she saw was ice except for a small pebble rock. Now that pebble rock looked strange amongst all the ice so she went near it to check it out.

When she lifted it up she saw a spherical piece of ice beneath it which she immediately realized that it is the hail stone because it was spherical and uniquely white as wanted by the competition. She picked it up cast a spell on it so that it does not melt while on the way and flew back to the starting point which was also the ending point of the race and won it.

The witches realized that although Catastrophe was young but she was intelligent enough to outsmart every witch. From that day on they stopped pushing her around and she gained new self respect.

TaLe 31 : ThE MaGiCaL cArT

During the times when pottery was in fashion, there lived an old man who was very hard working and very nice. This man's name was Fred. Now, Fred was very old and had no family. He earned his daily bread by making pottery. Pots he made were really nice. He did not fore sake quality for quantity. He not only made the pots but used his colour brush to make them look colourful and beautiful. Whatever he earned he spent it to buy food and timber. Timber he used to cook food and keep him warm during winter months.

To make pottery he had to dig in the earth to get clay. He also needed straw to make pottery which he got from backyard of his house. But to get good clay he had to go far to get it. So he had a wooden cart which he took to the clay digging area and filled it up with it. The cart was heavy but he had to use it as he had no other option. It took him three hours to reach the clay area and three hours to come back and therefore he struggled to reach there and come back with it. He could not do any other job because he did not know how to do it. He always wished if he had a helper he could spend less time in travelling, transporting and digging clay and more time in making pottery which would leave him with more money in his pocket. But since he was poor and barely made his ends meet he couldn't afford a helper. Thus he continued pulling his cart daily and working on his own.

Once it so happened that it was rainy season at that time Fred had to go through a road which had many puddles in it. He was always very careful to go through that road because he did not want himself to get injured and nor did he want anything to happen to his cart's wheels or cart itself. Now as he was coming back after filling his cart with clay and moving slowly he heard a voice "careful! don't kill me". Fred immediately stopped moving his cart which being heavy exerted a lot of pressure on Fred but he stopped it there and then. Then he wondered that where did the voice come from and he was actually in a shock thinking how could he or his cart kill anybody. Then he again heard a voice that said "down here". When he looked down he saw a beautiful pink starfish who then said "hi!". Fred first freaked out and thought if he has gone crazy because of his old age and that he his hearing things but then he again looked at the starfish and realized that it was really talking to him. Then the starfish said "thank you for saving my life". Fred asked the starfish that how did he save the starfish's life. Then starfish told him " by not squashing me". Then on moving forward the starfish told the entire incident to Fred. He told him that he was the son of the king of the starfishes and his name was Marer. He told him that he was always bound to the sea because of security issues but he always wanted to explore the outside world someday. So God fulfilled his dream today. Today he saw that it was raining cats and dogs so he decided that today was the time when he could explore so he moved up the river from the sea quickly and stealthily so as nobody comes to know. Then the river due to flood had washed onto this road and thus, he got washed onto this road too. He was exploring the area when suddenly the water level decreased and he gut stuck in this puddle. Now, he wanted to get off the puddle and go back to the sea but was afraid to do so. As there was no water Marer did not wanted to get spotted by any land animal and get eaten by it. So he waited in the puddle until Fred showed up moving his cart wheel over the same puddle where Marer was seeking shelter.

Marer then asked Fred if he could put him back into the river so that he can swim back to sea where he will be safe. Fred told him that he will be more than happy to do so. He left his cart filled with clay there, picked up the starfish and moved towards the river. He then blended and put the starfish safely in the nearby river. When starfish landed in the water it thanked Fred and asked Fred if there is anything he needed from him and that if there was anything that he wanted in his life. Fred simply said that all he wanted was a helping hand. Marer said that should not be a problem and went away thanking again and saying "Good bye! Fred".

Fred did not know what the starfish meant by saying that it should not be a problem but he went back to his cart thinking that he did a good deed by helping the starfish find his home. Now he went back pushing his cart towards home. When he reached home he was quite late but he still struggled to make few pots and keep them to dry. He slept late that night.

The next day he woke up thinking that he has to go again to get clay for his pottery. So he went near the cart and tried pushing it.

When he he tried pushing it he found it difficult to push saw there was way more clay than he had ever got that was sitting on the cart. He was surprised to see that and again wondered thinking about it. He thought that who could have put so much clay on his cart during the rainy night. Then suddenly he heard something. He heard the cart say"I did it master". Fred jumped with shock thinking that there was a ghost in the cart. But the cart calmed him down and said that there is no need to worry master, the starfish whom you saved life of had put life into me. He also told Fred that he was forever indebted to him because of that and his at his service forever. Fred kept quiet for some time and started feeling a bit relaxed. He then thanked God and the starfish in his mind and then immediately wet to his pottery desk and started making pottery. He now knew that he would be able to make more pottery than usual because now he had a helper which he always wanted. His happiness at that time had no boundaries.

That day he made double the pots because he did not have to go and get clay or straw himself. As time passed the cart became more and more useful. Fred then started concentrating on making more and more beautiful pots and thus getting higher prices for them and started saving money.

In a year or so he saved quite a bit of money. Then he thought of investing it on buying a farm. He knew that he did not needed any helper for him because his cart his companion was enough to help him in plowing and sowing the cart and it was true.

Fred bought a 5 acre farm land. He then bought seeds to sow . Then he bought a plow and tied it to the back his cart - the companion and then the cart was ready to plow the entire field. The cart plowed and sowed in a blink of an eye. Fred became richer and starting earning more and more money very yield. He then bought more and more farm land.

Whatever money Fred earned, he used it to help the poor people and poor kids by donating more than half of it. All he wanted was that since he had seen poverty nobody should see or suffer poverty because it's a hurting experience.

He died happily and seeing smiles on poor people faces. The cart still lives and sows and plows his entire acquired land. It then stores the grain in the granary. Poor kids and people come and take as much grain as they want and go away. They think that Fred before dying had stored so much grain in granary that it will never get over and they will never go hungry but they don't know that it is the cart who now does the work of Fred i.e. of helping poor people so that they don't go hungry in the night.

taLe 32 : A LiOn CuB tHaT mAdE A FiSh A fRiEnD

Once in an African desert lived a lion family. It was a happy family and it consisted of only one lion and one lioness. The lion protected himself and the lioness from the attack of other lions and thus both of them lived happily most of the time. Sometimes they used to have quarrel but that was okay it is what family is. If in a family there is no quarrel ever than this means that it is missing something is. This doesn't feel right but that's the truth.

Now one day, the male lion talked to the female lion about "missing something". The female lion who was his wife asked that what was the male lion missing. He told her wife that they were missing a toy that could be their's but they still don't have it. Her wife asked asked him "what kind of toy?" The male lion responded saying a living toy. By living toy he meant an offspring. But the female lion told the male lion that he already springs upon the land everyday why would he want a spring to go off? The lioness already knew that his husband was in romantic mode and wanted a baby from her. But she was teasing the lion because she liked the lion and wanted to have fun with him at that time. At-last she agreed and said lets have a baby. At they slept peacefully that day. The other day the fairy godmother of lions and lionesses blessed them and the female lion got pregnant.
The lion and lioness watched each other i.e. took care of each other until one day a lion cub sprouted off from the mother lion. At the time of birth, the lion cub looked very cute and her mother licked her whole body about 100 times. It was their first baby and they were excited about it. They then named the child Daffodil. It was a girls name but they liked their cub so much that they did not mind naming him with a girl's name.

Daffodil was very nice behavioured as a kid. He actually never quarrelled with his parents. Whatever his parents told him he listened to them and payed heed to their instructions. He never wanted anything out of the way. Whatever his parents could get, he accepted that and he was satisfied with it. He also always remained contented and happy.

Now as a child his mother used to take him with herself to teach home the art of hunting and protecting himself from intruders. Daffodil first was slow at learning but he slowly became good at it.

After getting to learn how to hunt land animals his mom told him that now it was time that he learned how to hunt a fish if needed, for survival. But his mom also told home that she will give her few lessons for hunting fish but he has to get better at it by himself.

Since it was a desert there were very less places in it where water bodies existed. So they had to walk quite far to reach an oasis which was very big and actually supported some marine life. When they reached the oasis mom told Daffodil to start observing and learn how she catches a fish. His mom gave him instructions. She told Daffodil that first is the "lookout" phase. In that phase they have to put their head inside the water until they can hold their breath and look for any fish. Then after finding a fish they have to use their paws to inflict a strong blow on the fish so that it not only comes out of water but dies too. Daffodil carefully listened to the instructions. Then his mom also told him to come there and practice that everyday. Daffodil agreed to it. Then they walked back home.

Next day it was again a long way towards oasis so Daffodil woke up early, had a hearty meal and went towards the oasis. He tried to sprint and reached there quite quickly as compared to the previous day.

Then he thought of practising his fish hunting skills. But the thing was that he had never actually seen a fish so he did not know how it looked like, but even then he started hunting for it.

He started doing as his mom had told him to do. He put his head in the water and started looking for a fish. For that he held his breath for quite long and put his head beneath the water but he did not find anything or anyone in it, so he was not satisfied with that. He then again took a huge deep breath and put his head in the water again. At that time he found a small tiny creature wiggling inside the water and not realizing it was a fish as he told the fish to get out of way as he was looking for a fish. Daffodil had though that like all animals that his mom hunted, fish would be a big size animal and never realized that the one whom he is asking to move away was actually a fish itself. The fish when asked to move away yelled at the lion stating that it was her kingdom and that lion no matter how big he was, he cannot ask her to go away. She told the lion that if the lion had a problem he should stop digging into other people's waters. But the lion did not listen and still continued looking for a fish whom he did not know that he had just talked to. Now the fish wiggled and moved further and kept on seeing onto what the lion was doing. She then realized that it was actually hunting for a fish. The fish whose name was Dessemay when realized that, got scared and suddenly saw a small rock near her wiggling spot and hid behind it. She the tried to swim away but as she tried swimming away she saw the lion cub and said to herself " I should not be afraid of that creature and face him". Then she turned back and went to the lion and asked him that what was his name? The lion said " why do you care?" Dessemay told her that she found something that he has been looking for. Daffodil first said "I don't trust you". Then she told him "trust me when you see it". Daffodil then though for a second and agreed. He asked her where is it? Dessemay told him that it was her. Daffodil looked at her for a while and laughed at her. He said that she could not be it because it was impossible that his mom would ask him to hunt for such a small piece of meat that would hardly fill his belly but Dessemay said that it was true. She also told him that it is not that fishes are always small its just that she is a young one and thus has not grown big enough like her mom and dad. Daffodil pondered for a while and then thought maybe Dessemay who told him her name and was inside water must be a fish and that she was telling the truth. He then looked upon himself and checked his size. He realized that even he was lesser in size as compared to his own parents. So similarly he thought that Dessemay must be a kid too. So he agreed to what Dessemay was saying and said " what should I do?" He said that since Dessemay was nice to him and had almost made him his friend by telling no lies, he will not hunt her. So daffodil offered her his friendship and asked her if they could be friends. Then Dessemay asked the lion cub that, what if he eats her and then she is no more. How would her parents feel. But Daffodil promised and said " I cross my heart and swear to die before I lie" Dessemay believed him and accepted his friendship. Now, it was already quite late and Daffodil told good bye to Dessemay and said that he should be going as he has to go a long way and if he gets too late his parents might get worried. So he left but he promised that he would come back again tomorrow.

That day when daffodil reached home he was a bit late but he was safe home. Now his mom asked the lion about his experience in hunting fish that day and asked him that how many fishes did he hunt that day? Daffodil became nervous when he heard that question and told his that mom since it was his first day he did not have much experience hunting a fish but he will definitely try the next day to hunt one and get more good at hunting fishes. His mom said that he should better get good at it because he will grow up soon and then he has to defend his family. So he should get good skills at hunting. Daffodil nodded and slept.

The next day Daffodil was excited to meet his new friend Dessemay so he woke up early and said good bye to his mom and dad and sprinted towards the oasis.

When he reached oasis he found Dessemay wiggling at the same place and waiting for Daffodil. Daffodil came there and said "hi!". Dessemay waived at him too . Now, Dessemay asked Daffodil if he had ever been under water and seen the beautiful world inside it?

Daffodil said "no". Then Dessemay told Daffodil that he should see it because it is worth seeing and different from the land world. Daffodil kept quite for a while and then told Dessemay that since he is a land animal he cannot hold his breath for long thus cannot stay under water for long. Dessemay thought for a while and said that her parents once told her that with practice comes power. So she told Daffodil that he should practice holding breath for some time and then he can see the wonders of water. Daffodil reluctant at first said that he will definitely work on it. So he started practicing holding his breath. Now by that time he kept on visiting the oasis and chatting with Dessemay . A year passed and Daffodil could hold his breath for an hour or so, which was great and sufficient for him to explore under water.

That day he told Dessemay that he was ready to go underwater with her and see her living place. They both dived and Dessemay immediately took him to see her home. Daffodil was shocked to see so much beautiful and awesome life in water. He saw many starfishes of different colours then he say octopuses who had many legs (tentacles) . He was really in a wonder to see the marine life. Then Dessemay showed him her home which was made of white coloured shells arranged on top of slanting green weeds and many fishes of her and bigger than her size lived in similar kind of houses. He was really pleased to see such beautiful place and wished that he could live in such kind of place too but he had to go as he was running out of oxygen. So they swam to the top of the oasis and he breathed then. Now Daffodil was glad that he made Dessemay his friend and got to see so much new.

That day he went home thrilled and excited. But when he went went home he freaked out because Daffodil's dad told him to hide because there was a group of 15 lion and lionesses who wanted to occupy their area and he might die defending him and his mom. Daffodil said that he would stand with his dad and protect their home but his dad did not agreed. He told Daffodil that they were too many and that three of them can't stand against all of them and he wanted his son to be safe so he told him to better hurry and find a safe spot to shelter himself. No matter how hard Daffodil tried to convince his parents about standing besides them during fight but they would not let him do so. So Daffodil had to hide. He then thought that where could he run and hide and be safe. He then though that hiding under water would be his best bet so he started sprinting back to oasis.

By the time the fight had started and two of the adult attacking lions had seen him flee. They followed him. Daffodil had seen that two of the lions were after him so he ran as fast as he could and reached the oasis. Dessemay who was swimming in that area at that time saw Daffodil and was surprised to see him so late. He said "take me under water". Dessemay without asking questions did that. They hid in the water for about 2 hours and by that time Daffodil could not hold his breath anymore and they swam up.

Also by that time the two lions chasing him and given up the chase for him and went back. Then Daffodil told Dessemay the entire story. Dessemay consoled him and told him that he was a lion and should have a brave heart and should not worry. She told him to go and check back his home and parents. Daffodil who was not sure went back immediately pacing as fast as he could. When he reached his place he saw that his parents were dead and had died defending their home. Suddenly he heard some foot steps. He hid and saw that the 15 lion and lioness were coming towards him. He wanted to fight and avenge his parents death but he remembered that his father had told him to live and not die and never be hasty and foolish in making decisions. So he slipped from there and ran back to the oasis hiding. He saw Dessemay, who was waiting for him and told her everything. At that time Daffodil and Dessemay wept for a while but they thought that past can't be changed so there was nothing that they could do about it. He could only keep his parents alive by living and keeping them alive in his heart.

That day he said goodbye to Dessemay as that area came under the ruling of the 15 lion and lionesses and if he lived there he could die too. So he left that place and went to some other forest where there was less violence and space for him.

tALe 33 : tHe piRaNhA hUnTeR

Let's start this story but before starting let's understand what is the meaning of piranha. Piranha is actually a fish. Although it is small but it is very deadly. Piranha hunts in a school. It is a meat eating eating fish. It does not ever show mercy and let it's prey go. This fish is a native of Amazon basin in South America. They are the deadliest of fishes. Although they are small in size but they exist in big schools so when they attack they don't leave anything behind. They can eat an entire buffalo or a land animal and are very very dangerous. They don't even spare humans. They have laser sharp teeth and when they attack they take a big chunk out of flesh of the thing they are attacking in a single bite as compared to their body size and keep on doing that until their prey is dead and there is no meat left on its body.

Long time back in South America there lived a man name Rocoo. He lived in a small village called Poonie. Where he lived was quite peaceful. The only threat that existed in that village was of piranhas.

It so used to happen there that the cattle herders needed to cross a river with their herd so that their cattle can feed upon the Pastures, which existed on the other side of the river. In that river existed schools of piranhas. Most of the time they could cross without being attacked by piranha because they were not hungry but sometimes they had to cross with deadly casualties. So sometimes out of a herd of 50 cows or buffalos one got slayed by the deadly piranha and there was nothing they could do about it. The river was quite wide and thus it was not possible for them to build a bridge over it that was strong enough to support the weight of their cattle herds. So this continued for along time. Fishermen had tried hunting the piranhas but they couldn't. Their fishing nets were of no use against the deadly piranha because they would cut the fishing nets with their sharp teeth and set themselves free whenever they were tried to capture.

Now, Rocoo lived with his grandfather all alone. His mom and dad had passed away in a forest fire long time back and his grandmother had also died of illness quite a few years ago. Rocoo loved his grandfather very dearly and cared for him. His grandfather was also very nice to Rocoo and did whatever he could to help him out in his daily activities. Rocoo was actually a wood cutter who rarely had to cross the deadly river to get his wood a it was available in the village itself. Rocoo used to enjoy his livelihood because he earned sufficient for him and his grandfather to get a good meal at the end of the day. They lived peacefully there.

One day Rocoo went to cut wood but he did not find any. Whatever trees were left had already been cut by the other wood cutters of the village for timber. Now he knew that from now on he would have to cross the river to get the wood but he was not worried. The only thing that bothered him was that he would be able to carry less wood than usual whilst crossing river. So he would have to cross the river twice or thrice to get the same amount of wood that he usually got before he had to cross the river. The idea was that he had to raise the wood up over his head and cross river so that it does not get wet. Because he couldn't afford a boat he had to make 2-3 rounds of crossing the river to get all of his wood from the timber cutting area across the deadly river back to the village.

This continued for a while until one day his grandfather decided to go with Rocoo and help him out in bringing wood from across the river. Rocoo told his grandfather that he did not needed help but his grandfather insisted on helping him that day. So Rocoo agreed to it. They crossed the river and Rocoo started to cut the wood and his grandfather started to collect it in a sack. So that day they made 3 sacks of wood as the timber Rocoo was cutting was quite big in size. After they had done cutting and collecting the wood it was evening and time for them to go back to their home. As soon as they finished packing and were about to move Rocoo's grandfather got a cut to his feet from one of the sharp edges of wood when he was trying to put the sack behind his back after lifting it from the ground. The wound was quite deep so it started bleeding. Rocoo saw that and immediately got a piece of cloth and tied it around the wound so that it stops bleeding. Then they thought it was not a good idea to cross the river because even though the wound is covered the piranhas might attack Rocoo's grandpa and may result in fatality. Rocoo's grandfather told him that he should not worry because he had covered his wound properly and so nothing of that sort should happen. Rocoo was not totally convinced but he respected his grandfather's view so they agreed to cross the river and go home. They took two of the sacks and crossed the river safe and sound. After crossing the river Rocoo's grandfather told Rocoo to start selling wood as it was already late and he would go and get the third sack of timber. Rocoo thought that it was safe for his grandpa to do so because they had already crossed the river without any attack from the piranha fishes. So he let him do so and started selling the wood there. His grandfather reached the other side of river, picked up wood and started to cross back to reach Rocoo. As soon as he entered to cross river holding the wood over his head his wound dressing slipped and went into with the flow of river. But Rocoo's grandfather was unaware of it and continued crossing river. When he reached the middle of the river he screamed Help! and got drown into the river. Rocoo who was seeing all this but did not know what to do because he saw that piranhas were attacking his grandfather and he wanted to save him but was helpless because if goes into the river to rescue his grandfather he would be eaten by the piranhas too so he stayed there seeing the horrific scene of his grandfather being eaten by Piranha till death. Rocoo stood their and yelled and screamed and did not know what to think of. He sat their crying and was in a deep remorse. He wept the whole night and did not sleep.

Three days had passed when he did not eat or sleep properly. But at the end of fourth day he decided to avenge his grandfather's death. He realized that piranhas were a big problem, not only for him but for the entire village. Sometimes they ate a whole cow or goat and this time they ate his grandfather mercilessly in front of him. He then decided that somehow these fishes should be eradicated from the river because they pose a great danger to the cattle and human life. He also had known that the nets the fishermen had did not work on piranhas as they tore them apart if anybody tried to capture them. He sat the whole night and though about a way to go around this. He then decided that just like a lion is hunted similarly the piranhas should be hunted. So he went to see the village head that day and told him about his plan. He told him that if they dig along the river a ditch and connect it to the river and then make a steel gate to shut the flow of river flowing to ditch whenever they wanted they might be able to lock down the piranhas and then eradicate them from that area. This would prevent the further loss of life in that river and in their village. The village leader thought for a while and said that it was a good plan and they should do it.

The next day Rocoo took 50 men along with him to the site where they had to dig the ditch and started digging it. It took a whole day to have a sizeable amount of ditch so they would be able to trap all the piranhas in it. After the ditch was dug they connected it to the river and installed a steel gate at its opening which can shut off the flow of water or anything from the river at any whenever they wanted. Now when the ditch filled with water they bought some bait which was an injured buffalo that was bleeding and thus releasing the scent of blood in the water which would be easily be sensed by piranhas. Then they put the buffalo in the ditch where it started drowning due to the depth of water. Now as soon as the buffalo started to drown they saw a big school of piranhas entered the ditch from the River and started chewing on and eating the buffalo. When they felt that all the piranha fishes had entered the ditch they shut the ditch with the steel gate and trapped all the piranhas in it.

It was a moment of celebration for all of them. Rocoo had avenged his grandfather's death and gave peace to the villagers but the hunting was still not complete. In a few days the water in the ditch dried and the piranhas got suffocated to death there. Since people wouldn't let anything go waste. They then took out the the piranhas cooked them and ate them. They had a hearty meal of killing and eating their enemy and thanked Rocoo and god that day.

TaLe 34 : ThE HyPnOtiZer

Long ago in Europe once there existed a person named Halucy who had mastered the art of hypnotism by practicing from his childhood. During those times hypnotism was considered to be impractical but he did not believe so.

Page 116

When he was a child he started reading many books which taught hypnotism. These books were hard to find and the authors did not themselves practice hypnotism. They only explained the concept of hypnotism and what all was possible through hypnotism. Some books also explained the possible ways to hypnotize.

Before Halucy, there was nobody who could hypnotize a person so deeply that the hypnotized person obeys the hypnotizer completely.

His training was unique. Before Halucy started training on human beings he started practicing on birds and animals. Although it was strange and difficult to practice on animals but he managed to do that.

One day he was sitting in a park near his house. At that time he was holding a magnifying glass tied to a thread which hung loose from it and was used by him to hypnotize. While he was sitting he saw a street dog come near him and bark at him. The dog's saliva was so much that whilst he was barking it feel on the ground and dirtied it. The dog was never going to pick the saliva up so Halucy decided to make him do that.

He took out his magnifying glass hanging to a thread so that he could hypnotize the dog. He held the lose end of the thread in his left hand and let the magnifying glass swing like a pendulum in front of dog's eyes. Then he kept on staring at the dog's eyes and also kept on saying " GET HALUCIFIED,.." for some time. In a little time the dog started feeling dizzy and totally became stationary as if he had been captivated in his thoughts by Halucy. Then Halucy tried to make him do something to check if he had been hypnotized. He told the dog to bend and lick his own saliva that was fallen on the ground through directions of his right hand. In a minute dog bended and licked its saliva and suddenly became active. The dog then started barking again and jumping.

Halucy realized that he had done something that no man could ever do. He had hypnotized a dog. He was happy about it but did not tell anybody at that time.

Then he tried testing his hypnotism on a bird some days later. What he did was he went to his room in his small hut and waited for any bird to come near his window. He had waited there for about 15 minutes when he saw a small sparrow come and started to dig upon the tree near his window so as if it has been looking for some worm or some kind of fruit or food. Halucy thought that this was the right time that he can test its hypnotizing skills. So he took out his hypnotizing instrument again and started his hypnotizing procedure on the bird. When he did that in a blink of eye the bird became motionless. Then he gave instructions to the bird to hop by movement of his hand in such a way that when he moves his hands up and down the bird should hop up and down and so it did. Halucy was happy at another successful hypnotism by him.

Now he wanted to test hypnotism on humans but was afraid that if he tests it on anybody they might think that Halucy has gone mad. So he did not just test it on any human but tested on his brother.

He told his brother to come near him at just look at the magnifying glass for a minute and concentrate on it. His brother asked him why? Halucy told that he just wanted to show him something. So his brother agreed. Then Halucy said "GET HALUCIFIED" and in a second his brother's eyes got fixated and still. He then decided to check his hypnotized brother out. He then told him to go to the kitchen and put house on fire. Halucy was very careful with his instructions because he would not let the house get on fire but he wanted to see how strong his hypnotism was. So his brother went to the kitchen lighted a match stick and then picked up oil bottle to open it. Halucy immidiately took matchstick from his brother's hand and told his brother to not light the house on fire anymore. His brother immediately woke up from his hypnotized state and asked that what he was doing? Halucy told him that he was just about to cook some food. "It's funny" his brother said that and that he did not remember coming to the kitchen and doing that.

At that time Halucy was satisfied that he had done it. He had become the only hypnotist and also the only one that could hypnotize both the animals and the humans. He rejoiced that day.

In a few years time when he grew up he joined circus and started doing shows and became famous as a hypnotist.

One day it so happened that in a nearby town there had been a fire in the zoo and the animals had escaped out of their captivity which was very dangerous for people living nearby because many animals including a lion had escaped and it was a threat.

The zoo people did not have time nor place to set up a trap for that lion and they were worried. The zoo people had heard about the hypnotist and they knew that he could hypnotize animals also so they went to him for his help.

Halucy told that he could help but he needs an eagle to help him out. They wasted no time and got him an eagle. Now Halucy hypnotized the eagle in such a way that it first flew away to locate the lion then came back. Then Halucy and the zoo people followed It. The eagle took them to a nearby pond where the lion was drinking some water . There was no time for traps and tranquilizer darts did not existed at those times so Halucy had to do magic of his own. He went near to the lion but to the opposite side of the pond which was closest to the reflection of the lion and started his magic. He took out his hypnotizing instrument and started hypnotizing the image of the lion formed on water. As soon as the lion looked at it, it tried pouncing on Halucy so as to eat him but to everybody's surprise the lion started licking Halucy's face. Everybody watching that was happy and dumbstruck to see what was going on . But they wasted no time and brought a cage and Halucy made the lion go in. The zoo people then closed the gate of the cage so that the lion does not escape and is captured.

The zoo people were surprised at this and thanked Halucy a lot.

Now in the course of time Halucy made many friends. One of his friends name was Halos. Halos was a very nice man and was philanthropist. He had helped many people during his life time.

One day it so happened that Halos and Halucy were walking on the road and Halos feet tripped and fell on the ground . The ground had another stone waiting for him. That sharp stone caused excessive bleeding at the forehead and he fainted. Halucy immediately picked Halos up in his hands and took him to see a doctor. The doctor had put stitches on Halos forehead but said that it would be difficult to treat him. He believed that Halos might have suffered a brain damage. So he told Halucy that Halos will have limited capability when he wakes up which was true. When Halos woke up he could not talk or walk and showed some abnormal behaviour. Since Halucy was very fond of his friend he determined himself that he will cure Halos anyhow.

So everyday he started coming to Halos house and started doing hypnotism on him to make he and his body remember and heel to who he was. It took him a many years when Halos started responding to hypnotism. He starting behaving normally and one day he stood up and walked properly then he said "Halucy! How long have I been disabled?" Halucy was surprised to hear that and was happy to hear his voice so he said:" Sun has not set yet so its must be just in the afternoon that you were hit and now you are the hit." Halos smiled and thanked Halucy for all that he did to get him back again on his feet.

Halucy and Halos remained friends forever during their lifetime and helped each other whenever any of them needed help. They became the best of friends ever.

TaLe 35 : ThE LoVe iNdUcEr

This is a story of a love inducer whose name is Lreffick. He was born in a world where magicians and magic existed. The magic in that world was caused by magical potions. He began his journey from there.

He got an apprenticeship position with a magician after many years of studying in the school of magic. He had studied hard enough so that he can become one of the good magicians in that world.

As an apprentice he learned many things while working with his magician boss. But one thing the magicians did not have was a love potion. It may be because nobody had ever thought about it. But Lreffick had once thought about it while he was studying in the school of magic and wanted to make one.

At that time he did not have resources to do that so he did not proceeded with this idea. But after years of studying Lreffick had been hired as an apprentice and had some money to spare for his experiment in his free time to make a love potion that can induce love to somebody. So he started thinking about how to make it.

After experimenting with many potions he finally made a potion which he believed was a love potion. So, he wanted to test it out. He took a drop of potion and went to a pig's pen and made it to have a sip of it. But he was cautious not to be the first face in front of the pig so that he must not be the first person with whom the pig falls in love with. According to Lreffick the person who drinks the magic potion, no matter in how much quantity will fall in love with the person or thing he or it sees first for first 5 hours of seeing that thing.

And so it happened, the pig was looking towards a wooden fence when it drank the potion. Suddenly something happened. The pig's face became big and small in a jiffy and colours sparked from his face for a second and immediately it fell in love with the wood of the wooden fence he was looking at. The pig came closer near the wood and started rubbing his back on the fence as being petted by the fence and made a beautiful face of kissing the fence and started kissing it and licking it. For five hours he kept on doing that.

Lreffick was seeing all this and he felt that he magic potion was in good standing and could be tested on humans too.

The condition was that the person fell in love with the thing or person whom he or she first sees after drinking the potion for only five hours and then the effect of potion will fade away.

Now Lreffick did not know how to sell it first so he waited for that day.

One day his uncle came and said that he has fallen in Love with a girl who works at a toy store and whose name is Ethemy. He told him that he loves her very much but has no guts to talk to her or even make her his friend. That time Lreffick told him that he could help.

So he told his uncle something. He told his uncle that he had developed a love potion that if somebody drinks it will fall in love with the one who he or she is looking towards at that time. His uncle was happy to hear that but he wanted to know that how would he make Ethemy drink the potion.

Lreffick made a plan and told him that even if it does not work out he should try it. He told his uncle that the next time he goes to the pharmacy he should buy 2 coffees and in one of the coffee put a drop of love inducing potion and keep it for Ethemy and other he should keep for himself.

He told him when he goes to the toy store ask her to have this coffee as it is good for her because she is working too much and would help her keep active. But he also told his uncle that he will have only five hours until the effect of potion dies out. He told him that he has to convince Ethemy in only five hours that he loves her more than anything in the world and to tell her that she is his blessing when he takes her out that day.

So their date started. Lreffick'S uncle whose name was Freddy did as he was told. He went to Ethemy and gave her the love inducing coffee.

Ethemy at that time was looking towards Freddy because he was right in front of him. After drinking the love potion dissolved in the coffee she fell in love with Freddy in a jiffy. Freddy then asked her if she could come out with him and so that they can go towards the woods. Ethemy agreed.

Freddy had already arranged for all the things that he and Ethemy together would do that day if the magic potion works

He first took her to a beautiful store in woods where clothes were sold. It was big store. So in that store they had an option of going underground and enjoy the underground water splash park.

Freddy bought some swimming clothes and accessories for Ethemy and then they went underground to enjoy the water splash park.

There they enjoyed the water rides and after 3 hours they were exhausted. But Freddy knew that he had still 2 more hours left for the magic potion to get over so he took Ethemy to a bowling alley and there they bowled for one more hour. Ethemy kept on enjoying that and after bowling Ethemy and Freddy walked on the streets where they enjoyed the cool breeze blowing and then in midst of it Freddy and Ethemy saw a little girl selling lemonade and ice cream. Ethemy asked Freddy that wouldn't it be wonderful if they had both of it? So they did. They bought a butterscotch ice cream and a grapefruit lemonade and shared it. It was about time the magic potion was about to get over and Freddy knew that. So he waited for that. When the effects of magic potion got over Ehemy realized that she had taken a big break from the job but also a wonderful date with Freddy. But at that moment she did not mind that and realized that she had already fallen in love with Freddy.

Then she asked Freddy that does he still like her? Freddy was overjoyed to hear that and said that even if the world comes to an end and the sky dies but he would never leave her ever and forever be with her, here and in heaven. Ethemy was happy to hear that and in a few months time they got married and lived forever happily ever after!

Lreffick's magic potion did work and helped his uncle. I just believe there might be some potion left with Leffrick for me!

TaLe 36 : ThE CaKe MaN ThAt bRoUgHt ThE rEvOLUtIoN

Is it possible? Let's go through a story about a cake man who brought a revolution in his country all by selling cakes.

Long ago there lived a person named Ratilof in a country called Flemin. This country in which Ratilof lived was a very small country. The population of Flemin was only 25,000 people. The area of Flemin was only 10000 square km. Ratilof lived in his small town named Denmef and worked in his own bakery as a chef and a salesman selling cakes. His cakes were famous in the entire town and country. He made the most delicious good looking cakes ever tasted by man. Ratilof was a hard working guy who spent hours in his bakery to make the best cakes possible because he enjoyed both his work and the appreciation. His cakes contained the perfect amount of sugar which was sufficient for kids and grown up, not too sweet not too less but awesomely best. The cakes he made were meant for all occasions and no occasions so people did not have to wait for an occasion to enjoy Ratilof's cake. He always talked to his customers very politely and gently and had not ever said any bad words to anybody ever. His customers due to his friendly behaviour and nature were also very friendly and nice to him. He never asked for tips but his tip box was loaded with tips at the end of day at the time of closing which he distributed for good cause.

Now, also in that town lived a very cruel king named Frugee.
He always tried to impose heavy taxes on whatever he wanted. Not only that he tried to find different ways to tax people. The most ridiculous of the taxes was Air tax. Air tax meant that since you are living in a country surrounded by trees in which majority of the trees including trees in the forest were on king's / government property thus you have to pay tax for air you breathe. Since trees in the kings country were taken care by king's workers which never was true so they had to pay Air tax. Frugee had calculated that 70% of the trees were on king's property and also he knew the population of the country which as said before was 25,000 so he had averaged that average breathing rate per person which according to him was every second of day which comes out to be 86,400 per day and approximately 32 million in a year. So according to him every person had to pay 70% of .01 cent per breath which amounted to approximately 2250 units of currency of that country per annum. The units of the currency in Flemin was Flea does not actually mean a flea. So everybody in his country had to pay Air tax of 2250 Fleas per annum. Even the new borns had to get registered to pay for Air tax. But since new borns could not work and were dependents and supported by parents so their parents had to pay for them which was ridiculous but it was the law of the country. This continued for quite some time until one night.
One night Ratilof was working late at night as he had an order for a very big wedding cake which was 50 tiers so he was taking his time to finish it. Suddenly he saw the king, Frugee outside his shop trying to enter in that late hours when he had closed shop for the customers. But since it was the king of the country knocking at the door Ratilof had to open the cake shop so that the king could come in. When Frugee came in he asked Ratilof if he had an orange flavoured cake ready as he wanted it urgently because he had a new taste developed for orange flavour. Ratilof had one orange cake left in his shop which he gave to Frugee. Frugee took the cake and did not even pay for it. When Ratilof asked for money Frugee rudely replied " I am the king of this country and my services are enough to pay for this puny little cake." After hearing this Ratilof did not know what to say. He got a little upset but let it go away.

Now when Frugee was at the door and about to leave the shop a small kid about 7 years old who was playing in front of the shop dashed into Frugee and made him drop his cake on the ground. Frugee was furious over this and slapped the 7 year old and the boy started crying. Ratilof was watching all this from inside of his shop.

Frugee knew that Ratilof did not have any more of orange flavoured cake in his shop and to make it would take some time which he did not have patience for so he went back to his palace. After Frugee left, Ratilof came outside of his shop and went near the boy who was crying. He consoled the boy and gave him a small candy and asked him to stop crying. The boy saw the candy and stopped weeping. The boy then went away. Ratilof also went back inside his shop and started thinking. He thought for a while and said to himself " This is not good, slapping a small boy is not royal and genuine". He realized after long thinking that the king had gone too cruel now and it's high time that their should be a people's government rather than a monarchy so he thought about bringing a revolution in the country. But how? He did not know.

That night he made 100 small fliers and wrote in them that a people of Flemin are invited to have a meeting discussing about tyranny of king. Then he slept.

Next day he woke up and went to his cake shop. Since it was very dangerous and illegal to speak or plan against the king he had already thought about a plan of distributing the pamphlets. He started making cakes and inserting the fliers in the cake so that they remain hidden and get distributed amongst people. He made 100 cakes that day and put in all the 100 fliers individually.

By the end of day Ratilof had sold all the cakes and waited for the third day to come when the meeting was decided to be held at his house.

About 200 people showed up in the meeting that day. Ratilof explained to all the people about what had happened that day with the 7 years old boy. People after hearing that became furious and mad. They wanted to overthrow the king and bring in people's rule rather than a monarchy as a government (which was Ratilof's idea).

But they did not know how to do that. Ratilof told them that a civil movement would be useless because the king would arrest all of the people and throw them in prison forever. Ratilof told people that Frugee had an army only of 5,000 which is sleeping most of time and only few 100's of them are at guard around the palace. If we spread the word amongst our people who are 25,000 that we can storm the palace during the night today and overthrow the king at night and throw him in prison we can start democratic government for our ruling.

So after the meeting ended people of Flemin spread the word to their relatives and friends about the plans to overthrow king that night and bring in democratic government for their ruling.

And so it happened. The plan was so effective that the total population which was 25,000 people accumulated in front of the palace and took the king unaware. The guards of the palace after seeing a big mob attacking quit their posts and left the palace. The king was captured and thrown in the prison. The king's palace became the parliament of Flemin, all because of wise decision of Ratilof and people and because of the tearful incident.

TaLe 37 : tHe GeRmAn sHePhErD

Long ago there existed a breed of dogs which was trusted the most by humans to take care of their sheep. The name of that breed of dogs which still exists was called German shepherd. It is sometimes called that dogs are a man's best friend but for shepherds German shepherd is a shepherd's best friend.

German shepherd's take care of sheep and cattle as if they are one of their own kin. The most important thing they do is protect the herds of sheep and cattle. They protect them by guiding them not to go too deep in the forest for grazing or if needed they will fight deadly animals like jackals and coyotes and don't let anything happen to the herd.

This is a story about a German shepherd named Frohen who was a breed of dog born of a mother who had died protecting her heard from a group of wolves. Frohen's mother was pregnant with frohen when this attack happened. The master tried to save Frohen's mother but could only save Frohen. Frohen had never seen her mother. All he knew was his master whose name was Dweny. Dweny was a very nice person and a good master for his companion, Frohen.

In the beginning when Frohen was a kid he used to sleep with his master who also had no other companion other than Frohen. Frohen slept on the same bed as that of Dweny. Frohen sometimes used to pee on the bed when it was winter and make it wet. In the morning Frohen used to see Dweny pulling up the mattress from his bed and putting it for drying in the sun. Then Dweny used to put a new mattress on his bed for the next night. Dweny never scolded Frohen but trained him by love rather.

Frohen learned everything slowly but steadily as he grew up. He learnt not to pee on the bed then he learned that he had to take care of the sheep of Dweny. Dweny also trained Frohen on different types of actions according to different type of whistle sounds made by Dweny alone.

Until Frohen turned to 2 years old he had done all his training and was proficient in it.

The daily routine of Frohen used to begin at 5:00 am when he went to the enclosure where sheep's were enclosed and it's gate was locked to prevent them from escaping and also to prevent any wild animal to attack them. Frohen had to open the gate by lifting up the latch and letting the sheep's come out. Then he took the sheep towards the pastures and let them graze their. After 2 hours he used to round the sheep up and bring them back. Then at 7:00 am Dweny used to get up and check that if any of the sheep wasn't missing from the herd. This was Frohen's daily job and he performed it with utmost care and responsibility. Dweny was always happy with the good job that was done by Frohen and awarded him with by giving him his favourite food Parmesan fish. Frohen enjoyed Parmesan fish very much as he would eat as much as he got and left nothing behind.

In those days there was an attack of wolves to one of his neighbouring friend's herd. The attack of wolves was becoming more frequent. Dweny had cautioned Frohen by explaining him through whistle sounds and Frohen knew it was dangerous out there during those times.

The day Frohen came to know about the danger of wolves he became more cautious and observant both during the night and the day.

One morning when it was time for Frohen to take sheep out for grazing he sensed something strange. He saw a wolf ready to attack him and eat up the sheep. The wolf looked hungry and wanted to really kill something. The strange thing was that wolf had its kids along with it too standing behind it. Frohen was strong so he tried to make wolf go away but the wolf was going for a kill. Frohen had to kill the wolf so that he can make sure the sheep are safe. The wolf kids were too small and tried to wrestle with Frohen but he did not fight with them and made them calm by showing anger and love. Frohen knew that wolves usually attack in a pack so he was cautious for another attack. He took the wolf cubs inside the shed where his master kept all the hay and locked the door of the shed from outside. Then he was on a tight watch for any other wolf and kept on high alert until his master woke up. That day the sheep did not go for grazing.

At 7:00 am Dweny woke up. When he came outside he saw that a dead wolf was lying outside the fenced enclosure. On seeing he realized that Frohen must have done this as a means to protect the sheep herd. Dweny was comforted seeing that. He then counted the sheep and not a single sheep was missing. Dweny was proud of Frohen and tapped him on his back.

Then Frohen toook him to the shed where Dweny used to store hay and made him see two wolf cubs. Dweny saw that and felt it was dangerous to keep the cubs so he tried to make them go away but Frohen stopped him and somehow gave him a message that the wolf cubs would be helpful in the long run as they would help him further to keep his flock of sheep safe when they grow up. Dweny then said ok and also conveyed to Frohen that from now on it was his duty to train the wolf cubs. Dweny then named one wolf cub as Ace and other as Xaf.

Bothe the cubs grew up to be strong wolves and considered Frohen as their dad forever. They learnt well from him. They learnt how to protect the herd of sheep and take good care of it.
The cubs also proved to be a very nice and lovable companions for Dweny after Frohen died. They took care of the sheep as gently as did Frohen.

TaLe 38 : tHe AnT sAviOuR

Ant's are a very communal and social beings. They all work together for a common cause i.e. for their community forever. Humans usually have a govt and are ruled by their elected leader but not ants. Ants are governed by a non elected leader who is a lady and is called the ant queen. In a colony of ants, the ant queen gives the orders which are obeyed by all the ants perfectly or somewhat sometimes imperfectly but they do are obeyed.

The colony of ants in discussion in this story had a queen named Acferia. Acferia was a noble queen. She did not allow her subjects i.e. her ants to loot from any house. She had strict orders that ants can only loot and gather food from public property alone which was from forests and parks etc.

Because Acferia was benevolent she knew that if her ants attacked a house and took all the groceries from there which she knew they had the capability for, then it would be difficult for people there to survive. She also knew that in the world of humans, money was important and if all the groceries were looted from house of a human they might be able to physically replenish it but the financial aspect may lead them to difficult situation. This proved that Acferia was a wise queen and always thought good of everybody.

Now, Acferia had a worker whose name was Drefftorim. Drefftorim was a nice worker and a friend of Acferia. Acferia always consulted Drefftorim whenever she needed advise on any situation. Drefftorim always tried to help the queen Acferia and his community by giving good advise. Although he was funny but his advise always had helped in one way or the other.

The strange thing was although the queen was very nice and friendly and cared a lot about all but the humans did not think the same way.

It was the end of autumn and about to get cold i.e winter was a few months ahead and ants needed to stock up. At the same time I would like to inform that the queen when built their colony they built it quite far from human civilization but due to rapid increase in population of humans and development of lots of industries they somehow had got nearer to the human civilization and many houses were near their colony.

Also along with their colonies they had other ant colonies. The ants and ant queens among other colonies were very mischievous and not good and benevolent as Acferia and her ants. They did not care about humans so when it was difficulty in finding food in the forest they raided human kitchens and fridges to get food for themselves.

Acferia had many times told them in there annual meetings that they should not raid human households as they had children like them and they have difficulty making their ends meet. But the queens of other colonies of ants never payed heed to Acferia's advise and always went to do what they felt right in any way.

That season was a rather dry one and the ants of other colonies had started raiding human households for their supplies quite frequently which did not prove to be good later. Due to frequent ant raids the humans had reported this to their local govt. and wanted something to be done to prevent ants from raiding them again. Due to more and more complains of ants attacking, the local govt. had to take some action and so they did. The local govt. hired some pest controllers to get to know where the ants came from and terminate their colony. The pest control people started to work on their task assigned. They found the colonies of ants which was in the forest so they started their work.

They got huge tanks filled with pesticide sprays, loaded their trucks and went to the place where the ant colonies were. When they reached their destination they started to spray the pesticide spray all over the huge colonies. Many ants who were sleeping inside the colonies suddenly woke up because of the ugly poisonous smell and because of suffocation came out of their colonies. Acferia smelt that too and tried to come out but got in stuck in stampede. Drefftorim saw that and tried to save Acferia but he had nothing in their colony that could stop her suffocation.

Drefftorim then immediately tried to come out of colony and wanted something to prevent Acferia's suffocation and get her to escape the stampede. When Drefftorim came out he saw that there was a unique material which was had fallen on his face and had covered it. While his face was covered with the plastic bag he did not feel the poisonous smell and was feeling actually better. He then realized that that material (which was a plastic bag) could also save Acferia. He felt happy with that thought and took the small plastic bag and went to the location above the colony on the ground where Acferia was trapped in the stampede and dead bodies of ants .

He then started to dig that area on ground and immediately dug enough to reach Acferia. He then tore a part of the plastic bag and covered Acferia's mouth with it.

Acferia who was getting unconscious regained consciousness immediately after getting the plastic bag put on her face. On awaking Acferia saw that Drefftorim was carrying her on her back and that a material was covering her face. She immediately asked that what was that thing? Drefftorim told her to keep quite and also told her that he will tell about it when they reach safety.

After they were away from the deadly fumes Drefftorim put her down and told her that the thing she wanted to know about was a unique substance that did not let the ugly fumes come in and had given them life. They were really impressed by that thing but they were sad too that because of the neighbouring ants their ants were destroyed and it would be at least a few days until they can go back to their colony to get food and claim it again.

Until that time they rested. In the meanwhile Drefftorim was checking out the forest when he saw a spine protruding animal which was a porcupine who also had escaped a snake attack by projecting its spines towards it. He realized that it was something unique and powerful unlike he had seen before.

So he went to the porcupine and asked if it could shed some spines and that then he and his group of ants who had come there after escaping a death attack could use it for their protection. The porcupine was nice and agreed to it and shed about 100 spines. The ants were called there by Drefftorim who quickly picked it up and went back to where Acferia was resting.

Now, Acferia was worried because she knew that winter was approaching and that whatever food they needed was stored in their colony. She knew that they could build up a colony quickly but to gather food was tough at that time. So she ordered some of the remaining ants to start building colony which was about 100,000 yards from there previous colony and was safe enough for their future. Then she and the remaining ants waited for 4 days and went back to their previous colony. When they reached the colony they tried to enter it.

But humans as we know are treacherous being. They were on the look out for any sign of infestation in the colonies again. One of them saw the ant queen moving swiftly. The ant queen was carrying the porcupine spine with her. The pest controller rather than spraying pesticide on the ant tried to squash it. Drefftorim who saw that cried and all the 100 ants started to attack that man with spines.

The man got brutally injured and bled for a while. The other pest controllers saw that and realized   that the breed of ants was of different kind and that they had never seen such kind of breed so they did not know what pesticide to spray on them to kill them. In a confusion they hurried back taking the injured pesticide sprayer to the hospital.

Now the pesticide sprayers were cautioned by this attacking and got a bit fearful. They did not think of going to that place again because of fear and lack of spray chemical for the special kind of ants that they saw that day.

In the meanwhile Acferia thanked Drefftorim and the rest of the ants who had attacked the humans to save her life. Then they picked up all the food and this time carried 100 times as they usually did and went to their new colony that was to be build by them. The ants that were already there had already laid the foundation for it.

After that they lived peacefully as they ate only from public property and not from private property and minded their own business as usual without interfering in other's.

TaLe 39 : tHe wiTcH tHaT gAvE cUrSeS oN hALLoWeEn

Long ago in hell when only witches lived in it there lived a witch named Aclifomy. Aclifomy was very fond of candies. But in hell witches got whatever they wanted except candies as candies are meant for kids and not for adults and all the witches that existed in hell were adults. So Aclifomy never got a chance to have candies. She only enjoyed the memories of it when she used to have it as a child when she was on earth. Whenever she tried convincing her friends to make candies her friends told her that they were adults now and didn't like candies anymore. They also used to advise Aclifomy that she should stop thinking about candies and concentrate more upon how to further enhance witchcraft. So she tried but couldn't concentrate on witchcraft enhancements.

One day she got real mad and decided that she would do whatever it takes to get candies so she decided to transform into a mortal body girl and enter earth's realm and get candies. But the only time she could reach earth was Halloween night which was a 5 days ahead. So she waited for that night very eagerly and impatiently.

After 5 days Halloween night came. She immediately transformed into a human girl and entered earth's atmosphere and then landed on earth without anybody knowing about it on earth.

As soon as she landed she saw a group of kids dressed up as ghosts and witches. Those kids were going from house to house and saying " trick or treat" and thus getting candies. Seeing that Aclifomy decided to dress as a ghost too and ask for candies. But since she did not had candies for more than one million years she was desperate to get candies and wanted all of them.

To do that she got mixed up with the crowd of the kids and went from house to house in that neighbourhood asking for candies. But her demand was a little different. Instead of saying "trick or treat", she said "trick or treat for me all" but the people who were giving candies did not give all the candies to Aclifomy. They only distributed the candies uniformly to all the kids. This made Aclifomy more mad and then she decided to take revenge.

At that time it was 5 to 12 and her portal to hell realm would be closed if she does not enter her realm before 12 am but at that time she had already decided to stay.

That night she spent alone in the dark underneath a tree dressed up as a plant. Whatever candy she got she did not eat it because she was not satisfied with few candies, she wanted a lump some. So she just saved them in her small but huge magical pocket.

The next day she woke up got a house for rent in the same neighbourhood and started living there.

Now, she made up a plan, she said to herself that the people of this neighbourhood never gave all the candies to one person because they either think they are too nice or they don't know if witches are for real. She had already decided to teach a lesson to the people of that neighbourhood so she waited for next Halloween.

Next Halloween she set up a poster on her door stating "Free hair cutting along with treats for Halloween". Children who saw that poster were delighted to see it and all went to Aclifomy's house first. Aclifomy was waiting for them. When the kids came she brought her magic scissors that cut in a second the hair of kids to the style they wanted. So there were 6 kids who came to her that night. She cut all of the six kids hair and gave them the previous year's candies. But they did not knew that the candies were cursed by the witch a night earlier.

When the kids went away she collected the hairs of kids and separated them with a blow of magic air coming through her lungs and flowing out through her mouth. Then she took one hair per child and prepared a cauldron. She put in it, a magic powder and lay a fire beneath it. Then she kept on stirring it and said the evil magic words " The owner of hair shall not pass until I get my wish alas. Let them turn into the ornaments of music till I pass". Then without wasting time she put the 6 hairs of kids in the cauldron. Poof! A magic happened. The kids who had eaten all the witches candies by that time were there at there home. They suddenly froze and got stuck to the ground. Then in a jiffy they turned into different musical instruments. One turned into a set of drums, other into a piano, next turned into harp, fourth turned into a trumpet, fifth turned into a bagpiper and the last who was a girl turned into a set of flutes.

The witch then decided to check her magic. She then strained the hair from the cauldron and started hitting each hair with her magical hands. As soon as she did that the whole neighbourhood screamed out, one, with the loud ugly noises that the kids turned musical instruments were playing and the second, the scream of the people itself.

People then realized that their kids were missing and did not know where the musical instruments had come from so they became worried. They wept all night wondering where their kids were.

Then the witch waited for 100 days and told in a musical tone that their kids were with them but they were turned into musical instruments because of a witch and the only way to get them transformed back into their kid form was that they had to give all the candies on Halloween to her.

Then the parents wanted to know how was that possible if they did not know who she was.

So she kept on making kids or the musical instruments scream many times a day until Halloween came.

Why she waited for halloween to get candies because in those days it was a tradition that candies had to be made at home and not bought from market for Halloween. So people used to collect the materials during different seasons and make tremendous amount of candies for kids`during Halloween distribution.

Then she said a musical message through kids that
" A hat will appear with a spear on the Halloween night dears, throw in as much candy as you clearly dear, only then the kids will come out of their musical fear, otherwise the wrath will be a player till the end of all of you dears".

The people knew then whom to give candies to during the halloween night.

So they made tremendous amount of candies to give to the witch and save their kids. As the Halloween night approached the witch sent her hat flying and floating in air to all the houses. When the people heard a knock from the spear they opened the doors and filled the bottomless witches hat with loads of candies and emptied all their stock.

When the hat collected all the candies it vanished and appeared in front of Aclifomy who did not waste time and opened a portal and went back to hell taking all the candies with her to enjoy for many years to come until she came for more.

The kids turned musical instruments immediately transformed back into kids and screamed a scream of happiness and thanked their parents for saving them from witch's clutches.

That night was a true Halloween night for parents, kids and the witch-Aclifomy.

tALe 40 : CaNdiEs bEaRiNg tReE

This is a story about a tree that gave candies instead of fruits. As much joyful it may seem but it wasn't at the beginning. Trees usually bear fruits or flowers but the tree god couldn't take away the wish of a child that under circumstances wanted candies for her well being. He altered nature's rules to do that.

Long time ago in a country named Xaeffy lived a very poor father and a child. Father's name was Westol and his child who was a girl, her name was Dammadan. Westol worked in rubber industry where he extracted rubber from tree. Westol always wanted to do his own business as the pay he got from extracting rubber was very meagre and with that pay he was not able to support his daughter's education.

In Xaeffy it was not easy to do business as only the rich people could do it. Why? Because the ruler of Xaeffy was a very mean person. He put tax on everything just so that he kept on getting richer and poor kept on getting poorer. His tax policies were so strange that they included tax on rubber and maple syrup trees which in turn supported the rich people and him. Many times people tried revolting against him but were always suppressed by the his huge armies. So nothing could be done against the king or his army.

Once Westol was working in the rubber farms. On that day it was the birthday of his boss's son. The owner was a miser too. Instead of giving a party to his workers he simply distributed candies (which were expensive too in that country but less expensive than a feast) to them.

Westol wasn't a big fan of candies but his daughter was. Westol took the candies home for his daughter. His daughter when saw the candies was very excited to see them. Her daughter took out the wrapper from one of the candies and tasted it. She liked it very much. But his daughter since she was just a kid wanted the taste of the rock candies forever and did not wanted to loose them. So she asked her father " How can I make more of the sweet rock candies that you have given me?".His father was a a bit confused and did not know how to answer that. His father jokingly told her daughter that the only way to preserve it was to make more of it which they could not.

The daughter then felt a bit sad but she was hungry too at that time. She wanted to eat food but the mouth watering taste she got from candies did not wanted her too have anything else so she started drinking water with her candies so as to at least fill her stomach. When she was doing that she felt sweeter in her mouth when the water ran down her throat so she did that again and again. She then realized that candy water tastier than the candies itself. She then got an idea. She thought that candies could be preserved by mixing them with water and making a syrup out of that. So she did. She picked up the remaining candies unwrapped them and then took a huge water jug. She then put the candies in the water jug ad filled it with water and started stirring it with a spoon. She kept on stirring the water in the jug until all candies got dissolved in it. Then she tried tasting it. It was beautiful! But lacked something. She tried putting lemon juice in it and the tried having a sip of it. When she did that, a perfect candy lemonade was made which she saved it till morning.

Now, she wanted her father to taste it but at that time he was asleep so she waited till the morning when her father got up for work. She did not sleep that night in excitement.

In the morning Westol woke up for work. After he got freshen up Dammadan filled a whole glass with candy lemonade and gave it to her father. She told her father to try it. Her father asked that what it was? But she said that try it first. When Westol tried it he found it that it was the most delicious thing he ever had. Her father in excitement screamed and asked what is that? His daughter freaked out and asked him "was he okay"? Her father said "yes" but he also said that he screamed in excitement and not other wise. He said that " He had never had anything like that before" he then asked her how did she make it? Her daughter then told him that she called it candy lemonade and made it by adding candy, water and lemons. Westol had always wanted to start a business but he never had an idea. This time he got one but due to laws of country he still could not afford raw materials in a lump some so he became a bit depressed then again and went back to work without saying anything to daughter.

The God of trees was watching all this and he became sad too and wanted to do something for Westol and his daughter, Dammadan.

So the tree god waited for a day and then disguised himself as a candy seller and went to Westol's house. He then knocked at the door and asked if there was anybody inside. Dammadan came out and asked the boy that what was his purpose of knocking the door. The boy told that he was selling candies and wanted to sell some of them to her. But Dammadan said that she could no afford candies as they were very poor. But the boy said that he never goes to another house without selling anything to the previous house or loosening the weight of his candy bag. So he said that since she did not have money to pay for a candy he would give her something that would get her candies without having to pay for it. He also said that he could accept anything in exchange for that. Dammadan thought for a while and asked him is it possible to offer him a special lemonade in exchange for what he has to offer. The tree god who was dressed as a candy seller said that that was okay and agreed to the offer.

Dammadan went inside and filled up a glass with candy lemonade and brought outside. She gave it to the candy seller. The candy seller tasted it and liked it very much. He then thanked the girl and gave her a seed. He told the girl that it was a seed that will grow a tree which will give candies. The girl though the candy seller was nuts but she did not refused the seed and took it and thanked the candy seller and then he left.

Many days passed but the girl did not planted the seed. Then one day she thought let's try planting it in my backyard what harm it could do. She hen took the seed from her drawer where she had kept it before and planted it an inch deep within the ground and waited for it to grow. Trusting the seed she slept that night very peacefully. The next day when she woke up she saw a giant tree where she had planted the seed. She then went outside to check it. When she checked it out she yelled just like her father did. The tree was bearing 1000's of rock candies. Seeing that Dammadan got excited and waited for her dad to come.

In the evening his dad came. Dammadan told her dad that she has something special to show her and took her to their backyard. When Westol saw the tree he was shocked too. He asked her daughter that how did it happen? Her daughter explained her the entire incident.

Now Westol was excited and said that there was no tax on candy bearing trees and lemon trees so they can sell as much candy lemonade as they want. And that night Westol got some lemon seeds and planted them in the backyard along with the candy tree.

Then what? They grew their business into a booming one and nobody ever came to know the secret of their lemonade. Not only that Dammadan was able to go to school and get expensive things of her desire, thanks to the tree god and her preserving trick.

TaLe 41 : Mr. PiNcHy

To a new born gifts are always precious but to this baby his new gift turned out be a bit bad for himself. To know this let us got through the story and find out how.

Once in village there lived a family with only husband and a wife as the family members. Both the parents wished for a baby boy but the local witch did not let them have a baby by casting a spell on them because once they had caused her a great ordeal of discomfort. This did not stop the parents from praying to the fairy godmother about them getting a child.

You know fairies are usually very busy creatures and they have long list of demands from people which they are always trying to fulfill. So after a long time the fairy godmother got a chance to know the wish of these childless parents. Along with that she also came to know the curse of the witch that was cast upon those parents that they won't be able to have a human child. But since the wish was given to the fairy godmother it had to be fulfilled. So she checked something. She analyzed that humans are usually of the size between 6 inches (size of baby in a womb) to a size of 6-8 feet so it will be difficult to give them that sized human baby be it a boy or a girl. Then thinking for quite a while she realized that she can give a gift of baby who looks like an elf but will be less than 6 inches tall. So she decided to do that.

She went to the husband and wife the that night and gave them a small box wrapped by a gift wrapping paper and tied with a beautiful ribbon. She then whispered in the mother's ear that this was the gift that she and her husband always wanted and then disappeared in the air. The lady felt a bit confused because she wanted a child and how could there be child in a gift box but she did not hesitate to open it. She carefully untied the ribbon and then opened the lid of the box. When she opened the lid she saw a beautiful small elf sleeping in the box.

She wanted to wake him up but she also did not wanted to disturb him by touching him so she gently blew air from her mouth over his body. Feeling the cool air the small elf started feelin cold and opened his eyes. When he saw that a lady was blowing air over him he felt a bit scarred and since he was just a little elf in his age as well he asked the lady that who she was and who he was. The lady did not lie to him. She said that he was a little boy who was gifted to him by the fairy godmother. She asked her if she could call him Pinchy. The elf said that it was okay whatever she names him because he was his son and she had to take care of him until he grows up.

The evil witch who was hiding behind the window where Pinchy was lying and suddenly came out furious. She said " I had cursed you people not to have a child, how then dare you get one?" She then had seen and heard that the lady had kept the name of the small elf who was her baby from now on as Pinchy and why because she liked his cheeks very much and wanted that whoever saw him should pinch on his cheeks to make him know that he was a cute boy.

The witch cursed that whoever pinches him and utters any work to be done will come true and went away. Pinchy's father who was standing behind his mother was also seeing this but was helpless and could not do anything so he, Pinchy and Pinchy's mother all became a bit sad and they said that Pinchy should not tell about his curse to anyone. Pinchy agreed to it.

Now Pinchy started growing up, not in size but in his age and started going to human school. He initially had difficulty getting along the tall human students but as time passed he learned to manage it. Pinchy was not a very bright theoretical study student but an awesome practical worker. So he continued getting good grades in his practical works but scoring poor in theoretical studies.

One day there came a new teacher in his class. This teacher was very strict. She gave an assignment to be done by all her students including Pinchy. This assignment was a class assignment so it had to be done in the classroom. When the time was over everybody submitted the assignment. Now, she was checking and giving grades to the students but as soon as Pinchy's assignment was given marks, she called him and pinched his cheeks in a negative way. She said " you have scored the least grades of all that I have checked until now, I wish that you had a bigger brain" and suddenly Pinchy's head grew bigger. Everybody who saw that freaked out and they realized that Pinchy had a curse on his cheeks and whoever touches it and wants some work to be done gets it done. The class sat for few moments and then suddenly they ran to catch Pinchy and touch his cheeks and ask for wishes.

Pinchy by that time had realized that his curse was known to all and thus it was not safe there. He ran towards home and when he saw his mom and dad who got afraid seeing his large big head. He then told them that his curse was not a secret anymore and many kids were after him to get his cheeks pinched. His parents hid him in a cupboard and whichever student came after him and asked for him they told them that he was not at home and that he had gone somewhere far. Pinchy stayed in the cupboard for a while and when it was safe he came out.

He and his parents were very worried and did not know what to do. They then again prayed to fairy godmother for help. Fairy godmother who heard there prayer and immediately ascended to their house and asked "what was wrong"? Pinchy told them the entire incident and the story and asked how he could get rid of the curse. Fairy godmother told him that since the magic cannot be fought for through magic so it is time that he had to do something for himself by himself. Pinchy asked " what could he do"?

The fairy godmother told her that she will send him to a magical place and there he will have three tasks to do. First one will be to cross a huge mountainous range that would be the size of all mountain ranges on earth combined in 7 days. Secondly he will have to find water coloured eggs born of a fish and take one of its egg and break it. Thirdly he will have to kill a flying snake. Then she said that if he could not complete the tasks he would die and never would be able to see his parents. Pinchy was brave and said "yes" he could do that and that when can he start.

The fairy godmother took her magical band out and waived it in the air and suddenly Pinchy was transported to that magical land.

Now, Pinchy saw the mountain range which was a mile ahead of him. He did not know how he would be able to cross the huge mountain range but he was determined to do so. On the was he saw a huge flying pig whose wings were the cutest wings of all. The flying pig was digging in the ground to find something. When Pinchy saw that he asked that could he be of any help? The flying pig who was busy digging up the mud stopped doing that and turned around. The pig said that he was such a tiny creature and so how could he be of any help. Pinchy said that although he was tiny he was more maneuverable so he might be able to help the flying pig.

The flying pig then told him the incident. He said that he was sleeping and rolling over his back too much and thus a feather from his wings had fallen somewhere there on the ground. He then told Pinchy that without the feather he would not able to fly. Pinchy told him that let him search for it if he does not mind. The pig said " go ahead ". Pinchy then started searching for the feather. He then told the pig to lift his belly that was touching the ground. When the pig lifted his belly the feather that the pig was looking for was lying there right underneath it. Pinchy picked up the huge feather and gave it to the flying pig. The pig was very happy to get the feather and thanked Pinchy for that. The pig first attached the feather and then asked if he could be of any help? Pinchy told him his whole story and also told him that crossing the mountain range was very important for him to get his life back.

The flying pig then held Pinchy's shirt with his mouth and turned his neck towards back and then released him so that he gets seated over his back.

The pig was so big that Pinchy and the pig flew and crossed the entire mountain range in less than a day. Pinchy thanked the flying pig for that.

Now, the next task was that he had to find water coloured eggs of a fish. But there was no ocean or lake to found nearby. The pig then told Pinchy that the fish eggs he is looking are found in the oasis in the desert. Pinchy then decided to go toward the oasis. The pig again helped him. He and pinchy flew to the desert and found the oasis.

They found the oasis for sure but was difficult to find the fish that laid water coloured eggs. Pinchy asked the pig for his help again. The flying pig told that the oasis was too small and that he can drink all the water and filter out the solid things if Pinchy wished that. Pinchy thought for a while and said that they should go ahead with that idea and they did.

The flying pig drank all the water and left the solid things behind in the oasis. Pinchy then started looking for water coloured eggs and suddenly he found them. He then took one of the egg and broke it and suddenly a star got shone inside the egg. It was so bright that the flying pig shadowed it. In the shadow they saw that it was nothing but a sword shining in the desert sun. Pinchy thought that he could carry and use it, so he took it.

Now suddenly a flying snake attacked them from air and tried to bite Pinchy but he somewhat escaped. Suddenly the pig held Pinchy's shirt and made him bounce so that he gets seated over his back. The pig then Told Pinchy that let's fight the snake together. He told him to aim for the eye with his sword and so Pinchy did. They fought a great battle and in the end pinchy took out both the eyes of the snake and punctured his head with the sword. The snake died.

Pinchy had just completed all his tasks given to him by the fairy godmother when suddenly she appeared and said that now his curse was removed and he would be able to live normally but then she asked does he want to be of same height or wants to be of human height. The boy replied that all this got possible because of his small height so he would prefer to have the same height that he had. Fairy godmother smiled and waived her wand and went away.

In a second he was magically transported back to earth with his parents. His head was not big or large anymore but of normal size and his cheeks were not cursed anymore. Thereafter he lived happily ever after with his parents.

TaLe 42 : ThE BaBy WhALe

So do fishes go to school too? Usually fishes don't go to any school. Whatever they learn is from their mom and dad including the art of hunting for food, art of escaping predators and art of communicating, that is, learning their mother tongues.

But in the wilderness of waters their existed a whale family to whom a female baby whale was born. She was the cutest looking fish. Her parents were very happy the day she took birth because all they were missing was a daughter which they got. They named their daughter Whalefic. Whalefic as other baby whales did, started to grow up and learn several things.

As Whalefic started to grow she came to know about something from his whale friends that the wilderness where his parents and relatives spent most of the time was not a very safe place. Although they were the biggest mammals to rule the waters but still they had carnivorous predators who were jealous of their aura and wanted to take over them. She came to know that all her relatives including her parents were attacked by the bad sharks quite frequently.

There were good sharks too who were friends with the Whalefic's parents and relatives but were less in number and always needed the support of the whales to help defend themselves and the whales territory.

Since whales and sharks have different mother tongues they communicate differently. They could not understand each others tongues so they had to communicate with sign gestures. Whalefic came to know about this.

She was young so she knew that she her brain was still developing. So she though since her brain was developing and in her learning stage she thought that she could learn the languages of the sharks and dolphins.

The dolphins did not actually protect whales because most of the time they were away from the wilderness where the whales lived thus they could not help in protecting the whales village.

But these dolphins had the art of producing signals and sounds in such a frequency range that sharks can not tolerate and thus they swam away after hearing such frequency of sounds. Those sound frequencies were dangerous to the ears and brain of the sharks.

Now Whalefic knew all that.

To learn the languages of shark, Whalefic used to slip away from her parents sight while they were in the meetings with the other whales. Whalefic did not wanted her parents to know that she is going to her shark friends to learn shark's tongue because she did not wanted them to get worried.

Every evening she used to sneak away from her parents and and go to her shark friends. She started learning the tongue of sharks and how they communicate. It took her some time until she was proficient in speaking, reading, listening and writing shark tongue.

Now it was time for her to learn the the dolphin sound weaponry. Since dolphins were far away from their home she had to escape her parental home for sometime. For that she had think of a plan to escape.

By that time she had grown to be 5 years old and at that age she thought that she could ask her parents if she could take a vacation and go to see the dolphin land.

After taking permission from her parents she left but she could not leave alone. She had to take 2 whale bodyguards with her. So she agreed to this decision of her parents and decided to leave.

It took 4 weeks for Whalefic and her two bodyguards to reach the dolphin land. Until they reached the dolphin land Whalefic kept on practicing the shark tongue in her mind whenever they took rest from swimming.
After reaching dolphin land Whalefic started making dolphin friends of her age group.

One day she told her friends that she wanted to learn the art of dolphin's sound production that freaked out the sharks and protected them. Her dolphin friends told her that it would be difficult to mimick their sounds but Whalefic told them they she is ready to face the difficulty no matter how tough it was. So her dolphin friends decided to teach her.

Whalefic was there for only a year so she had to learn the dolphin's technique of sound production that was dangerous for sharks to hear in a very less time frame.

She started her training. Initially it was very tough to adjust her voice pitch to produce the dolphin's sharp frequency sounds but she practiced it a lot and then started producing that kind of sound frequencies which was required. She was happy when she perfected them. It was almost a year by that time. She then thanked her dolphin friends and left for her village.

When she reached her village and met her dad and mom she told them everything. Her parents were shocked and surprised to hear that. But then her dad asked her to show some of her skills. When she did, her dad realized that Whalefic was telling the truth. Her dad starting thinking and told Whalefic that he was happy to have a daughter to like that and then he left.

He immediately called for an emergency meeting. All the adult whales in the village came to attend the meeting. Then Whalefic's dad told them about a plan to get rid of the sharks attack forever.

He told them that her daughter had learnt to speak in the shark's voice and also she could produce sharp frequency sounds like that of dolphins that renders the sharks helpless. Everybody was amazed to learn that.

Her dad then told everybody that they had no time in teaching everybody those skills so they should currently use Whalefic's skill to attack the sharks and make the sharks know that they can't attack the whales anymore because now they have the dolphin's skills to defend themselves and also that they could understand their language.

The plan involved Whalefic to say what her dad had told her when they reached the shark's town.

When all the whales reached shark town Whalefic's dad brought a big shell which increased the sound as in a microphone attached to speakers. Then he told Whalefic to speak into the shell " We the whales warn sharks to leave and let them and they be in peace otherwise they would have a very deathly attack on them which will not leave any shark alive" which she said in shark's tongue

Sharks first got scared that how were whales speaking their language but then the sharks said that " They were evil and will not leave".

Then Whalefic's dad told her to produce the dolphin's sharp frequency through the huge shell that was dangerous for the sharks. Whalefic said "yes dad" and with all her strength produced a deadly frequency of sound.

The sharks who were coming to attack after hearing the declaration of war by whales when heard the sharp frequency produced by a baby whale got freaked out. They could not handle the frequency and swam away.

After that event, sharks never came back to attack the whales as they knew whales now had a sound weapon with them which they can't penetrate.

By that time all the new born whales were compulsorily taught shark's tongue and dolphin's sharp frequency producing sounds by Whalefic. The learning was important to protect their family and school and to remain at the top of water food chain.

From then on all the whales learned the different languages and forever remained safe and secure and nobody ever questioned their authority or supremacy.

TaLe 43 : ThE tiMe TrAvELLeR

There are many time traveller stories in the world but this one is precious because this one came in my dreams, hahaha!

Now let's tell you this story of a time traveller that came in my dreams.

There was this time traveller who before becoming a time traveller was a very smart mechatronics engineer. Mechatronics engineer means a robotics engineer. He was hired by the king to make various contraptions to help king to do different kinds of work.

The king of that country who had hired him was a very rude person and was not fit to be called a king. He was also a very miser and a mean guy. The king had named the country as Frugle meaning freely ugly or the meanest country.

Oops! I forgot to tell the name of the time traveller. The time traveller's name was Grealifo. Grealifo although had a royal job but he did not used to get salary from the king. The king used to say to Grealifo that whatever he makes is for the country and although he did not get payed he was getting honour for that. This disgusted Grealifo.

Grealifo couldn't leave the job because if he did he would be thrown to the lions and in the prison.

Now Grealifo had made so many machines for security of the mean king that its was difficult to overthrow him by means of mere force by humans. So Grealifo sometimes remained depressed too. All the people of the country including him were really angry against the king and were always looking for a way to overthrow the king.

Grealifo was also looking for something on his part through which he could overthrow the king and make people form a government which was for the people. All he knew that when everything fails God and books help a person to achieve success. So after finishing work at the king's palace he used to go to the local library to get more knowledge about what he could do to overthrow the king. He explored and studied many books but could not find a way to fulfill what he and people of the country wanted. One day he was scrolling through the books when he found a history/archaeology book. He picked that book up.

Usually future changes the entire course of history but this history/archaeology book was going to change the entire course of the future.

In that book he saw pictures of huge giant carnivorous looking creatures which he studied and found that they were called dinosaurs. He then further studied and went through the book. He found out that there were many types of dinosaurs that once ruled the world. The most ferocious of the dinosaurs was called Tyrannosaurus rex. After knowing that he found T-Rex(Tyrannosaurus rex) to be a very impressive and a warrior. So he set out to make another contraption the one that would change everything.

Since he was an engineer he had read Einstein's theory that if one could travel more than the speed of light he would be able to go to past or future. He thought that since he had made many contraptions in his life, to make this should not be impossible so he set out on this new task.

Everyday after returning from work he went to the local shops to pick up parts and supplies. He picked up few parts everyday and started making a time machine, part by part and day by day.

After many unsuccessful attempts one day his attempt was successful. He then tried going to the dinosaurs ages and return back in a second which he could. That moment was the happiest of his life. Because first of all he had made a time machine and second of all he could go into the past.

His time machine was a very accurate machine in which he could also place the gps coordinates so as he can decide the exact location as to where he wanted to go.Then he tried again this time he programmed the machine to send him to a particular gps coordinate at about 25000 feet high from surface in the air and bring him back in about 30 seconds.

It then happened exactly as he had planed. He went back to the dinosaurs age and this time when he did he took a gps marking machine. When he was in the air he checked out some spots where tyrannosaurus rex's nest were and marked them on his gps tracking machine.

After coming back in the future to is time he prepared himself. He took a bag and rope and a knife for security purposes. Then he again marked the gps coordinates where he wanted to go and then pressed the start button on his machine. As soon as he pressed the start button on his machine he was immediately sent back in time to the dinosaurs age and to the exact location where he wanted to go i.e. to a T-Rex's nest. As soon as he reached there he picked up 5 T-Rex's eggs put them in a bag tied it with the rope which he had got and took them back to his time.

He after reaching his present time put the eggs in an incubator designed specially for the T-Rex's eggs.

It took about 5 days for the eggs to hatch. When they hatched he had already come back from work and was siting in front of the incubator and staring at the eggs. When they hatched small baby T-Rex's came out of the eggs. He was so happy to see them come in existence in his time.

Now as soon as they hatched they started saying mama, mama and Grealifo did not know what to do at that time so he took all the five of them which were 10 inches in height in his arms and embraced them. He murmured and told them petting on their heads that he was their mama and he will take their care forever.

He used to give them lots of fishes everyday and trained them for war by teaching them attacking and defensive techniques. Everyday he came home he saw them grew about a millimeter and he used to be very happy to see them grow.

Now, since they had to grow more than 50 feet tall he had already planned a place where he would keep them so that nobody notices or gets a hint about them until they were ready for battle. For that he had built huge barns all with his inheritance money. There these dinosaurs played and got tamed for battle.

It took them some time to become war ready but the day Grealifo realized that they had grown up and were ready he called an emergency meeting of the town where he lived . He told them all about dinosaurs and told them that they were the only one who could break all the security contraptions that he had built for the king. People for once were happy to have a hope.

They the planned a battle. The battle lasted for 5 hours but ultimately the tamed dinosaurs who were like kids to him broke all security contraptions of the king and king was thrown in he prison. They won the battle and all the people were happy.

People then brought into place a people's government of whom Grealifo was appointed the President.

As long as Grealifo lived, he remained the President. He helped bring prosperity amongst people who also lived happily and peacefully ever after.

TaLe 44 : tHe mOuSe AnD tHe mUsiCIaN

Long time ago there lived a musician. His name was Menry. Menry was not a very rich guy. He was actually a struggling musician. Before, Menry lived with his old parents until one day he had to move to a new but old house. What happened was the place where he lived with his parents was leased under his parents name and one day both of his parents passed away because of heart attack. The heart attack that occurred was sequential. That day Menry had bought a mouth organ and had just started playing when his dad heard and said that such a ugly tone player his son his and suddenly had a heart attack. His mom followed suite. After seeing Menry's father in great distress and in a condition of lost consciousness she got a heart attack too and died.

Menry was very sad to see them go. Since he was not earning that much that he could continue the house lease so he had to leave and move to his ancestral old broken home.

Now, Menry was not educated much and was not that smart but he had started to learn music all by himself.

When Menry had moved to his old broken ancestral home it was new to him as he had never lived there before. Because of its broken condition he used to hear some noise coming out of the house as if somebody is running, colliding and falling. But that somebody was creating noise only as if it was a small creature. So he was not too much concerned about that initially.

One day after keeping his stuff in order in the house he was upset and depressed. So he went to the market and got some used musical instruments with some of his money.

He then put those musical instruments on a platform in his house. He then sat on the piano seat. Since he was depressed he did not know what to play. He kept silent and did not play anything on the piano at that time. While he was sitting he heard the same running and falling noise that he heard when he had moved to the house. So he started pressing a key every time and a new key tone whenever a new sound came from falling or running of that creature and realized that very beautiful music was being produced because of that.

Later that day he wanted to know more about the creature was that was producing these sounds and noises so he started looking for that creature that was producing the sound.

To check that he put some bread crumbs in front of the door which was facing the platform where his musical instruments were kept. He then sat on the piano seat and did not play any music but waited for the creature to appear. After few hours of waiting he saw a small mouse ran from one side of the house to another and picked up a small bread crumb while running and went away.

Although Menry was afraid of mice but he felt pity for that cute little mouse and did not know what he could do to help him out. He then realized at that time that the mouse had lived in his ancestral house all alone for quite a long time and was used to its peace. Now that since he had moved in, the mouse had gotten worried and therefore kept on running and colliding with the wooden walls of the house. Secondly Menry also realized that the mouse might have some poor eyesight. But at that moment he could not do anything about it.

That day, Menry was happy that he had found the mystery creature who had created so much racket in his house.

That day he also remembered that he had played beautiful music while the mouse was creating racket and he was hitting the keys on piano to sync with the noise. He had also realized that the mouse who he then named Freny kept quite during the night and he felt that it was because he slept at that time. It was difficult to comprehend that as all mice are usually nocturnal. But this was how Freny was.

Next day Menry woke up early and sat on his piano. He then waited for Freny to create some racket. In about few minutes of getting up he started hearing the racket. Now this time he was ready to make music. He then did. He created a master piece of music that resonating with the racket which sounded as beats to the music.

Menry was now confident that he could create music and that he cannot make the same music again because every time Freny created different noise through the house.

Menry then decided that he will call audience from the town where he lived, to listen to him playing music and get to know what they think about it.

That day he created hand written tickets and signed them off. Then he went to the town centre and distributed them for free amongst the people.

The show was in the evening. About 100 people showed up. Although his home was old and broken but it was quite big and thus it accommodated 100 people easily.

Menry waited few seconds and then started playing music with the sounds of beats of Freny running and falling as usual.

People were wonderstruck after hearing such different kind of awesome music. They cheered until Menry stopped playing music. He received a great applaud by the people who had come to hear his music. Menry was happy about that.

Now he decided that this time he will sell tickets rather than distributing for free. He then made more tickets and went to the town centre and sold 150 tickets which was a full house for his house's capacity. People had already heard about the praises of Menry's music and were eager to his different type of music .

He earned quite a bit that day.

From that day on he started selling tickets everyday and did shows everyday.

Menry started making good money. He then thanked God and started refurbishing and rebuilding the house. He did it bit by bit so that his partner, Freny does not leave the house.

He made the whole house a musical house. He made a small room beneath the basement for Freny with all kinds of fun equipment including vertical wheel/carousel for him to enjoy his running. Not only that he attached beautiful chimes to the vertical wheel so that whenever Freny runs on it sounds of chimes along with the sounds of beats are produced which were appeasing to both his and Freny's ears. Then he put a small swimming pool in that small room meant for Freny. Not only that he decorated all of his room and gave him candies every a day to eat.

Later Freny and Menry became close friends and Freny started understanding Menry and they became the best of friends. Also whenever Menry went outside in the town to shop Freny climbed up his shoulder and they did shopping together. Whatever Freny wanted, he pointed it out to Menry and he used to get it for him. Menry always introduced his best friend Freny to the people and used to tell them that he was his partner in making music and people just smiled.

Menry and Freny were the talk of the town and they lived till peace.

Tale 45 : ThE wAtChMaKeR AnD tHe tiNy bEiNgS

Once there lived a watchmaker who used to work very hard and meticulously every day to earn his daily bread by fixing watches. He had a small watch shop and a small house attached to it where he lived. This watchmaker had turned old fixing the watches therefore he was very experienced in it . He was thus able to fix every type of watch that was ever made.

Now one day he was fixing a watch but in amidst of it had to go to the nearby shop to get something. When he came back and got back into his shop to continue fixing the watch, he found that one of the gear of the watch which he was fixing which was also the smallest gear of the watch was missing. He then wondered for a while . He was amazed to see that why only one gear of the watch was missing. He checked everywhere where he was working to find the gear but could not find it. He looked beneath the table and in his pockets but could not find it there too. He then thought that if somebody had to steel why would he steal only one gear why wouldn't that person steel the whole watch or other watches which had come to him for repair as he had also checked other watches which were intact.

Then he just forgot about it and let that moment go unremembered. After few days he was working again and found another gear of watch which he was working on was missing. This made him remember the other day when the smallest gear of one of the watch got missing and that he to order a new gear for that watch. But how were the gears of watches missing. In his entire life of fixing watches such incident of missing gears had not occurred in his shop.

But what could he do he just ordered the part and went to his house in the evening. He then had his dinner and slept.

During the night when he was sleeping and heard lots of racket in his kitchen. So he woke up and was on high alert. He slowly crawled towards his kitchen. He then stood behind a door and saw that small beings just an inch high had his refrigerator open all the way and were transferring food item through slides and ropes from the refrigerator to more of their kind of beings who were standing down on the floor. When he counted, there were 50 of the tiny beings in all working on stealing the food.

He was shocked and totally surprised to see them and to see them do that. He then realized that these beings were the one who might have stolen the gears from the watches. So without fear he came out of the door and said "Hi! little beings". The beings tried to run away from there but he caught the ear of one of the beings with his finger and got a hold of him. He then said that "I am not going to harm you, I just want to be your friend". All the tiny beings that were running stopped and saw that indeed he was telling the truth.

Then they came near him and told him that they were sorry that they were stealing his things. They then told him that why they were stealing his goods was because there was a marriage in their house of the eldest daughter of the family who lived in his house and they wanted supplies for the celebration.

The watchmaker then asked what was the schedule of the events in the marriage. The father of the daughter who was listening then came forward and told him that the events gonna last for 2 months and that there will be 10 events for her daughter's wedding.

Then the watchmaker had a question. He asked the family of tiny beings that how long had they been living in his house. The father of the yet to be bride told that since the time he had moved there after its brand new construction. Then the watchmaker exclaimed and said" Hmmm!"

He then told the tiny beings that no matter how tiny they are, stealing is not a way of life. So he asked them if they knew how to work. All the tiny beings said yes. He then asked them to tell him about the field of their expertise. All of them told him that they were skilled to do mechanical work. He then asked that was that the reason that they stole the gears of the two watches? They said "yes" and "no". They then told him that they had a small well in their house which was beneath the floor of watchmaker's house and that well's pulley had broken and they needed the two gears to make a pulley for their water supply.

The watchmaker then thought for a while and said that if you know mechanical work then you can surely fix watches and also it will be easier for you to do so as you can sneak your little fingers in them to do the fixing. The beings confirmed that they could do that.

So the watchmaker exclaimed and said that was good. He said that from now on they don't have to steal to earn food. He has found a perfect job for them. He told them that they could work in his shop from now on and whatever food or things they need will be provided to them by him.

The tiny beings agreed to it and did as they were told.

The tiny beings used to work inside a room in his shop and fixed watches quickly. The watchmaker's work also increased. Whatever watch came he used to put tiny notes on a paper and attach it to the watches for the tiny beings to read. While the tiny beings worked inside the watchmaker worked outside.

He told the tiny beings that they don't have to hide anymore from now on in his house. The watchmaker had three rooms in his house. He made one room as the bedding area and put beautifully made tiny beds in it and in the second room he made a recreation/ sports/games room for his tiny friends.

He made a small swimming pool with slides attached to it and kept it in their sports room. Then he made all the playable swings in that room. He put an electric carousel there, then he made a small roller coaster in that room for his friends to enjoy. He also put many playable things like jumping swings and to and fro swings in that room.

The tiny beings were wonderstruck to see all that was made for them. They thanked him heartily but the watchmaker used to say that it was all the hard work of the tiny beings and not of his. He used to tell them that they had earned it.

The tiny beings had a wonderful marriage party and all the relatives forever lived in the watchmaker's house and earned their bread and enjoyed there.

Tale 46 : ThE gArBaGe PiCkEr

Let's tell you about a weird story about a garbage picker who once picked up gold while picking up garbage.

In those days garbage picker used to come in a horse cart to pick up garbage. The garbage in those days was collected very week as nowadays in some places. In those times there was no concept of recycling so everything that was left was totally garbage.

This garbage picker was a person with modest requirements in his life. He was poor and owed a lot of money to the money lenders as he had got a small house in the town for he and his family. His family consisted of only him and his two kids. One of the kid was a boy and his name was Zulu and the other kid was a girl whose name was Alpha.

The garbage picker did his daily duty without delay or miss. The horse cart he rode had 4 horses and a big cart attached to it where he put the garbage that he picked up. His cart was sufficient to pick up the garbage of one entire neighbourhood.
So he continued his work peacefully.

One day as he was working he came near the garbage of a house and tried picking it up but as soon as he did a gold nugget fell on the ground towards his feet. He saw that piece of shiny thing and thought "could it be gold?". First he was afraid to pick it up but then bended over and picked it up in palm of his hand. He then folded his palm so as to hide the piece of gold in his hand and also so that nobody sees it. Now he took another piece of metal out from his pocket and tried scratching and rubbing it with that piece. He rubbed it for quite a while. He then saw gold did not show any sign of wear. That made him sure that it was gold.

But he was surprised to find such a big chunk of gold in form of a nugget in garbage. He wanted to return it but was afraid and skeptical about it. So he continued his work.

He then put the garbage of that house on his cart while holding on to the gold piece. He then put the gold piece in his pocket and rode away collecting the garbages of the other houses.

After reaching home he showed the gold nugget to his kids Zulu and Alpha. Kids were in aw and wonder and asked his father that where he had got that from. They were so excited seeing it that they wanted to keep it. Their father told them that he found it in garbage kept in front of a house when he went to do his duty.

He then told his kids Alpha and Zulu that it looks pretty strange that a gold nugget could be found in garbage. So he told kids that since it is strange that a gold nugget could be found in garbage they have to now find out what's going on in that house. He told his kids that they will all have to work together to get knowing about what was going on in that house and thus they will have to play a spy game.

He told his kids that they should start playing in one of the park in that neighbourhood and keep an eye on the house which he will show them the next day. He told his kids to keep a keen eye on that house and that they should keep passing on the road around that house very frequently.

He then waited for the next week to come. As soon as it came he took his kids along with him in the horse cart and showed them the house.

From next day the kids stopped going to school for a while until they found out what's going on. They then went to a park near that house and started playing there. They frequently walked on the road that was in front of that house where their father had found the gold nugget.

First and second day they did not find any clue while playing around that house. But they did not stop keeping an eye on it. The third day they were playing and they found a mouse running out with a shiny thing in his mouth which was nothing other than gold . The kids freaked out and thought that how it could possibly be again.

They then made up a plan. Zulu went to the door of that house and knocked at it. Nobody opened it but Zulu did not stop knocking and in a while a man opened the door.

The man asked in a shrewd voice "what do you want". Zulu told the man that he and his sister Alpha were playing outside and that he has to pee very badly and his sister wanted some water to drink as she was thirsty while playing in the scorching sunlight.

The man tried to refuse but due to excessive pleading he let them in. He then gave them strict instructions not to peep here and there and do what they had come in to do and go away.

It was a big house and the washroom was at the other end of the house. So Alpha told Zulu to peep wherever she can stealthily and that he will go towards the washroom while looking into other things.

Zulu did as she was told. She secretively looked here and there and so did his brother. The man was waiting at the door for both of them and it was already 5 minutes so he screamed at the top of his voice for the Zulu and Alpha.

The kids by that had done what they had come there for. They then thanked the guy and went out through the door . But they were in utter shock to see what they had seen.

They then immediately returned home gasping for breath. Then they waited for his father to return home from his daily work. When their father returned home they told him everything that they saw.

They told him that first of all they saw a mouse carrying a gold nugget in his mouth and then they went inside that house. There they saw that through a wide tap in one of the rooms in that house gold was dropping with water and that two people were working in the house. They told him that those two men who were working were so busy that they did not have time to see them and so they went by unnoticed. Their father became suspicious.

The next day he went to the local authorities and told them what was going on. The authorities immediately raided that house. They found that the gold was being transferred from the gold reserve of that country.

What some of the people who were working in the gold reserve had done was that they had built a huge underground pipeline connected directly to that house and everyday they threw lots of collected gold nuggets into that water pipeline which reached that house about 500 miles away. The pipeline was directly connected to that house. There the thieves collected the gold and shared it amongst each other. The authorities also told that there plan was to collect as much as gold they could and disappear. But due to help of Alpha and his brother Zulu and also because of their father they were able to save a lot of money of people of their country.

The garbage picker and his kids were rewarded with good amount of cash and their father then gave back all the money that he had borrowed to get a house and started a business of his own - A spy agency. His agency helped him earn a lot of money in the long run and one day was one of the renowned person in his country. Ultimately he became the president of that country and governed it fairly and wisely.

TaLe 47 : ThE rAcE bEtWeEn A sHiP, tRaiN aNd A dRaGoN

Once upon a time there lived dragons and men together, where dragons ruled the world.

They were considered to be the strongest, mightiest and fastest beings alive. Not only that, during those times they were the only beings alive that could fly.

But during those times steam engines had also been invented. In that era steam engines were being used to do a lot of things that needed power. Steam engines delivered more power than the conventional source of energy which was at that time was horse. Dragons at that time could not be tamed to do work because they did not wanted to work as they had a free life of their own and wanted to enjoy it . They were like free birds that could chirp on whichever branch they wanted. Also dragons were more intelligent beings than horses. Not only that they had defensive armour and offensive fire power to protect themselves and their freedom.

Now, lets come back to steam engines. As the steam engines developed people got more comfortable as they could travel long distances without relying on biological sources of energy which were horses. The steam engines never got tired. They kept on generating power as more and more coal was put in the furnace to generate heat and steam. The main purpose of the steam engine was for locomotion. They used it in trains and ships and to run heavy machinery.

Mankind was happy with what it had created and used to boast about its power and potential.

One day four people were sitting together. The four people were a set of workers amongst whom two were drivers and two were mechanics. One of the driver was a train driver and the second was a ship captain. Similarly amongst the two mechanics one was a train mechanic and the other was a ship mechanic.

Now they were discussing the greatness of the steam engines and they believed that they were the mightiest of all things. Then one of the driver sprang upon an idea. He said that why don't we have a race between our equipment and a dragon. There was utter silence at that time. All thought that that driver had gone crazy. They then said that since dragon can fly it will surely win. But the person who had put forward that idea told that even though the dragon has a flying advantage it will only win if it flies at a high altitudes over the obstructions. Then he said "what if he has to fly near the surface and with obstructions". Everybody got confused as they knew that there are no obstructions in the air. Even if they wanted that how could they possibly create obstructions or hurdles for a dragon in the air.

The driver who was a ship captain explained to all of them in detail. He told them that when the race begins the ship will travel through the tunnels beneath the mountains. The train will travel around the mountains and the dragon will have to travel near the surface and around the obstacles. Thus it will have to turn around the mountains or hills as many times as the train will have to to reach the top of mountains or hills and then only it will be an even race. Thus he showed the other three men the hurdles for flying. Everybody thought for a moment and said "yes" to it.

This race had now gone tricky because of the train which would take time to go up the hill but when it goes down the hill it will have great momentum and thus will come down faster and thus have a greater speed which might leave dragon behind. Also a dragon is biological. It will feel dizzy and tired after travelling long distance thus might have to slow down for a while even when in the air. This might be advantageous to either the ship or the train.

Then they decided a day to have the race. Then they gave an invitation to a dragon for a race with them and explained him the rules. The dragon understood their rules and calmly said yes to there invitation.

The race was to be held on the 50th day of that next season. It was a 5000 km long race in a mountainous region where existed water as well and tunnels inside the terrain for ship to travel. It was a unique terrain but it was fit for the race.

Til the day arrived everybody prepared except for the dragon. The ship mechanic finely tuned the engine and checked for any flaw. The train mechanic streamlined the train and also checked for any flaws. The dragon who was pretty confident that he would win the race did not practice for the race or anything until the race day.

The race day finally came. All the teams were excited except for the dragon who was in a sleepy mood and said that no matter what you do "I will win it". He also told the ship captain and the train driver that it was a peace of cake for him. This did not decreased the moral of the competition.

The race then began at the sound of the third thunder because that day it was cloudy and it had started to rain. The dragon had not expected this kind of weather during that season and so he could not do anything about it.

The ship fired up its engines and started moving forward and so did the train. The dragon also started flying forward and at low heights as had been decided in the rule book.

The train was faster at first but as soon as mountainous terrain came it started to loose speed but it still continued forward not loosing hope. The ship also was tackling rough seas due to the storm but it tried to remain perfectly steady on the course without altering it as the shortest distance will help it reach faster. The dragon who was flying had a good speed initially had started to slow down as the rain was falling on his eyes and when he was turning around the hills and mountains it was getting hard to do that. Sometimes the dragon had to hide behind a hill in the mountains to avoid a fall due to bad weather conditions . He was also doing that to escape from getting unconscious because he was feeling dizzy due to continuous circling of more than a 100 times around different hills and mountains.

The race continued and dragon was loosing its traction in the race because of the severe weather. To everybody's surprise the ship was quite ahead and was currently winning. Now till that time most of the climb by the train had finished and it was on the descent. The train started picking up speed and started gaining on in position.

50 meters were left for the race and the dragon was nowhere to be seen. The train had gained in on the ship and had left the ship behind.

So ultimately the race finished or had to be finished. The train was first, the ship was second and the dragon who was nowhere to be found and was declared as disqualified because later it had come to everybody's knowledge that he had gone to his home after crossing the starting line backwards.

Everybody had a great laugh at its folly but they did not mind it all. After all they had won and had proved that the steam engine was the most powerful thing at that time and was a boon to them all.

TaLe 48 : A fLeA aNd iT's PeT DrAgON

Long ago there were only fleas living on earth along with few other animals. The fleas were so many and they always used to fight with each other over many things. Sometimes they fought over food, sometimes they fought over things they wanted to play with and sometimes over over-speeding. The fight over food and playable things is imaginable but fight over over-speeding is not.

They fought over over-speeding because simply if some fleas flew faster than the other than the fleas behind would loose their group and in times if there is a fight with other fleas the fleas that are left behind may loose lots of blood during fight and at those times it was sometimes difficult to find a donor flea of the same blood group.

Therefore fleas as usual were always fleeing and nothing more.

Now, one day a flea meeting was going on and in that meeting there was a young but a smart flea. The agenda of that meeting was protection. The fleas were discussing how to protect themselves from other fleas and stay uninjured. The young flea said that why don't we hire some animals to protect ourselves. All the fleas had their mouth wide open after hearing what it was saying.

So the fleas discussed with each other and asked the flea who had given them that proposal that "do you want us to hire goons". The flea replied not goons but friends. Then the other fleas said that " we fleas never had anything common with other animals and had never talked with them. How can we be friends and ask for their protection".

Then the young flea said that we can discuss this later but first of all let's go to the animals and ask them that what say they? The fleas than talked to each other and said okay.

The next day a military squadron of fleas along with the leaders of those fleas went to see the animals.

The animals asked them that what was the matter and why so many of them with their full battalion of army had come there. The fleas said that they needed protection. The animals laughed and said what kind of protection? Then the fleas explained them that those fleas were less in number and they wanted the animals to fight and protect them against the other fleas so that there is no flea causality amongst the fleas that they will be protecting.

The animals thought for a while and said that they could do that but they need some rewards in exchange of protection. The fleas were prepared for it. So they asked them that what kind of rewards do they need.

The animals told them that since fleas had a good detection capacity, they need a supply of sweetest fruits from the forest where they lived. Secondly they stated that should not bug them ever. The fleas agreed to it. Then they signed an agreement with the animals.

Then there was an era of peace for the fleas that had got animal protection. This era was not for long.

For few years the animals were true to the contract but after that they started cheating. They started helping other fleas out for some other favours that only those fleas could provide like flower nectars and fruit nectars as those fleas were more technically advanced than the contracting bees. And could provide those favours and gifts.

How the fleas detected the flaws amongst the animals was that they started showing less skill in the their fight and therefore more of the fleas that were to be protected were getting injured.

Then they questioned the animals who had signed the contract. The animals replied that they had signed the contract to protect them but had not signed that they will remain biologically profound all through their life and exhibit the same fighting skills all the time.

The fleas were upset hearing that and did not know what to do. The young flea who had given the idea for protection was then asked that what they should do now?

The young flea was upset at that time and though that the idea was good for sometime only and wasn't working anymore.

It then wept for a while and left its group of fleas. It was not long when she was flying and then she suddenly saw a dragon who was lying injured and there were many fleas of the opposite groups who were attacking its wound and drinking the infected blood out of it and digging deep into the flesh.

The young flea felt very sad to see it. So she thought that even if it cost's it's life it will protect the dragon no matter what it had to do. The young flea immediately flew near the fleas that were affecting the dragon and warned them. It told the other fleas that if they did not leave the dragon in peace it will call all the animals who had a contract for protecting it's flea group and will cause them to attack them. It also said that no matter how much blood falls on the ground, it will not let anything happen to the dragon.

The fleas who were attacking the dragon's wound then stopped and listened to that young flea.

At that moment the fleas had already had enough to eat and drink and were well satiated and did not want to fight. Those fleas then left harming the dragon.

The young flea then went to the dragon and told it that it would be helping the dragon out to recover. The dragon softly replied " ok ".

It took 5 days for the flea to treat the dragon's wound and to get him well and standing. The dragon thanked the flea and asked if there was anything that it could do. The flea then replied " yes". It said that if they could be friends and that it could protect it's flea group and friends from other fleas with its fire power that could be really beneficial". The dragon laughed at said " you saved my life and therefore I consider you as my friend and also I am indebted to you for my whole life". It also said that " I swear that I will forever defend you and your flea group and will not let anything happen to them.

That day the flea sat over the dragon's head and rode it towards it's flea group.

It was the first flea to ever ride a dragon who remained its friend for life and protected the young flea and it's friends forever.

No flea ever dared to attack the young flea group as they knew that if they did, the flea who rode the dragon would command the dragon to blow fire which will burn any flea that comes and disturbs the young flea's group.

The other fleas were not only afraid of the dragon but were also afraid of the flea who rode a dragon. Dragon came to be known as a pet of the flea. There was thus peace in that entire flea group due to that young flea and it's pet dragon (as it was known).

TaLe 49 : ThE tELePhOnE rEpAiR gUy

I was sitting and waiting for somebody. Suddenly I heard a knock at the door. I went and opened it and saw nobody so I said " Hello, who knocked at the door ?"

Suddenly I saw a small tiny guy went passed my eye and said " Hi " to me. I was shocked to see such a small guy jumping in air. This person was wearing small shoes to which springs were attached that helped him jump to such a height. When I checked his height, he was no more than a inch tall but was wearing a uniform. Then suddenly he jumped and climbed at my shoulder and told me that he was the telephone repair guy and had come to fix my home phone.

At that time I did not know that they hired such small guys to fix phones. So I asked him that how many of his kind were there in his industry. He politely said " None" and told that he was the last one this planet. I was not surprised to hear that.

Then he asked me that where the telephone was? I immediately pointed him towards the Telephone's direction. He then hopped with his springs that were attached to his shoes until he reached the phone that was kept over a table. He then stopped hopping and stood still. Then he took out a small music player, attached the headphone's wire to it and put the headphones around his ears on his head and started listening to music. Then he took out a small instrument which he was carrying inside a backpack behind his back and then started testing the phone with it. After few minutes of testing he found out that the wire inside the phone's receiver was a bit loose thus was causing disturbance while attending a phone call. So he opened the phone's receiver with a motorized screw driver which had a big head and had a good torque. Then he looked for the wire that was loose and was causing the problem. It took him no time to find it. He found the loose wire, changed it and then tightened the connection.

Then he again reached the back of his bag pack and took out a paper and wrote something on it. He then told me to sign it. When I held the paper I tried reading it. The writing was on the letter head of the phone company and was very small so I got a magnifying glass and read it. That writing described the problem and also that it had been fixed. Then he jumped on my shoulder once again and told me to sign it. I then signed and returned the paper to the telephone fixer.

He then hopped from my shoulder and jumped on the ground and went out of my house. I was looking at how he hopped and jumped to reach his destination. He first hopped over the stairs and then he jumped with huge leaps to reach the bus stop near my house. I kept on watching him for a while through my window. The bus for which he was waiting came and he hopped in it along with other passengers and since he was very small he was not noticeable to the bus driver who did not ask for a ticket from him. He then went inside and the bus doors closed. That was the end of what I could see.

Later I enquired about that guy from the telephone company and they said that that that telephone repair guy was the best they had and he lived in the company itself inside a vacated phone which was kept on the managers table.

I wondered that how smart that guy was even though he had a tiny brain.

So few days had passed and I had lost the memory of that telephone repair guy.

After, another few days I was reading the newspaper and I saw a news that said " Brave little telephone repairer fixed a huge problem ." I then though for a while and wondered could it be him ? So I checked that newspaper article out.

The article was an interview with the tiny telephone fixer who single handedly had crossed the Atlantic ocean to fix 5 major cracks in the telephone line from Canada to Great Britain. What he did was that day he was sleeping in his house which was a vacated telephone when suddenly the manager knocked at the phone and he got up because of the disturbance. Then he came out and asked what was going on? The manager told Alen which was the name the telephone repair guy that they had a huge problem at hand.

Due to overload some underwater lines that connected Canada to Great Britain had sparked and had developed cracks and there is requirement to fix them immediately due to an emergency issue amongst the governments. He then told Alen that he was the only one who could do that in such a short time. Alen kept quite for some time and then he said " I need some equipment to do that but it should be provided quickly so that I can finish the work in as much less time as possible ".

He then took out a paper and wrote on it the list of things required. The manager called his engineers and told them to prepare all those things for him.

What he asked for, were some unique things. He first of all asked for a rocket engine sufficiently big that he could attach to his back and maneuver. Then he asked for a soldering wheel which he could pedal while sitting on it over the wires that have to be fixed. Also he asked for under water diving suit having an oxygen supply in it. The manager asked for 1 hour to get all that for him.

By that time Alen got ready. He packed food and other essential things that would be needed by him to do the job.

It was about an hour and Alen was ready to leave. At that time the equipment arrived. A set of four engineers were carrying the small equipments who then gave it to Alen and wished him good luck.

Alen then wore his spring shoes and hopped out of the table to the ground and then went out of the office carrying the engine and the supplies. Then he went to the garage and loaded the back of his tiny car with jet engine and sat on the driver's seat to drive the car towards the east coast of Canada. The coast was only an hour drive from his place. He then reached the coast and put his diving gear on and attached the jet engine at the back of his body and then sat on the pedalling wheel. (Even though the wires were underwater they were beneath the ocean bed where some air was available for functioning of engine but for safety he had to wear diving gear.)

He then turned on the jet engine while sitting on wheel. He had already calculated the distance for each broken point and marked each point on his map. When he had turned on the engine he was already underneath the ocean bed with it. Then he started speeding the engine up and maneuvering it to follow the path of the underwater telephone wires that were broken.

The wires were broken at intervals of one hour each. So he had marked that time on his watch and whenever an hour passed he checked to see if he had reached the broken point of the wires. His planning went perfectly. He never missed a broken wire. Whenever he reached the broken wire he put fire on his wheel and moved over the broken wires pedalling back and forth with the engine off at that time and thus soldering them. Thereby he fixed all the cracks like that in the lines and came back home safely.

TaLe 50 : tHe RaDiO tYpeWriTeR FiXeRs

What is a radio typewriter ? Does anybody know? Well it's a close kept secret. After typewriters had been invented it took a long time for them to become radio typewriters.

But where did they exist? They existed in the office of top leaders of all the powerful countries. These radio typewriters were just like telephones amongst leader of the countries or telephones amongst a leader of a country and his associates. The unique thing about the radio typewriters was that they transmitted signals wirelessly and needed no power externally. All the power required to transmit was produced by typing alone. Because of that, the range of the signals was limited.

Now, let's come back to the story. In the office of president of The USA there was kept the most advanced typewriter. It was also a typewriter that worked with the fastest speed and was the most accurate. That typewriter consisted of 101 keys which is more in number than the keys of a standard typewriter.

The typewriter which was with the President was operated and fixed(repaired) by exact and only 101 tiny men which belonged to the secret service of The United States and were only an inch high.

How the typewriter worked was, first numbers had to pressed which connected the typewriter to the other specific typewriter/ typewriters where the signal had to be transmitted. Then the " ENTER" key had to be pressed. The paper was optional. It was only to keep record of the transmission. Signals could be transmitted by typing the numbers for connection and then typing the secret passcode for the typewriter.

What the president of USA did was that he used to dictate his message and the tiny people who were standing on the keys of the keyboard just jumped on their respective keys and these tiny people were so smart that they knew when it was their turn to press the keys even at such high speeds of communication .

So the work continued everyday without stopping.

One day the tiny people were typing on the typewriter when a secret service agent came and was sweating. He told the president something that caused the president to sweat too. It came to know that the 10 metre wide keyboard that sent signals automatically to the headquarters about the enemy activity in the south stopped sending signals and they were afraid that it might have been captured and thus war could be looming over their heads.

But before the president could make a decision he wanted to make sure that typewriter was indeed captured and was not malfunctioning.

So he thought for a while and then came to a decision.

The decision was to send the 101 tiny secret agents to that area and check out what was happening there. But there was a difficulty. The area was at the southern border and was at the top of a huge mountain amongst a very large mountain range. Sending big planes to make those tiny secret service agents land via parachutes over that area was like initiating a war. The tiny secret service agents had to be sent secretly without the enemy if it was there noticing their arrival.

So they had to built small planes that could fly to that mountain range and not only that could land vertically wherever the tiny agents wanted.

The army got in the job of building those small miniature planes and the tiny secret service agents got training from special Air Force pilots to fly planes. Special equipment was installed in the human Air Force Planes which helped the tiny typewriter secret agents to learn to fly those planes while sitting on the pilot's seat.

It took 3 months for the tiny secret agents to learn to fly jets and it also took the army exactly 3 months to make tiny planes for the tiny agents.

Then the tiny secret agents were ready to fly to the mountain and find out what was going on.

They were ready to take-off for the mountain at exactly 3:00 am and had planned to reach there by 5:30 am.

The plan was followed.

After navigating properly they reached the location by exactly 5:30 am when there was just the correct amount of light required for the operation. Now, they were instructed to land at a location which was a bit away from the exact location of the mountain.

After landing they went to the mountain checking for enemy sight. When they reached the mountain they saw that 5 men wearing enemy uniforms had captured the station where the typewriter was and had dismantled it. They had a radar that they were checking quite frequently to see any enemy aircraft. Their radar did not detect the small aircrafts that came there because the aircrafts were too small to detect. Even if it had detected the small aircrafts they might have thought that some birds are coming through because of very less metal on them.

So this was a time for action. The only thing that could be done was that some of the tiny secret agents would have to distract the enemy men and other would fix the typewriter and send a distress signal to the USA headquarter's office.

So they did it. Five tiny agents jumped on the noses of the enemy men and put their nose hair on fire which created a huge distraction for them. This distraction caused enemies to run here and there. By that time the remaining tiny secret agents fixed the typewriter and sent a distress signal which reached the headquarter's office.

After getting the distress signal the Air Force immediately dispatched fighter jets who passed over the mountain and the enemy men who were busy extinguishing the fire in their nose saw the fighter aircrafts. They freaked out. At that moment they could not do anything and became helpless. They then ran away back to their country seeking shelter.

So the tiny secret agents fixed the huge typewriter and helped the country get rid of enemies no matter how less they were.

TaLe 51 : tHe mOuStAcHe mEAsUrEr

Long time ago there was a very miser man that lived in a town called Axiz. Everybody in that town had a very difficult time dealing with that guy because he wanted breakdown of earnings and profits of other businesses whom he was dealing with so as to make more money and make his business prosper.

There is nothing wrong in making one's business prosper but the evilness with which it is done is not good. It generates bad vibes. He made a lot of money for himself but left little for his suppliers and his employees.

Now this person whom every called Stinky (as his ways of life stunk) had a very peculiar habit. He used to measure his moustache and keep it to a size of 6 cm always on each side of his nose and used to keep it twisted and rolled up. People knew this fact because he always carried a scale and scissors with him. He measured the moustache many times a day while he was anywhere. He measured that even when he was in a washroom.

Few people out of polite anger had got chance of asking him that why he measured the moustache always and why did he keep it to perfect 6 cm on each side of his nose?

It was actually what he liked and was very stringent about it but did not wanted to share with people why he did that because he did not considered anybody close to him or his friend. So he simply used to say that why he kept his moustache that way was so that when he looks down through his moustache while his chin high up, even the stars should look shorter than his moustache and why perfect 6 cm on each side? For that his reply was that that he was humble creature and did not wanted wanted stars to be too short than his moustache.

It was always awkward when he trimmed his moustache in front of people (remember he trimmed only when they grew more than 12 cm in total and beard does not always grow during night.) but he was a very rich person and had lots of political contacts so nobody dared utter anything against him.

Now in course of his business he had done lots of different types of events. It so happened that the country where he lived was a cold country where it snowed . Thus it did not have tropical animals, especially elephants.

One day he came upon an idea of bringing an elephant to the town and country, not for mere exhibition but to give rides to people and kids on that elephant and earn even more money.

He knew that it would be costly to transport in and out an elephant from a tropical country and keep it for a day but he had calculated that he would earn him quite a lot of money and would be a great lucrative business venture.

So he did that. He started advertising that an elephant will be coming to the town and people can book elephant rides. People went crazy hearing this and started to book for the rides. He had also advertised that the rides will be served by first pay first serve basis. Kids and people started queuing up behind the booking room. So he started getting money from people all over the town for elephant rides.

The day came and people were waiting for it eagerly. It so happened that the ones who paid for the tickets first and who were supposed to get ride first were 5 poor kids who had spent their entire savings to buy a ticket to ride a huge gigantic creature which was the elephant.

But it did not happen like that that day. Due to wicked nature of Stinky he started giving rides first of all to kids of his connections in high political places. This aroused anger amongst the kids who should have been the first one to be served.

The kids ultimately got ride but they had to wait for 6 hours to get it. That day those kids had to miss work because the ride which was scheduled to be in morning happened in the evening and was totally unacceptable.

These kids since missed their work that day had to skip a whole day's meal and thus went hungry that day.

The kids did not like that and were very mad at Stinky and decided to teach him a lesson. They came up with a plan. They thought that the most precious thing for Stinky was his moustache and what if they cut half of one side of his moustache? It would be very insulting, funny and would ruin whatever ego Stinky had. Secondly it would be fun for everybody to see and would be a favour to whomsoever Stinky has troubled ever.

Now the plan had to be executed. They decided that this plan could only be done during night by going to Stinky's house when he was asleep.

The next night all of the 5 kids walked from their homes wearing flip-flops in cold with no socks and dirty black feet towards the mansion of Stinky. They reached their destination after some time. When they reached Stinky's house they climbed the huge gate of his mansion and went to his room after picking the front door's lock.

One of the kid held the right side of moustache of Stinky without him getting disturbed and the other cut half of it with scissors. Then they wasted no time and ran outside Stinky's house keeping their laughs and giggles mum until they reached their own cottage. When they reached their small cottage they laughed to their heart's content and for hours to come.

These kids were so happy that they had taught Stinky a lesson and were very excited to see what will happen when Stinky goes to meet people as a part of his business.

The next day Stinky was the giggle of the town. Stinky even if he wanted could not skip his business meetings so he had to go and when people saw Stinky they laughed to their heart's content.

Stinky realized that day that he had been a very mean person and his way of life was not a very good one so from that day he started becoming a better person and changed his ways of living. He became a nice person later and gave free elephant rides to every body once a year which he thought was a good deed.

But for that day and time until his moustaches became even he left his moustaches like that and let people see it and amuse themselves as a part of his punishment which he thought.

tALe 52 : tHe cLoUd siZe GrApHiC cALCuLaToR

This is a story about small tiny people called CHOPs. CHOP meant Cute Hopping Over Powered with less cleverness. These people were very friendly people who lived together but as the name suggests they were very cute and hopped most of the time which was also their favourite activity to pass time but had very less intellect, cleverness and smartness.

They worked in their offices peacefully without any worries of any threats or dangers towards them. But the thing was they were so less intelligent that for example to teach a set of students in class there were at least 50 CHOPs per class. This was because that one CHOP could calculate using only one calculator. Because if there were more calculators per CHOP the CHOPs would became nervous and start to go mental and crack. This was because of two reasons.

One was that they could not design a graphic calculator with more functions in it and second of all there hands were so small that they could not hold it.

So it went like that for centuries.

After 100 centuries there was born a baby amongst a family of CHOP called Enigma. His parents named him Enigma not because of his intellect at that stage but because he was always in a mysterious spot whenever anything was occurring. For example after his birth his father came to see him but Enigma was nowhere to be found. His parents got worried and scared. After quite a lot of searching they found Enigma sleeping under his mom's hospital bed with no toys around him. After few days whilst Enigma and his mom were still in hospital his dad came from work looking for him but he was nowhere to be found again. After quite a while they found him sitting and playing with a baby girl.

Now, to understand this better, you should know that new born babies are usually sleeping and they barely walk around. But this kid was different so they ultimately named him Enigma.

Now Enigma grew up playing with kids of his age but sometimes even his friends used to see him lost in his own dream world and they sometimes got confused that was he really a CHOP or somebody else as he used to think too much and put up questions that were out of kids and grown ups knowledge. But nothing could be done about it and thus he continued like that.

As he grew up he became a teacher. Too know, he was the most awesome teacher ever. But when he started teaching he started thinking that why his people were not smart enough and why could not they do multiple things at once. So he started devising a plan.

After school every night he started sketching something on paper. It looked like a big typewriter first but actually he was drawing a huge graphic calculator to help people of his kind i.e. CHOPs.

He had realized that his people liked to hop a lot and were deprived of intelligence. In fact in government offices if a person had to get drawings of his house approved he had to go to different clerks to get different shapes and structures measured and approved. So it was very pain taking for people.

Enigma wanted to put everything in a hand held calculator and could have done that but he did not.

He wanted to see people enjoy working and increase their intellect so he started making that huge machine. Funding was no problem because he was the smartest of his kind and thus he was approved and got a government grant.

For building the huge machine which was the graphic calculator he required a lot of help but could not get it because CHOPs would not understand how to build something new like that. So he had to work alone.

Enigma started following his paper designs and drawings. It took him 50 years to build such a huge machine for calculating but he made it bit by bit diode by diode, gear by gear.

The calculator he made was a calculator that would help kids learn and gain more intelligence during their childhood and become smarter.

To test it out he requested the government to make a huge 10 km by 10 km wide park and put that 8 km by 8 km dimension calculator there.

Now what this graphic calculator did was that for example if one had to draw a circle on the big 1 km by 1 km wide screen the kid had to hop on the circle sign once and then other kid who wanted to increase or decrease the size of the circle would first hop on the type of measurement required for consideration like inches or centimetres and then another kid would jump on the plus sign or negative sign to increase or decrease it in increments or decrements of set minimal value. Same was with squares and same was with triangles.

Then there was no end to designing the shapes. They just had to hop on a different buttons for drawing a line then give it angle, increase or decrease its size and finally give it shape.

Also this graphic calculator could scan and measure shapes of different things.

After the calculator was successful CHOPs started building more and more calculators   and keeping it in different cities and neighbourhoods.

After sometime, not only kids but CHOPs of all ages started going to the places where those cloud size calculators were kept. They hopped and learned new things and thus started improving their intellect.

The cloud size calculator gifted by Enigma increased the IQ level of CHOPs and thus new offsprings were smarter than the previous CHOPs and thus they progressed to a great future.

All the CHOPs needed was a mental exercising machine while having fun which increase their intelligence and smartness in every field.

TaLe 53 : fLyiNg fiRe

Who does not have a wish to see fire flying in the sky without it hurting anybody?

Once there was a kid who also always wished this and dreamt of making it happen but he never knew how to.

This kid was born in a family of very poor people who had to work very hard for their survival. His name was Gaouteiy. This name was given to him by his parents. Gaouteiy's father was a Lumberjack. In those days wood cutting was not a very profitable business as very other person who lived in that area was a lumberjack and therefore there was much competition for this trade thus money fetched through this job was not very great.

Since Gaouteiy's father was a lumberjack he had to follow the same trade as that of his father. Gaouteiy just like his father was very hard working. Merely at the age of 10 he started helping his father in cutting wood. His father was always impressed with his son but could not bring riches to him as much as he wanted. One day Gaouteiy's father asked his son that what did he wanted in life?

Gaouteiy replied that the only thing he wanted in life is to see fire flying in sky. His father was highly impressed with the thought. He then told Gaouteiy that he should pursue his dream and never let it go away thinking it was impossible because he said " Impossible it may sound but it will not be, because it's not a dream, it is life".

That day Gaouteiy was highly motivated by his father's words and thought that it was possible. So that day he asked his father that if he could save money from wood cutting to go to school. His father happily said "yes".

Before Gaouteiy had given all hope of achieving his dream but with his father's words, inspiration crouched upon within him like forest fire.

From that day he started to save money to go to school. He knew how to read and write so he started from grade 5. There he studied with his full concentration and as he went to grade 6 he started attending science classes where he learnt lots of chemistry.

One day he was sitting at his home with few matchsticks in hand. He then decided to do an experiment with the matchsticks. He brought a bowl and filled it with some oil. Then he triggered fire at the burning tip of match stick through friction. He then put the other end of matchstick in the oil without completely submerging it. Then a whole minute passed and the match stick did not go out of flame. He was surprised to see that. He wanted to know why it was happening like that. When he checked he saw that matchstick was absorbing the oil from the bowl as it was partially submerged and touching it and was burning only the oil and not the matchstick. This made him excited and he did that experiment again and again. The results were the same. Only the oil that was being absorbed by the matchstick was burning and not the matchstick itself. He was very happy with the experiment and remembered the results.

As Gaouteiy progressed in his school life he learnt more about fire proofing materials i.e. that don't catch fire and are light in nature.

One day after giving his grade 12 exams went to his class lab and made a fireproof material. He then after seeking permission from his teacher took the material to his home. On the way to home he also picked up a small helium cylinder. After reaching home he made a kite. He then filled helium gas in the fireproof material which was of bag like in shape and formed a shape of a balloon when helium was filled in it. He then tied a knot at the mouth of that material in such a way that the helium gas in it does not leak and does not leave the fireproof material which had formed a balloon.

Now he attached the helium balloon made up of fireproof material to the kite.

Also with the same fireproof material he made the string from which he would tie and make the kite fly in air.

He then brought a bow and a blunt arrow and started the experiment.

He made the kite fly in the sky. When the kite was high up in the air he let the string which was attached to lower end of the kite with which he was controlling the kite to fall in an oil can. Then he picked up the blunt bow and put it on fire. Then holding the arrow stretching on the bow he aimed at the kite at threw it towards the kite that had absorbed oil through the string by that time. When the blunt fire arrow touched the kite the whole kite was lit up with fire and it burnt until the oil in the entire can got empty.

Before doing that experiment he had remembered his matchstick experiment in which the oil burnt first and then the matchstick burnt.

This flying fire experiment was done again and this time in front of his father who was nothing more that impressed. His father than suggested Gaouteiy to show this magic to people.

Gaouteiy agreed to his dad and stuck a poster in the town centre about flying fire show. At that time he did not knew many people would be interested in seeing that.

But on the day of the show which he conducted in a very big open empty space almost the entire village population showed up.

He was nervous that day but did not hesitate to do the show. That day he had arranged for five kites to be lit on fire and so he did.

When he did people were no less than amazed to see the flying kites lit up on fire and not getting burnt up for quite a long time. People did not know how he was doing that and thought it was magic. They kept on saying that we want more but Gaouteiy had not expected this.

Gaouteiy then realized that he could earn an handsome income from this kind of show exhibition. He then started charging people for his show. He earned lots of money by showing fire shows to people in the village and in the entire country.

Whatever money he earned he donated some of it and rest he kept for his dad, mom and himself and lived life peacefully and happily.

TaLe 54 : tHe rAiNbOw tHaT wAs bLaCk AnD wHiTe

We as humans are used to and frequently enjoy 24 hours shops on planet earth. People who are living in metropolitan cities have many 24 hours shops at their disposal and also they can't live without it. When people want things they go to these 24 hours shops and get them. This gives them peace.

This was not the case with many nocturnal creatures in this story. These creatures were called Naoughteiy. These creatures lived on a tiny planet whose name was Laouteiy and was about a million light years away from earth. That planet had a sun and a moon and had life supporting characteristics.

These creatures as already told were nocturnal and therefore did not come out during the day to work and run their shops and livelihood. Their shops were built on the surface of that planet but their houses were built underground. Their shops and houses were nothing less than spectacular. They were decorated beautifully. Even if they did not like sunlight they still built their shops on the surface of that tiny planet. This was because they separated work from enjoyment. They did not wanted to work and get disturbed after hours.

Now as their civilization advanced some of these creatures wanted to come to surface even during day (which is sleeping time of nocturnal creatures) to do shopping. But two things hindered them from doing so.

First was that nobody worked during day in the shops and second was the sunlight that inhibited them from going on the surface. These creatures had created many sources of artificial lighting which did not bothered their eyes or their body but could not prevent something like sunlight from disturbing them or their eyes. (These lights were also used to decorate their shops and homes.)

Since many naoughteiys found money in the concept of 24 hour shops their government started funding some scientists to make something that could prevent the sunlight from bothering them so that they could also do shopping during day and have 24 hour shops on their planet.

Naoughteiy scientists started working on making something that could make shopping during day happen. They tried many things but could not succeed.

After few years their was born a boy in the naoughteiy community whose name was Saoumeiy. He knew what was going on in their community and about the massive funding that was being given to develop something that caused naoughteiys to do shopping during day. As he grew up he did not see anybody make anything like that but what could he do so he continued attending his classes first in school and then in high school.

Since he also wanted 24 hour shops he eagerly awaited for that day. While he used to attend his school he used to think what if nobody during his lifetime could invent something that could make shopping on surface during day possible. He used to get depressed thinking that and wanted to do something about it.

That night he was sleeping in his room in his underground home he looked up to the sky and saw something. He saw white clouds floating in the sky and sometimes coming in front of moon and thus creating a shadow from moonlight.

At that instance he thought that what if he created a cloud or smoke that encompassed the entire planet and did not allow the sunlight to enter the visible zone then it maybe possible to do shopping during day.

Next day he went to his school lab and started working on it. He started skipping all his classes from that day and only concentrated on making the cloud which he thought, in the lab. He started experimenting on making a cloud that filtered the sunlight and allowed only the good light which was possible for naoughteiys to tolerate.

Saoumeiy did many experiments. Sometimes there was a blast. Sometimes there was nothing. And sometimes it formed a solid rock out of many experimental reactions that he did.

Sometimes his teachers used to worry about him and used to ask him if he was okay. Whenever asked that Saoumeiy replied that he was okay and continued doing his experiments and skipping classes. He also said that he did not mind missing classes even if his teachers thought that it was a waste of time for him to just experiment without learning the theory.

One day he was working on creating the same cloud when suddenly an explosion of gas occurred. The gas that was formed was formed when he mixed some unique chemicals in a definite ratio.

His eye glasses which he was wearing were completely filled with the material that was exploded out of the mixture. Saoumeiy got scared and worried and thought that he would not be able to see anymore but something came in his mind and he remembered that he was wearing glasses so he touched the glasses and removed them. He was very happy that he could see. But to his astonishment he saw that he could see better through this fine cloud that was formed and the colours around were visible too. He suspected that this cloud could be answer to his efforts.

The chemicals he had put in to test tube he had already kept a record of them so he did not have trouble finding the chemicals which he used to do the experiment when he did it again.

He then took same chemicals in same amount the next morning and went to the opening of the surface. There he sat in shadow underground and let the same chemical reactions to occur.

This time he was at a distance from the reacting substances. When the gaseous explosion occurred the gases spread out in the open air on the surface. He then tried checking if he could see in the sunlight without blinding himself or causing harm to his body.

When he checked out, he saw that even though it was morning and sun was shinning brightly he could see clearly the shops and lights in them and his body did not become uncomfortable during the sunlight.

He cried Awesome! Yes! I did it.

After making sure that this cloud chemical was good to go he went back to his school and told his teachers about it. His teachers did not believe at first but then told him to show it to them.

When all of them went and he did the experiment again and showed it to his teachers they were really surprised to see it and said that yes it was true and was working.

Saoumeiy's teachers told about this to the society of naoughteiys who tested the chemicals and confirmed that yes it was true that the cloud formed by the reaction of those chemicals was good enough for the naoughteiys to go to surface during day and see through it without harming their eyes. They also confirmed that it was safe for everybody including kids of naoughteiys.

The naoughteiy's society awarded Saoumeiy with a huge amount of money and certificate of achievement and excellence.

Now since these creatures had artificial lighting they failed to realize that the sunlight also produced colours.

Also since these creatures started coming out during day they started seeing rainbows formed in the sky during day but always saw it black and white. At that time they did not know that rainbows had colours in them too but still they enjoyed the beautiful shaped thing that got formed and called it a blessing. The rainbow although was black and white but was something that they could not have seen without going in the shade of the sun.

TaLe 55 : tHe cLoUd tHAt sToLe rAiN

As everybody knows that clouds are born and they die or pass away in the atmosphere of earth and everywhere where there is moisture. In this story we will be talking about clouds that exist on earth. Also, I will be telling you that clouds have a life of their own and are living creatures who give shade and rain so that crops grow and we don't go hungry ever.

But now question arises that why can't we detect that they are living? This is because they live secretly by forming only regular circular oval shapes that scientists think are formed because of water cycle that exists in nature including other factors.

Now far far away in a family of clouds near the north pole was born a baby cloud called Caoutestriphcy. Caoutestriphcy was a very naughty baby cloud. He liked his family of clouds but never listened to them. He used to do enormous mischiefs.

Once this cloud was moving in air around North Pole (as he was not allowed to go anywhere else) he saw a huge oil tanker which was moving over the seas in the North Pole. At First, he did not come to know what it was as it was something he had never seen before so he continued looking at its shape and tried to understand it.

He was very much intrigued by it and wanted to form a shape just like it but he knew the golden rule of clouds which said that a cloud should not form anything strange that humans detect and which in turn could be harmful to their kind. So he tried to stop himself to not form the shape of that oil tanker but since he was a very mischievous and a small, he could not resist himself from doing that.

He formed a shape exactly that of oil tanker and moved in the air by having formed that shape feeling very happy. He let the his shape be like that for some time but later changed back to his original shape.

That day he was very happy as he had formed a new shape and wanted to do it more. He was lucky that day that none of his family members saw him form that cloud shape otherwise he would have been severely scolded for that.

Now after success of making a oil tanker shape Caoutestriphcy everyday used to look for new things to form shape of. Most of the time his family of clouds who were all adults used to leave their homes and go to work. (The work of these clouds involved causing rain to some regions for relief from heat or just for giving water to crops to grow). But that day Caoutestriphcy brother had high fever and he was unable to go to work so he stayed at home floating in air. Caoutestriphcy was unaware of this as he woke up late and with his half open eyes hurried to his favourite place which was where he had seen the oil tanker to look for more unusual shapes.

When he reached that place his brother who wanted to say good morning to him followed him from behind. When Caoutestriphcy reached his favourite spot he saw a weather balloon floating in air. He was further intrigued by that shape and again without noticing that his brother was following him he changed shape to the weather balloon. As soon as his brother saw that he was shocked to see that because Caoutestriphcy had broken the golden rule. He hurried towards him and held him by his hands and asked him " What are you doing?" Caoutestriphcy who was unaware of his brother was taken by surprise and said in a shrewd tone " I have done nothing wrong". His brother than scolded and lectured him that forming shapes like he did today was not in the code of conduct of clouds book and that he should not do that again. He also told him that doing this could threaten the life of all clouds on earth.

But since Caoutestriphcy was a very naughty cloud he did not listen to his brother. Caoutestriphcy's brother who thought that his brother would listen to him and would not do anything stupid like this any more did not tell to his family at that time. He thought that a warning was enough for his brother.

Caoutestriphcy did not change to any other shape for two days but he could not resist his temptations. After 2 days he again went back to his favourite spot but this time his brother somehow came to know about it and skipped his work that day. Just to make sure that his brother was not doing the same mischief again and to stop him from doing it, if he plans to do it, he went after him.

That day there was another oil tanker floating in the sea on which he saw a person, who was riding a bicycle on that oil tanker. Caoutestriphcy was again excited to see something like bicycle so he wanted to form that shape and did it it in a second. Now his brother got scared seeing that and got really mad at him. He came near him and started scolding him again.

This time he went home and called for a meeting of all the North Pole clouds and told them what Caoutestriphcy was breaking the code of conduct of clouds and it could be dangerous for other clouds.

The verdict came from the meeting and they all decided that Caoutestriphcy should be grounded for the entire year until he learns the code of conduct of clouds and follows them properly.

Caoutestriphcy was then grounded but he did not like that. He started hating his family and wanted to do something to harm them. He used to sit in his house and cry a lot. He used to think everyday that how he could take revenge from hi family. So he thought about a plan. While thinking about that plan he saw that there was a slight opening beneath the door of his house through which he could escape. So next day when all the clouds went to work Caoutestriphcy escaped from his house by slowly diffusing through the door's opening below. He then immediately went went to a witch and told his whole story and that how he would like to take revenge.

Since witches love to take revenge she agreed to help the cloud. She gave her a potion and whispered something in his ears. By hearing that he came to know that the most important thing of clouds is to work which mostly is causing rain so he decided to steal the rain.

He drank the potion and became enormously large and invisible. Now the witch had told him that where were the clouds that were causing rain to occur. So he went there and descended just near the surface, quite below the rain causing clouds and since he was invisible nobody saw him.

The clouds started causing rain and when they rained no rain water touched ground as all the rain was absorbed by Caoutestriphcy who took all the rain and flew away. The clouds who realized that no rain had touched ground did not know what was going on . They could not do noting at that time and went away.

Caoutestriphcy took all the rain and dumped it onto a river without realizing that what would happen further.

As soon as he dumped all the water in the river, the river water level rose and caused a lot of flooding in the towns around it. This lead to huge amount of loss of life and property in that area.

Caoutestriphcy was just about to leave that place but when he saw people dying he got scared and started to cry realizing what he had done.

But nothing could be done at that time so Caoutestriphcy went away crying and reached his home and told what he had done, to all his family. He apologized deeply from his family and said that he was ready to accept all the punishment that would be given at him. He cried deeply all day awaiting judgement.

After seeing that Caoutestriphcy had realized his mistakes and had become a better cloud, his family forgave him and told him to follow the code of conduct forever from there on.

So the cloud realized his mistakes and never made any mistakes from there on and forever followed the code of conduct of clouds.

TaLe 56 : tHe pEnGuiN tHAt fLeW

Penguin! What is a penguin. Penguin are birds that can't fly but they do have wings, which are featherless and just act as arms thus, they can't fly. Also, penguins mostly live in cold climates usually poles.

What do penguins eat? Penguins are a lover of fish and they eat mostly that. They might not be able to be afloat in air but they do swim very beautifully in water which is were they catch their food from i.e. fishes.

Now do penguins want to fly. This is a hard question to answer because penguins have been living like that for many years and thus it is very hard to say that if they ever have dream of flying. They might get interested in flying if they knew they could and how it felt like in air. There was one such penguin that starting liking floating in air so much that it had a dream that it wanted to fly. Let us read this story about that little penguin.

That penguin's name was Aoucripen. This penguin was a female and was born to two penguins who loved her very much. From the time she was born they took a lot of care of their daughter. Although they don't have penguin schools but still she was given the best teaching of morals.

Now as Aoucripen started to grow up she was allowed to leave the sanctuary of her parents and roam freely. At that time she started making friends belonging to her age group.

She used to feel very happy with her friends and they all became close friends. Now she and her friends started exploring places and things (as all little ones try to do wherever they go) everyday.

Everyday they went to different directions to search for something new and different.

Once Aoucripen and her friends were exploring a new place they found a big hill and just below it was a small water body which was a pool. They did not know what to do with it. So while they were thinking one of their friends climbed up the hill and jumped in the pool from the top of the hill. When he did that all the penguin friends saw it and first were afraid to know if the penguin that had dived into the small pool was okay. But after diving he came out of the pool and said that it was the best experience that he (who was a male penguin) had ever had.

This intrigued all his penguin friends who wanted to try themselves diving in the pool from such a height. So all of them did, turn after turn.

When Aoucripen's turn came she was a bit scared at first but she gathered some courage and asked her friend to push her to fall down the hill because she was to afraid to do that by herself even if she wanted to do so. Now as soon as she was pushed she screamed and fell in the small pool. But more than the splash in water she was excited about her time in air. She was exhilarated for that time and was totally lost in the excitement of being in air.

That day she was super excited and kept on diving for a very long time. She dived for about 50 times from that same hill and wanted to keep on doing that forever but it was late and she had her friends had to go back to their respective homes.

Aoucripen was in love with air. She thought of being in air forever but she knew that she can't fly even if she wanted. This thought made her even more determined and she wanted to do something so that she could fly. It was night at that time thus was sleeping time so she tried to sleep standing with high hopes.

She tried to sleep but couldn't sleep. So while she was awake she saw a star that flew across the sky and disappeared. She wondered, that how could a star break from sky and fly because she knew that stars were always fixed and never moved. But at that time she could not get any answer but hope.

Next day when the sun rose she wanted to go and do the diving but did not go there. Instead she went near the sea and started looking for something different that might help her fly.

She searched for hours and hours but could not find anything. After sometime she got depressed but she did not give up hope and continued walking along the icy path along the sea waters. As she was walking she saw a pole and something attached to it at the top which was a flag. She saw that as the air picked up speed that material started moving and waiving in air at almost the same speed of the wind. At that moment she got scared and though that it was a wild animal and would eat her. Then she tried running and hiding behind a rock and saw   if that moving material was following her . But few minutes passed and nothing happened. That thing remained tied up on the pole and continued its movement as before.

Aoucripen gathered courage and moved near the pole. She then realized that the material was just a cloth like feather and was non- living thus was nothing to be afraid of.

She then realized that something that was so responsive to the wind must help the person who holds it to float in air. She then decided to take off the flag and use it for herself. But how? She first wondered. Then she saw that as the wind was blowing and the cloth which was a flag fluttering, the thing which was a pole to which it was attached to was shaking by the pressure of wind on the flag. She then also realized that the pole was not permanently fixed to ground and could be removed.

It was too late at that time so she had to go back to her parents . When she went back home she told about the fluttering material to her friends and also asked for help from them to remove the pole from ground. Her friends were very close to her so they told her that they will help her all the way to get the flag off the pole and also if required, to take down the pole.

Morning came and she and her friends got up and went straight to that flag area. All her friends saw the pole and started hitting and pounding by smashing into the pole. The pole started loosing ground. After many attempts of hitting and smashing the pole fell. This made the flag cloth accessible. Aoucripen removed the flag from the pole, picked it up and then they all went to the big hill where they were diving from, the previous to previous day.

There Aoucripen pricked up some strong ice rods and tied the flag to it to form shape of huge feathery wings as she knew. Then she went up the hill and held the huge wing frame with her hands and jumped off the hill. When she jumped it was the most awesome experience she ever had.

Aoucripen actually flew. She did not fall in the pool but flew way past it to a great distance. Aoucripen was in air for an whole hour and floated because of the winds pushing the cloth frame up for a very long time . She never wanted to come down. But since the wing frame did not have any engines in it she descended down and landed slowly. She yelled and screamed for another hour with the excitement in her lungs. Nobody in their family had ever flown in air except her and she was very happy with that feeling also.

She then went home and told her family about that who wanted to see her fly again and teach them and her friends how to fly too.

This marks the end of story as you now know how once a penguin flew.

TaLe 57 : tHe rUnNeR tHaT nEvEr fiNiShEd tHe rAcE

It sounds funny that a runner never finished the race he started but it is true!

There was once a man named Draouwseiy. He was always fond of running marathons and drinking liquor. Usually he drank very little liquor before running a marathon but this was not the case with the marathon he was going to run next.

Before the marathon day, he came home after getting supplies for next week. After putting the grocery supplies aside he decided to watch TV for some time. He watched lots of shows before going too sleep. He watched some drama, some action and finally some cartoons. But as he was about to turn off TV his thumb slipped and instead of turning of TV, he pressed the channel 1 button on the remote and which resulted in showing a new type of liquor advertisement on TV. The advertisement showed a new type of liquor which was called hallucinating liquor. They were advertising that the hallucinating liquor was a unique liquor available at nearby stores in the entire country and was of a different effect and taste. This advertisement was very appealing to Draouwseiy. Draouwseiy after seeing the advertisement decided to try the liquor early in the morning before running in the marathon.

So next morning he woke up, got ready to taste that liquor and also to compete in the marathon.

He then went to the liquor store to buy the hallucinating liquor. He bought it, opened the bottle and tried to drink it straight up sip by sip to check the taste and it's effect. As soon as he had the first sip it was truly appealing to his heart's tastiest desire. He liked it so much that even though he knew that he had his marathon race and should not be drinking more but he drank the complete 700 ml bottle till it was empty and that too neat.

Now, was the time for the race as he looked at his wristwatch so he ran towards his car and hurriedly drove to the race. But he never knew that the alcohol was going to effect him in a strange and a funny way.

He wore his gear and reached the starting line of the race. At that time the liquor had not started to intoxicate him that much, so he was in his senses.

Suddenly the judge said " On your marks, get set and GO !" So the race started and also did Draouwseiy.

Draouwseiy was first running at a good speed but suddenly he started having the liquor's intoxication effect on him. He did not even realized that at that time liquor started taking control of him rather than he taking control of himself.

At first, he started feeling very thirsty and also starting to forgot about the race. As he was running he took out his phone and checked the nearby juice shop. His phone's GPS showed him a nearby juice shop that was about half a kilometre away from his position. He then decided to go there. He at that moment just walked to the juice shop.

In about 5 minutes he reached the shop and ordered one huge juice pitcher. When the pitcher came he drank the entire pitcher without even using a tumbler. He felt nice after it. Then he did not know what he was going to do next. So he first thought let's stand up at-least and then he thought he will think of something to do next. As soon as he stood up he felt pain in his feet which he did not realized at that time were because of running so he thought that it might be because of bad shoes he was wearing. He then decided to go to the nearby shoe shop.

He had lost his memory at that time so he did not know where the nearest shoe shop was. So he decided to ask the person who served him juice to tell him that where the best shoe shop was. That boy directed him to that shop.

After reaching that shop Draouwseiy went inside it. There he saw all the shows on display and then asked for the most expensive shoe they had. After seeing those pair of shoes he bought them. That shoes were worth a fortune but at that time he did not realize that he was spending so much money on shoes.

After wearing those shoes he felt good at heart might not be good at pocket which he did not realize at that time.

After buying shoes he realized that he was still feeling hot. He did not know why. He then thought maybe his clothes were causing him sweat so he thought of changing his clothes. Since he did not have spare clothes with him he decided to go to a cloth shop and this time by searching for it himself.

And so he kept on doing stupid things and ultimately when every marathon racer had finished the race he was nowhere to be found.

He actually was still doing shopping somewhere to make himself comfortable. At night he slept on a sidewalk as he felt very sleepy and did not know where to go at that time after the long day all because of the liquor.

Therefore he never finished the race and spent too much money on wasteful things because of drinking excessive liquor that caused him a lot, later.

tALe 58 : tHe oStRiCh bAbies tHAt tAsTeD hOnEy wAtEr

Once there lived a group of ostriches in a dry part of Africa. Food was scarce but the ostriches somehow managed to survive there. (Just to inform ostriches are omnivorous animals and can eat both plants and some animals like reptiles.)

Where these group of ostriches lived, there was no rainfall ever in that region. Whatever water their bodies needed was derived from eating their food which was mostly snakes and some dead mice. Therefore none of those ostrich had ever tasted water as a whole. But this did not matter them much. They continued their daily lives without any trouble until the mating season came.

When the mating season came all the ostriches mated with their partners and laid eggs in a short time. Usually ostriches have bout 7 eggs and so all of them did except one couple. The female ostrich in this couple gave birth to about 35 eggs which was astounding but not good for the ostriches living in a food-scarce area. When the leader of ostriches came to know about this he became surprised and worried because to see that every ostrich was getting sufficient food was his department.

So he went to that couple. The name of the male ostrich was Fritto and female one was Fremna. He went to them after quite a lot of thinking and asked them that how will they manage to feed their babies. Fritto and Fremna at that time had not thought about this because they were lost in joyousness of having so many kids. When this question was put up they themselves became worried and started thinking about it.

Then the leader of the flock told them very politely that they should take good care of the eggs and let them hatch first. After they have been hatched they should take the babies and go away from there to find a new home because it would be very difficult for he and his flock to arrange food for all their babies as food was already scarce there.

The gentle couple agreed to what the leader of the flock said to them and agreed to leave their dwelling and find a new home for themselves and their kids after their kids hatch.

It was not long before they hatched. The first baby to hatch who was also the eldest one was named Ricko. Ricko was 15 seconds elder to the next hatched ostrich baby.

So that day that ostrich couple had all their babies hatch out of their shells and made the family complete. After checking, their parents were happy to know and see that all the babies were healthy and fit.

The next day as was requested by the leader of the flock they left their dwelling. Before leaving they had already arranged for some food for their kids and themselves for the journey. 20 kids jumped and climbed the back of their father and remaining 15 kids including Ricko climbed the back of mother and their started their journey.

As both the parents had not left their zones of dwelling ever before they did not know to which direction to head to. Since they had to choose any random direction they asked their eldest son Ricko to point to a direction. Their son pointed straight north. The family then decided to head to that direction to find a new home.

They travelled for about 45 days until they had crossed the desert completely and why they had travelled 45 days was because their eldest son Ricko was not satisfied with the desert alone area. So in hope for finding something different they continued travelling for 45 days and finally reached some greenery.

When the family reached the greenery they were shocked to see such beauty in that area as it was something they had never seen before.

There were trees there, many colourful fruit and flower bearing plants and many ponds.

The family decided to stay there and make that place their home, thanks to non stop will of their son Ricko to keep on pursuing their journey for a better place.

After they had rested their kids wanted to go and check out that region so all the ostrich brothers and sisters went out looking for something special. As they were roaming around they saw bee-hive with bees flying all over a bee-hive.

That bee-hive was sticking to a tree that was near a pond and was oozing with something which those ostrich babies never had a taste of, which was honey.

As ostrich babies were looking at the bee-hive they saw some honey fell into the pond and they all wanted to try it out and so they did. As soon as they tasted it was like they had a taste of heaven. It was the most sweetest and wonderful things they ever had.

They took some of that honey that had dropped in pond water and put it inside their beaks and went to see their parents. After finding their parents all of them straight away went near them. Some went to mom and some went to their dad and put that honey water into their mouths.

When parents tasted that they also found it very nice and tasty and asked them all about it. The kids told them everything about where and how they found it.

Parents were happy at that time that their kids had found a paradise and a safe haven for rest of their life where there was no shortage of food and sweetness.

tALe 59 : tHe bUbBLe tHAt tRaPpEd a hOuSe

Long ago there was a scientist whose name was Cloud. He was a funny scientist who used to do various types of stupid experiments everyday. Mostly he did not succeed in getting the outcome but he still never lost his heart and hope.

Once he was trying to make a bubble that would be able to surround the whole house and therefore would look beautiful from outside-In.

So to make that, he had to think about the properties of the bubble that would make his dream possible. The properties of that bubble, he thought should be something like :

1)   It should allow the flow of fluid or a body in and out of the bubble without breaking the bubble itself.
2)   Secondly, it should be sturdy enough so that it does not break for years to come.

So he started working upon this idea. He did lots of experiment trying to make a bubble like he wanted but initially did not succeed.

He did various experiments. Sometimes he made bubbles that were very colourful and sometimes he made bubbles that kept on making sharp squeaky noises. Some bubbles he made burst and left him flooded with the material they were made up of which was a waste of time to cleanup.

So whatever he did, he did not succeed in making the bubble that he wished for.

But one day something unique happened. Cloud mixed some chemicals together and put them in a test tube. Then he made a small lightning conductor and attached it to the table where he had put the test tube. He had at that time thought of producing lightning through a small spark and it getting it absorbed by the lightning conductor. The main idea involved in this was that he wanted to produce a different kind of electromagnetic field near the chemical mixture he created to form the desired bubble by producing a lightning spark and it getting absorbed by the lightning conductor.

The experiment was all setup and he went in the store room of his house where he was doing the experiment to get some batteries and produce a spark by discharge.

As soon as he went inside suddenly he heard a Big Bang and saw that roof of house was ripped apart through the centre. He immediately came out. He saw that the lightning from the clouds had struck the mini lightning conductor and caused a chaos. The table where the lightning conductor was placed broke and the test tube in which the bubble forming chemicals were kept had also broken. He saw that a huge bubble started forming from there and in a matter of seconds engulfed the entire house.

When Cloud saw that he was excited and dumbstruck! Something that he had been working on for a long time and had wanted it desperately was right in front of his eyes.

Then he tried testing it. He tried walking out of the enclosed bubble but could not. So he tried breaking it by poking it with a sharp knife but that did not succeed in that too.

His excitement turned into fear as he did not wanted to get chocked to death in that bubble. At that moment he did not know what to do. He sat on the ground and thought of breaking that bubble somehow. Since the bubble did not pierce so he thought it should be blasted away.

He mixed all the chemicals through which he could cause a blast or an explosion and cause the bubble to break. Because if you can't pierce a bubble you can at least blast it off. Then he barricaded himself in a room and caused the blast to occur.

One, two and three BOOM! an explosion occurred. Cloud was very much sure that bubble would break through such a strong explosion. So to check that he came outside of his barricade and looked up through the crack of the house in roof to check if bubble broke away. But to his frightful astonishment nothing had happened to the bubble and it still surrounded the house as if had form an unbreakable prison wall. The house although suffered some damage.

Cloud had tired whatever he could to break the prison but he had failed. He then realized that since no chemical reaction was working on the bubble, there should be some other way through which he could break the bubble.

It was night time already and since he had not slept for two days he was very tired and wanted to sleep even if not for long. He then went to his bed, laid down on it and closed his eyes. But before he went to sleep he set an alarm for 5 hours from then. He was much tired at that time so he just slept without thinking that what would happen tomorrow. He had given up all hope that night.

After 5 hours the Alarm clock beeped and Cloud opened his eyes and sprang out of his bed. He then thought that if he can't break the bubble why should not he try to modify it. At that time he did not know how to do that.

He went to library in his house and tried looking for some answers. He kept on looking through the books and throwing them down the shelves. What he was looking for even he did not know. He kept on doing that for a while until he had made a mess of all those books on the floor and until no book was left on the shelf. He stepped down the ladder and again checked the books but to his hopelessness he did not find any chemical formula that he thought might be worthy to help him to break the bubble. He looked confused and was looking here and there when he happened to have a look at a book.

The book's title was shape shifting and there was a square drawn over a circle. This gave him an idea. He realized that a spherical shape gives the most strength to a structure and it is difficult to break that structure because of the shape. Just like the shape of a oval shaped egg which is naturally strong because of it's shape as it is difficult to break by compressing it with the palm of one's hands.

He screamed YIPPE! He decided that even if the bubble was very strong, if the shape of it is altered to a cubical or a cuboidal shape then it might be possible the weaken the bubble and then ultimately break it. He then started working on this task.

He brought 2 steel polls and extended them by cranking them such that one aside of the polls touch the ground and other side touches the inner membrane of bubbles. The poles were kept in an inverted "V" shape extending from the centre area of the house. He then added some soap to the walls of the bubble by his hands.

He had added soap to the walls of the bubble so that when he causes an explosion the greasiness of soap causes the walls of the bubble to bend to a different shape.

Then he caused a great explosion once again. This explosion was bigger than the previous one. He caused it only after he had barricaded himself properly inside one of his room.

To his wonders, after the explosion a magic occurred and the bubble distorted its shape to an uneven shape.

What was next? Cloud brought a small harpoon weapon and fired the harpoon towards the bubble's wall and Loo! The bubble broke and he literarily had a sigh of relief.

That day he realized that he had learnt a lot and should be careful with what he wanted and experimented upon.

TaLe 60 : tHe dOLLhOuSe

There are many fathers in this world that take a lot of care of their kids but the father in this story is somewhat special. He took a lot of care about his daughter whose mother had died while giving her birth.

This father's name was Laoungeiy. Before her daughter whose name was Queaoniy was born Laoungeiy and her wife had always dreamt of having a daughter. But since there financial status was not very good they did not have any child. Both of them worked hard to improve their financial profile so that they could afford a kid and give him whatever he/she wanted.

After 5 years of marriage they finally were able to afford a house and have some free cash in their hand so they decided to have a baby.

Laoungeiy's wife got pregnant and in nine months she was to have a baby. They both wanted a girl baby but did not mind even if it was a boy. At that time Queaoniy's mother stopped working and started staying at home and making gifts for her son/daughter that would be born very soon.

That day at the time of delivery Laoungeiy came from work and Mrs. Laoungeiy gave a huge scream. She was at the upper level of house and was about to step down the flight of stairs when she slipped. Laoungeiy had just entered the house and he ran to catch her but could not quite save her. She fell on the stairs and was immediately taken to the hospital. An ambulance came and took her right away where the doctor gave Laoungeiy a bad news that her wife could not be saved but he also consoled him saying that before passing away she gave birth to a beautiful daughter.

Laoungeiy remained sad for sometime because the dream of having a daughter was both he and his wife's dream. But then he consoled himself and said that even though his wife was not with him anymore but he will take good care of his daughter as he and his wife had decided.

He went to the room and picked up his daughter whose eyes were just like that of her mom's.

The next day he performed all the rituals for her dead wife and bid her ashes good bye.

Now Queaoniy was also very fond of her father who cared a lot for her. He gave beautiful gifts for her every birthday which were not found in the market. These gifts were all hand made by Laoungeiy himself. Now, his daughter was going to turn 4 next year Laoungeiy wanted to give her the biggest gift of lifetime. He wanted to give her a doll house which was unlike anything available in the market.

After much thinking he decide that he will give him a doll house made of honey which she can also use as a cake for her birthday. He was confused at that time and did not know how to proceed with that idea because whatever honey he will use to make the house it will fall as a puddle and wont stick together.

After few days of thinking he decided that he will use a honey bee itself to make the doll house.

So the first step involved was getting a bee. He went to the forest that day and somehow trapped a bee in a jar and got her home. Now, he told the bee and requested her that if she could make a doll house for her daughter from honey. The honey bee at first was very mad at Laoungeiy. She asked him that how dare he trap her. Laoungeiy then explained her everything. After listening to Laoungeiy's plea she decided that she will do what he has asked for but he should help her in doing so. Laoungeiy agreed to the bee.

The bee then asked Laoungeiy that if he had a garden of flowers around him. Laoungeiy told the bee that he does have a garden but not very many flowers in it. The bee then told him that it will be a problem if there were not much flowers in his garden. So then, Laoungeiy asked the bee that what should he do? The bee told him that in order for her to make a doll house of honey she needed lots of flowers and him to be there with her for an entire month with a hair dryer to form the house. Laoungeiy thought for a while and told the bee to give him a day's time so that he can take a leave from his job and help her out in making the doll house. She said "okay".

Now next day Laoungeiy's leave started and he started helping the bee out. Everyday he used to get a kilogram of fresh flower petals from the flower shop and put it in the room where the bee was making the honey doll house. Then he used to plug in the hair dryer and whenever the bee dropped a small amount of fresh honey he used to turn on the dryer and dry that. The bee kept on working for 30 days non stop and so did Laoungeiy. Whenever Queaoniy needed something he took a break and helped her daughter out. Meanwhile the bee rested too. All this happened in a room so Queaoniy never came to know what was going on and also since she was too small she could not have guessed anything.

After 30 days the doll house was complete. A beautiful glowing doll house made of honey appeared which was further decorated with beautiful and colourful flower petals.

Then Laoungeiy thanked the bee who was also happy at that moment that such a beautiful doll house was made. Laoungeiy then promised the bee that he would never trap any bee again. The bee also told him that in future if he wanted he can only request for help from a bee but not trap them. Laoungeiy agreed to it and said good bye to the bee.

Now, for Queaoniy whose birthday had a few months left continued snooping around for her present for her 4th year but could not find it. His father had done a good job of hiding it in a place where she could not find.

Now when Queaoniy's 4th birthday came and she was super excited. She asked her dad what he had planned for her on that birthday. But his dad said nothing but "honey".

And so it was. On her birthday Laoungeiy took out a present which was covered with glossy net and paper and told her daughter "it's for you honey". When Queaoniy opened it she was in tears and said to her dad that it was the sweetest present ever and that she would never forget it. Laoungeiy was also happy hearing that.

That night was a very good night for Laoungeiy and her baby doll because they had the sweetest dollhouse ever.

TALe 61 : tHe biRtHdAy oF A hApPy mAn

Long ago in Norway lived a man named Raffaelliy. H was the most noble, kind hearted and a caring guy of all. He loved and took care of all of his friends, neighbours and anybody who needed help in his town. He had no shortage of money as his businesses ran good. But this was not always the case.

When Raffaelliy was a kid he had a tough time to face. His father and mother who were his only family had died when he was young. How? His father and mother were crossing a bridge while riding on their horses back when suddenly the bridge collapsed and they fell in the river whose bodies were later recovered. Along with them many people too died that day falling from the bridge.It was a sorrowful movement for many.

Since Raffaelliy was left with little property and some cash he decided to go to school during the day and work as a shoe polisher in evening because the amount of money he was left with was sufficient to support for his school tuition but not for his daily living expenses. He always thanked God and never had any grudge against him ever. All he wished was that when he grows up he can be as much helpful as possible to others and help others be less worried about their problems.

As he grew up he became well educated. He had got six degrees until the time of his marriage. One of the degree was his master's degree in business which helped him prosper through his business ventures.

At the age of 35 he got married. His marriage was not a common one. It was a huge party with lots of pomp and show. He had got married to the daughter of the mayor of that town at that time and there was nobody in the town and country that did not know about it. The chefs that prepared the food in the wedding were called from far and wide. Whoever had the food and wine that day said that it was beyond comparison and was the best they ever had.

So life of Raffaelliy was always happy and he never held any grudges against anybody. Even his employees never left his companies and always stuck around it as they always felt at home working in his companies.

Usually people get badges for best employee of the month but here it was Raffaelliy who used to get the badge for best employer of the month and this did not stop there. Since his employees used to honour him with the badge he used to through a lavish party every month for all his employees. In his businesses both the employer and employees used to enjoy the company of each other and always were happy and got rejuvenated seeing each other.

Raffaelliy had every thing a man wanted, money and happiness. Even his wife used to tease him that how is it possible to get so much happiness in life? All he used to tell her was that he never held any grudges against anybody and always thanked God. He also told her that he always worked hard, honestly and that this was all God's grace that he had given him so much.

Once Raffaelliy had got cancer but he survived the serious diseases. At the age of 53 he had got cancer but he did not cared. He spent his time happily with his wife and his daughter whose name was Frex. When he was going through cancer treatment he had gone hairless and thus he had gone bald. He never minded that. His daughter who was still young at that time used to laugh at him and used to say that his hair has been stolen by "Hair

Fairy" just like tooth fairy steals the tooth. Both his father and mother used to laugh at their daughters remarks. Raffaelliy was never worried even if he had Cancer because at that time although treatment was not that much advanced but he tried spending his present happily and without worries of any kind even about his future.

While spending life happily and in a jolly good way came his 87th birthday and he had forgotten all about it. His daughter had grown up at that time who tried wishing him " Happy Birthday" that day but Raffaelliy did not paid heed to it because he had finished an important work the previous night and was sleepy in the morning when his daughter wished her.

Now his daughter Frex thought that since her dad had completely forgotten about his birthday let's surprise him with a party and so she did.

That day she removed the calendar from her father's room and made great arrangements. She invited all their relatives and neighbours and told everybody to not tell Raffaelliy who promptly agreed to it.

In the evening when Raffaelliy returned from work, there it was, a big noise and huge wishes poured in from the crowd standing and waiting to sing him "Happy Birthday" song. TO everybody's surprise it was the first time that Raffaelliy felt a little sad. He sat on a chair with not much expressions on his face. He did not look happy to all. When his daughter asked him that if he was okay, he replied that usually birthdays make people happy and not only that he used to get happy too but when he checked his age today he realized that he was 87 years old that day and about to get 90 in three years and so he would have to leave his people and his happy family someday. Everybody after hearing this laughed at him and said "you Goof, you had never been sad in most of your life, even when you had cancer you were still always in a joyous mood. Now when it will be time to go to Heavens and maybe see God whom you have always loved you are sad."

Raffaelliy at that moment realized that yes he had always trusted The Almighty and loved him very much so when it's time for him to go and meet The Almighty sometime in future "I am sad". " I should not be" he said to himself and regained happiness and blissfully started enjoying birthday. He also realized that life and death cycle is something that everybody endures so should be only thankful to God that he had given him a joyous life and that who knows how many more years he has to live, maybe forever, he thought.

TaLe 62 : tHe AiRcRaFt mOdEL mAkEr

Long ago but not so distant ago there was a king and his ruled country. This country he ruled was not a very big country and was known as Rhiofania. Rhiofania, although a small country had incomparable beauty.

It had beautiful trees and gardens which were kept as a secret sometimes just to be gifted to a near and dear one. Yes! it's true in that country people instead of giving flowers as present gave whole beautifully decorated gardens with a rare collection of flowers growing in them as presents or gifts.

Rhiofania was like heaven on earth. In this country the water that was brought down through the mountains which flowed as rivers was sweet as sugar and people never needed sugar to put in lemonades because the water in it was itself very sweet. Not only that ground water was also sweet as the river water. Also people remained fit in this country because of the effects of natural beauty.

Rhiofania had all types of weather and weather conditions. It was sometimes cold sometimes warm and sometimes it had fall and sometimes it had spring.In some mountainous parts of Rhiofania there used to be snow as well where people of Rhiofania went to ski and play with snow.

Now in Rhiofania there was no militia as it believed in having peace without war forever. It practiced this principal by politically keeping strong ties and friendship with it's neighbouring countries. The king of Rhiofania kept expert negotiators in it's monarch government who were experts in talking and negotiating with the kings and ambassadors of other countries. The king of Rhiofania and his previous generations who had ruled Rhiofania for many centuries never invested funds in militia. All they invested was in people and and in maintaining beauty in their country. They thought that money may buy might and then buy happiness but its a waste if might becomes mighty further leading to more investments thus leading to waste so let money give happiness straight away without spending anything on might which is always might. Also they believed that friendship and having allies. They believed in demilitarization of all the countries.

Now also in that country lived an aircraft model maker who was expert in making aircraft models and replicas of smaller sizes by merely seeing the pictures of the aircrafts. This aircraft model maker's name was Jaouckreletiy. Jaouckreletiy was the only aircraft model maker in Rhiofania. His models were well sought after and were sold at very high prices. Sometimes due to less supply and more demand he had to auction his aircraft models, which got him lot of money. His profession was worth spending time in as it was highly paid and not everybody could do it.

In amidst of this discussion something happened. Their was a country neighbouring Rhiofania whose king was jealous of Rhiofania's beauty. This king wanted to takeover Rhiofania by force and make its own. He had a strong desire to rule there although it was nearly impossible as it was bound by strong legal ties with Rhiofania and it's allies and thus could not do it.

At that time although Rhiofania did not have militia and it did not believed in one but it's allies had lots of militia who believed in investing in militia and believed that talks are for fools and actions are more fruitful and practical. Difference of views never let there be any question in their friendship because views maybe different but that's what makes people people and goodness makes friends and thus difference in views don't matter.

The king of the jealous country who wanted to take over Rhiofania by hook or crook started spending money secretly on building secret weapons like boats where aircrafts can land and takeoff and also which could be submerged with the aircraft if required and whenever required at will.

The militia of that jealous king succeed in making such kind of sea vessel. They then started making aircrafts land and take off from that boat which they succeeded through practice.

Now since Denick (which was the name of the jealous king) could not send even 10's of fighter aircrafts to attack Rhiofania because of fear of getting attacked by Rhiofania's allies itself so he made a plan.

His militia loaded one fighter aircraft in that submergible boat and send it to scout near the shores of Rhiofania.

It happened that the aircraft model maker that I had told you about in this story also lived near the shores of one of the town of that country where the submerged boat with a loaded aircraft was sent to scout.

The submersible boat of Denick's militia reached the shores of Rhiofania in about 3 days and was told to remain submerged until further notice. When the vessel was submerged for about a month it got some technical problem and thus had to come up and open its hatch so that the aircraft was visible.

When this happened Jaouckreletiy was working on an aircraft model sitting in his workshop and looking at the sea and the shore through his window. Suddenly when he saw that a huge naval ship was floating on the sea waters with a fighter aircraft in it he was more than shocked to see that. He already knew that it could not be his country's militia as it had none. He then decided to warn the king but he had no time and something had to be done at that time and so he did.

He had about 25 aircraft models at that time which he was making to be sold in an auction. He wasted no time in arming them. Although those planes could not fly he had thought of something in mind that would make them fly.

He made small rubber sling shots, stretched them, loaded them with small marbles and tied to the top of aircraft models. Then he filled same number of rubber balloons with helium and attached a thread to them.

Now he brought the aircraft models who were attached with loaded sling shots and the helium balloons together. He then tied the thread of the helium balloons to the aircrafts and let them float. But before that he had also tied threads to slingshot so that he could release the sling shots whenever he pulls them. He had also attached a third different colour thread to the aircraft models so that he could somewhat maneuver them or change their pointing direction if required. The helium and air mixture in the balloon was measured by him before filling them with it. He had filled only that amount of helium and air in the balloons so that they hang at altitude of about 1000 feet which should be the maximum altitude gained by the actual fighter aircraft that he saw in the huge ship near the shore when it takes off and reaches the shore.

Now since there was a trouble with the ship and it had to come up. It did not remained secret anymore. So the king Denick ordered the pilot of that plane to take off and attack Rhiofania with all its power. The pilot agreed to it and took off. When he did the model planes were already floating in air. When Jaouckreletiy saw the plane coming towards the land he waited and as soon as it came near enough he pulled the threads and let go of the marbles in the slingshots. Some marbles missed and some hit the engines and the aircraft's frame and windows. Both the engines of that aircraft were on fire and it suffered sustainable damage and crashed on the ground with pilot in it. (Since it was at low altitude pilot had not gotten any time to escape the aircraft via a parachute).

By that time the king of Rhiofania had come to know of that and he had informed his allies about that. His allies who when heard this sent thousands of fighter aircraft to protect Rhiofania. The aircrafts sent to Rhiofania by it's allies were ready to fight a war if required.

That military aircraft was down and also the models he used to fire sling shots at the planes were brought down safely. These models got sold at a greater price than usual at the auction as they had saved Rhiofania and had a story behind them.

Thus the aircraft model maker saved the day. He was thanked by king and the country.

TaLe 63 : tHe mAgiC bOw AnD it'S OwNeR

This is a story about a boy who was a little different than others. As human civilization progressed all men including women progressed and amongst whom women started wearing ornaments including jewelry and earrings. During those times only girls and women used to wear earrings and they were liked very much by all but men never wore them. Not only that it was a taboo for men to wear earrings so no man wore them except this boy.

This boy's name was "Rather". Rather who was although very helpful to everybody was a bit different and unique in his nature. When he first saw an earring that was worn by a girl he immediately ran towards the girl and asked her that what was hanging onto her ears. The girl asked him " Don't you know", Rather said "No." the girl then told him that it was an earring. He then asked the girl can a boy also wear it. The girl told him that she does not think that it was meant for men and went away.

Now Rather was so impressed by the earrings that he decided that he would wear them too. But for that he had to have a hole in his ear and to get that it was a bit difficult. He somehow got a hole in his ear and was ready to wear an earring.

The earrings that were available in the market were not of his choice. Therefore he decided that he would make an earring all by himself for himself. For that he thought of exploring the market for a material that was unique and impressive for him to make an earring.

So next day he went to all the shops but could not find anything that he would make an earring with. So it was evening by that time and he was very upset. He was still walking and checking shops for a material when he saw something hanging outside one of the shops. That thing was shining even when there was no light. This intrigued him and he went inside the shop. There he asked the shop keeper what was the material that was shining outside his shop even when there was no light. The shop owner told him that that material was a photo-luminescent material called strontium aluminate and was a costly material to buy. Rather had already made up his mind to get that material. That material was worth pay of whole month when worked at minimum wage and that too 24 hours a day. But that was not going to stop him from buying that material.

He told the shopkeeper that he will get 50 grams of that material and get it by next month. The shopkeeper said "ok" and then Rather went away.

Rather worked sleepless for a whole month in a coal mine and earned sufficient money to buy that photo-luminescent material and to make an earring out of it.

After he got his pay he went straight away to the shop where strontium aluminate was kept and then bought it.

He then purchased exactly 50 grams of that material and went home. Then he had to decide that what kind of earring was he going to make of it. He thought for a while and then decided to make something that he liked the most - "A bow."

He spent 5 more days sleepless and carved a beautiful bow earring out of that Photo-luminescent material. In that earring not only the bow frame was made of that material but also the string of the bow earring was made of the light emitting material. Then he attached a hook to it and immediately wore it.

After wearing that he slept for 2 whole days undisturbed and woke up wearing that earring.

Wherever Rather used to go he kept wearing that earring. Some people like that earring and some laughed at him and mocked at him asking him that if he was a girl. But that did not discourage him and Rather never stopped wearing that earring.

The special ability of that material was that it use to absorb light the whole day and emit back multicoloured neon lights the whole night which was very unique on its own.

One day after listening to talks of people that Rather wore girl things his father got really mad at him at scolded him a lot. Rather felt very sad that day and went away from his home to a calm peaceful lake shore.

There it was dark and he sat for a long time crying thinking that everybody was a enemy of him and nobody appreciated him. He kept on weeping when suddenly he heard a voice " Hello! Can you help me?" Rather who had his head bent down between his folded knees tilted his head up and asked " Who is it?" The voice told him that I am a gnome. Rather first felt scared but then asked that how could he be of any help. The gnome said that he is looking for his gnome brother who was forcefully made to drink a magical potion by a witch that made him go invisible and soundless. He also told Rather that his brother would die if a light source does not touch him. The only light source that would be able to touch him without causing harm to gnome's brother was not candle flame but the light emitting substance that Rather was wearing.

Rather immediately told the gnome that he would love to help him to get his brother back and save him.

The gnome immediately took the earring from Rather's hand who had removed it for the first time from his ear. Gnome then uttered some magical words and then a flash of lightning occurred and loo! gnome's brother became visible. Both of the brothers jumped with excitement and yelled "Jolly good, jolly good!"

Now the gnome who was given the earring to save his brother thanked Rather and asked that who could he ever repay his debt. Rather was a bit confused and said " I don't know, I just like doing good." So the gnome gave back his earring rubbing it with his hands and saying that since you like doing good, whatever you throw after placing it in the bow and stretching it with its cord which touches both the bow frame and it's string will bring some life and happiness to the thing it touches. At that time Rather did not know what to make of it and so he took the earring and thanked gnome for his magical blessing.

Now it so happened that after a few years a huge monster threatened the city. He came and started destroying it. Even the king's army was not able to stop it. The army threw lots of arrows at the monster but he would not stop and kept on destroying the city.

Rather who came to know about this wanted to help his city and country from the destruction. He then remembered the gift he had in his ears that would bring some life and happiness to the thing that is javelined through it. So he decided to test it.

He took off the bow earring from his ears and picked up a needle and aimed it at the monster. When that needle touched the monster a huge apple fell on the ground. At that moment the monster stopped destroying the city and started eating the apple. People were surprised to see that and realized that the monster was hungry and not mad so they brought lots of food and kept it in front of him. The monster ate all the fruits and started behaving friendly and went away.

Even though the monster went away the destruction was still left behind and people did not know how to fix it. There came an idea in Rather's mind. He picked up 25 needles and javelined through his bow in space together. The needles touched the ground and wherever the needles touched, the destroyed area disappeared and there emerged an area or building which was beautiful looking.

Thus he restored his city- All thanks to the magical bow and him.

People thanked Rather and never mocked at him. The king appointed him his Prime minister and from there on he lived his life happily and without any trouble.

TaLe 64 : tHe fiRe bEiNgS

Long ago there lived 2 gremlins together in a house along with other gremlins in the neighbourhood. Actually in that town where these gremlins lived had a population of only gremlins.

The 2 gremlins that I am talking about inhere were husband and wife. They were as evil as it could get. They also had evil powers like bringing negative luck to whoever they wanted. These gremlins were evil but they were evil only to things other than themselves or other gremlins. Also they were social only amongst themselves.

Just to understand, they are very evil creatures that can cause great deal of harm to machinery and other beings physically and/or by their magical powers.

Now gremlins although evil but are creatures and they feel cold too, so during the night they used to burn log of woods in their fireplace to keep themselves warm and cozy. These fires which were burnt by gremlins were a bit magical in nature and were very pleasing to the beings known as fire beings.

These fire beings were called fire beings because they enjoyed fire i.e they bathed in fire for long hours and did not burn themselves even a little bit. Just like people and gremlins use water to have a bath so as to get cleaned up so did these fire beings. These fire beings loved to bath in fire and that was also how they got cleaned up.

In that house where these 2 gremlins lived also lived 50 fire beings. These fire beings were about a centimetre high and used to come out during the night when the magical fire place was burning to enjoy and have a bath. Since the gremlins at that time used to be in deep sleep they never came to know about the fire beings. This continued for many years without the fire beings getting noticed by the gremlins.

As years passed the gremlins became a bit old. Since they got old and they did not have any offspring they took care of themselves and each other whenever any sort of help was needed.

It so happened that during one night the female gremlin started to cough a lot and so she asked her husband to help him out by getting some water and some medicine to stop her cough. Her husband got up and went out of the room towards the kitchen to get those things for her wife. As he walked into the lobby where the fireplace was burning he saw that the fire looked as it was cracking, with colours coming out of the fire. He was astonished to see that. He then went a bit closer and saw that some beings which were of the same colour as that of flame were inside it and dancing and playing in the fire. As they were doing that colours were being produced which looked magnificently amazing. He immediately hid behind the pillar near the fireplace so that the fire beings would not be able to see him. He stood there for about an hour and enjoyed the show while his wife kept on coughing and shouting for him.

After watching those beings for an hour he moved away from the pillar stealthily and went to the kitchen to get water and cough medicine for his wife. When he entered his bedroom he immediately kept the things on the table besides her wife and jumped on the bed, excited. His wife was a bit surprised to see his quickness and excitement. So she asked her husband that what had happened. The husband then told her about the fire beings. His wife also got excited after hearing about them.

Then they thought that if those beings don't burn in fire and are magical, what if we they were eaten ." We would become fit, healthy and younger and diseases might not be able to make us ill again. Thus we would remain in good health and shape forever".

Her husband listened to what she said and totally agreed to it. Now she wanted to know that how should they do that.

Then they both made a plan. The next day they both got a fishing net sort of equipment made of magical threads. That night they did exactly as the did the other nights. They turned the fireplace on by burning logs of fresh dry wood in it and waited for the fire beings. Then they hid themselves inside a secret location in their house.

Now it happened. At about the 12:00 am in the night the fire started cracking again and both gremlins saw the fire beings playing, dancing and bathing inside the fire. The gremlins took their magical net out came out from their secret location and stealthily moved near the fireplace. As they were moving to get near the fireplace, the female gremlin stumbled and fell on the floor. This created a loud noise and caused the fire beings that were in the fireplace to get cautious. The male gremlin realized that the sound of her wife falling would make fire beings cautious and so he ran towards the fireplace and threw the net on the fire. Since the net was magical it did not burn but because the fire beings had become cautious when they had heard the noise most of the fire beings had already ran away from the fireplace but some were still preparing to run away from there. Therefore some fire beings got captured in the net.

Now was the female gremlin's turn. She picked up the fire beings caught in the net and took them straight to the kitchen.

By that time, the other fire beings had raged a war in the house. They brought there huge catapults and crossbows to fire at the gremlins. But to their surprise the shots fired were all failing to miss their targets because by that time the male gremlin had cursed the machineries with bad luck.

The male gremlin somehow managed to save himself from the firing weapons but it was not too late that the fire beings had realized this. So they went back and got some other stuff to attack the gremlins. They rode on unicorns and drew a sword on their hands and yelled "Fire" and started to attack the gremlins.

By that time the female gremlin had also realized that it was impossible to cut the fire beings. Whatever she tried to chop the fire beings she couldn't.

Those fire beings were not only fire proof but also shred proof. In fact the fire beings which were held by the gremlins were actually enjoying the massage.

The gremlins failed and they surrendered to the fire beings who then fled their house never to come back.

Even though they were fire proof and shred proof but they did not enjoy their freedom to be taken away. So they went to some other place were they could enjoy fire forever without being disturbed or captured ever.

TaLe 65 : tHe mArShMaLLoW cAr

Every boy in his school wants to be praised. To get the praises he needs he has to do something great and admirable. So is the story of this boy who wanted to show that he is the best in his school and wanted to win everybody's heart. He wanted to be praised and admired by everybody. To get this admiration he had his eye on the "Creative cup" of the school. This cup was given to that high school student in his school who made the most creative thing of all in that competition.

The name of the boy in this story who wanted the "Creative cup" from the time he was young was Crealo.

The junior school which he attended also had a high school built in where students who graduated from junior schools went to high school at the same location.

Crealo had got to know about the Creative cup when he was very young. It so happened that he was in school and attending his English class. The teacher who taught that English class was a high school teacher. That day 2 students had come to her class and were talking to the teacher about the Creative cup. They were asking the teacher to suggest her with ideas for the Creative cup. That day Crealo realized the importance of that cup as the teacher had told that whoever wins that cup also get's his photo published in the leading newspaper of that area. This made Crealo excited who wanted to win the Creative cup and get his picture published in the newspaper.

From that day, although he was young he started studying hard and reading a lot of general knowledge books so that one day he can make something that would honour him with the Creative cup. He wanted to get lots of knowledge and ideas so that he can create something new.

After few years he graduated and started going to high school. By that time he had become smart enough and was ready for the

Creative cup. He had made all the preparations to win this cup as he had thought of a unique thing to make.

The creative cup was exactly after 9 months when he had to show his unique creative project. Since he had planned about it from the beginning he started working on it.

He wanted to make a bright colourful car from a single piece of marshmallow without sculpting it through a knife. Now colourful marshmallows were available but they were not bright as a neon colour. He could have painted the marshmallow car with neon colours but he wanted them to be eatable and should have uniformity in exhibiting neon colours through out the marshmallow i.e. both inside and out.

For it he had thought about a plan. He had studied that to produce eatable neon colours he has to get them from wild flowers that grew in a forest near him.

So he started his work. He went to the forest near him and took a paper bags with him. There he started plucking various bright coloured wild flowers that he liked. He put them in his paper bag. After collecting them he went home and took those collected flowers with him.

In his home he had a big mortar and a pestle. He then put all the wild flowers of the same colour in it after separating them from their stems. Then he crushed the flowers that were put in the mortar using pestle until they formed a paste and a liquid started oozing from them. He separated the liquid from the paste and put it in a jar. He did the same for all the wild flowers he had got and separated their bright colour liquids and put them in separate jars.

Now the liquid separated was of wild flowers and so was a bit poisonous. To counteract the poison he added an agent in them that neutralized the poison and made the colours fit for human consumption.

He had already gotten sugar and gelatine from the market to form the marshmallow paste but the tough part was to make a mould in which he will freeze the liquid mixture of marshmallow paste. The mould could be carved so he got a wooden block from market and carved a mould out of it. The mould was such that a car would form if a liquid is cast in it. He made a marshmallow mixture with sugar, water, gelatine and added the bright liquid of colours derived from the wild flowers separately to form different parts of the car with different colours.

Then carefully and artfully he cast the marshmallow liquid into a car. He was very happy when the mixture dried. A beautiful car formed which had a neon orange base colour and three neon coloured stripes on it running from front to back. The car looked magnificent.

Doing that nine months had passed and it was the day of showing his project for the Creative cup. When Crealo showed his car everybody was wonderstruck that how could it be possible? An eatable neon coloured marshmallow car that was 22 inches long, 12 inches wide and 6 inches tall attracted everybody's attention and was a show stealer.

Next day when Crealo woke up first thing that he did was check the newspaper and loo he saw his picture on the front page of that paper holding a huge trophy and his marshmallow car. Yes, of course he had won fame and name because of his creativity.

TaLe 66 : sUgAr sWeEt

Now, is this tale sweet because of it's story or is it sweet because sugar is involved in it? Let's read this tale to find out the truth.

Long time ago there was a peasant who had a small piece of land that was not much fertile. The peasant that owned that land had his name as Grallick. The land was so less fertile that his profits were less than his investments that included seeds, time and labour. Since the land was cheap there, there opened up a candy factory which produced candies of very fine nature. In fact, the candies that they produced in that factory had to meet the standards set by the owner and policies of that factory. They should be of perfect size and shape and only then they were packed to be sold.

These things Grallick came to know when he started working in that factory. At that time he had no choice but to work at the factory as he had to feed himself and live for a better day. When the candy factory was being built there he was actually thrilled to know about it as he knew that candy factory would need workers to make it run.

As he started working in that factory then he came to know that the candies that were not up to the mark were thrown in the garbage and used to go waste. Those candies were not recycled at all. But what could he do at that time about the candies when he came to know.

Page 209

One day as he was working in the candy factory he saw a fresh batch of candies being dumped into the trash to be disposed off. An idea came to his mind. He thought of talking to his immediate supervisor.

He went to his supervisor and asked him if it was possible for them to give the candies they were trashing to him. The supervisor asked Grallick that what would he do with the discarded candies as they would not be allowed to be sold in the market. Grallick said " Don't worry Sir, I would not sell these candies but would utilize them for healing something." His supervisor then talked to his managers. They allowed Grallick to take the discarded candies with him whenever he wanted and as much as he wanted. The managers thought that since Grallick would not sell them it would not hurt company's reputation and not only that it would help them reduce their garbage bills.

From that day Grallick started taking the discarded candies home. Now, what he did was that he started sowing fruit tree seeds in his small uncultivable land and started throwing candies on that land-area uniformly. He then purchased some manure and fed his land with that too. He then waited for rain to happen and also used little bit of ground water to water his would be trees.

By that time he kept on working in the candy factory and kept on bringing discarded candies home. At night he used to throw candies on his land where he had sowed fruit tree seeds and kept on doing that every week.

What used to happen was that as rain fell on the ground it also dissolved the candies and this made seeds absorb the sugary sweet water. To his surprise, in about 2 years time the fruit trees grew and started to bear fruits. He had only thought for a possibility of that as his land was very less fertile but thanks to God and his wise thinking it happened. He did not stop throwing candies on the ground for the trees to absorb its sugar and give it to their fruits. The fruits were then ready to be eaten. He then tried checking them out. He went to one of the fruit tree which was an apple tree and plucked an apple out and tried eating it. When he tasted it he was like what in the heavens has he had! The fruit was as if he was eating sugar itself and the juice of the fruit was all oozing out. He could not believe it and so he went to another apple tree and tried eating it's fruit too and same thing. All fruits in that land were as sweet as sugar and he was so happy that day that he cried thinking that he would not have to worry about his meals anymore and nor about his future.

That day he went and got few men to gather all fruits from trees and told them to sell those fruits at a price 5 times higher than price of regular fruit of that kind. That day he made all his fruits sell out completely because he had guaranteed that his fruits would be sweeter than any of the fruit that people had ever tasted otherwise he would not charge a penny for his fruits. And it was true his fruits including apples were so sweet that the men that were selling his fruit had a huge line up of same customers who were so excited to eat such sweet fruits that they could not stop buying more and more.

At the end of day he earned a lot. He also gave some extra money to the men along with their regular wages who sold his fruit. That day there was no limit to his happiness. He rejoiced that day by giving money to poor people and by also saving a lot for himself.

He never stopped working at the candy factory where he still got lots of candies. Slowly but steadily he started getting more farm land and started growing more fruit trees and feeding them with candies. Slowly he started making so much profit that he bought the entire candy factory where he went to work.

Although he had bought that factory but did not change the company's policy of dumping the candies that did not meet the company's standards. He still used the candies to feed his fruits trees and expanded his business by building more of that candy factories and growing more fruit trees.

TaLe 67 : fAtHeR oF cReAtiON

Have you ever thought that who could be father of creation? If not let me tell you who he is. He is the one that takes care of everybody, which some people might doubt. Why some people would doubt because if He really took care of everybody than people would not be in poverty and people would not die in pain due to cold or heat or any other disease.

Let me tell you something, maybe everybody has heard that He who is God has lots of positiveness and many people say all things good about Him? Is it because he really does good or is it because he is good. God has done so much good but things like poverty are also given. It is true poverty hurts and it brings sorrow. But to tell the truth that although poverty is there but people still live and this is because life is a never ending gift which keeps on unwrapping everyday with other tiny gifts.

How does a person live? There must be something that causes a person to live. Things like stars in the sky and sun and moon which motivates and causes one to rise and live.

Let us tell something about stars. Tiny little kids who see stars are not much sure what they are until they are told about it. Scientists say that stars are massive fire balls that are most of the times bigger than earth itself but why are they so tiny when seen through naked eye. I think they are tiny because kids including adults who see them sometimes are helped by them. Not that they give you light to see but they actually are so small that when measured through scale while viewing they are the size of one's eye and as eye's differ so do their sizes. I think that tells everybody that stars can be touched and are just the size of one's eye.

Now, sometimes people say the sky forms an umbrella. Is it true? Let us find that out. If all the stars that are seen get connected through ribbons of various sizes shapes and colour they might form a spacious umbrella in space and with space(gaps) in it. Would that umbrella be beneficial? Well, yes because it powered our imagination to form.

Now why is the sky blue? Is it because of science or because God wants that way. I think its blue because it means the maker thinks that B - etter L - eave U - mbrella E - ndless.

Now, where is the umbrella's notch that ties all of it together. I think the top notch at night it is moon and in the morning it is the sun. Now sun always helps, no doubt about that but let us understand that is the moon a really helper too? Two things yes and yes. First it gives light during night except sometimes when it hides and sleeps away. The light gives hope and also some power to see. Secondly it says I am stronger than a regular umbrella and also a top notch because it, through aura of its gravitational field has stopped pouring and raining of meteorites on earth many times avoiding destruction of earth. But many don't know about it because the moon is shy so it stays far and therefore no one sees the meteorites marks on it through naked eye. Whatever marks are visible get so well concealed by the moon that they look like eyes, and smile of the moon.

So, rest assured their is a master who is - Father of Creation. He rules and rolls the sky and the stars.

TaLe 68 : wiTcH's cArE!

Well, as everybody knows that witches have lots of magical powers and can do a lot of things with that. One thing they can't do is generate money with magic. That is why most of the witches are not very rich and live very poorly. Now all witch's are not bad some are good too therefore they sometimes help too.

Long time ago there was a village where lived many peaceful people who were happy and content with what they had and what they got. The only problem that village had was that there started attack of some giant monsters that destroyed almost the whole village whenever they came. They used their clubs to destroy houses and small buildings. Sometimes so they used to play games with each other that would destroy the entire village. But this game came at the cost of death and destruction in the village. When the village people asked those giants that why do they came and destroy their houses, they used to say that they liked destructive games and therefore they like having fun this way.

The village people were very upset and they had a meeting one day. The village leaders decided that at all costs they have to stop the destruction of the village because it costs a lot to build back the houses and buildings every time they get destroyed and also they can not accept more deaths in the village.

Then they decided that they will use the help of witches by paying them so that they can stop the monsters and possibly finish them or drive them away.

The witches demanded huge amount of payment for that task and also told the villagers that it was non refundable. The villagers were in so much distress that they agreed to their demands and paid the witches the amount of money they asked for.

The witches then prepared for war. A great battle was fought between the monsters and the witches. In this battle many witches died but a few survived too. Amongst the witches that survived only one was badly injured. This injured witch cried for help from other witches but witches are evil and cruel too so they did not help her. They thought that, the lesser the witches are the less the amount of money they will have to share thus each of them will get more money. So not only did they leave the injured witch in pain but also they broke her magical broomstick which made her more upset and ill.

Now people of the village were seeing that battle and all of them knew that one of the witch was badly injured in the battle and was forsaken by all other witches. Even though some people had pity on her but nobody wanted to take care of that witch.

But their was one little girl whose name was Fin-niay. Fin-niay asked her mom that if she could take that witch to her home, keep her there and take care of her until she gets well. Mom looked at Fin-niay's eyes and could not refuse her request so she agreed to it and let Fin-nay keep the witch.

The witch was heartbroken and unconscious but when she opened her eyes she saw herself lying on a bed and a small girl asking her "are you okay?" The witch at first was a bit shocked to see herself alive but then started feeling happy about it. She still was not completely well but was getting there. Then the witch replied " yes, a little bit." Hearing that and the witch's voice the little girl felt happy. Then she asked the witch " do you want anything?" She said, " only peace". The little girl replied that i don't know if I can give you that or not but I do can give you some care." The witch looked at Fin-niay's face and smiled.

Now in the following days Fin-niay took a lot of care of that witch. The witch started getting better day by day. The little girl in her free time used to draw beautiful sketches and paint them with water colours. Once the witch happened to see her paintings. After seeing that it gave her utmost peace and happiness and therefore she wanted to learn to draw and paint.

Next day when they woke up in the morning the witch requested Fin-niay to teach her to draw and Fin-niay said "okay". She carefully got some paper and pencil and held witch's hand softly in order to teach her to draw. She at first taught her to draw straight lines, then curved lines and woo! The witch started to draw. This healed the witch physically and mentally. The witch no longer needed a magical broomstick to fly. Now, she was flying in her dreams by sketching on sheets of paper. Until the witch got completely recovered she continued to stay in Fin-niay's house and Fin-niay and her mom did not mind that at all.

Years passed and Fin-niay grew up. During that time they started facing some financial difficulties as Fin-niay's mom had grown old and the taxes on the land had increased. Fin-niay's mom worked very little and could get only that much money that put bread on the table. Seeing this Fin-niay wanted to work. She wanted to start her own business with whatever she had saved from her childhood. She could not see her mom and the other household member to suffer because of money.

Since she had just entered adulthood she was a bit confused and did not know what business to start. The witch then told her to start a coffee shop and put one marshmallow in each coffee she served. It took some time to open a small shop but it was done.

Now she wondered that why the witch told her to put one marshmallow in each coffee that she served but since she trusted her so she started adding one marshmallow in each coffee that she served. Now when she put a marshmallow in the first coffee she was surprised to see that as soon as the marshmallow touched the coffee it dissolved to form a beautiful coloured painting unlike she had ever seen before. Even the man who was buying the coffee was shocked to see that but was excited about it. The coffee was for one penny but the buyer of that coffee gave her 10 cents for that. Fin-niay was thrilled to get 10 cents for one cup of coffee. She could not have dreamt that ever. Then she remembered the witch.

She then immediately left her shop and went straight to her house to thank the witch. But when she went she saw that only her broomstick was left and she was gone. On the broomstick was written "Take Care!"

Her coffee shop became famous. People came from far and wide just to see the paintings in the coffee cups. Sometimes they did not even drink those coffees, they just took them like that as souvenirs.

Fin-niay became very rich but never stopped helping those in need.

TaLe 69 : tHe bOnE bReAkEr

Hi! How are you doing folks. I have told many stories about witches, giants, dragons and dwarfs but this story is somewhat unique as it involves none of the above. Actually, this fairy tale is about people known as Baouneiy. So let us begin it!

Baouneiys were a set of species of people who lived on a planet other than Earth. Even the animals that lived on that planet had a property of their lives similar to Baouneiys and what it is I'll tell you later in this story.

Baouneiys lived very peacefully amongst themselves and were also in peace with the animals that were there on their planet. Also most of the animals that lived there were very friendly creatures except for some. Some animals like Fieraouy's were violent animals but they did not attack other animals or Baouneiy's that much.

Now, Baouneiys although were a separate species but they were not much different than humans in terms of developed civilizations. They were just a little behind. Why they were called Baouneiys and what was the trait that they shared with animals was something to do with their bones. They had a unique muscular and bone system. They could have their bones broken and fixed automatically in very short time. No matter what bone they broke it got re-formed in a very short time. The drawback of their bone system was that although broken bones re-formed but the twisted bones did not which they twisted often and this lead to their deaths.

As I told before that Baouneiy civilization was somewhat advanced but they could not develop a cure for twisted bones and save Baouneiy lives. This had continued for a long time.

So years passed and no cure for fixing twisted bones had come to in their worlds. Many researchers were working to get a cure for that but still nothing could be found.

Now let's tell you about a boy named Raoudecliy. Raoudecliy was a Baouneiy boy born in the suburbs of Laouceiy in the same planet. Baouneiy was a very ambitious and loving boy. He went to a small school because his parents were poor and thus could not afford a big and expensive school for their kid. Raoudecliy knew this but it never bothered him because he knew that if he wanted to achieve something big, expensive schools don't matter that much. He knew that whatever he wanted to study was available in the library as books and he spent lots of time finding what he wanted and then studying them.

As Raoudecliy grew up he started knowing that Baouneiys had a big bone problem about the twisted bones. He knew that once a Baouneiy got his bone twisted he had to start counting days of his life. This, he did not like and wanted to do something about.

So he aspired to be a medical doctor. From the time he decided to be a doctor he started working real hard on his studies and scored the maximum possible marks in his subjects in all his grades and thus cleared high school and his medical school this way. He became one of the leading medical doctor.

Even though he was successful in the eyes of others but he knew that he still could not decipher a cure for twisted bones.
Realizing this he started becoming depressed day by day and one day due to depression he took an year long leave and sat in his house doing nothing.

In his house he had an aquarium in which he had a small fish. One day he started observing it very closely. He saw that although the fish wiggled sideways but it's movement led it to move forward and same was true for its fins. This started intriguing him and he kept on looking the fish for hours and hours and noted down something. He looked a bit satisfied. At that time he also thought that this happens in nature a lot. Like a seed is planted on ground but it grows upwards towards the sun and not towards the ground from where it gets all the nutrients from. Only roots are formed in the ground but most of the plant is above the ground. He started thinking about it whole night and day until he thought about something. At that time he was walking back and forth randomly in his house and immediately went to his lab which was in his house itself.

In his labs were some test rats and test animals of which he wanted to break bones of but not for mere fun but because he had realized something after studying the fish movement and plant growths and by going back to his medical books and noting down some points for application of his new theory.

He picked up a mouse and broke one of it's bone and in a short time the bone was re-formed and fixed. He confirmed that the mouse was healthy and thus an experiment could be done on it. He then took the same mouse and twisted one of it's bone and he knew that since mouse was of the same species of animals that were on their planet whose twisted bone could not be corrected so he had to fix that fast. He did not wanted the mouse to die of his hands so he picked up a small hammer and then broke a bone which he thought was connected to that twisted bone indirectly and was responsible for that bone's untwisting. As soon as he did that the bone that was twisted started to untwist and got corrected.

Raoudecliy was thrilled to see this and yelled in excitement! He then did the same for all the bones in that mouse carefully one by one checking their indirect connections and he practised it for a while until he became confident that he could now fix the bones of Baouneiys.

He then took a leave from his leave and started to go to his clinic and attending his patients. He waited for a case of twisted bone. In evening a case came. A small boy had twisted his bone and wanted it to be fixed if possible. Raoudecliy immediately pounced upon that case and asked his parents if he had permission to break some of his bones to untwist his twisted bone. Parents first thought that Raoudecliy was kidding but he said that he could fix their child if he got their permission. That child's parents thought that the doctor was out of his mind and had gone crazy but he begged them and told them to trust him so they agreed.

The child was immediately admitted to the clinic's operating room. Raoudecliy was so excited to perform surgery that he forgot to give anesthesia and started breaking bones right away. The child yelled and screamed but he was too busy in fixing him and did not care about his screams. The child's parents who were standing outside were hearing the screams too and they knew that something's gonna happen. In few hours that doctor came out and said that your boy is fixed. The parents who were shocked at that time asked Raoudecliy that what did he mean by that. He said that what he meant was that their son's life had been saved i.e. he had untwisted their son's twisted bone and he he is free to go home the next day.

The kid's parents did not believe what they were hearing and requested the doctor if they could go and see their son. The doctor said "Yes" but also told them not to disturb the patient as he still was recovering from broken bones.

Parents thanked doctor and went inside to see that it was true that their son looked okay to them as he was not groaning with pain anymore and was on lying on bed relieved.

The doctor became real famous and came to be know as " The Bone Breaker" and his theory came to be known as " The Art of Bone Breaking."

TaLe 70 : ThE LoLLiPoP diStRiBuTeR

This is a tale about a very naughty and mischievous child. The child's name was Fretty. He was found of lollipops but not just any lollipops. He was found of homemade lollipops that his mom made specially for him. His mom did lots of effort to make those lollipops from all basic ingredients

She made homemade candies then melted them and attached them to a stick. Later she froze these melted candies while them being attached to sticks separately and a lollipops got formed. His mom although loved making lollipops for his son but she always did not have enough money to support herself and her boy. She worked very hard all day long as a labourer and earned just a few pennies which she did not mind. She just thanked God and believed that they were pennies from heaven. But she was also were strict and a traditional woman. She never gave her son more than one lollipop a day. She did not ever wanted her son to become hyper or get induced with sugar coma.

Fretty although small was very naughty, as told earlier. He loved his lollipops so much that he could not ever imagine a day of life without lollipops. He always wanted more lollipops to eat everyday but his mom never gave him more. This he could not resist.

One day what he did was that he hid in a cupboard just behind the kitchen so that he can watch his mom make lollipops for him. He actually wanted to learn how to make lollipops and then make unlimited number of them for him to eat and lick whenever he wanted. He waited in the cupboard with a one of it's door open just a little so that he can peek through it properly. He also had a pencil and paper in his hand so that he can write down the ingredients ad steps that his mom did to make lollipops. He kept on seeing and writing down the entire procedure of lollipop making and also remembered it.

Now it was time to put it into practice. The next day his mom as usual woke him up and told him to get ready for school. He obeyed his mom and did as he was told but not completely. He acted as he was getting ready to go to school but he did not go to school that day. He just said "Good Bye! Mom " and hid again in one of his closet in his room. Fretty's mom thought that he had gone and so she hurried for her work.

Fretty then went in the kitchen and started the procedure to make lollipops. He was successful with his first try.

That day he had made about 50 lollipops. He was so thrilled and excited that he ate 15 of them and hid remaining under his bed. He then felt like he was intoxicated with sugar and just jumped and cheered all day watching T.V. And playing games with lollipops in his mouth.

Next day came and he was excited to go to school because he wanted to give his homemade lollipops to his friends who ate all of them too. His friends loved those lollipops too and wanted more.

That day when he went home he was in a shock. His mom had been checking lollipop supplies in the house and she found them missing. Also the pan in which she put the ingredients was found to be sticking with lots of candy when she tried to clean it up. She had realized that she never made that much candy for lollipops so it could only be her son that did it.

So his mom come to know that Frett had been making lollipops and she scolded and grounded him for 2 months. He could only go to school and come back. If required he could go to his friends house to study and that was it. Frett felt very bad when this happened but things had gone out of his hand. He sobbed for a while but he had made other plans by that time.

The next day after school he requested mom if he could go to his friends house for study. His mom agreed and let him go. That evening he took one remaining lollipop to his friend's house and gave it to him. That friend had not tried his homemade lollipop before and when he did he was on his feet wanted more. He said " What is that?" Fretty then told him that that was a lollipop that he made. Then he told him the whole story and his plan.

He told him that his mom would not allow him to make any more lollipops at his home. Then he told his friend that if they start a lollipop business they can get enough money to make more lollipops and eat them as much as they want and as many as they want. He also said that if while distributing it in their neighbourhood his mom catches him he would never see the light of day.

So he told him of his plan. Fretty told him that he would make lollipops at his friend's house and distribute via paper planes to neighbouring kids and get their price in form of money, back through the paper planes. Fretty's friend was excited about that because by this way they could make enough money to get supplies for their lollipops and make them as much as they want and eat as many as they want.

The problem lied in that how could they make paper planes travel far so that more kids can have them and they can get more money for their lollipop supplies.

Fretty devised a plan. He said that they will add a small streamlined hot air balloon to their paper planes and then make the paper planes fly. This will allow them to go further and would be more profound than just pushing paper planes by mere force. Fretty's friend agreed to it. But the deal was that they have to have 50% partnership for gobbling lollipops. Although it was an ill deal but Fretty agreed to it.

Now they started their distribution. First they distributed their homemade lollipops for free and then when kids liked it they started getting money for them, which meant more lollipops for the manufacturers and more sugar induced comas,.!!!^^^$$ $???!!!!!!.

TaLe 71 : tHe pOoR mAn'S giFt

This is a very heartfelt and an exciting story about a poor man who gave such an incredible gift to the ruler of his country that tears rolled of that poor man's eyes and my eyes.

Once there was a beautiful country named Selcko. This country had lots of mountains and lots of valleys where people lived. It's beauty was par excellence and people living there were happy. Although it was a big country but it had very less population. People's nature was as usual.

Now amongst the people of that country there lived some poor people also. Amongst those poor people there was this poor person whose name was Sam. Sam was a very nice person. Although he was poor but was not homeless. He loved helping people with whatever he could.

Every year there was held a festival which occurred on the king's birthday. That day everybody gave a gift to the king out of respect and love for the king and not because of fear from him.

So the festival was only 2 months short and people were eagerly waiting for that day. During that festival on celebration of king's birthday people enjoyed the food, music and wine etc. Children enjoyed the carnival.

Sam also gave present to the king on his birthday every year. To buy the presents every year he worked overtime and saved penny by penny until it accumulated to a good amount enough to buy a gift worthy of consideration. So just like the previous years he started working overtime two months before and started saving money for the present.

The king's birthday came and the festival was ready to be showered. Like others, Sam also got an appointment for the evening to meet with the king to give him his birthday gift. So he got ready in the morning picked up his cash and was on his way to buy the present. That day it so happened that it started pouring cats and dogs and so he had to take shelter. When he was standing in the shelter he saw a homeless guy who was handicapped (without one leg and a arm) and was getting severely wet and was coughing and sneezing badly. He wanted to seek shelter but it was difficult for him to move in such heavy rain as he could slip and fall on the rough ground and get further injured. Immediately without thinking for another second he went to an umbrella shop and bought 2 umbrellas, one for the poor man and one for himself. He then rushed towards the homeless person and sheltered him and himself with those umbrellas. He then held that person's hand and let his body support him and slowly walked him to a nearby restaurant. There Sam made the homeless guy have a warm cup of soup. Then he bought some food for him to eat there and packed some of it with him for that night.

In amidst this he had forgotten that the money he had used to buy umbrellas and food for the homeless guy had to be used to buy a present for the king. He realized this after he left the homeless man in a shelter.

Sam got worried thinking about this but he had to give a gift to the king so he decided to do it. He went to the newspaper stand and bought the comic section of the newspaper with the remaining money. Then he bought three different coloured ribbons (neon orange, neon dark pink and neon purple) each of one metre length. Then in the same shop he also bought a small empty packing box and was out of money at that moment. He then wrapped the small empty box with the comic part of newspaper and glued it artfully and wonderfully. Then he wrapped it with the three different coloured ribbons that he had bought elegantly.

By that time it was evening and was time to meet the king and present the present to him. He stood in the waiting line to meet the king. When he was called for his meeting to present the gift to the king, he was a bit shy but he took the newspaper wrapped present and went to present it to the king. People who were seeing his present were confused and a bit amused but Sam did not worry about that.

Before giving the present to the king he told him "Your Highness there is nothing in this wrapped box only the art exhibited by ribbons on the newspaper and the present is itself is empty." The king then looked at the present and took it. Then he said " Sam the present maybe empty but your heart is not and I appreciate it, secondly it is the most beautiful wrapped gift that I have ever seen." Then the king took his crown and placed it on the stool besides his throne and kept the small present inside the crown and said that gifts from heart matter and that's all that it is and matters. Saying that he wrote Sam's name in his diary of contacts of friends and thanked him. Then Sam said good bye to the king and so did the king.

Sam was happy that his present was presented well and became a real present. He was also happy that his present was worthy enough for the heart of the king.

tALe 72 : tHe tOrTuRoUs pAtH mAdE eAsY

If the path was so torturous why was it something that had to be taken? Why couldn't it be avoided? Let me tell you why. Sometime's nature gives you life and sometimes it tries to take it away too, by infecting you with disease or illness. Those diseases or illness are very painful but one tries to fight them and survive. Who helps one when very strong illness affects a person especially when one is just a kid? It's parents who are the angels, the guardians and the one's who help their kids through bad times and illness.

So let us begin the tale....

Have you ever heard about chicken pox? If you have not let me tell you that it is something that does not happen to chickens but to kids or older people as well. It is a very uncomfortable disease in which a person suffers from fever and small or big rashes or dots coming from body at the same time. Mostly people recover very quickly but this kid who got chicken pox took 2 months to recover. What happened in the process of recovery?

This boy's name was Riltomanit. Riltomanit was a loving kid and always cared about others. His parents were also very loving and caring and could not see their son upset because of any reason whatsoever.

One day Riltomanit was coming from school and he felt a bit more tired than usual and did not feel quite well. So in the evening his parents took him to see their family doctor. He sat outside in the waiting room with his parents until he was called for to see the doctor. When the doctor checked Riltomanit he told his parents that the kid had chicken pox and there was nothing he could do. He also told his parents that they would have to make him remain strong until he gets cured from chicken pox. He also told his parents that there was no cure for this diseases only the good news was that since once he has got this illness and gets cured from it he will have immunity developed against this disease for future infection.

His parents were worried and a little sad and so was Riltomanit. But parents and the family doctor told him to remain strong and face it like a brave boy. Riltomanit and his parents thanked the doctor and went back to their home.

Since Riltomanit could not do go to school anymore for some time, he stayed at home. His parents also took off from work. Now, his parents decided to take care of their son and help him pass the torturous path happily and peacefully. They then decided to do something beautiful for their kid.

Next morning they went to a store and bought lots of bubble making soap solution. They then also bought a bubble making machine. It was evening by that time and when they came home they filled the automatic bubble machine with the bought soap solution and started it. The whole house started getting filled with bubbles and Riltomanit who was sitting on his bed started seeing the bubbles come in his room and got super excited. He started playing with the bubbles and felt very calm and happy. He then shouted in excitement and said " wow, what is all that?" He was happy to poke bubbles and see them burst or go away. For that moment he had forgotten all his pain and was feeling very happy. His parents were also happy to see him thrilled and excited.

Next day they did something different. They got a pool for him. As soon as Riltomanit saw the pool he jumped in it splashed the water all around. He played in it the whole day and passed his time jumping and swimming in it.

As his chicken pox grew more severe he started feeling more and more pain and had difficulty walking and sleeping. Then his parents thought of something else that would help their son.

The got a shoemaker and asked the shoemaker to make shoes with holes in them exactly at the points where their kid had developed rashes. The shoemaker did as he was told. He checked the feet of Riltomanit and folded a piece of paper. Then he marked the points of holes on Riltomanit's feet on the folded sheet of paper and went away. Next day he brought a pair of shoes and flip flops which would fit Riltomanit's feet and would make him comfortable. When Riltomanit wore those shoes and flip flops they fitted perfectly over his rashes and did not hurt him while wearing them. Then he thanked his parents a lot.

He was then able to walk around and get a relief from pain. But his parents did not stop at that they kept on giving him beautiful toys and gifts and he kept on playing with them until he got cured.

So his torturous path towards life was made easy by the help of his parents. He still remembers those days and asks himself were those days, days of suffering or of surfing? Were those days happy or were those days sad?

Sometimes life is not easy, it is made easy.

tALe 73 : tHe nEvEr eNdiNg dReAm Of A FaiRy

So do fairies dream? Yes they do and they dream a lot but not during daytime. Because during daytime if they dream of something they get it and the things they had dreamt of and gotten are not right or something that they don't want they just make it disappear or go away.

Today let me tell you a never ending dream of a little fairy who freaked out from her dream until she was made to get up from her own scream.

This little fairy had her juice and then she had a small kiss from her mom and slept and this is where she entered into a world of never ending dream.

She dreamt that she lived on the moon with her parents and enjoyed that place except for one thing. She used to see the Earth from there and always dreamt of going there. She always thought going to the Earth would be exciting and always wanted to see that place. Since she was very far away and could not see what humans did she thought that all humans would be very nice creatures as they lived together on the same planet and the planet never blew up. So she thought that it was safe to say that the humans were peaceful creatures. She also had seen the blue and green colours on earth from the moon and had thought that how lovely it would be to touch blue and green colours if she ever got a chance to go there. She had tried producing those colours on the moon but only shades of orange could be produced (which many people see sometimes) there and no other colour. Maybe she then used to think that it might be because moon cannot handle those colours and thus its magic to produce those colours on moon remained ineffective.

One day she was sitting and gazing at Earth when a tiny little creature sitting on her left shoulder that looked like very evil appeared and told her that let's go to Earth and see what it is like there. But she knew that no matter how much she wanted to see that place it could be risky and dangerous to go there. So did the thing that looked like an angel who was on its right shoulder told her. After much listening and debating she thought what's the worst that could happen. She said to herself " I have magic and if I get into any trouble I would be able to get rid of any trouble whatsoever through my magic." Then she decided to leave. She went to her dwelling that was rock formed house and packed some clothes. When she was done packing her clothes she said " small you go" and the clothes turned small. She then picked up the clothes and put them in her pocket and left for Earth.

As soon as she jumped from moon to reach Earth she started to fall and kept on falling and she got scared but that was nothing. She kept on falling and getting scared and after sometime she entered the realm of hell. She did not know where she was so she asked a Hell associate. The Hell associate told that she was in hell now and also told her that if she had plans to get out of there it would take some time as the associate who departs one from Hell is having a baby so he is busy. The fairy freaked out. For few days she had to live in Hell but she could not do anything about it so she went into a room and sat down. There she put on the TV and saw nothing but "how bad people are tortured", " how to torture yourself", " what is the best way to torture". The fairy was nothing but freaking out and could not see all that. There were no cartoons or funny shows on the TV. She shut the TV off and tried to sleep but she could not as she heard screams and shouts from outside where people were being thrown in fire and roasted or whipped with a fiery whip. She just sat on her bed trembling and shaking and waiting for the day when she leaves.

After some time the day finally arrived and the Hell associate let her go.

After she jumped from hell she entered the realm of a devil. She did not know what to do know. Her magic did not work on the devil. The devil made her do all sorts of things that she did not like. She was made to sharpen devil's nails so that they are pointed enough for his prestige. After she used to finish sharpening devil nails she was made to go to the forest and get only those grapes and apples that had worms in it because the devil liked to eat those fruits cooked with the worms inside them or just coming out of them with lots of salt added, that would be enough to make a person suffer from high blood pressure and die at once.

She used to ask the devil that " when thou shall leave me?" The devil used to lie to her by saying " sooner than thou think. "

Fairy kept on working for the devil night and day and she did not see any sign of the devil letting her go. She thought that she was screwed. That night when she was cleaning the devil's house the angel and the evil creature appeared again and both of them told her that she should slay the devil for good but she did not know how? So they both told her to put a sharp pointy object in both his eyes together and make him suffer and then he might let her go.

She did as she was told. She went where the devil was sleeping and picked up two needles and inserted them straight into the eyes of the devil. The devil screamed in pain and then let her go.

After she jumped from devils realm she was about to say " No more" but then she entered the realms of the ghosts. There she saw ghosts passing through her and other things around her. She could not take it anymore and screamed in pain. Suddenly she started to feel cold and woke up. She saw that her parents were lying besides her and did not look worried at all. Then she realized that it was nothing but a nightmare and she never knew that fairies had nightmares too. So from that night she slept on her mom's lap until she grew up and was ready to face the nightmares on her own.

So those of you who did not ever had a nightmare let me tell you that nightmares do exist and scare a lot!

tALe 74 : cAnDy tHiEf

So have you ever heard about a thief that stole candy? I guess not. All kids are found of sugar filled sweet candies but all kids are taught never to steal or to rob anybody of anything. The story I am going to tell you is about a kid who although had enough money to buy a whole store of candies but he did not stop stealing them. He liked candies very much and could not see them with anybody and just stole them away from that person. This is not a good thing to do but it happened. To know more about it let's begin with the story.

There was a place called Minty which had lots of small mountains and had a vey rich person who lived there and ran the place like a king. The person's name was Higlocks. Higlocks was a very nice person. He had decided not to marry because of his own personnel reasons and neither did he have any girlfriend ever. But he was fond of kids and wanted a kid. So one day he decided to adopt one. He choose a kid from a foster home in his town who was an orphan and started taking care of him after adoption.

When he brought the kid home he was only 3 years old. He kept nurses and a nanny to start taking care of that kid. The kid's name was Ellnox. Ellnox was taken care of very carefully and lovingly by his nurses, his nanny and by Higlocks himself.

As Ellnox grew he started to go to school. In the school he made some friends. While going to school he developed a very bad habit of stealing candies. Stealing candies gave him a thrill that he could not withstand. He used to steal his friend's candies, his classmates'

candies and also one of the teacher's favourite chocolate. This happened everyday without a break.

One day Higlocks came to know about this. Higlocks became very furious when he heard that Ellnox stole candies. He called his son Ellnox the same evening and asked him that why does he steal? He also told him that his dad has all the money in the world and could buy him whatever candy he liked and wanted so why did he stole? Ellnox then told him that he liked candies so much that he was very possessive about them and could not see them in anybody's hand, therefore he steals them from whomsoever he find's having them. Higlocks did not know what to say and told him nothing at that time.

As time passed Ellnox did not stop stealing the candies or eating them. This made him gain lots of fat and he became obese. Higlocks kept on observing that and decided to do something about it because he thought that if Ellnox had gained so much weight at this young age it would be difficult for him to survive as he grows up. So he made a plan.

Next day he went to the wholesale store of candies and told them that from now on whatever candy they got from the factories he will buy all of them until his son becomes fit to eat them again. He had something unique in his mind to help his son get rid of stealing candies and become fit.

As I had told earlier that the place where Higlocks and Ellnox lived had lots of small mountains and this had made Higlocks work upon a trick. As soon as candies coming in from the wholesale shop of candies to Higlocks place he ordered them to be put in huge helicopters . Then he told the helicopter pilots to fly them to the mountain tops and keep them there separated by their classes. For example he told that lollipops should be kept on a separate mountain and chocolates should be kept on a separate mountain. His helicopter pilots did as they were told. Things were about to get changed now.

That day when Ellnox went to school he did not see anybody having any candy of any sort. He found that strange but later he came to know that his father had bought all the candies and there was none left in the stores. Ellnox did not know what to do then. He was half excited and half worried. In the evening he went to see his dad. During the meeting his dad then told him the truth. He told him that he had ordered his helicopter pilots to keep the candies on the mountain tops which he sees from their house. He also told him that he does not know which candy is on which mountain and he has to find that himself if he wants to eat candy. He told him that to get candies he has to climb the mountains himself and no help of any kind would be provided to him. If he loves and wants to eat candies, this was the job he had to do.

Since Ellnox had turned obese he had no strength to climb the mountains to eat candies. Two days passed and Ellnox could not resist being without candies so he decided to climb the mountains to get candies. Next morning he woke up early and geared up to trek. The mountain he decided to climb that day was the smallest of all mountains that were visible from his house and was about 1000 metre in height. That mountain had lots of stones laid on the track on the way to the top. He slowly trekked and at the end of the day and finally reached the summit. He was happy that he reached the top of that mountain and that he could eat some candies now.

This continued for many days until Ellnox discovered all the candies and became fit and healthy. He also became mind healthy and realized that he has to resist his candy stealing tendencies because that is not a good thing to do. Whatever candy he wants he can get them from summit of the mountains or stores when/if they get them.

After he became a nice boy his dad stopped sending candies to the summit of mountains and let the candies be distributed to the stores and then be bought by whomsoever liked them.

Thus Ellnox's dad not only made his son fit physically but he also made him mentally sound.

TaLe 75 : tHe MAgiCAL tEAcHeR

Once on a planet lived magicians and non-magicians together. There appearance was no different from humans only their skill made them different. Non-magicians did not like the magicians because they never shared the knowledge of magic and kept it among themselves. They shared it only amongst their kind. Secondly those magicians did all the fun by doing different kind of tricks on things and sometimes on non-magicians too. The non-magicians did not like that because it looked somewhat illegal and intimidating for the non-magicians with magicians around doing all sort of tricks which sometimes got uncontrollable.

One day the heads of magicians and non-magicians had a meeting. The non-magicians told the magicians very politely and calmly that staying together is not working out altogether. They told the magicians that their magical powers sometimes got very intimidating to them and therefore some non-magicians lived in a lot of fear from them. Then the non-magicians also told them that is not right and it should be stopped because life is given once and if a person spends his life in fear from anything then his life is a waste.

Therefore the non-magicians and the magicians decided to separate. Half of the planet was given to the magicians and half was given to the non-magicians. The magicians were then forbidden to enter the the other half of planet where the non-magicians lived for everybody's safety and peaceful life. Also they were forbidden to use magic in the non-magician's share of the planet. This continued for a long time.

In the land of magicians there was one very peaceful and a nice magician who did not like his own kind because he thought that they were mean and selfish and thus did not wanted to stay with them. He used to think that what he could do about that. One day he decided that he will leave the magicians' land and go to the land of non-magicians and live there by disguising himself as a teacher.

Then he left his land and entered the land of non magicians and started looking for a teaching job. In a few weeks he found of teaching job. The job involved teaching grade 1 students. He was happy to get that job and thus he started teaching there happily. He loved the non-magical kids and taught them lovingly and with care. He even spent hours after school to teach students something they were interested in knowing that was beyond the curriculum of that class. Not only that he used to treat children everyday with lots of cakes and candies. The extra sugar that he sensed in the body of kids he just made it disappear magically so that no harm ever touches the kids.

Although he was a careful teacher but he could not stop some of his students get bullied by grade 5 students. When he used to talk to the teacher of that grade 5 class, their teacher used to laugh about it and boast about the kids that bullied saying that it was their right to bully and his kids to get bullied at. The magician who was disguised as teacher did not like all that but he did not argue with the grade 5 teacher.

One day as the grade 1 teacher was walking in the lobby of the school to reach his classroom he saw that the same grade 5 students started bullying a kid from his class. They took the spectacles of that student out form his eye and started playing with it and teasing the boy. While playing the child whose glasses were taken away could not see anything properly and was in a very sad spot. The grade 5 students after torturing that student finally broke his glasses and went away. The teacher seeing all that cold not hold himself anymore and he decided to avenge his students bullying, mockery and teasing.

That afternoon he went to that teacher of grade 5 and challenged him to a quiz on literature. He told the teacher that if he thinks he is a smart guy and has taught his students well they should be able to win the literature quiz against his grade 1 students. That teacher laughed at the grade 1 teacher and said " Of course!" He then asked that when does he plan to have the quiz and where does he want it to happen? The disguised teacher said that this quiz will happen in front of the principal of the school and the whole school would see it. The grade 5 teacher agreed to it.

The quiz was on a novel. In that quiz anybody from each side will ask questions about any instance of the novel or the complete novel itself and whichever side answers most questions wins. They were given 2 weeks to prepare and both of the teachers agreed on it.

Grade 1 students of his class when heard that were scared because they thought that would loose the quiz and would be more than ever bullied by grade 5 students after that. The disguised magician who was their teacher consoled them and told them not to worry at all. Grade 1 students of his class were very polite and nice kids. They simply obeyed their teacher and did not worry at all.

Now from that day the disguised magician started teaching his students about the novel. But this time his teaching style was quite different. He used to close the classroom's door and cast a spell on the students so that they do nothing but concentrate. Then he used to start writing the novel on the white board, line by line until the space on the board finished and then something unique used to happen. Whatever he wrote for example if he wrote "During nightfall and day the boy worked." He wrote all that in cursive writing. The writing he wrote came to life and the connecting ink that formed the words of the sentence used to come in 3D space in air and form images from that ink like a running rope. This happened all day for about 2 weeks until the kids of his class had learnt the novel by heart and were ready for the competition.

The other teacher just told his grade 5 students to read the novel themselves and ask if they had any questions from the novel or any doubts they want to clear so that they can win the quiz one to nothing. He was very overconfident that his grade 5 students would win easily over those grade 1 students and with flying colours.

The day of the competition came and grade 1 students sat on the right side and grade 5 students sat on the left side of the stage and the competition started.

That competition was a nightmare for grade 5 students who scored so little that everybody doubted that if they were actually fit for grade 5. All the students and the principal applauded at those little grade 1 students who won. The principal congratulated them on having such a great teacher who never gave away his secret.

After that day no grade 5 student ever dared to bully grade 1 students. In fact they were a little scared of grade 1 students and their teacher and sometimes respected them too.

TaLe 76 : yEnNi AnD mEnNi

Once on Earth lived humans, animals and witches. Although they lived on the same planet they did not live together. Humans and animals lived on a separate part of the planet and witches lived on a separate part of the planet. Humans and animals had formed a country together which was called Danmerkiy. Witch's lived in a country called Sleeping Deathmare.

Sleeping Deathmare was a very dangerous place. No human or animal dared to go there ever. Even for witches it was a very dangerous place. Different witches that lived there had different levels of evil magical powers. Some were more magically more strong, some were less. They lived, learned and practiced magic there. Most of the times they were peaceful but sometimes they got really angry at each other and tried to kill each other. The most powerful witch amongst them was known as Voodoodoll. She was not only powerful but was also the oldest of all the witches. Nobody ever tried to mess with her because they were afraid her immense evil magical powers. Even the witches that lived there lived in fear from her and that they did not like at all.

One day all the witches except voodoo doll had a meeting together. They talked to each other and discussed about the danger in their lives which was nothing other than Voodoodoll. They said to each other that although they don't ever say any bad thing to the Voodoodoll and do not ever disturb her but what if somebody mistakingly disturbs her or troubles her then what's going to happen? "She will not spare anybody" one of them said. First she will kill the witch that disturbed her and then she will destroy all other witches for having failed to stop the witch that disturbed her or troubled her. So that day they decided that Voodoodoll would have to leave Sleeping Deathmare and find another place to live. During that day in the evening all the witches wrote a letter of request to Voodoodoll and signed it stating that she had to leave Sleeping Deathmare forever and that all stood by that decision. When Voodoodoll received that written request in form of letters from all she became helpless and decided to leave Sleeping Deathmare.

She decided that she will go to Danmerkiy. Without any hesitation she sat on the broomstick and said "fly Voodoodoll stick" and the stick flew. Then she landed at Danmerkiy. There she openly declared that she was the most dangerous of all the witches and plans to stay with humans and animals. She then made her intensions more clear by saying that she needed house in Danmerkiy to stay. When humans and animals heard that they got extremely intimidated and said "no" to her. Not only that they also threatened her with knives and fire to leave that place forever or she will face consequences. When Voodoodoll heard that all this she was extremely enraged and cursed them by saying that " Even though you may live but will live worse than death." She then flew away.

People when heard that did not know what she meant and did not bother much about it. They continued to live their life thinking that the witch left for good.

Now two animal kids had heard all that the witch had said and took it very seriously. They told everybody to be careful about it but the people did not pay much attention to the curse.

The name of these two animals kids were Yenni and Menni. Yenni was the son of parrot and Menni was the son of a pig. They were very good friends and trusted each other very much. Now they talked to each other and asked each other that what should they do? Yenni told Menni that this curse could be a fake because nothing happened until then. But Menni said that witch's don't joke around and that they are very dangerous to do both humans and animals. Then Yenni agreed to it. Now Menni asked Yenni that what did the witch mean by the curse. Yanni said "I don't know and we can't find out until something bad happens" so that evening they went back to their homes and slept.

When they woke up the next day and went to school they felt something weird happening. All the teachers were behaving as they were heartless creatures and were only doing the work and did not exhibit any emotions, feelings or compassion for the students. They behaved as if they had no heart and witch(which) was true.

Their hearts were taken away by the witch. She came that night, stole the hearts of all the teachers and then put them in a sack and went away. This happened every night until only the kids hearts were left to be stolen and this was going to happen that night. The kids got afraid when the Yenni and Menni told them about this. They told them that they should help them destroy the witch but all the kids were afraid to do that and thus did not help them.

That evening before nightfall, before the witch came, Yenni and Menni packed their bags and decided to go, destroy the witch and save people's hearts and people themselves. When they left Yenni took Menni to the opposite direction of witch's dwelling. Menni got a bit confused and asked Yenni that why were they going in the wrong direction? Yenni then told Menni that it was impossible for them to destroy the witch themselves so they have to seek the help of God of thunder and lightning and so they went to see him. Menni then followed Yenni to the god's temple. When they reached the temple they prayed and asked God of lightning and thunder to help them save their people. Suddenly there appeared a huge Giant standing in front of them who was thundering while talking. He was no other than the God of lightning and thunder himself. When he saw the kids standing there he asked them that what did they wanted? The kids told him the entire story. They then requested him that he has to save their parents and people.

The God of lightning and thunder sat down and told them that since there is magic involved in it he can't do much because he has to take care of the union of evil magicians and witches. But Yenni and Menni did not listen to him and kept on begging for mercy. Then after much thinking the God of lightning and thunder said that he could not help them but since they appear nice he can surely give gifts to them that further can help them in their quest. Yenni and Menni were happy to to hear that and said "Thanks" to God of lightning and thunder.

He gave them three gifts.

One was a small lightning bolt to break the lock of the cage where the witch had kept the hearts.

Second was a huge lightning bolt. That was to be used to destroy the witch and the place where she kept her magic potions.

Third one was a unique gift. It involved set of wheels which got attached to their shoes magically. He then blessed them and told them that this would help him reach the witch's dwelling quickly. Yenni and Menni thanked the God of lightning and thunder. They were about to leave when the god told them that when they use the bigger lightning bolt to destroy the witch's dwelling , they have to implant it in the ground and run away from there as fast as they could because it would explode in a few seconds and if they were near to it they would get hurt.

The wheels attached to the shoes helped them reach the witch's dwelling early. When they reached the place it was night and she was about to leave to steal the hearts of all the kids. She sat on her on her broomstick and said "Fly the Voododoll stick" and the broomstick started to fly but as she was about to leave she remembered something. She had forgotten to lock the cage where she had kept all the stolen hearts. She then locked the cage, made the key magically disappear and then flew to steal the hearts of the kids.

Yenni and Menni could have broken the lock with their mini thunderbolt and could have gone away with those hearts. They could have not worried about the kids who were sacred and failed to help them but they did not. They waited that night till the witch got all the hearts. When she came she put all the stolen hearts of the kids in the cage, locked it and made the key disappear. She then lay on the grass between the trees and went to sleep. Soon she was fast asleep. Yenni and Menni wasted no time. They implanted the mini thunderbolt in the cage's lock where the hearts were and in a few seconds it burst the cage open. The witch was so fast asleep that she did not hear the sound. Then they put the hearts in a sack and tied it to the witch's broomstick. After doing that they implanted the big thunderbolt in the ground where the witch was sleeping. Then they sat on the broomstick and said " Fly Voodoodoll's stick" and loo the broom stick flew faster than it had ever flown before. In a few seconds the thunderbolt exploded. It killed the witch and also destroyed all her magic potions.

By that time Yenni and Menni were far away from the explosion. They saved themselves and all the hearts.

Later they just unloaded the sack full of hearts over Danmerkiy and all the hearts went to their owners. Life was back on track for everybody. Nobody, except Yenni and Menni ever knew what had happened.

TaLe 77: tHe PiLLoW FiGhT cLuB

Once there lived a very evil witch called Ewiny. Ewiny was so evil that she could not find a servant for her huge house. Whatever servant she hired ran away after seeing how evil she was. This evil witch had a dragon name Festrox. It was her pet dragon and she loved her dragon very much. Both wanted something that was very difficult to get. Dragon wanted young human meat to feed upon and the witch wanted servants.

Day by day it was getting difficult for them to survive not only because they could not get what they required and wanted but also because people were becoming more and more aware of evil power of witches and thus they were trying to get rid of them with all means. Everyday Ewiny and Festrox were hearing stories about people burning witches and destroying there witchcraft. This made them more scared and they started becoming helpless every day until one day. On one occasion the witch became very angry and decided to do something about it. She at that moment thought that most of the young ones that were of appropriate height and age and had lots of flesh in them to the universities to study. She then made a plan and said that it is only universities where I can hunt for my servants and also get meat for Festrox and therefore decided to go there. She then disguised herself as a teenage girl fit to go to university and took admission in one of the biggest university of that town.

Their she started going and attending the classes and also started checking out the girls. She looked for girls that were healthy and could be used for both her and her dragon. She started making friends. Then she started inviting those friends which were all girls and were fit for her cause to her house . But those girls somehow sensed an evil aura around Ewiny and did not go to see her in her house. Thus she was avoided. But the witch was cunning and evil and did not fail to realize that. Whomsoever she called, that girl never showed up. This made her mad and she decided to do something really severe about it. She thought for a while and made a plan on what could be done.

To nab the girls Ewiny did something very wicked. She started a pillow fight club which was meant for girls only. It was a paid club and thus all the girls that wanted a pillow fight had to pay for it and get a band tied to her wrist. The club used to be in the evenings after university lessons. Whichever girl wanted to play pillow fighting came to that club. The band on the girls wrists indicated that she had paid for the ticket and can enter the club's room where they played pillow fight.

The witch was cunning and evil. After opening the club she started inviting those girls that previously had refused to come to her house to see her in that club and have some pillow fight. Most of the girls came to the club for pillow fight. The girls thought that what harm could it do.

The evil witch then started working on her evil plan. She used to choose one band and cast a spell of entrapment on the band after dipping them in special magical potions made specially for that purpose. Whichever girl wore that band got trapped in the evil magic of the witch and followed her instructions without hesitations. She started doing this and bringing the girls to her house enchanted with the spell everyday. When she used to bring the girls to he house the dragon magically devoured them and spit the soul out. The souls of the girls that were released still had the bands of entrapment attached to their arms. The witch then used the souls of those girls as her servants and made them do all the work. This continued but not for very long.

The news of disappearance of girls from that university reached the king. The king then immediately sent his men to check out what was going on. His men started to track the last location of the missing girls. They then came to know that the last location of the missing the girls was the the pillow fight club in the university. After much inquiring they came to know that the pillow fight club was run by a girl named Ewiny. They sensed something fishy about that girl and started to observe and track her secretly.

What they saw one day was something very shocking to them. They saw that a girl wore a bracelet given to her by Ewiny and immediately started doing as she was commanded by the witch. She immediately started obeying her as if she had become a servant of Ewiny at an instant. They then followed Ewiny and the entrapped girl. They saw that Ewiny took the girl to her house. There mistakingly the Ewiny left the door of the house open. The king's men who were following her looked though the open door while still hiding and saw the evil witch's work. They saw how the dragon ate the girl and spit out her soul leaving the soul of that girl helpless and fully entrapped by Ewiny.

This shocked them and they reported this to the king. When the king heard about it he really got angry. He knew that it was difficult to fight a witch so he choose five of his best knights and told them to destroy the dragon and kill the witch by all means. Those five knights took a huge army of men and marched towards Ewiny's house. They then surrounded the house and told the witch to surrender but the witch was not going to surrender that easily. The witch ordered her dragon to attack the knights and destroy them and their army. She also told to get rid of them for once and for all.

The dragon came out and started breathing fire. It killed all the army men and four of the knights. Only one knight managed to survive the dragon's attack. He fought with the dragon using his sword but the dragons scales were steel-like and the dragon did not seem to get hurt from the blow of that knight's sword. At that time the knight was exhausted and did not know what to do or how to kill the dragon therefore he stood bravely yelling and cursing the dragon after he realized that dragon could not be killed. When the dragon tried to eat that knight the knight immediately saw that dragon's inside was flesh and that it could be harmed. He then pierced the dragon's inner neck with his sword and not only that he also jabbed the heart of that dragon before coming out from the dragon's mouth and thereby killing it completely.

After he had done that, occurred a huge flash of lightning and the dragon disappeared casing the souls of the entrapped girls to form flesh. The witch then tried to run away but at that time the neighbouring people who had come to know that a witch was living there had surrounded her. They came there holding sticks in one of their hands and torches in other. The witch after seeing all that got scared and surrendered. The witch was then ordered to release the girls from her curse and enchantment. The witch out of fear did as she was told and the girls got free from the enchantment.

The witch was then thrown in a never ending well. Sometimes screams are heard from that well and people say the witch is being damned by a more evil and sinister evil than her.

The girls were then returned to their parents. Their family thanked the knight, people and the king for their heroic efforts . They then also prayed to god to help them keep away from such kind of evil.

Everybody lived happily thereafter and ever after.

TaLe 78 : OnCe A BiLLiOnAirE, fOrEvEr A BiLLiOnAirE

Once there lived a man who had lots of assets. It included, having lots of expensive properties under his name and having tremendous amount of money in his bank account. This man whose name was Ralph was a very big business tycoon and was also a billionaire. Ralph was not only rich but he was also very fair in his dealings. He dealt very honestly be it personally or officially and was a true businessman. He was known for his fairness in doing business with people. The only thing he did not have was a wife. He had been busy doing business and making money for so long and that he never got time to date. After years of hard work Ralph had accumulated much wealth and was ready to date, get married and keep that girl which would be her wife happy for rest of her life. He therefore started looking for a girl to date.

He went on many dates but did not find any girl nice enough to continue his relationship with. This made many girls who he dated him, angry. One of the girl got so mad that he she hired a witch to do something about Ralph.

The witch's name was Exan. She could have done anything to him but she wanted to meet him first and then decide what can be done to him, accordingly. She had to destroy him without killing him completely as that was what was requested by the girl who hired her. So she tried meeting him.

She turned herself into a beautiful girl and met Ralph. When Ralph saw that girl he got really attracted towards her and started thinking about her. He then asked her out for a date. This was what Exan wanted so she agreed to it and they went out on a date to a candy shop.

That candy shop was one of the favourite store of Ralph. Ralph although was in his 40's but he still liked candies very much. This might had been the reason that he could not find a girl to marry. The witch who hated candies got real angry at him so when they came out of the candy shop and when nobody was looking towards them he cursed Ralph by saying " Be a rat, you candy eater. Stay like that forever until you get something that I have. If you can't find that in your lifetime you will age like humans but die like a rat." Ralph then immediately turned into a rat. Exan then took out some magical powder from her sack which was tied to her waist with a cord and sprinkled it over her body. This made her disappear.

Ralph who was now a rat had gotten really scared with his new body shape and the curse that was upon him. He did not know what to do. Feeling scared he tried hiding in a hole in one of the walls nearby but the hole was very dirty and Ralph felt disgusted to stay there. Since he had been a very rich man he had always lived a life of royalty so it was difficult for him to live or stay at a dirty place like that. At that time it had also started to rain so he had to find shelter somewhere quickly.

He then remembered a store which used to sell toys, books and candies and was a good hiding place. This store was meant specially for the kids but the book section in that store had some books for the grown-up people too which was perfect for him and therefore he decided to go there. He then jumped and pounced on the ground and ran on the side-walk hurriedly to reach that store.

It took him a while to reach that store. When he finally reached that store it was very late in the night at the store was closed. This made him feel sad and he got more and more afraid but then something in him said " you are a rat and rats can enter whichever place they want." This made him feel positive about himself which made him look for a way in. While searching for a way he found a drainage pipe going towards the top of the store's building. He then reached to the top of the store crawling through that pipe. When he reached the top of the store he found lots of ducts going from the air conditioner to the inside of the store. He then entered the air conditioner from a small opening and through that entered the ducts and finally reached the inside of the store.

When he reached inside there was very less light but since rats can manage to navigate without light he tried to go to a shelf which he remembered from his human form. When he reached that shelf he was too tired so he slept.

Next night after the store had closed he wanted to read the books of magic so that it can be helpful to him because he knew that was the only thing that could help him now. So that night he went to a shelf that had a small flash light kept on it. He took that flash light turned it on and hung it around his neck.

From that night he started going to the book shelves to find books of magic and started reading and learning magic there. Not only that, he also used to go to the toy area and turned "ON" some of the toy rides there. He used to enjoy being there by riding on toy merry-go-rounds, toy trains and toy roller coasters. At the end when he used to get exhausted he used to fill up his tummy with chocolates and lollipops available in that area of the store and used to dispose off the wrappers in the garbage cans so that nobody comes to know about it. Also before leaving the toy and candy areas he turned the toy rides off to maintain secrecy of his presence there. He almost started enjoying his life there.

One day after going through many magic spells he learnt a spell that could help him see during night and not just only navigate. He wasted no time and casted that spell upon him. Now, he had the capability to see at night. But there was still a problem. Although he could read books during night he had to throw them on the floor from the shelves so that he can open them and read them. Since the books were too heavy and he had no help, he could not pick them up and keep them back on the respective shelves so he left them there on the floor itself . This made the people who worked there during the day get suspicious. They thought that there could be some kind of infestation in the store so they reported this to the store owner. Ralph got aware of this and was worried about this but he did not loose hope.

One night he was learning magic and stumbled upon a spell. He got some toothpicks and bundled them with a cord. Then he attached some bird feathers to the blunt side of the toothpicks and said " Flappajack, Flappajack be strong. Let the feather make the toothpicks fly along, when I like and where I want."

That contraption immediately turned into a flying broomstick. Ralph made it so strong by his spell that it could carry 1000 times it's own weight. This made Ralph's life easy. He then not only continued with the reading of the magical books but this time he could also keep the magic books back to their respective shelves by tying the books to his broom stick and then towing them back to their places and thus it did not look as if the store was infested.

One night something happened. Ralph somehow triggered a mechanical alarm. This made the store owner come to the store and investigate. When the store owner came, he was surprised to see a rat reading books and then towing them with his flying broomstick back to their respective shelves. Ralph was so busy in reading and towing books that he did not see the store owner watching him. While the store owner was seeing all this he struck upon an idea. He immediately said " Hello there" and Ralph heard that. Ralph got scared and tried to fly away but the store owner calmed him down and said "I am not here to harm you in-fact I have a proposition for you." Ralph then sitting on his flying broomstick flew near the owner and starting hovering around his face. The store owner then asked Ralph " will you work with me? I will make you my business partner." Ralph immediately got a paper and pencil and wrote yes on the paper with the pencil. The store owner was delighted to get the answer as yes. The store owner than explained him the work.

He told him that he has to unload truck every other day with the help of his broomstick and place the items on their respective shelves. Ralph then again wrote on the piece of paper that it was not a problem and that he could do that.

The next night that store owner brought all the paperwork that was to be signed by Ralph. Ralph read the papers and happily signed them.

From that night both of them started their work the store owner removed his workers from store and Ralph did the unloading and loading. They made the store fully automatic and worker-less.

For example for billing, the customer had to dispense the exact amount of change that came on the mechanical machine's print out. (How the machine worked was that the person buying an item used to move to move gears to the numbers that were marked on the item and then the machine told the price and the customer dispensed exact change and the item was marked sold in the inventory and so was the system with the returns) .

Ralph did not stop at this and continued learning magic. One night he learnt the magic of "multiplication." Through that magic he could convert himself into 50 Ralphs and do work more quickly and efficiently. Then he told about his capability to his business partner who after hearing it was impressed and happy.

They then both opened more stores where Ralphs worked . This made them earn more money.

After few years Ralph had learnt lots of magic and had become truly a professional magician. This made him remove the curse on him and he turned himself back to human form.

After turning back to human form he found out the witch who had cursed him. The witch was then sent to a witch's prison after he filed a complaint against her.

Thereafter, he lived his life happily and married a beautiful girl. He was better than ever because he was rich financially and mentally.

tALe 79 : VaN aNd SiM

Long long time ago there lived a man named Sim. He was a good man who worked hard to serve people of his country.

But how did he do that ? Sim was an adventure seeker. During his trips to far far away lands including The Land of the dwarves and giants he happened to save a giant eagles hatchling once from falling into prey.

What happened was that he was walking up the mountains in the giant lands when he saw a giant eagle fighting a giant creature to save her hatchling from being taken away by that evil creature as an entertainment object (as he heard the giant say that). During the fight both the giant creature and the giant eagle were injured very badly but the giant was less injured than the eagle.

The fight continued until the giant killed the eagle. After killing the eagle the giant was severely wounded and so he sat and tried to cure his wounds by licking them. Sim had already decided to save the hatchling from becoming an entertainment thing for the giant and being trapped in a cage for rest of it's life. So Sim decided to hide the hatchling. He went near that baby bird and picked it up. The hatchling was double the size of the regular eagle but he somehow managed to put it in his bag in which he used to collect things and hid it along with himself.

When the giant felt better he picked up himself and started looking up for his prize which was the hatchling but he could not find it as it was with Sim, hidden. After looking for a while the giant could not find the hatchling so he got frustrated and stopped looking for it. He then went away. Seeing him go, Sim waited for some time, picked up the hatchling and took it home in the same bag in which he had hid him carefully.

He carried it all across the mountains to his country where he started taking care of the hatchling as is own whom he named Van. Van grew to the size of a small hill in that year. Sim was favourite of Van. Sim took care of it everyday. Not only that Sim helped Van learn to fly.

How he did that was when Van started to grow up, his wings grew in size too. Now eagles soar very high but they first have to learn to how to fly. So he used to take Van to the top of the mountains but before that he used to keep padding below the mountains so that if Van falls on the ground while learning to fly it does not hurt itself. Then he used to push Van by hands from the top of the mountain and see if it could fly. Initially van only glided and that too intermittently but later it learnt how to fly like no bird ever before or after it did.
They relationship was like that of a father and a son. They cared and protected each other.

Slowly Van turned into a full-grown giant eagle and Sim started to ride van and work for the people there.

What they did was that during those times mining was a huge business and many people were in it and working for it. But in those days there was a problem. During those times only cheap construction material was available and was used to build mines. This cheap material made mine collapse often.

The job of Sim and Van was that during collapse of mine or mines they had to supply fresh air to the people trapped inside and also help in removing mine debris.

How they did that was during collapse of mine they were called in. As soon as they were called in, they immediately took some empty balloons to the mountains to get fresh air filled air in them by pressure and then they came back and blew the air into the mines by compressing the balloons in the mine slowly and and also removing debris with Van's claws to clear the way for the miners and workers.

This continued for quite a while until on one occasion saving people's life was no piece of cake. After doing the regular task of removing the debris and supplying fresh oxygen people were still trapped in a mine. It was getting very difficult to get the trapped miners out of mine. This was happening because of the structure of the mine and secondly because it was too deep. The mine's structure was that that it was first slanted, then it ran down through long spirals and then it was vertically down so no rope or ladder could help. The family members of the people trapped in the mine were very scared and nobody knew what to do at that time.

Sim thought for a while and then made a plan. He told the workers who were there for help to take lots of small nylon balloons and fill them with air. He and Van had then flew to a huge lakes and filled their regular huge nylon balloons with water.

Meanwhile, he had also told the workers to write notes on paper like an instruction manual that should say to tie the small air balloons to their waists with the nylon cord that is around the air balloons. He also told them to write, informing them that they will be pouring in water slowly and allowing them buoyancy through the balloons tied to their bodies so that they can float and come up.

After filling in the calculated amount of water in the huge balloons by Sim and Van there process started.

After throwing in the air balloons in the mine and giving sufficient time to the trapped miners inside to tie those small air balloons to their body so that they worked as a life jacket Sim and Van started slowly pouring the water in the mine by opening to mouth of the balloons hoping everything goes well.

Things happened as they were planned and the miners were brought up and saved, thanks to planning of Sim and efforts of Sim and Van.

They were both honoured by their country and were loved by everyone.

TALe 80 : WiTcHeS bRoOmS' tiCkS

Witches are usually the worst beings ever and could be the worst dreams ever too but as the generations progressed they became from worst to worse and then bad and then sticked to bad but bad wasn't that bad. They remained in this state of evilness but also started being friends with people. In some time they would know that the deeds of past witches will haunt them some day and that will come soon.

Meanwhile the new generation of witches started to mingle with regular people. On one occasion a witch was flying over a horse race track and a horse rider saw that. The horse rider who was riding a horse shouted saying " Witch, why don't you try a race on your broomstick with horse riders on the ground?" The witch heard that but at that time flew away. When she reached home she told this to her witch friends. She told her friends that a horse rider wanted to have a racing competition with them while they were on there broomsticks. When the witches heard that they got very excited and told her that why didn't she tell them that before and that they should do that.

So the next day all the witches that had heard about that race went to search for that horse rider and finally found him. After that, they told the horse rider that they really liked his offer and were looking forward for a competition or competitions. The horse rider was also happy to hear that.

So the race of the witches on their broomsticks and and horse riders on their horses started. Sometimes the horse riders won and sometimes the witches but as I have told you that something was coming to haunt them.

One day there was a race being held on a race track and a witch was about to win that race but suddenly her broom started swinging here and there like something was itching the broom badly and that witch lost the race.

That something that caused the problem was a magical tick of the broom. Witches did not know about that. But where where had they come from?

Few years back when the witches were worst they had cursed many men and women with evil curses who had died a very painful death. Before dying those men and women had sworn that they would avenge their plightful death come what may and in any condition. At that time God was seeing all that and heard them. So he granted them their wish and let them teach a lesson to the witches but in their next life. Those men and women and promised to themselves that they will cause more pain and havoc to the witches then they had ever done to them.

So it happened that the one tick that started the trouble grew in population. The population consisted of souls of previously cursed men and women. Those ticks joined hands in causing trouble and caused lots of harm to the witches .

Flying on broomsticks was the one of the favourite things for witches but falling was not. The witches troubled the brooms sticks so much that many accidents with the witches occurred. For example, many witches fell from their broomsticks while flying as they could not stop their brooms from swinging here and there or getting inverted and shaking them off and getting away.

After many such incidents with the witches they became furious but they could not understand what was going on and what had happened to the broomsticks.

One day all the witches decided to have a meeting and discuss about this issue. Nobody could come with an answer except for one old witch. The elderly witch told the other witches that this time only a saint would be able to help them. So they all thought about it, scared at first but finally decided to meet a saint.

When they went to meet the saint, the saint pulled out a twig from one of the brooms tick and put it in his pocket. Then after feeling and realizing something, he told the witches the their broomsticks were infected with magical ticks that were nothing but the souls of past cursed people.

He then told them that the only way to get rid of them was by apologizing to them and also promising them that they would never hurt or curse people ever.

The witches did as they were told. As soon as they did that all the ticks came out from the twigs of the broomsticks, got collected together and vanished in thin air.

The witches were glad that trouble had gone and evil ended for both, of the witches and for the witches.

tALe 81 : ThE mAgiCaL gLoVeS

In a magical century there once existed a magician. This magician had grown so old that it was difficult for him to do his daily work like carrying stuff or moving things from here to there. He did not know what to do about it so he continued his life living with quite a lot of hardships.

One day a kid knocked at his doors asking for candy. The magician somehow opened the door after walking through great difficulty. After knowing that that the matter involved a candy he felt a bit bad because first of all he had to walk all that way and second of all there was no candy in the house. The kid who had asked for candy was wearing gloves in his hand. This had came to his notice when the kid said bye and then a polite thanks with a sorry coming out of his mouth for causing the trouble to the old magician for coming to the door. The child then went away but that gave the magician an idea. He said to himself "as I need an extra pair of hands so why not get them". He then started working on something to get that first.

During that night he sewed a pair of gloves. In the morning he took those gloves in a dark room which was pitch black and then he casted spells of goodness and poured on them some magical potions while keeping them in a cauldron.

After he had done his work of magic, he suddenly lit a matchstick. As soon as the matchstick was lit the gloves jumped and said "Hello master!" When the magician heard that he was very happy that he had actually got "helping hands". So the magician replied back, "Hello! Jam". (At the spur of movement the magician had named these magical gloves as "Jam"). Jam replied back saying thank you for the lovely hearty name and said "How can I help you?"

The magician at that movement passed away to heavens in happiness and satisfaction. Those gloves did not know what to do at that time so they went outside looking for help but people got scared when they saw those gloves. They got intimidated and ran away after screaming and yelling. Jam later realized that why people were scared off him. He realized that he had no human form. He could not do anything about that so he left the magician alone and went away sorrowfully . The magician was then buried by the people of that town who came to know abut his demise several days later.

Jam had moved to a new town until that time while travelling in night and darkness. At that time Jam did not know what to do so he just sat on a tree deciding about his future. In a few days he came upon an idea. He had already realized at that time that he was born and made to help and that is what he will do.

"But to help was difficult in there too
because of having no face or a body at all too."

He then made a plan and looked for a boy who was good at heart and was not very well-off. To find out a boy like that he set up a fire putting some logs of woods together beneath the high canopy tree where he was staying. Then he put lots of magical chemicals in his hands and put it in that fire. The fire then sparkled with colours. Near that fire, he made soap bubbles to come out of the tree. As the wind blew, it picked up magically seeing the scene.

This visual was seen by the people of the nearby town. Many people with their kids came to check the beautiful wondrous scenes that were being caused in the vicinity of that tree.

Jam who was hiding in the tree also started his look out for a "good at heart" kid. He saw that all the kids and teenagers were afraid to go near the fire except one. Those kids only played with the bubbles. This one teenager kid went near the tree and touched it with his left hand. Jam realized that that kid was pure of heart. Jam decided that that will be The kid with whom he will be friends with and so he did. As the show continued everybody admired it while watching. After it ended they started to return back to their homes and houses and so did the-boy. Jam followed the boy to his home secretly.

And so the process of meeting and friendship began. As soon as the little boy went to his room Jam also entered his room by passing through the walls by being not opaque.

Now, Jam had came to know that the kids name was Jillo. When the kid was about to sleep. Jam said "Hi! Jillo" and Jillo said "hi!" back but a little curious at first to hear the voice. But before Jillo tried asking that whose voice it was Jam immediately sprang upon his bed and starting tickling Jillo. Jillo started laughing and then realized that the thing that said hi!" could not be a bad thing so Jillo said "ok ok, I am not scared of you so stop your hilarious movements and tell me why are you doing this?" Jam had seen that Jillo was from a poor family so Jam asked Jillo:" Is it possible to help me and you by me." Jillo said ." what do you mean by that and then he said "maybe".

Jam told Jillo that he was not only mobile but magical too. He then told Jillo that he was made by a magician to help and so he wants to help people out. Jillo at once agreed to it. Then Jillo told him that he didn't have enough money for himself or his family and that they have to struggle with their life everyday. Jam said "l know that and that's why I will help you". Jillo then asked "How'?

Jam by that time had come to know that he cut trees for living. So he said that tomorrow when you go to cut wood which is your daily job put one of me in your right hand and put the rest of me in your right foot.

Jillo did as he was told. After doing that Jillo was surprised because that day he had cut 100 times more trees than he usually cut and not only that he had also carried all of them across the river. Jillo was very happy that day. He earned 500 times more than his regular pay and didn't know what to do with that. Jam then told to keep his earnings for himself and for his father and mother which was his family.

Now, Jam told Jillo that he has to help him now as promised. Since everybody was afraid to see Jam alone therefore Jillo wore Jam in his hand and his feet as he did for cutting the wood. Then they ran across the town checked for people with short food supplies and then kept lots of food outside their houses after having magically produced food for them by Jam and went away. When the families saw the food there happiness had no bounds so they thanked god for jam and bread and lots more and had there food.

Jam and Jillo did that forever and secured their future there and thereafter.

tALe 82 : tHe mAgiCiAn AnD tHe GoLf SticKs

In olden times there was no term of retirement or no term as retirement especially for magicians. So this is a story about a magician who had to actually fool his pupils and fellow magician friends to escape his working life and retire. Well, to let you know he actually retired without playing golf or did he? He never played golf ever but still this story is about him and golf sticks.

Once this magician whose name was Jaoumenia was teaching his students magic, outside his house in his backyard. Suddenly the sun became too bright for him so he closed the class's session and started going inside his house for rest.

As soon as he was trying to go inside his house a fellow magician who was also his friend came to meet him. When the magician came he said "hi" to Jaoumenia and took out a smoke pan pipe and put tobacco in it. He then lit it after taking a match stick out from a match-box and rubbing it to Jaoumenia magical hat. Jaoumenia was very surprised to see that. He could not understand that how could anybody enjoy in such a scorching heat with sun shining on your face. But it was as it was.

Jaoumenia said to his fellow friend who was also the head of magical society that he would like to stop working and rest till he rests in peace. The head of the magical society said that, that was possible only when he goes to heaven.

At that time Jaoumenia got really angry at him and so he asked his friend whose name was Laneck that how far do you think that heaven would be? Laneck the head of magical society said that." must be very far". So Jaoumenia replied back in rage without thinking much saying " so you think sun must be on the way to heaven?" Laneck said "of course!" Jaoumenia did not say anything further. He kept quiet maybe because he did not have anything to say or did not know what else to say.

Then Night came in. Jaoumenia closed his eyes while trying to sleep on his bed but the thought of smoking pan pipe and the burning sun kept on bothering him. He then thought for a while and decided that he needed some entertainment.

So, he got up from his bed immediately and crafted a tin shaped and sized bag and then made five slender slicks out of pan pipes that looked like tiny golf sticks. Those things which were golf bag and golf sticks looked very beautiful. There are many beautiful things in the world but how was entertainment possible only through beauty. So he put magical spells on the golf sticks and the golf bag while waiving his hands in air. While he was doing that he heard a screaming voice of a girl that caused the window pane to break.

The magician said in a shock:" what, what? "The magic bag and the sticks had come to life at that moment. The bag had a girls voice and the golf sticks had a voice too but it was boys' voice which was shut in front of the screaming girls voice.

The magician when saw that he said "hello" to them and immediately asked what do you want to do in your life?
The golf bag and golf sticks said things which were as follows. The golf bag said I like talking and the golf sticks said we like to hit, something like a round thing which may be spherical. The magician then immediately produced a ball out of magic which was the size of a small cherry but was surely spherical.

Now, these golf sticks used to play golf in magician's room and the golf bag used to do a commentary. This used to entertain the magician a lot. One day the magician was watching the golf sticks play with the ball. They were hitting it so fiercely that that it looked like that tiny ball would catch fire. Then magician asked the golf sticks "how far do you think can you hit". The golf sticks said that so far that nothing could beat us. Magician was happy to hear that and at that time an idea struck him.

The next day he called all the magicians of the magical society and told them what had happened between him and Laneck.

Laneck had told Jaoumenia that he could only rest if he goes to heaven. Jaoumenia then confirmed with everybody that after life only a part of one's life (soul without body) goes to heavens and to that everybody agreed. Then he also said that Laneck had told him that the sun was on the way to heavens which thus was true.

Then he asked everybody that if a part of me will reach the sun and later heaven then he should be allowed to rest i. e retire. Everybody looked at each other and then said "yes."

Laneck was in jeopardy because everybody agreed to what Jaoumenia had said.

Jaoumenia then took out a pair of scissors and cut a piece from a strand of his hair. Then he cut opened the small golf ball with knife. After that he put the piece of hair that he had cut before into it and sealed it magically. Everybody saw him doing that.

Then he called the tiny golf sticks by name: "Jack, Jim, Jeff, Jimer and Jykno". They all came hopping outside with the golf bag . Then he said to the golf sticks "hit this ball as far as you can" and they agreed.

Then they took positions in the sky hitting towards the sun as was requested by Jaoumenia. They then took turns in hitting. Jack hit it first. He hit it so hard that the ball passed from the Troposphere to the Stratosphere. There Jim was waiting. When the ball reached Jim he hit it further away such that it passed the Stratosphere and entered mesosphere. At the beginning of mesosphere Jeff was standing. He further hit it so bad that it reached thermosphere passing mesosphere. Now Jimer was waiting for the ball there. When it came, he hit it again so that it burned catching fire in the thermosphere while passing through it. Jykno who already knew that that's what it's going to happen did nothing but wrote a letter to the magicians while watching from below that the ball had passed the sun burning and had reached heavens.

All the magicians who were watching with their mini telescopes were dumbstruck but still nodded and said "yes it was true". the ball carrying Jaoumenia's hair had indeed reached heavens while passing and burning through the sun. Everybody was utterly shocked and blissfully surprised.

As had been decided Jaoumenia rested till he finally rested in peace and that was when the process of retirement for people took shape. So sometimes you don't have to play golf to retire. Only seeing it or a thought if it can make you retire or maybe sometimes a magic trick can help.

TaLe 83 : sUgAr cAkEs

Once there was a country where lived many bakers. Regarding that this story is also about a baker who lived amongst them but a little far from them. This baker had a small shop outside the city therefore it earned little customers and profit. The other reason for his marginal existence was that he was not a good baker. He had opened a bakery only because it required a cheap set-up and the raw materials that were required to operate were also not that expensive. Secondly, according to area he had that was the only type of shop he could open. So his life continued as a struggle both financially and personally. Why personally? Because he did not have a wife or kids. (For dating too one requires money which was a scarce thing in his pocket.)

Days passed but he did not while owning the bakery. One day he was sitting in a coffee shop when he heard on radio that the government was providing student loans to anybody who wanted to enhance their skills in a college or University. The baker who was known by the name Cefno decided at that moment that he would go to school to learn bakery and be an excellent baker.

Then he went to a nearby college and applied to it for a bakery course. It took two weeks for the admission process and the college accepted his admission in the school of bakery. When he got the admission letter is his hand he went to apply for a student loan from the government. Since he already had a business he was approved for a student loan.

From next month Cefno's school started and he started going there with full eagerness and enthusiasm. He started learning how to bake different types of delicacies and so did the other students. Since other students were also doing really good Cefno realized the other reason why there was tough competition in market. So he thought that if everybody was making deliciously baked goods why would anybody leap 10 miles to come to his shop that was so far away from the city. So he decided that he needed on edge for his baked items that would make people come from far and wide to enjoy his baked goods. So as they say" knowledge is always there to be explored", therefore he started thinking in this direction.

He then started going to the library of the college and started reading various kind of books which he thought might help him develop an edge for his baked goods.

One day he was reading a baking book. In it he learnt that sugar was mostly derived from sugar beet in non-tropical countries and from sugar cane in tropical countries . This made his brain think. He knew that all the sugars contain glucose and fructose and therefore have the same chemical formula but he also knew that since being derived from different sources they have different chemical signatures and thus should taste different and which was true as he confirmed it with his teacher.

Cefno was happy at this discovery and was content with the knowledge he got because there he had got an idea that would would make him rich.

After completing his bakery courses and passing with high grades he went back to baking in his bakery.

In those times he already knew that in their area many tonnes of oranges, strawberries, apples, blueberries, etc. were dumped every year in the earth because there were no buyers for it. (They produced more than it was required). So he contacted those fruit farmers . He then asked them that if they would not dump the excess food in earth and instead give him at a very cheap price. Those fruit farmers immediately agreed to it.

By the time these discussions took place he had already set up a small machinery in the backyard of his house to make sugar from molasses of fruits like apples, oranges, blueberries blackberries, pineapples etc. This was a revolutionary idea as nobody knew that sugar could be made from fruits too. Conventionally people used to think that sugar is needed in massive quantities so it should be made from something that has high sugar content so they can make more.

He started making sugars from apples, bananas, blueberries, oranges and many other fruits. What he did was that with these sugars he started making cakes. He used to make these cakes by melting those sugars and cooling them in a specific way. Then he sold every cake for 50 times the price of a regular cake of same size and weight.

First it come in the News and then it was everywhere. People from far and wide came to try it out and buy it. People used to buy in lump sums and pay heartily. They knew that these were the cakes that would not harm them because they were made of unbleached and natural sugar - which was actually made of fruits that are healthy for body.

TaLe 84 : ThE kEtChUp LoVeR

"Pop!" the balloon bursted and a boy took birth. This was a day of celebration as a baby boy was born to a very rich family. He was named after his grandfather who had died few years back. He was called Bonny.

Bonny started his life drinking baby milk and eating baby food but one day he grew enough to have a hamburger. He tasted this delicious dish when his mom took him to a burger place and his mom had told him that he will try something new today from this fast food burger restaurant. He did not know what it would taste like but he had agreed to what his mom had said. The burger was ordered and he ate it the very first time in his life. It was like nothing he had ever had before. It let so juicy tasty, buttery but wait a minute what was that red thing that everybody was dipping their burgers with? His mom then explained to her son that, that thing was called ketchup and she could get some for him if he wanted. The boy knocked his head up and down and made his tongue swirl around saying "yes". His mom got up and got some ketchup for him in a small paper bowl which the boy tasted without dipping hamburger in it and then he again tasted it again without putting hamburger in and he did that again and again and kept on doing that until all the ketchup was over from that small bowl. He and his mom left the burger place without the Bonny having any burger but ketchup. The burger was tasty but the ketchup was tastier.

The ketchup taste was so overwhelming to him that he had dreams about it all night and whenever he slept. It was the tastiest thing he ever tasted and wanted it more everyday. He would not go anywhere or eat anything without ketchup. In fact ketchup was the only thing he ever and mostly had.

Now, he was a rich kid and had no worry about money i.e. he did not have financial problems. One day he turned 18 and his dad asked, "Do you want to go to college or start a business of your own?" He told his dad to give him a day's time to think about it so that he could decide upon it and then would let him know. His dad firmly said "Okay."

That night he tried sleeping while thinking what do in his life and the thoughts of ketchup again overwhelmed him and thus he could not sleep properly and so he had decided something. He decided that since he loved ketchup so much there must be others too that would like ketchup very much and would do anything for it so he would open a ketchup fast food restaurant.

The difference in other fast food restaurants and this fast food restaurant would be that in Bonny's fast food restaurant everything that will be made and served, would be from ketchup.

Next day he woke up from whatever sleep he had and went straight to his dad's room telling him that he wanted to start a business which he would start by hiring some scientists and so he needed money. Without listening more, his dad was thrilled to learn that his son was trying to start up something very unique as it involved research from scientists so he said "Yes" immediately and lended him out some money from his vault.

Bonny was thrilled that he had got money for his heart's desire. Then he interviewed and hired some food scientists to make him buns, patties, vegetables and all other things required to make burgers from ketchup and ketchup alone.

The food scientists were at first amazed to hear that but since they were getting lots of money for that they agreed to what Bonny had asked for and decided to make ketchup buns, ketchup vegetables and ketchup patties etc made only from ketchup and ketchup alone for his fast food burger restaurant.

It took them 2 years to make the things requested by Bonny but they surely got up running some processes to make those things.

The burger restaurant was opened in a busy market intersection. Many people were amused by it. But many kids were attracted towards it too because it was a restaurant where everything made out of ketchup was served. So with kids, parents came in and tried out some burgers. They were actually very tasty so the burger shop was in a lot of financial profit. He grew that burger restaurant to many new shops and chains of it were formed. It was a very profitable business after all and Bonny had monopoly over it. It kept on opening more and more across the town and country and Bonny was very happy with that.

Days passed then years and Bonny was sitting in his own restaurant trying his own burgers one day. He did not feel something right about it. He realized that his burgers were missing something and it was really true. His burgers were all missing essential nutrients required by the body. He felt very uncomfortable understanding that so he thought and said why am I making people eat junk food?

So from that day he first started advertising that junk food is not good for health and then slowly but steadily he turned his restaurants into actual food serving restaurant business and thus made people realize and eat healthy, not junk food.

TaLe 85 : tHe AdJuStAbLe sHoEs

Once when the world was developing, in some parts of this world shoes was an expensive commodity. Therefore everybody could not afford it thus some did not wear shoes. Also during those times child labour was acceptable and was very cheap. In that world lived such a boy named Sfity.

Sfity was such a boy that worked hard all day long just enough to make money for his food. This chap lived alone and had no parents as they had died some years back. He struggled hard everyday to earn his bread.

Since he was a poor fellow he could not afford shoes. He worked barefooted wherever he had to work and wherever his job was. Because of working barefooted his feet used to get black as coal and also sometimes get ruptured and injured. He did not mind that but still wished for shoes.

One day he was 12 and thus had worked for about 5 years in a row. This means that he had quite a lot of job experience but his pay wont budge even a little bit but he had become ambitious by that time. So he decided that day that he will work two jobs so that he can secure enough money to buy or make some shoes from raw materials if required and so he did.

He worked 19 hours in a day and thus started saving some money. In a years time he made enough to get raw materials for making shoes. It took some time to make a pair of shoes by him but he made those shoes. Now he wanted to relax and cut back job hours so that he could sleep well for at-least some time.

But the next day there was bad news. The government had passed orders that people would have to keep on working the same amount of time as they used to work and also their pay would be reduced. That hurtled Sfity a little bit, thinking that he would not be able to sleep much because of the new law but he was happy that he had at-least got his shoes made.

Now a year passed and he started feeling pain in his feet. He realized that his feet had grown in size. Thus the shoes he was wearing could not be worn anymore as they had become too tight to fit.

He felt very bad at this situation and did not know what he could do. His pay had been reduced but the working hours were same and thus he could not work anymore. Something had to be done about it. He then decided to meet a witchy magician.

That magician lived out of town and was a day's walk on foot. But he had realized that only a magician could help him this time no matter how cunning he was. So he took 2 days leave and went to meet that magician.

When he entered the magician's mansion the magician asked him what was his purpose of entry in his house. The boy politely said that he wanted something so that whatever financial crisis he may be in he should always be able to wear a pair of shoes which would fit him forever. The magician looked at the boy and said "Boy, do you see my feet?" The boy looked at his feet and said "Yes, I believe they are 20 inches long." He said again " Do you see my body?" The boy looked at the huge figure the magician had. He then thought that he must weight 500 pounds, if not less. The boy then replied " yes sir."

The magician then told him that I can give you what you want but in return you have to give me what I want. Sfity looked puzzled but then he said to himself "Anything for shoes"and said "Okay". The magician then told him that Sfity should devise something for him which covers his feet and that he remains fit forever with his stomach tugged in.

At that time the boy was thinking about shoes quite deeply and then an idea related to that came into his mind. He then asked the magician that could he bear some weight. The magician said " Yes I can." Then he told the magician that he will devise some shoes that will be heavy and would fit him perfectly for his life as his feet won't grow anymore. Then the magician asked the boy what about my fat stomach. The boy then said that, that will be in control too. But the boy said I need some raw materials to make your shoes. The magician asked "What would that be?" The boy said "I need steel to make your shoes."

The magician at that time looked surprised and then said "Okay" and in a spur of the movement he produced some some beautifully magnificent shining magical steel through a spell.

It took only 3 hours for the boy to make shoes from that steel as he was in desperate need of his own shoes.

He added hinges to the separate parts that he made from the raw steel and gifted it to the magician. The magician then asked that how would they help him remain fit? The boy then replied that since steel shoes are heavy therefore whenever he steps up and move his fat will reduce and thus make him thinner than he his and if he keeps wearing them forever he will remain fit forever. The magician then realized what the boy meant.

He then immediately took out a fibre from his pocket and gave it to the boy. He then told the boy that that fibre was special fibre and whatever thing he makes with that fibre would be adjustable including shoes if he makes from it.

The boy was happy and thanked the magician for that and went home.

The boy then made shoes from that fibre which really turned out to be adjustable. Thus, no matter what his feet size ever would be he could wear his beautifully crafted and well earned shoes forever and never go barefooted ever.

tALe 86 : JaCkJoT

Long time ago there lived an old man named Highsti. Highsti was quite an aged guy who always wanted a companion which he never had. He had no companion because in his neighbourhood only young folks and kids lived who were least bothered about him. As he was very old he stayed at home and continued his life as it is and in it. One night he was very upset and saw a shooting star. After seeing the star he wished if it could give him a companion which may be in any shape, size or form.

The shooting stars that were passing by, actually consisted of two fairies that were fighting while flying, so, the shooting aspect of the stars. But while they were fighting they heard the wish that was made by the old man. They were in utter shock to hear that wish as that wish asked for a companion in any shape size or form. This made them think because they did not know that there could be such loneliness amongst humans and in their hearts. They then realized that they were way better off than those without friends because they had each other with whom they could talk, play, quarrel, fight etc. At that moment they immediately stopped fighting and started thinking about the wish made by that old man. They then thought about a gift that they could give to the old man. After much brainstorming and after quite a while they thought of something special.

By that time the old man was sleeping and the two fairies had already thought about a companion that they could give as a gift to the old man.

They had planned to give the old man a talking magical pencil. So, during that night they came into the room where Highsti was sleeping. They sweetly slipped a magical pencil which was just born, into the pocket of Highsti's shirt and immediately went away disappearing. (The magical pencil which was just born was also fast asleep and had not opened it eyes yet).

Highsti woke up in the morning and twisted his body such that he lay on his chest. He then felt something twitching where his shirt's pocket was. As soon as he tried touching it he heard a huge scream that was quite funny. That scream made Highsti get up in a jiffy. He was surprised and shocked to hear such a loud scream in such a kiddish tone.

He then shouted " Who is it?"

The pencil immediately jumped from his pocket and said "it's me - The mighty pencil and your pal."

Highsti then said " I don't have pals, where did you come from." The pencil said that I am sent as a gift to you by some magical beings who heard your prayers. After hearing that, Highsti felt a bit happy and peaceful.

Highsti asked very politely " Can you tell me a joke?" The pencil whom he had named Jackjot then tried thinking of a joke. While he was trying to think about joke which he knew none, he kept on behaving in a weird manner and kept on showing that he is really trying to remember a joke. He was changing his face gestures quite rapidly and coughing while doing that. Every other second it looked like he was going to pop up a joke. This created a hilarious sensation for Highsti who started giggling and then burst into tremendous laughter. At that moment he laughed so much that tears came out of his eyes. He had not laughed for about 25 years and suddenly he laughed like he had never laughed before.

Jackjot was confused seeing Highsti laugh. He said "I did not crack a joke or said any funny thing. Why are you laughing then?" He kept on asking but Highsti did not tell him the reason.

Highsti then suddenly got up and yelled in a extremely loud, sharp and happy voice " Yes! I found a companion!" Jackjot when heard that, it changed his mood from confused to being happy and got satisfied with what was going on.

He then asked Jackjot " What else could he do for him?" Jackjot immediately said " Draw anything on paper using me   and see what happens." Highsti at that time did not know what will happen if he draws anything using Jackjot but he did not seem to be worried with that at that point.

Suddenly he remembered that oil for his light lamps was getting finished so he asked Jackjot what he should do now as all shops were closed for the night and they needed light for the night. Jackjot said " Just draw using me." Highsti listened to his companion and drew a can of kerosene oil. As soon as he finished drawing the lamp with his crooked hands the oil can came to life. Highsti then understood the capabilities of that pencil. He then filled oil in the lamps and thanked his companion for help.

Highsti was happy that from now on he would not have to use his meagre life savings for buying any thing. Whatever he wants he just would have to draw and that would come to life easily. He then drew candies, fruits, vegetables etc. and they all came to life.

Next day he distributed candies to the kids in his neighbourhood who thanked him later.

Then he made a flying cart which he used to send across the town at night. That cart distributed fruits and vegetables to the poor as it had its own hands and could fly endlessly.

The pencil lasted as long as Highsti did and gave him company till the end of his days. Both the companions died at the same moment. Highsti went to heavens and the pencil took human form and met him there. They lived happily forever.

TaLe 87 : tHe KiNg AnD ThE dWaRvEs

Long time ago there once lived a miser and a cruel king. There also lived his subjects which included people and non subjects that included dwarves.

To understand this story better let me tell you that kings have power because they have wealth. If they lose wealth they don't get to have power because the world runs on money and if there is no money the world does not run. All the king's soldiers, his ministers and other subjects withdraw a salary from king. The king in turn rules by putting taxes on quite a lot of things that people use and then allows flow of money within his kingdom. Most of the times it is affordable to pay taxes but some times like in this story, the king levied such high taxes that people were not left with enough money to even buy food for their families and that they did not like.

Also, amongst people lived many dwarves who were always on the wanted list by the king and many of them had been captured by him.

The dwarves were really angry at the king. They including the people of his country were fed up of his rule so they were thinking a way out of it.

At those times the king was in search for a "wisdom minister" that gives him some good ideas to rule his kingdom and levy more taxes. So he sent his soldiers all across the kingdom who spread the word that the king needed a wise guy to be his "wisdom minister".

Now, the dwarves heard that too and they got an idea from it. They choose the oldest of their kind to go and apply for that job. Since that dwarf was old he had so much beard on his face that he did not look like a dwarf instead he looked like a regular old man with short height who used a stick for walking.

Since very few people liked king, very few applied for this job and so all those who applied got interviewed by the king. All of them failed except this dwarf. The king had only one question in his mind. He wanted to know from the men and women that were being interviewed that what could be the favourite colour of a king like him. All of them tried but ended up in wrong answers except the wise old dwarf.

The wise old dwarf said that since the king is mighty and rules the day so their should be no other, other than light blue colour- the colour of endless visible sky which should be his favourite. Although the king had some other colour in his mind but hearing that light blue coloured sky was endless and that that should be his favourite colour he liked it and made the dwarf who looked like a short old man as his "wisdom advisor."

Now king was happy that he had a new advisor with him who was wise and that he would make him more powerful and richer. He used to keep on asking silly questions from him everyday like when will i grow more rich? Or when will i rule the world? The wise old dwarf used to satisfy him with calming answers.

Meanwhile the dwarves knew that if the king loses all his riches he will be nothing more than a pauper who would not receive any thing even if he begs. But since the king was miser he had put all his gold in a huge treasury which was so secure that it could not be robbed. So they made a plan. They told their oldest dwarf who was serving as an advisor in the king's court to somehow ask the king to move his gold to a different storage so that they can rob his gold while it was outside the secure facility. When the old wise dwarf heard it he made up a plan to fool the king wisely and force him into moving his gold to another location.

Next day in the morning all the advisors and the king had a meeting. In the meeting the wise dwarf told the king that a great omen has fallen and that if the king does not change the location of his gold he will be robbed of it .

He then explained to the king that if he plans to change the location of the gold to protect himself and gold itself it should be done in three parts and in three days. Then he said that those 3 days should happen very soon when they see shooting stars. These shooting stars would fall for three consecutive nights beginning from the 5th night from that night.

(This plan was made like that because dwarves were less in numbers and they won't be able to rob all of the gold at once so they needed three days time to do all that and his they had asked for from their old wise dwarf. The falling of shooting stars was a separate plan.)

"The king when heard that knew the old man was very wise and would not be telling a lie because shooting stars are a sign and if the do fall let him not."

He then immediately ordered his soldiers to start packing gold. This gold, then he told his soldiers should be ready to go to a another secure building across the town in 3 shipments. The soldiers obeyed his orders

Now the second plan of dwarves came in. They were going to make artificial shooting stars fall from sky by using their huge catapults.

The day came and they parked a huge catapult outside the kingdom's boundaries. They then took a huge rock, put oil on the rock, loaded it on the catapult, set it on fire and then threw it across the sky during night from the far end of the kingdom.

Meanwhile the king's men where waiting to see the shooting star so that they can transfer gold to the new location. As soon as they saw the sign which was the shooting star they started transferring gold (which was laden on the horses) to the secure location. But, they did not know that the dwarves would be waiting for them and the gold. When the soldiers and their horses carrying gold passed through the dense part of forest the dwarves passed a sleeping potion through the breeze that only affected humans. All the soldiers fell into sleep and the dwarves looted all the gold.

Since the old wise dwarf was in charge of gold transportation he did not tell anything about the disappearance of gold to the king . All he said was that the gold had been shifted to the new location safely and that they should wait for the next shooting star to come so that they can transfer the next shipment of gold.

In three days the dwarves created three shooting stars in the sky and robbed all the gold of the king. They then distributed it to their true owners - the people of that kingdom. The king was reduced to a pauper and had thus lost all his powers. He was therefore unable to punish anybody. Thanks to the dwarves, the kingdom and its people were saved.

TaLe 88 : tHe mAgiCaL gEm

This is a sad story about a gem that remained unhappy during all his life until one day he found freedom. So let's begin it

Once there lived a poor man by the name of Kroton. Kroton used to remain very upset with his life as he could not earn enough money to live his life properly. The reason for that was that he was neither skilled nor educated. He lived his life doing labour jobs but that barely filled his belly. So he was very dissatisfied with it. One night he came from work and the oil for lamps of his house had got emptied and thus there was no light in there. Tired and frustrated, he went to get oil from an oil shop that was a little far away from where he lived. Since he was poor he could not afford a horse or a buggy therefore he had to walk all the way to the oil shop.

Disgusted with his life, as he was working he saw a shiny thing lying on the pathway. At first he did not dared to pick it up but then he got so attracted and influenced by the shine of it that he could not stop himself from picking it up. So he went near it and picked it up. When he checked it out closely he realized that it was a gem. Happy with that, he put it in his pocket while looking around and confirming that nobody else had eyes on it.

He was so happy with that, that he wanted to go back home and hide it some where but then he realized that he needed light in his house to do that and for that he needed oil for his lamps. So he had to go to the oil shop and he tried that.

As he was heading towards the oil shop he said " I wish that this gem fetches me good money when I sell it." At the same moment he checked his pockets to see if it was still there. As soon as he checked he found something weird going on. He realized that the 10 coins he had to get oil were missing and the gem had turned to a black rock. Seeing that he got afraid. He did not know what to do next. But it looked like that black rock was the only thing left with him at that time. Without much thinking he turned back and went home realizing that he won't be able to buy oil anymore.

When he reached home he took out the black rock from his pocket and asked it "what are you?" Then when he did not get any response he he threw that rock towards the floor angrily. As soon as the rock hit the ground it said "Ouch" and Kroton heard that. Kroton immediately asked him " So you can talk?" The gem that had turned into black rock said "Yes and I have sweared to do the opposite of what is asked of me." Then Kroton realized that when he had said "Fetch good money for the gem," the gem had done opposite of it and robbed him out of whatever money he had in his pocket and turned itself into a black rock. Kroton then thought carefully that if that gem has sweared that it will do the opposite of what is asked of him then he might be able to turn it into good for him.

He then said to the gem "I wished I had no money at all". The gem immediately gave him so much money that his house overflowed with money actually. Kroton wasted no time and before anybody saw it he put all the money in sacks so that there sight is obscured. He then wasting no time and immediately said "I wish that I did not own a beautiful palace." When the gem heard that it immediately brought a huge palace to life just where his house was.

After getting all that he kept on wishing negatively, for things that would keep him happy and prosperous life long. But after some time Kroton realized that it was a little sad that the gem keeps on doing the opposite of what is asked of him?

One day it asked the gem "why are you so negative in your thinking?" The gem then told him the entire story of his life.

He told him that once he was a slave and his name was Gem. He was a very obedient slave and obeyed his masters orders promptly but he did not know that his master was an evil magician. One day after having seen, that the slave was very obedient and obeyed all orders of his master his master-magician turned him into a real gem which had magical powers. Gem was really trapped being a gem and had lost all his freedom and life. Gem did not liked that. The magician took him wherever he went and forced him to cast evil spells on good beings. Gem really got angry at the magician one day and that day magician was trying to get a dragon of his back. So the magician forced the gem to magically turn the dragon into a rat but the gem did not do that this time and the dragon killed the magician. Before the magician died he cursed gem that "May you remain magically bound forever and serve as a slave forever."

Then the gem told Kroton that this was the reason why he did negative things and thus did opposite of what others wanted of him. Kroton felt bad for him and then asked him that what did he want in his life now? Does he want to turn back to human again. Gem said that that would be impossible now. He then said that that he wanted to be free both physically and spiritually forever.

Kroton then kept on thinking about a way for that . It took him 10 days to think about a way to get Gem freedom from his cursed life. So on the 11th day he said to Gem that" I wish you become unbreakable and don't break yourself into million pieces". The gem at that time did not know what started happening to him. A light shined out of the gem and Gem got broken into million pieces that then looked like shiny metallic dust. He then carefully picked up all the dust of the gem and kept it outside on the ground. The dust was so small that as the wind blew it got carried away by the wind and was free to go wherever the air went.

Kroton then realized that Gem's soul found peace and his physical form got freedom from the treacherous life.

tALe 89 : tHe eScApE

Once there existed Eeknocks and men together on earth. Although they existed together they did not go well along. Eeknocks were very notorious and selfish minded beings and always wanted to rule the entire earth. To explain their physical attributes, they were short creatures who had a cubical nose, pointed ears and a short tail with no hair at all whatsoever towards their tail's end.

They had always tried to overthrow human civilization but were not successful ever. So this one last time they prepared. They planned and planned and also made their forces strong. After 15 years of preparation they were ready. They declared war on the entire human civilization and almost completely defeated them.

There were two places where they could not lead or have a victory . One was an island named Stringyheld and the other was a small country named Flimnopee.

Before the war had started people of Flimnopee had already had come to know about Eecknocks' evil plans and had made their country very strong by making their defences extremely powerful. Any Eeknock that even tried to come near their extended boundaries was instantly killed through arrows and a special magical potion which once inhaled by Eeknocks would give them instantaneous death.

Since Eeknocks had seen that they had failed to penetrate the defences of Flimnopee they gave up attacking Flimnopee but the thought of attacking Stringyheld was something they could not resist and therefore, wanted to do it very badly. So before attacking that island with their powerful weapons they thought of torturing people that were on that island. Then they would kill them so that they could avenge the death of their people in that battle.

People of Stringyheld were not prepared for what Eeknocks had in their minds. Eeknocks surrounded Stringyheld and started pouring acids in the waters of the lake surrounding that island so much so that it became poisonous for marine life which started dying. People who drank water from that lake in which their island was started falling sick.

So many people fell sick that medicines became short of supply. They found that water had gone acidic suddenly. Everybody was confused and did not know the reason for that. They then sent scouts out looking for the reasons.

The scouts then went out to the far ends of the lake with their boats and checked out the area with their monoculars. They saw that Eecknocks had surrounded them completely by laying their defences on the outer periphery of lake and that they were pouring acids into the lake continuously. This shocked them. The scouts then came back and informed this to the leaders of their tribes. All the leaders of that island then had a very long meeting that lasted 2 days. In the meeting they decided to move the people of Stringyheld to the only un-captured place on earth which was Flimnopee, but how? To move 10,000 people which was the population of that island was very difficult, but they had a genius plan in mind.

They dig a huge underground space beneath their island which took them about 10 days. Now in that place they started making feather houses with huge cluster of feathers (which formed a wing shape) attached to them. The feathers required to make the feather houses and the feather wings were derived from birds that were available in a great quantity on the island. They did not kill the birds to get the feathers rather fed them so that they can get more from them.

Second thing was to make a huge coal engine that was powerful enough to carry a load of 10 million tonnes. (They had actually planned to fly those feather houses out of the island without the Eecknocks coming to know of it with the use of that coal engine). That single engine would be used to flap feather wings that would be attached to the feather made houses.

It took them about 2400 hours to make that coal engine. The coal engine was designed in such a way that while flying, the steam and smoke released from it would engulf all the external areas of those feather houses in such a way that it would look like a big cloud and nothing more. Thus this would protect the people of Stringyheld from getting noticed or attacked by Eecknocks from ground when they would be flying in air.

But the main problem was how to get the house off the ground as the engine could only cause motion in air if it was in it already.

For this they also made a plan. They planned on using the pressure of volcano to slingshot them in the air while keeping them hidden from the eyes of Eecknocks.

It took them a day's time to build a huge wooden platform that would be able to support the weight of the feather houses, the people of stringyheld and that of the engine. This would also cover the mouth of volcano from the middle portion of its neck at the interior of it.

After it was built they covered the volcano's mouth with that platform at the required location and then kept the feather houses on top of it.

As soon as it was done the pressure started building in the volcano beneath the platform. In a day's time so much pressure got created that the volcano bursted with smoke, steam and dust. The feather houses that were kept on the wooden platform covering the mouth of volcano at the middle-interior were slingshotted towards the sky. As soon as this happened the people of Stringyheld that were inside the houses started the coal engine and the feather wings of the feather houses started flapping and producing lift. Since coal engine worked perfectly it camouflaged the entire feather houses and their wings so that they looked nothing more than a cloud formation. They safely guided that huge structure to the strongholds of Flimnopee and landed there with no harm done to anybody. People who were suffering from the affect of acidic waters got treated there. Everybody was happy that they were in a safe place now.

Later, People of Flimnopee and Stringyheld made their defences so strong that Eecknocks never dared to attack them again. Although Eecknocks captured the earth but they could not capture homes and hearts of People of Flimnopee and Stringyheld.

tALe 90 : tHe giAnTs AnD tHe TiNy SkieS

Everybody knows that quite a number of giants lived some time ago. But how did they survive and go on living happily for so long without entertainment or somebody to do work for them? Giants are lazy beings, so how did they manage their lives without working hard.

To answer all this let me tell you that Giants lived their lives happily because they had workers who worked for them. These workers also entertained them. These workers were called as Tiny Skies.

Why they were called so was because each of them was like a tiny sky as they carried burden of a sky or several skies with them (sky herein refers to giants). Secondly also they were called as Tiny Skies was because they measured only about an inch but worked like (actual) skies without any rest. Thirdly the reason why they were called as Tiny Skies was also because they were always near their masters (Giants) as and whenever needed just like sky was at an arms distance for the Giants (which they thought). The fourth reason for calling them Tiny Skies was also because they could be put to death any time just like sky could by the shattered anytime by the Giants (due to its proximity, as they thought) with their hammers and will. Giants thought that the actual sky was useless as it only gave them shelter from God's anger and therefore was also a slave to them. Therefore the name for those tiny creatures - Tiny Skies.

But how did the slaves go on with their life and what were their work orders.

Tiny Skies were responsible for causing daily activities of the Giants to happen. For example : in every instrument or an automobile there worked one or many Tiny Skies. In music systems there existed trained Tiny Skies which played fresh music as per the taste of the Giants or current audiences' demand. Tiny skies that played music while being inside the boom box or a stereo were trained in musical schools specially taught by Tiny Sky virtuosos. These training schools like other things were run by Giants. Just like factories manufactures parts and puts them together i.e. assembles them, similarly these training schools were like musical factories. Tiny skies were herein trained to use their specialized instrument or vocal voice. They were then put into a stereo which was shipped to stores or houses of the buyers.

The automobiles had a similar structure and story. The engines of the automobiles consisted of strong and trained Tiny Skies inside the automobile's engine. They rotated the shafts attached to the gears which further rotated the tyres of Giant cars and the Giants commuted and enjoyed while sitting in them and driving them. To accelerate the Giants only pressed a pedal from their foot which gave a signal to the working Tiny Skies. After receiving the signal they used to start rotating the shafts attached to the gears with more pressure and speed and reduced or stop doing that when the pressure was released accordingly.

These things happened because giants were dumb and had the ability to pressurize whomsoever they wanted to be their slave. But this had a cost to pay. Many Tiny Skies had suffered death and pain under the tyranny of Giants.They had lost many of their loved ones because of evil rule of Giants.

(Tiny skies processed food just like plants i.e. they made their own food but they were biologically fragile just like humans who can easily get hurt with a slap of giant or their sharp nails.)

This all continued for a while until the Tiny Skies realized that the torture by giants has to end. So the leaders of the Tiny Skies sent secret paper mails to all Tiny Skies telling them about their plan. They clearly wrote to all Tiny Skies that the Giants were strong creatures but they can be easily beaten by their wits. According to the plan they told their counterparts to amplify whatever the giants wanted them to do so much that they get freaked out and shocked into trauma of what was going on.

Next day the plan came into application.

For example. On road whilst on the drive when the Giants pressed the accelerator to speed up the cars and motorcycles they got speeded up at a drastic uncontrollable rate which got difficult to control. And, if they applied brakes the brakes were so sudden that it jerked the screams out of Giants. This happened to all Giants that day and they all got freaked out and confused about what was happening.

This was not limited to cars or other automobiles alone. When the Giants played music it was played at such a high pitch that it caused the ears of Giants to ache.

Now, as tension gathered among the minds of giants. They realized that Tiny Skies were all working their 100% as they had been told to do (if they wanted to avoid getting tortured or killed).

This was something that Giants were not prepared for. They did not know what to do as their whole civilization was in great danger from the skies.

As this discussion was taking place a child of Giants said " Maybe you already torture Tiny Skies too much and that maybe I think, they don't like that". It took a while for the giants to realize that but the Giants did realize that. Then they discussed and said "What other options do we have?" A tiny sky then suddenly jumped out from one of the microphones' and said "We can make actual car engines that would run on something called fuels and not us!" Giants were in a shock to hear that and did not believe at first. But later when Tiny Skies made those things they apologized to them and peace prevailed after.

tALe 91: tHe VaLuAbLe GiFt

Once there lived a magician who at the age of 50 created a son magically. He named his son Ace. His son was inherently a very powerful magician. Even his magical father's magic who created him was not as strong as compared to his son's magic. Usually with so much power one boasts about it but Ace never boasted about it and always maintained a low profile. Ace liked playing with animals so he had a favourite animal pet which was a dragonfly. He called it Elf.

One day a very evil sorcerer came to his house and challenged Ace to a duel but he gently refused it. The sorcerer was very upset about it and decided to do something really bad about it. He had seen through magic that Ace loved his pet dragonfly - Elf very much.

So one night when Ace was fast asleep he went in his house and captured the dragonfly. He then released the soul of dragonfly and divided it into 11 parts.

The 11 parts which were : dragonfly's mind soul, its heart soul, eyes soul, ears soul, wings' soul, skin soul, nose soul blood soul, blood vessels soul, lungs soul and flesh soul. He thought if as the people say that Ace was really gifted and a very powerful magician he should be able to free the dragonfly's soul from these traps. He then wrote a letter to Ace stating what he had done to his dragonfly.

When Ace got that letter he was furious and decided to save his favourite pet Elf from the clutches of the evil sorcerer anyhow. He was also sent the blueprint of the curses and trap he put Elf in.

After reading the blueprint he found out that Elf's mind soul was tied through a magical thread to one of the fish's fin that would be found in the biggest ocean of the world.

The heart soul was tied to one of a wild camel's shoe. That camel would be moving aimlessly with or without its herd in the deep hot Sahara desert.

The eyes soul shall be further cut into as many parts as there would be humans living in the world at that time. Then it would enter their stomachs and stay there forever hiding.

Ears soul would mix in the worldwide ink used for writing.

Wings' soul would be attached to a pen that would never be able to write.

Skin soul would be put in the air which people use for speaking.

Nose soul would hang loose at the point on earth where "the sun begins to fall as soon as it begins to rise."

Blood soul would get tied to the bench where the sorcerer used to sit in his free time after performing sorcery.

Blood vessels soul was put in an egg that would never produce a hatchling but still would be under protection.

Lungs soul would be given to the army of tiny men who would be told to protect and safeguard it or else their entire race would perish.

Flesh soul was given to the the evil sorcerer Evilicka to protect and use it as its walking stick.

Now, the only thing that could be done to release his pet's soul parts was that all parts had to be found out and released physically with or without using magic so that all soul parts combine to form one single soul of his pet - Elf and then later he could combine it and put it back in Elf's body so that he could be alive again.

Ace would do anything get his pet's soul back. So he got determined to release all the soul parts of his pet from the evil veil traps that the sorcerer had put on the various soul parts.

To do that he locked himself in a room for a week so that he could devise a plan to release his pet's soul from all the traps and treachery.

At first he had to untie the soul part from a fish whose whereabouts in the biggest ocean of the world had first to be found out.

Now, to do that he made a pair of extremely fast running shoes through magic that would float and could make him run on water without drowning him. These shoes were so fast that they could make person run at about 100 times the speed of sound without falling. After he had done so it was required to find that fish that had his pet's soul tied to it. Now since his pet's soul was tied to it and the soul part was still in the human world the soul would have to breathe i.e. needed air for survival. So he used his fast running shoes to run all across that ocean (which was the biggest in the world) and see for a fish that comes up often.

He found many fishes that did that. Mostly all of them were huge fishes except for one which was a tiny golden coloured fish that kept on coming up (as it was forced by the soul to come up and let it breathe) for no reason at all. Ace thought that that could be the fish to which one of the soul part of his pet was tied too. So he got hold of that fish and chanted a spell on it. By doing that he came to know that it was that fish to which his pet's soul part was tied and that was the one which he had been looking for. After making sure that that was the fish he cut a small part of the fin of that fish to which his pet's soul part was tied to and let his pet's soul part free through magic.

Now to free the next part of his pet's soul he used the same extremely fast running shoes to find that camel that wandered on the hot Sahara desert. Now the trick involved in this was that since it was hot where the camel walked and the soul part was tied to the camel's shoe, it would scream a lot as his pet could not tolerate much heat. So he looked for a camel through whom lot of screams could be heard while running across the entire desert. He found such a camel that was quite old and was limping and also would feel a bounce when he kept one of his leg's shoe on the desert. Not only that Ace was able to hear a different kind of scream coming through that leg's shoe. Ace confirmed that that camel had his pet's soul part attached to its shoe. He took no time in replacing the camel's shoe with magic and releasing his pet's soul part from there.

Now to release his pet's soul part from stomachs of people he made several magical bees. These bees would attack the exact point of all people's stomach by an exact amount of fixed spiritual magical force that would release his pet's soul part from the stomach of people. It took a while to do so because first of all Ace had to make that many bees and then had to keep them in control. Also bees would take quite a lot of time to travel around the world to attack stomachs of people. After bees were successful in releasing Ace's pet's specific soul part he came to the next challenge.

Now it was time to release his pet's ears soul's attachment from the ink of the world. No matter how powerful a magician he was but to do this he took help of one of the magician and used a spell during night time and when no one was using ink to write. His pet's that soul part was also released safe and sound.

The next challenge involved finding a pen that would not write. This was a little tough for Ace because how could he find a pen in the world that would not write. After much thinking he sprang upon the answer to that question. He realized that the only pen that would not write would be a pen that was magical and if its master would not allow or use it for writing and also it would be an evil pen so he knew. The pen he was looking for was the same cruel sorcerer's pen that had divided his pet's soul and to which his pet's wings' soul was trapped and tied with now. He then hunted that pen down at night and opened it up using magical force. Then he located the place on the pen to which his pet's wings soul was tied to. After locating it he uttered a spell which released wings soul of his pet and the soul of the wings was free then.

Now, it was time to release his pet's next soul part which was soul of his his skin from being attached to the air that people use for speaking. For that he did another trick. Since everybody likes a beautiful smell so to get his pet's skin soul to get released from the people's speaking air he with his magical might produced so many beautiful smelling flowers on earth that forced the larynx in the people's neck to change the air they speak with. As soon as it happened Ace's pet's next part of soul was also released.

Now there are two area on earth where sun falls before rising. These are the poles of the earth. During that season according to the curse, his pet's nose's soul would be lying in the north pole. This time he again used his sprinting magical shoes and located the exact point where his pet's nose's soul would be hanging. It took him 7 days to find it but he did found that out and used another spell to let his pet's nose soul part free.

Now came the turn to free his pet's blood's soul by getting it free from the bench it was tied to. Ace wasted no time and broke all the legs of the bench with one blow causing the release of his pet's blood's soul.

It was time to release his pet's blood vessel soul from the egg that will never produce a hatchling. This was a tough one. But since it was tough to locate an egg he summoned a mighty magical dragon. This dragon was commanded to collect all the eggs in the world and keep them on an empty land which had suitable temperature to hatch eggs. He waited for 8 months until all eggs produced hatchlings except one. So that was the egg Ace was looking for. Ace was careful not to shatter the egg into 2 but many pieces so that his pet's blood vessel's soul could be released.(Why he did not wanted to break into 2 but more pieces because according to the curse "if they somehow find that egg and broke it into only two parts Elf would die forever and for eternity.") (So Ace was careful with that). Now as soon as it was done Elf's blood vessel soul was released. He then ordered the dragon to return the hatchlings to their respective parents so that there was no disturbance or destruction of peace and order on earth.

Next he had to collect Elf's soul part from the army of tiny men. That he thought would be easy. He tried using physical and magical strength on them but they would not die. They would regenerate and keep on coming for more. But as the day ended and fighting stopped because it was dark but not hopeless Ace got worried and therefore during the same night did some brainstorming and thought of another way to deal with the tiny men. He came to know that these men may not fall to might but they did fall to music. So next morning he amplified the sounds of gushing waters in the oceans, chirping of birds and blowing of air and let the tiny men fall into state of trance. Then using magic he entered their brain and got to know where they were keeping his pet's lung's soul. It was being kept tied in their chief's refrigerator to prevent it from dying (which they thought was like meat because it was a body part and would get spoiled if kept outside). He then stealthily shrinking himself entered that house where the refrigerator was and released his pet's lung's soul. After that he again grew back to normal size and ran away from there.

Now it was time to get his pet's last soul part released from Evilicka's hand and stop it being used as a walking stick. To do so Ace went to Evilicka and offered her a deal that involved use of magic to give her a new leg and in return she would have to return his pet's flesh soul. The Evilicka agreed to it and since Ace was a very powerful magician even more powerful than Evilicka he gave Evilicka an actual human leg to walk or run with. The deal was obeyed from both sides and at last all the soul parts of his pet were released. Then his pet's all soul parts combined to form one soul which was of Elf and he was then put back in his body and given life again. The evil sorcerer then had to submit to Ace's will who was then banished from mortal earth zone.

Ace gave himself and his pet a valuable gift which made him and his pet happy. Also, he realized his true potential.

tALe 92 : tHe sAviOuRs oF A fRiEnD

Once there lived a very old magician. That magician's name was Wiktoy. This magician although was old but was very fond of playing sports. Wiktoy always cursed God that he did not give him a child. So no matter who talked to him about God he used to be always be pessimistic about Him and would say that He does not exist and would continue with his somewhat sad life. Although Wiktoy had become old and grumpy he still had some vivid tastes. He liked wearing special clothes when he would go out to play soccer, tennis, cricket or whichever sport he wanted to play with his friends.

One day it so happened that Wiktoy tried wearing his favourite neon bluish green shoes. But that day these shoes were tight to fit and he could not find a reason for that and also since he was in a hurry he did not think much and casted a spell on the shoes to fit him "properly or suffer forever." The magic was so powerful that shoe adjusted its size and fitted almost instantly to his feet. (Why his shoe were not fitting his feet because they were made of cloth and this cloth due to excessive washing had shrunk causing the entire shoe including the sole which was also made of cloth to shrink to a smaller size.) After seeing that shoe fit his feet he felt excited again and went out to play soccer. Since he was in an excessive mood of excitement he tried to play a bit more actively i.e. more than his health would allow. In doing so he had an injury. The joint between the right hip and the thigh of his right leg broke and he was immediately taken to a hospital. There the doctor told him that only way to save his life was to remove the entire leg and put an artificial leg in its place. The doctor said that if that was not done Wiktoy could loose his life or be bed ridden forever. Wiktoy who had to make a decision at that time decided to get an artificial leg then.

After 15 hours of surgery the doctor put an artificial leg and took out his real leg. The doctor then asked Wiktoy that what would he like to do with the real leg. The magician replied that he would like to keep it in a bag preserved and take home as a souvenir. The doctor agreed to it. After Wiktoy got used to walking with his artificial leg in the hospital he went home taking his souvenir with him. Now he kept the souvenir in a wooden box with a glass in it so as to preserve it. But to let you know his souvenir was not that ugly it still had the shoes on its foot, the one he was wearing when the leg got injured. The doctors could not remove that shoe as they said it was way too tight to remove and also they did not needed to remove the shoe as they were planning to remove the entire leg. Therefore, the leg still had that shoe on its feet.

The magician used to watch the leg daily and see it decompose. One day it so happened that the entire leg decomposed completely leaving behind something that shocked and changed his eyes. After the leg had completely decomposed he found a small boy siting in that shoe which did not decompose with leg. The boy looked towards Wiktoy and said Hi! to the magician. Wiktoy looked surprised but he was so excited that his happiness had no boundaries. Seeing a little boy in his house even if it was in a shoe he was thrilled. Wiktoy immediately opened the door of that wooden box and picked up the shoe. The boy seeing the magician said Hi! again to him. The magician this time responded to him in a very sweet voice and also greeted him back saying "Hi , wonderful boy". Wiktoy was very excited and asked the boy his name . The boy said that since he does not know his name Wiktoy could call him whatever he thinks it would be appropriate to call him. Wiktoy thought for a while and named him Faourreiy.

Faourreiy was a very sweet boy and was only 3 inches tall. Wiktoy was so happy that day that he actually thanked Almighty for his blessings. Almighty had actually given him a companion for which he had always wished for. Now this boy - Faourreiy had some special property. Since he existed because of magic he had a special ability to give life to somethings that he liked. Faourreiy did not know this until one day when he was sitting and gazing at a fallen flower. He had started liking that flower. He looked at that flower and thought if it could be brought back to life. It was just matter of his thinking that the flower got lively and started to bloom. Faourreiy was astonished to see that and realized what he could do. But at that time he did not know that if he needed that power so he continued his life playing with his guardian- Wiktoy in the house.

One day it so happened that Wiktoy suffered an heart attack and without saying anything to Faourreiy he passed away. Faourreiy was very sad seeing that but he could not do anything about it and wept. Once he tried to bring Wiktoy back to life but he could not because wiktoy's soul and conscious had already left his body and thus he could not be brought back to life a he had a human life. Now, he woke up after quite a short sleep realizing again that he had nobody to take his care or nobody he could call his friend. It was daytime so he looked outside for help. As soon as he looked outside he saw the same flower which he had rejuvenated with his powers. He felt a bit comforting seeing that.

He then realized that he could give life to somethings that he liked and was very happy thinking that. He then choose 5 things to which he would give life to and make them his friends. The five things were : a boy made of breadcrumbs that was lying on the table, second one was a paper rat that he had made in his free time and liked very much, third was a small parachute made of handkerchief, fourth was a small tree that just looked like an actual huge tree and fifth one was something special. The special thing was a bubble whom he wanted to give life to, as he was a big fan of soap bubbles. He used to see them shine and glow in light while floating in air and so he wanted to give life to a bubble and make it also as his friend.

Now to do give life to those 5 things he simply wished that in his mind. But when he did that he was careful. He wished at that time when there was only one bubble in that room which he formed from a soap solution. As soon as he put all the things in place he wished for them to come to life and woo! the things came to life.

Now when the 5 things/toys came alive Faourreiy knew that these are talking things and the world might fool them and take them away from him or make them do bad things if people got to know about them. So he thought of giving each of them a conscious which would be helpful if such circumstances exist.

For the breadcrumb boy who was now alive and active he made some real small roller blades from wood that would fit that breadcrumb boy's feet and would also be his conscious and gave them life. This conscious could was only meat for him.

Secondly for the paper rat creature who now had a life he gave him a set of talking wings that could attach to him and also make him fly if he wanted ever.

Thirdly for the parachute made of handkerchief who was now active like any human being he made a small firefly and made it alive. That small firefly was the conscious of that small handkerchief parachute.

Now came the turn of that small tree. To give that tiny little tree a conscious he brought a flower from the garden that was outside his house and gave it life which was then told to be the conscious of the tree that would help him in his treacherous times.

Also for the bubble he picked up a small arrow attached to a showpiece in his house and gave it life. The arrow was smart and immediately understood its duties as a conscious.

He used to call all his toys by their common names.

Now, why he choose small things and gave them life to help his real toys was because small things in the world have often been crushed by bigger things in life and so they are very careful in making any decision about their life or life of others as they want to continue their life and life of their loved ones and live peacefully and in harmony with others. Now for that arrow. Arrows are usually attacking device but was still given life as a conscious because the bubble was soft in physical and moral nature so it wanted to give it something that would protect it physically and in a sharp manner too if required.

Faourreiy was very happy with his playful toys and their conscious' and used to play all day with them excited and thrilled to get such toys that were not available in world.

But in the coming days an old enemy of Wiktoy came to know that Wiktoy had adapted a boy who was still living. This made Wiktoy's enemy whose name was Ablax and who was also a magician (although not a very powerful one) very angry. He had always wanted to make Wiktoy suffer even in his afterlife so he decided to make his dream come true. To do that he then went to Wiktoy's house as a friend of Wiktoy enquiring about Wiktoy. When he went there he saw Faourreiy playing with impossible things. He really had a shock of his life when he saw the creatures and toys with whom he was playing with were alive. When he further inquired from Faourreiy after telling him that he is Wiktoy's friend, Faourreiy told him that he had given life to those toys themselves for his fun-time. Ablax did not like that at all. After he knew that, he was more determined to destroy Wiktoy's loved one and his friends.

Since he was cruel he wanted to brutally destroy those things including Faourreiy. So he set up a trap and kidnapped Faourreiy. He then wrote a letter to his toy-friends that if they wanted to see Faourreiy alive they should go through a series of tests and traps set up by him and pass them. If they clear those then they could get Faourreiy back. These traps which Ablax was talking about were severe traps which were very torturous and had the capability to destroy and make his friends die. Now Faourreiy toy friends discussed this with their conscious' that what should they do? First all of the conscious thought for a while. These conscious did not want to loose their owners but they also knew that Faourreiy was a very nice person and their creator and so whatever it takes they should bring back their friend Faourreiy back from the clutches of evil Ablax.

They then together went to Ablax and asked him if they do clear all his traps then he would have to banish himself from the kingdom and would never return and try to disturb them or their life. The deal was made and was made magically bound.

Ablax was wicked and since he had decided that he would torture Faourreiy he was going to make Faourreiy see all the traps through which his friends would go through, through a magical glass ball. This would make Faourreiy feel bad and sad and would be a kind of severe torture for him too.

So the traps were set.

The first obstacles were for the breadcrumb boy. He was to survive a falling aerobatic plane. Now the boy sat in the plane and the plane was remotely controlled by evil Ablax. As soon as the breadcrumb boy sat in the small toy plane, it started to roll on its wheels and begin to take off. The breadcrumb who had its conscious which was roller blades hanging around its neck with laces told him not to worry and be cool headed if he wants to get out of this misadventure. (since roller blades are a kind of sport equipment which are used for aerobatic tricks on ramps his conscious was ready to guide its owner through the the treacherous tricks of that evil man, Ablax.) Now the plane started to ascend and suddenly breadcrumb heard a voice which was no other but his conscious' voice who told him to wear a seat belt because otherwise his master would fall and hurt himself badly. Breadcrumb wore the seatbelt immediately. The radio controlled toy plane was a vey powerful and an expensive equipment so it reached an altitude of approx. 1500 feet. Now sometimes Ablax caused the plane to spin sometime he caused it to spiral out and sometimes he made it to turn steeply for quite a long time. It looked like there was no way out of that plane but death, but still breadcrumbs conscious which were roller blades told him not to worry and not to fall unconscious. After quite a number of spins and spirals Ablax wanted to do steep dives next. While doing so he kept on making the plane go over a huge lake and then kept on turning back and ascend to great heights. At that time the conscious was ready and told his master to be ready too. As soon as the plane dived to just near the lake surface (about 75 feet over water) breadcrumb boy's conscious told him to immediately take off his seatbelt and jump (bail out). Breadcrumb boy did that and thus survived the torturous plane ride. The breadcrumb boy had thus cleared that trap.

Now came the next trap. This trap involved putting the breadcrumb boy in the cylinders of a car's piston engine and he would have to escape from there. Breadcrumb boy said okay and accepted the trap but before accepting the trap it was agreed that no combustible liquid would be used to run the engine. Ablax was smart so he had decided that he would use a gas inside the cylinders of the engine and would make it compress through pistons by running the through battery causing harm to the breadcrumb boy. Ablax had a choice. It was up to him to choose which cylinder he would like to enter but still he had no choice as all cylinders had same diameter and same volume. So he jumped into one of the rightmost cylinder. Now this time he wore the roller blades on his feet so as to help him run around the cylinder on its piston's surface. The pistons started running up and down and a gas started pouring in which was not oxygen. This gas was supposed to make him dizzy but the breadcrumb boy was too fast and was protected from that because breadcrumbs face all kinds of heats and hot gases in the oven so the gas was not going to bother or hurt him. (Breadcrumbs are hard headed). Its conscious told him to skate towards the exit valve when the compression stroke occurs and jump and hang on to the exhaust valve there and then and his master obeyed it. As soon as the exhaust stroke occurred the exhaust valve opened (moved down) and then the breadcrumb boy jumped out from the piston and this way he survived the cylinder compression threat. Ablax was getting a little tired of the tricks that breadcrumb boy was performing on him but he said there are more traps to go and the "Breadcrumb boy shall fall." So this time he tried putting him under a trap which he thought was more dangerous.

This time Ablax said to himself that I will put this breadcrumb boy in between the gears of a wall clock so that he gets crushed with the gears while they rotate in a clock. The breadcrumb boy had to accept the challenge of getting out of gears of wall clock safe and sound otherwise the deal of saving Faourreiy was off. So since he had to see him get crushed with the gears Ablax told him to jump in the gears of a clock within the next hour. Before that, breadcrumb boy's conscious told him to wear his conscious on his shoes which were the roller blades and be ready. Breadcrumb boy wore his conscious and was ready. He then jumped in the gear box of the clock within the time and was just going to get killed when he felt that he has to skate fast and not get stuck into the gears. He kept on roller blading and jumping through the gears until at last he was out of the clock escaping from a very small opening and saved himself and was thereby free of that trap. But Ablax did not give up and gave one last try to make him suffer torture. He watched all that and also showed it to Faourreiy through his magical glass ball. Faourreiy was getting very upset seeing all that but could not do anything because he was all tied up on a wall.

The last task for breadcrumb boy was to escape from a river entering waterfall. To perform that task he would have to jump straight in the river heading towards dead end - which was a waterfall. Breadcrumb boy had gotten smart by that time. So as soon as he jumped in the river he took of the wheels of the roller blades which were heavy and threw it on the river shore. As soon as he reached the end of the river he jumped and used the inverted shoes of his roller blades as a parachute while falling down which further became a bit more air buoyant . He was hurt a little bit but he did not mind that and after that he swam to the shore hereby completing that torturous path.

Ablax had no other option but to start putting task on the paper rat and make him fail by giving him tougher tasks.

The first trap for the paper rat was that he had to escape a cat. The cat would block a small opening while trying to eat him and the rat would have to escape from there if he could. Now to deal with a cat is the most difficult task for a rat but it had a conscious which were talking wings. The conscious (talking wings) told it not to worry. As soon as they were left in a room the talking wings flew in air by themselves and whistled causing the cat to get distracted and stop it from tearing off the paper rat. As soon as the cat got distracted and stood in a certain position the talking wings attached itself to the cat and lifted it up, applying full strength to do so. This made a pathway for the rat to go out of the room from a little opening in the wall which the cat was initially blocking.

Now Ablax had seen the drama for quite long that the conscious kept on saving its master from trouble so this time he decided to put the rat and its conscious both in trouble. It told them since the rats conscious could make it fly, they would have to cross through a ring lit on fire. They both thought that it should be easy but he put rat in such an atmosphere that made it loose sense of uprightness and thus was difficult to fly. But the conscious told its master a trick. It told him that he should just somehow try to keep its body horizontal no matter what direction it is in i.e to be straight and rest will be taken care of by him. The master of that conscious obeyed it and the wings took no time in clearing and passing through the fire lit ring holding his master from the back. When Ablax saw that he had no other option and so he jumped on the next candidate which was a parachute whom he thought would be easier to kill and demolish.

The parachute had to pass only one trap set by Ablax which was that the parachute would be made wet and then a huge mass would be tied to it which if it could not support would lead him to fall heavily and cause its death. Ablax made sure that the mass was quite heavy even for its conscious which was a firefly to support. So the challenge started. The parachute was made to drop from a height of 15000 feet. Now, the firefly was smart. As the parachute which was its master, was dropping it knew that since it was drenched it could not make itself float and neither the conscious could open the knots as the knots the strongest when they are wet due to high friction between them. The firefly did a trick. It flew so fast around the parachute that it made the parachute completely dry. This made the knots to open up easily and with much less pressure by the firefly conscious. The parachute was free and thus it glided smoothly towards the ground and landed there softly. Now parachute completed that task with the help of its conscious safe and sound.

Faourreiy was watching all this through the magic ball and kept on feeling upset about it but he had nothing in his hands to help or protect his friends or toys. But after some time he realized that the conscious' given to his friends were helping their masters a lot and they had already cleared a few of the hurdles. So even though he was feeling a little bit sad but was a little bit happy too on the accomplishments his friends and toys had done.

Ablax seeing that even a cloth was able to save itself, he got really frustrated and jumped to the next contender. The next thing/toy that had to face traps was the small tree.

Now the next trap involved removal of chlorophyll from the leaves of that tree . The tree had to then survive for 5 days without chlorophyll in its leaves. Tree's conscious which was a flower said to his master - the tree not to worry and that they shall survive and live through these 5 days. The main challenge involved in this trap-task was that the tree should not loose a single leaf otherwise it would fail. The test started but it was a hard one. The flower told the tree to try converting all its leaves to thorns so strong that even if they had no chlorophyll and would dry out, but they should keep sticking to the tree itself. The conscious also told its master that this would help him to conserve the food and water and so his master - the tree did as he was told. The small tree survived the five treacherous day without loosing a single leaf and thus passed the test.

Now came the next trap which demanded that the tree shall get itself rooted to the ground and shall face a flood. Also it should not fall while doing so. The small mighty tree was ready for that. The tree got itself fixed to the ground and the magician poured in heavy rain. The water was so much that it was causing the soil to get eroded and make the tree fall. But the flower then told the tree to keep on extending its tap-root towards the earth which would help him to hold the earth firmly and thus it would not fall. The tree obeyed its conscious and did that. The magician then was tired of pouring water and he could not pour more. The trap ended and the tree was successful.

Now the trap for the last toy was left which the magician thought of giving the most challenging one according to its functionality. Ablax wanted the living bubble to fail so that Faourreiy can never be set free. He was already into deep worries seeing all of the living toys succeed.

The bubble's first test was that it would be compressed from all sides and forced to change its shape thereby trying to give death to the bubble. So it started. The bubble was put in a chamber which was getting compressed from all sides. But the bubble was smart. It shrinked to a size of molecule and escaped from the compression chamber through the gap between the two adjacent compressing bars. Ablax was dumbstruck seeing that and he did not know how he he will beat the bubble that he thought would be the most weak thing and thus would be easy to defeat. Ablax gave up. Since the deal of releasing Faourreiy was magically bound he could not cheat that deal. Faourreiy was released and Ablax got himself banished.

Thereafter Faourreiy and his toy friends moved to a new house secretly and lived there happily forever.

tALe 93 : MiNi fLyiNg pUmPkiN

In the age of piracy, pirates and stealing there once existed a group of pirates. The pirates had a captain whose name was Fol. Fol was a very evil and a wicked captain. Since Fol was a captain of pirates he had stolen many things from the world that were very rare. One of the thing that he had stolen and now owned was a mini flying pumpkin.

That mini flying pumpkin when stolen, was a baby born by magic from a witch. Fol had come to know about the birth of that baby pumpkin. It was very rare thing   and therefore he wanted that anyhow and in all ways.

He told his pirates to steal that baby pumpkin and bring it for him. So, the pirates attacked that witch and since they were too many for witch to handle she could not defend herself or protect her things. The pirates locked that the witch in her house and stole the mini flying baby pumpkin. The mini flying pumpkin grew under the care of Fol. Fol taught him to steal. That pumpkin was like a son to him and was treated like one amongst the entire crew.

That pumpkin used to enjoy his life on the ship where pirates and his crew worked and lived.

Fol had built him a mini roller coaster and a mini carousel on the ship's deck. Those rides were built high up on the ship and were supported by a single pillar so nobody could do mischief including Fol and use the roller coaster for themselves. It was only meant for that mini flying pumpkin. Whenever the mini flying pumpkin wanted rides on the coaster or the carousel he flew by flapping his wings to that high location and enjoyed the rides.

Now since the all including the pumpkin were pirates, Fol used the pumpkin for his mischievous and bad work. He used that pumpkin for stealing special things which were difficult for pirates to steal, like stealing things from royalty. This was known to all the royals and they were fed up of there precious gems and jewellery getting stolen by that mini flying pumpkin. They had tried catching that pumpkin but it was too smart and tiny so it could not be caught easily.

Since all royals wanted to be in peace and safety, once, one of the royals asked his advisor to make a plan to catch that thief pumpkin.

(Pirates did not dare to enter the royal areas, like their palaces, etc. but only this little flying pumpkin had the guts to do so.)

So a plan was made. They made an announcement that the King of Slacknock would be bringing a special coloured jewel to show to the people of his country. This news was also heard by the pirates. Fol after hearing that it was a unique jewel had got determined to get that jewel at any cost and the only one that could do it was that little flying pumpkin. So the orders were issued to the pumpkin who prepared and waited for that day.

The day came soon. The king was to show that jewel in an open area with crowd all around.

The day came soon...

The pumpkin flew so high in the sky above the area where jewel was to be brought for showing that he could not be seen through naked eyes. While flying and hovering high up he saw the king coming and that he had kept on orange coloured shiny thing in his coat's right pocket. As soon as he made sure that it was the jewel that was to be exhibited, he dived at blazing speed and picked up the jewel (which he thought) and tried flying away. When he tried to do so he could not. He had got trapped in the claws of that jewel. That jewel was actually a trap which had claws and was activated by a spring when touched. It was especially meant for the flying pumpkin to get trapped in. As soon as the pumpkin touched it the spring shut the claws of that gem which caught the mini flying pumpkin. That trap was safe and did not harm the pumpkin other than just catching it.

The mini flying pumpkin was then brought to the court of justice where he felt sorry for what he did. He then told the court that since he was raised by a pirate he did not know any other way of life other than stealing. Seeing that, court decided to have pity on him. They showed it mercy and give him a new life.

It was decided that he would be given a guardian to take care of him for his entire life. Secondly he would have to go to school and learn morality and nobleness in there. The pumpkin was happy to hear and obey that order and judgement.

The mini flying pumpkin learnt different things in school and made new friends. He had changed his life for good and had become a completely different pumpkin.

As far as Fol was concerned he missed him but could not do anything about it because the mini flying pumpkin had changed the way of his living. Also, Fol had realized that it could not be forced to do evil things anymore, now that he knows difference between good and bad.

tALe 94 : tHe sEvEn nOt sO gOoD viRtUeS

Once a fairy lived in her fairyland, happy and content. She had nothing to worry about except her happiness. She was a very nice fairy but an idle fairy. She used to go and roam in the shopping centres of that fairyland and get whatever she wanted for free and that she enjoyed very much.

One day as she was going through the books in a book shop of fairyland she came to know through a book that in the human world there are seven deadly sins which were pride, covetousness, anger, envy, lust, sloth and gluttony. Since she was a fairy she did not understand even little bit by why they where sins and how dangerous they could be. After reading and knowing them she went to other shops and then later she went home.

When she went home she sat and had some coffee and then the thoughts off seven deadly sins started popping in her mind and she could not help herself stop thinking about them. She then decided that she will try to adapt to these sins and see how it goes in the fairy world. She did not know that it could be dangerous even in the fairy world to adopt these sins but she was idle and so could not stop thinking about them.

She then stared with the first sin - pride.

To feel pride within her she thought to dress up as queen of the fairies and so she tried to do. Since she was not the queen of the fairyland she could not get the gems and jewels that the fairy queen wore to feel as a queen and get pride in her noble ways. So she thought for a while and kept on thinking. She thought that what could be the closest things to the gems so that she could wear them. After much thinking and hitting the ground with her feet she thought that balloons in fairyland were made of fairyland magical rubber that shines during the daytime. She decided that she would wear balloons on herself and look like a queen and be pretty and feel pride.

She filled quite a lot of small balloons with air and then wore a dress to which she attached the balloons. She looked pretty but funny in them and the air of fairyland could not tolerate all this so it blew air containing sharp weeds which hit the balloons and they bursted one by one. As they bursted Doolemiy which was the fairy's name, heard lots of popping sounds which almost bursted her ear drums. She soon realized that not only pride but thinking about pride was very dangerous thing and she should not let pride thoughts or pride take over her .

Then she thought let's try covetousness.

Since she could not get the jewels of the queen she decided to try covetousness and steal the fairy queen's jewels. So she went straight to the palace of the queen. As soon as he tried entering she was stopped by the palace's guards who asked the purpose of the visit. As we know fairies speak the truth and are humble may not be wise sometimes so Doolemiy told the guards the truth. She told them that she was going to steal the jewels of the queen. The guards got really angry at the fairy and pinched her really bad which made her body sour for weeks to come. She then realized that covetousness was a bad thing to adopt or get adapted to so she quit the thought of that.

Now came anger.

She had read that anger was something that is aroused and for that you need a reason. So she thought like a human and said that what other reason there could be of getting angry other than the reason of not getting the jewels to wear. She then decided that she will raid the fairy queen's palace. To do that she did some magic. Now, the magic put a horn on her head just like a unicorn but vertically up. She then thought of testing it before she went to the palace. She said that let's try it on something that already has some horns and should be a legitimate rival. She went to the forest and saw a porcupine. She then took positions and darted straight toward that porcupine pointing the horn towards it. Now the porcupine's pines were too sharp and way longer than Doolemiy's horn. So when she hit the porcupine with her horn she screamed and realized that getting angry and doing things with it is senseless and dangerous too. She also realized that when one is angry it unscrews the nuts and bolts of the brains and thus one faces painful consequences. Then anger was also struck off the list.

Now came envy.

She thought that how could and against whom could she have envy. After going through the previous bad virtues she was already brain-broken and was quite free too so she thought let's develop envy against humans because they have money which fairies don't have. She decided to steal some money and keep it for herself even if it was of no use in the fairyland. Now in envy she had forgotten that she could not exit fairyland no matter how much she tries (for security purposes) or what she does. She therefore stared preparing for that. To do that she cut her wings and dressed like a human. Now when she tried to do magic and reach human world she could not. This made her remember the rule for fairies that they can't go to the human world. She felt sad as she had already cut her wings and thus could not fly around but only walk or run. Her baseness was destroyed just by having the thought of being envious. She realized then that how deadly was having envy by her side.

Lust was something that she did not understood so she put it aside and thought that it must be a human thing which she could not decipher.

She then jumped to being "sloth". Now she said to herself that how could she be lazy? She said only way to be lazy was by keep on asking help from others and not doing anything by oneself. She then tried this. Whatever she needed she kept on shouting and screaming and yelling from her home for help to other fairies. It so happened that the fairies that lived near her house and were helping her, got fed up of helping her for no reason and kept on magically shifting there houses ¼ of a meter everyday from Doolemiy's home until they hit a 10 metre mark and Doolemiy's voice could not be heard there as it did not reach that far. Doolemiy soon realized the trick played and felt bad for that and said to herself that how will she adopt gluttony if she can't have friends helping her but it was so.

She tried to eat as much as she can to get a taste of gluttony. But the more she ate the heavier she became and even if the wings had grown back on her back in a few days even then she could not fly as the wings could not lift her weight and not only that it was difficult for her to walk or to talk as she felt lazy and sleepy all the time. So that was it! She gave up! She realized that sins or bad virtues are something that never should be thought about or adopted so she gave up the thought of the sins, no matter how tough they were and got back into being a nice fairy as before.

tALe 95 : tHe MaGiCaL mOuStAcHe

Once there lived very simple people in a very simple country. The country's name was Simpleton. In this country it was only sometimes that people tried to lie and do bad things and not all times.

Since all beings in this country including animals were simple, the king was simple too.

But to protect simple beings from getting robbed by evil the fairy godmother of the king had given a magical moustache to the king to give it to whom he trusted to wear. Now, king would not wear that moustache himself because the moustache had powers and he would look like an idiot to have that magical moustache. So he gave it to his most trusted servant - the gatekeeper of the palace.

There was a ceremony in which the gatekeeper's original moustache was cut and the magical moustache was bound to him where moustaches grow on the face below the nose through a magical glue.

The powers of the magical moustache were as below:

1)   Since it was job of the gatekeeper to record with pen and paper, what happened in the palace that day and also who came to the palace, everyday, the moustache acted as third and fourth hands to write or signal people when to go in and out if the gatekeeper would be busy doing other stuff like writing, drinking, eating etc.
2)   The second job of the moustache was to catch intruders by elongating as much as it can to work around the palace and catch those who could not be caught by king's guards.
3)   The third job was to catch people telling lie and then to tickle them with the slightest might to know the truth from them.

This all kept an order in the kingdom and peace prevailed because of the magical moustache.

But in doing so the gatekeeper of the palace to whom the magical moustache was bound started becoming more popular than the king. This made even the simple king to be jealous of the gatekeeper.

Now, he asked the fairy godmother that what could he do? The fairy godmother told him that it was bad being jealous and since you have given it to the gatekeeper it is rightfully his now. The king would not listen and stole the magical fluid from the fairy godmother to unattached the moustache so that he could use it for himself.

One night he went to the gatekeepers house himself when both the moustache and the gatekeeper were asleep. He then after entering the gatekeeper's house through an open window made his move. He went near the gatekeeper confirmed that he was sleeping and poured in the detaching fluid over his moustache little by little so that the gatekeeper and the moustache does not awake.

After 5 minutes he was successful in removing the moustache from the gatekeeper. Then he took it to his palace.

When he reached his palace the fairy godmother was waiting for him. She scolded him and in a fight the king got mad and glued the moustache to the fairy godmother with the magical glue. The fairy godmother went away in anger and the king later felt what he had done.

Fairy godmother got the moustache removed from where usually the moustaches are i.e below the nose and did not return back.

The simple people who sometimes were wicked too started doing more bad things as they could not be caught now as they knew that magical moustache had magically disappeared. Crime grew in that kingdom. The king did not understand what to do. Even his palace sometimes use to get robbed sometimes.

After much thinking he wrote a letter to the godmother and told her to return the magical moustache if not for him but for the peace of the kingdom. The fairy godmothers had a long meeting and they decided that if the moustache had to returned it will only be returned to the gatekeeper as it was rightfully his. They told this to the king.

The king agreed to the fairies and told them not to tell that he had stolen the moustache in the first place. There was a mutual understanding about this and the magical moustache was again bestowed upon the gatekeeper in a huge ceremony.

Thus peace was then restored in the kingdom all because of the magical moustache, king and the fairies, I believe.

tALe 96: tHe tiNy WoOdEn ToY giRL

As it is known that just like humans witches celebrate too. They celebrate their own amongst own. So not too far away from mainland of a country on an island, witches were celebrating birthday of their grandest witch. There was bonfire and fire-works on that island which could be seen from the mainland area which was near to that island but everybody knew that it was witches' works so nobody went near. One of a girl carrying her wooden toy doll was watching it secretly from backyard of her house. But since the celebration show was quite long she got tired and went to sleep. When she had gone to sleep she had mistakingly dropped her wooden toy girl in that garden's backyard.

As witches were celebrating it so happened that while flying on their broomsticks and celebrating around the bonfire in a merry mood, a witch while flying over the bonfire dropped her glass of wine over it. It had slipped from her hand as she was quite drunk.

Now, the wines that witches drink are very special because they are made from blood of animals after being cured magically. As soon as the glass of wine fell on the bonfire there was a huge burst of fire and some part of that fire landed directly onto that wooden toy girl that was left in the backyard by the girl that was watching live show celebrations. This burst of fire as soon as it touched the doll made it alive and soon the doll opened her eyes. As soon as she opened her eyes she saw the live world around it which was so dark but still utmost beautiful. She felt thrilled having life.

She walked around the garden secretly so that nobody comes to know about her and that she was blessed with life. In that night she saw the fireworks (which were not over yet) occurring far in the island. She was thrilled to see that and wanted to escape that garden to see that. She crawled from beneath the fence and tried going towards the fireworks. In doing so she she saw many pairs of people walking, holding hand in hands, kissing each other and having a good time while chatting and playing with each other.

But since she was attracted towards the fireworks she kept on moving in that direction . As soon as she was walking, running and moving in that direction she saw a wooden toy that was just like her but was a boy toy lying abandoned on the ground. She went near it and felt happy seeing it but it would not talk or move or shake hand as it was not alive.

Then she realized that the toy was just not alive. She liked that boy toy so much that she wished the boy toy had life too so she could play with it, dance with it, jump with it and do many amazing things with it i.e. be his partner for rest of the life.

When she was wishing that she saw a shooting star pass through over her in the sky. The shooting star heard that wish. Since shooting star are secure homes of fairies (as they are fiery and can't be caught) her wish message got delivered to one of the fairies that lived inside the shooting star.

Now when that fairy saw the tiny wooden toy girl who wished to have a partner she decided to give her what she wanted. She came out of the shooting star and appeared in front of the wooden doll. Th tiny wooden toy girl felt more alive than before after seeing the fairy.

The fairy than told her that she was a fairy and that she would fulfill her wish but since she wanted to see that how much did the tiny wooden toy girl really wanted that wish to be fulfilled she had to do two things for her wish to come true.

One was that that she had to make a round trip around the earth without using a boat. Secondly she had to create a heart for that wooden boy toy doll whom she wanted to give life to and who would come alive later.

The tiny wooden toy girl agreed to what the fairy had asked from her to do. She was given one whole year to figure out and do those things.

The wooden toy girl thought for 3 nights and 3 days that how would she be able to cross the world without a boat. As she was thinking a bird passed above her chirping. By seeing an object fly (which was the bird) she got inspired and thought of doing so to cross the earth. So next day she decided to make her own flapping wings and fly across the globe by it. Also, since she was made of wood she couldn't get hurt easily-if she fell down of being tired of flying or due to storm.

To make wings was the next step. She then went form door to door from one bird's nest to another and asked for used and fallen feathers of those birds. After knowing the reason for donation, many good birds donated their used feathers for the cause. When she had sufficient amount of feathers which were about 25 she used natural thread and glue from trees to tie the feathers and to form two wings sturdy enough to carry her load.

She then flew tirelessly flapping her wings across the globe stopping very little just for food and some rest, which was mostly done on fruit trees and some on land including islands for getting drinking water. It took her about 5 months to travel across the earth and be back to her home-place. Just so that nobody steals that wooden boy toy with whom she fell in love with she carried it all across the world with her.

The fairy watched all this and was happy that the tiny wooden toy girl did her first task.

Now came the second task which was creating heart. She though about it for 5 days and 5 nights and came upon an idea. She decided that she will make a heart of rolled up flowers which would be like a candle wick. This wick she would create every night so that nobody steals her boy toy's heart ever. To make the heart function she would light it up everyday. The warmth of fire and the scent from the wick would make the toy feel life and would make it alive until the wick gets changed every night by her with different flower when he is asleep.

The fairy was impressed with what the the tiny wooden toy girl had done and what and how she wanted to give life to the wooden toy boy.

She granted her wish and soon the boy toy was alive when after the tiny wooden toy girl put a flower petals made wick in the boy toy and lit it.

The boy toy and the tiny wooden girl toy lived fun fully hiding and playing, loving and eating and drinking and never came a time when the boy toy's heart could get stolen ever.

TaLe 97 : pOoR gEeSe

In olden times the jobs of geese was to deliver parcels but times changed. Due to their inefficiency and slow delivery system and rather an impractical system it made the geese lose this work and become jobless. Humans took charge of the delivery systems. Actually they realized that birds had nut brains and so it was they were inefficient liking missing parcels and wrong deliveries.

Since all geese had lost their only jobs and they became jobless and home bound. It got difficult for them and their families to survive. They did not know what to do so they had a very big meeting. In the meeting they decided that they ought to earn money anyhow. Through intense discussions one of the goose sprung upon a plan. He said that we have intense flying skills and may not be other skills and so we can start a drama company.

Other geese did not know what that goose meant by that. That goose then explained. It said that we can form any type of formation in the sky while flying. Then he said, this gives thrills to the kids fate world when we do it for our fun or practice purposes. The goose than said that we can sell tickets for our shows to people who would like to see them in a more beautiful way and this would earn us money. This made geese happy as they found the idea, brilliant.

They then divided into marketing and flying teams. The marketing team of geese contacted the mayors of separate towns region wide to get permission for aerial shows. The mayors were happy to give them licences to do that as it looked quite interesting to them. They were allowed to do aerial shows only at particular spots and particular height so that they don't obstruct the migratory bird or other air traffic. The geese agreed to the conditions and got their licenses. As soon as they got their licences they started selling tickets to their respective regions.

The geese had actually hit a jackpot by this plan. They did many shows in their regions and earned great amounts of money. Theses shows kept on happening for quite a long time man got advanced and started doing such shows for free through their aircrafts.

Thus it became difficult for the geese to show their shows and they stopped. But even today many a times or every time they fly in some kind of formations as if advertising their shows and asking for a comeback.

Life is a mystery but it passes away with time which passes away too. Sometimes bad things happen in life and sometimes good. Sometimes life is sorrowful and sometimes it is happy, sometimes it it is both and sometimes it is none but always, it is meaningful.

So let me begin with a story of a boy who grew to be a man and whose name was Drandrum. He had lost his parents at a very young age. This led to him start working at that age. He worked for a while but at his young age he started suffering from a very serious illness that even he did not know of. So this lead to a disaster.

Once he was working and a co-worker had not payed him his borrowed money. Drandrum kept on asking him politely for some while and later one day out of nowhere he got mad and hit that person. The person whom he hit got mad at Drandrum and called upon the police at him. He was then sent to a penitentiary. Drandrum later realized that he had done something which he never wanted and did not know how it had happened and how did he flung his hand to hit a co-worker. But what had happened had happened and it could not be reversed. So he suffered seriously because of that.

After he was released from penitentiary he became homeless. He did not know what to do at that time. After leaving the prison he walked for a while and then he could not walk further. He stopped and found a place on the street where he could sleep. All he did there after that was sleep and sleep. As for food to eat, looking at his condition, people used to throw some food over him and he survived on that. After some months of only sleeping and some eating Drandrum realized that he suffered some form of illness that was eroding him mentally but he did not have funds to go to a doctor and so he could not go. But he realized that sleeping won't help him solve sadness in his life so he started some work. He used to clean the horse wagons that ran on the streets and the wagon owners used to give him some money which he started saving. It had been quite sometime that he was saving money. Now after having saved some money he started feeling what life is and what could be done with it. He had forgotten about his illness and wanted to enjoy little bit.

To do that one day he went to a restaurant and tried to order something but he was thrown out of that place before he could do that. But he did not give up hope and tried going to another and another and another but all in vain. He was kicked out from all of them even if he had money. He felt bad because of that and did not understand the reason. Nobody wanted to talk to him or even come closer to him. One day somehow he cornered a man who was in fact a scientist and asked him that what was wrong with him? The man said politely "you stink as hell" and then Drandrum realized that what he had been missing. "Is there a way out?" Drandrum asked. The scientist told him "hell ya." He gave him a chemical and told him to rub it on his body and his clothes and then rinse it with water . He then told him to do that for at least 5 times before he goes to sit in a restaurant.

Drandrum obeyed that scientist and did as he was said.

After he had done that next morning he went to the same restaurant where he was initially refused entry but that day nobody refused his entry. All he needed was a bath which he took after 5 years. He did not stink anymore and then continued his work as a wagon cleaner.

Later he used to enjoy ice creams, pizzas and had a train ride across the continent after saving some money. Then he made sufficient money to open wagon cleaning shop of his own and used to go to see a doctor as and when wanted. He started a good and a clean life, realizing what conscious or unconscious defects he had in his life.

TaLe 99 : MaiL ExChAnGe

Once in a neighbourhood there existed some neighbours as it is supposed to be. These group of neighbours were divided into 2 groups, group A and group B. They are categorized according to their relationship between each other. Group A friends were friendly but group B friends were sworn enemies. The bad relation among group B friends was because of some misunderstanding which occurred quite a long time back which they did not even remembered now. The thing they remembered was enmity with each other. This had resulted in their sons and daughters to be enemies too. Therefore this lead to lots of noise and commotion in the neighbourhood in which lots of swearing against each other was done.

This could not be tolerated by the group A people of the neighbourhood. Group A people then had a meeting. In the meeting there was also a postman who had a plan in mind to make the group B mortal enemies to be friends. He said to the people who were in meeting. He said that he could do a thing and group B people could start meeting each other and then would eventually forget there enmity against each other and would hopefully be friends. Group A people listened to the plan and agreed to it.

The postman that delivered mail in the same neighbourhood started with the plan next day. He knew that group B people although did not like each other but knew each other's addresses and names.

Now to start his trick the only thing he needed was that there should be community mail boxes for the group B neighbours and which were already there. Then he purposely started delivering the mail into wrong community mail boxes but all belonging to group B neighbours addresses only. When group B neighbours started receiving each other's the mail they first did not return their mails but later realized that it was wrong and could be illegal if they did not do so. So one by one they went and started visiting each other's houses and started giving each other there respective mails which had got wrongly place in their community mailboxes.

Thus they started swearing less and less at each other. There were less fights, less commotions and less noise in the neighbourhood. Peace started to exist between group B neighbours and in fact all of them. Group B neighbours started being friends and later when the postman realized that group B neighbours now have become friends and so that he does not fall into trouble himself he started delivering to the right addresses. But now the group B neighbours missed how they used to go to each other's houses and meet.

So the group B neighbours came together and with group A neighbours started to barbecue together every weekend. Even there kids met and enjoyed together in the barbecue. This led to a healthy environment for neighbourhood and all became good friends until they died all because of exchange of letters and trick of the postman.

tALe 100 : ThE mAgiCaL tOy gLoBe

Once there existed a family in which there were two daughters of teen and almost of the same age. They were bright but they did not have money to study or to start a business. Fortunately they had an uncle who was a magician and was form their maternal side. They had rarely seen him on Christmas giving them presents. But not this time! It was Christmas time this year again and this time they saw there magician uncle who people used to call Dricodaf. There uncle looked very sick that day and it is believed that he and all his family members and relatives knew that those were his last days.

Dricodaf came near the teenage girls whom he used to call Ment and Fent and gave them a present which was a toy globe but the girls did not knew that at that time. He told them that that present was a magical thing and if they ever got into trouble by this just remember him and this day. Those were his last words for them. Those girls listened to their uncle and took the present. They then thanked their uncle and took that present to the room. After keeping the presents they came out of the room and celebrated Christmas with their uncle and all their family members. Next night including other nights and days the girls were busy cleaning their house and doing other important things of the houses so they only had opened few presents. They had not opened their uncle's precious present at at that time as they were a little afraid to open the present because their uncle had said some fishy tings about that present.

After 3 days the news of demise of Dricodaf came. The family including the girls wept. That day the girls gathered courage to open the present. So, they went into their common room and unwrapped the gift paper and saw a box with small toy globe in it.

As soon as they saw the toy globe they were excited to see it and immediately took it out of the box. Ment and Fent were holding each other's hand and Ment went forward and touched a part of the globe while holding its frame in her hands. The area which she touched was in China. As soon as she touched it they reached that exact geographical and political place where they had touched and suddenly a tricycle cart puller immediately passed though their side yelling "rangkai xie" (which means "move aside" in English) just missing them because they had landed on the road. Hearing the yelling, remembering and the seeing the set up of that country they realized that they had landed in China, the part which they had touched. They were shocked and really surprised to see that and immediately ran aside to get off the road.

After few moments the realized that indeed their globe was magical as their uncle had said and they were very happy with that but now they had to return to their home. How do they do that? They felt sad at that time and flapped their hands over their thighs. The girl which was the youngest of the two and whose name was Fent felt something hard in her right pocket and it had hurt her when she had clasped her hands onto the thigh. She immediately put her hands in the pocket to check what it was and wanted to throw that thing out. When she did that she saw it was that same globe which had travelled with them.

Fent and Ment both were happy when they saw that. So now they knew how to return back to their home. Fent then holded Ment's hand and then touched the area on that globe where their house was and loo they immediately reached their neighbourhood from which they walked and reached their home.

They then discussed with each other saying that it was a wonderful thing and they should do something with it i.e. utilize it in a way that would lead them to make money and would also be a source of enjoyment for them. So they did that .

They initially travelled around the globe seeing various different things. Somewhere they saw ice cream mountains , somewhere they enjoyed rains of juice and somewhere they got into pizza fights. Then they decided to earn some money for themselves and their family.

They started pizza delivery business. According to their advertisement they told they could deliver a hot and ready serve-able pizza to any location on earth in less than 15 minutes. This business took up. Many people who had relatives staying in different parts of country would make pizzas and give it to the girls who delivered them in the exact time frame they had said. People were happy with it and the girls started making loads of money. After some time they started delivering not only pizzas but any item to any part of the world just by holding or touching that thing while touching the part of globe where it had to be delivered. It was fun and good business as they charged a reasonable amount of money for that.

One day Fent went near the globe and just out of enjoyment touched the ocean of that mini magical toy globe. And as the globe does she was immediately thrown into that ocean water and she started drowning as she did not know how to swim. She started screaming while struggling to stay afloat. While doing that she tried to take the globe out of her pocket but it slipped and went deep inside the ocean. She tried to look at at it while drowning so that she remembers where it was falling but a dolphin came and swallowed it. She wanted to stop the dolphin. She put hands in her pocket to get something that she could give to the dolphin like some food in return of the globe. As soon she put hand in her pocket she did not find any food but found an orange coloured paint. She immediately threw that towards the dolphin so as to mark her. The paint touched the dolphin and left a mark on her head.

By that time a boat had seen the girl shouting and drowning and came to her rescue. She was then brought onboard the boat and rescued but she was worried that how would she reach home. She again put hands in her pocket and found quite a lot of money which was that day's sales.

When she reached the nearest port she got a ticket for a passenger ship and reached home safe and sound with all the money she had in her pocket.

Meanwhile Ment was worried and when Fent reached home she hugged her and asked her that what had happened. Fent told her the entire incident. But Ment who was the elder one told Fent not to worry.

They then with their savings bought a huge fishing boat and reached that part of the world travelling on it. They searched for the orange marked dolphin everywhere but could not find it. They tried there level best and used all kinds of traps to find that dolphin and their magical globe but they could not. It was like finding needle in the haystack and the haystack was the earth. Therefore it was impossible to do so.

They then gave up and cried on that fishing boat, but Fent remembered her uncle and that day and wished if he was alive. Suddenly a tiny sized soul of there uncle popped out of nowhere and it whispered in Fent's ear " check your pocket." She unconsciously listened to it and checked her pocket and loo! she found that globe.

But then they realized to play with magic is bad and so they used it only for work and some enjoyment but never fooled around with it and later they flourished again and they and their family stayed amongst the richest people on the planet earth after that and the girls never revealed their secret even though parents had found out so but they kept mum about that.

TaLe 101 : tHe StArS aNd ThEiR sToRy

Ever wondered why there are only 12 stars that affect the seven continents on the earth and why was there a Pangea at first. Also ever wondered why did it break up but still moves? Why is the earth made of 7 large tectonic plates which further move shorter plates? Well it's just not for fun or theory, there is a reason behind it.

The reason is a story that took place quite a long time ago after the earth had formed and there existed only a single landmass called Pangea. God had made a single landmass so that all people could live in harmony and peace with each other and be together in time of need but this was not going to happen. To test the earth God sent few of his demigods at first. Initially amongst them were 2 gods, one was Sagittarius and one was Capricorn.

This all happened during the spring time when everything was appropriate and beautiful. This today is represented as the Aries star or constellation. Now after the 2 gods came to earth they played and enjoyed there but the gods have feeling too so there aroused a mixed feeling among one of the gods which is called as Pisces and represents two fishes swimming in opposite directions i.e. one wants to go towards fantasy and one wants to go towards reality. Since Sagittarius who is half human and has a lower body of a horse and is a Demi god developed a feeling that he could be the real God on this mortal land and universe. He had seen and known that the real God had created planets, moons and stars etc. He wanted to create some planets of his own too because he boasted about being the real God of earth with Capricorn.

Capricorn after coming to earth liked and lived in the waters as his most of the body was fish-like. He could not stop Sagittarius for this reason and secondly Sagittarius was stronger than Capricorn in god powers so Capricorn did not come in his way at first.

At first Sagittarius decided that he will break the earth into 7 parts and would thus form 7 earths and they would all be for his future family on mortal lands. He knew that when he would break the earth the water would leak and thus Capricorn would have to go back i.e. he will die from earth as he would not be able to live without water.

He started his quest. He tapped the earth hard with his godly hoofs and started to break it. Capricorn at first though that it would not be possible to break the earth but Sagittarius was determined to do so and he cracked the landmass which was Pangea into seven land masses. Seeing that Capricorn became horrified and made a magical poisonous crab (which is now called cancer) that at night went and stung Sagittarius with the poison but the poison would take time to effect. The next thing he did was that he prayed to the almighty God. God who heard Capricorn's prayers sent four more gods to the earth. He at first sent a bull and a lion god. These gods came on earth and told Sagittarius to stop doing what he had planned to do but he did not listen to them. So there was a huge godly battle between them and of course the lion god and the bull god won. They subdued Sagittarius and by that time the poison of cancer had put him to silence too making him go back to where he came from where he realized his folly. Then came the two peace gods Aquarius and Virgo who restored the earth and brought food and peace there. After that a balance was restored among many things and almost everything. But since they were only Demi gods they could not make it 100 percent right like God does so the earth's continents still moves and still there are droughts etc. But majorly everything goes almost okay.

So these gods are now represented as stars while some in their forms still rule the earth kingdoms in animal forms and take care of their civilizations.

That is why Aries stars though although looks like an axe but is the first zodiac sign and tell about the spring that was sprung and started it all. Similarly other star constellation that look a bit different but are what they are and how humans perceive them because the gods affect them sometimes.

TaLe 102 : FLyiNg hEdGeHoGs AnD tHeiR wiLL tO sUrViVe

On earth there once lived flying hedgehogs. Along with flying hedgehogs there lived their enemies and some neutral people too. The enemies were vultures and eagles. The neutral people were men and women living as tribes who wanted to maintain peace amongst every being be it animal or living being.

Now it so happened that even though the hedgehogs were able to fly and even though they have pines on their backs but they are fat creatures thus are slow in movement. This character made them loose fight with their mortal enemies, the vultures and eagles. Thus it costed life to the hedgehogs. Their numbers were getting greatly reduced.

Seeing the condition of their population the leaders of flying hedgehogs had a meeting. They all wanted to do whatever was possible to prevent them from loosing their near and dear ones. The meeting lasted for 12 hours. After spending so much time one of the hedgehog came up with an idea. She said that why don't we ask the humans who live in tribes to help us. Then she told that all the humans believed in peace and if we tell hem our story they might be interested in saving us. The hedgehogs agreed. They then decided that the best person to talk to them would be the person that came up with that idea which was the lady hedgehog whose name was Cassandriona. Cassandriona then made a plan that how would she meet the tribes.

She flew to a tree near a lake and sat their next morning waiting for any human or human kid that would come near that lake and try to play. After much waiting their came a boy who first used his hands to throw stones in water so as to play and have fun. Initially he was alone but then came his other friends and they started doing it too. But the stones were not going were far. So one of them took out a strange thing. This strange thing was a catapult and he starting throwing stones throw it on the water of the lake using it. Now those stones crossed distance and seeing that other kids started asking that boy about the thing he was using. The boy told that he needed something in return for that help. So every kid went back home and brought some kind of gift for that kid. Some got money, some fruits, some honey and some got vegetables. The boy then taught them how to make that catapult and told them about the material used to make it. Cassandriona understood how the humans worked.

Next day she then went to the human chiefs. She talked to them and told them that if they could help them fight eagle and vultures so as that they could live they would be really thankful to them and would forever remain friends with them and would come in help in time of need. The truth was that that they would be highly indebted to them for generations to come.

The humans agreed but they had a problem. They said that "we would love to fight and help you but we can't carry those many arrows in our quivers as there are birds of prey in the sky and secondly even if they carried it would be too heavy and that would be dangerous during battle. Cassandriona understood and then she told them them that they need to make special bows in which they could fit the spines of hedgehogs in them and also throw them through it if required. The humans understood what Cassandriona meant.

So to every human there were assigned 25 flying hedgehogs. They hovered around that human like an angel and the war began. Humans had already made special bows to shoot hedgehogs spines through. The war started. When the eagles tried to attack the hedgehogs, they used to shed one of their spine and give it to the person loading and firing them from their bows as arrows. Sometimes even hedgehogs got injured while fighting directly trying to save humans. Those hedgehogs that got injured were flown and carried away to safety by those flying hedgehogs that had finished shedding all their spines for fighting with eagles and vultures. At the end the humans loaded and shot about 50000 arrows/spines towards the angles and vultures and finally the humans and the hedgehogs won.

The flying hedgehogs were now safe from the evil eagles and vultures who were going to destroy them all just for filling their stomachs. Then the humans and hedgehogs lived and still live peacefully except for sometimes the hedgehogs attack but it is very rare all thanks to the help given to their great great great grandparents to help them save their generations and race.

tALe 103: A mAgiCaL ChriStMaS pReSeNt

Once there was a boy named Straf. Although he was from not a very rich family Straf was always nice to the people around him. In fact he was too nice and did extraordinary deeds of goodness and kindness for kids of his age and for older people as well. Due to this he always got whatever practicable gifts possible from Santa that he wanted. (Remember by practicable gifts I mean, non magical gifts i.e. those gifts that did not cause or produce magic from them). He was always happy with the Christmas presents he got and always loved them very dearly. Straf was very fond of Christmas not only because of presents he got but also because it was a festival of lights and people gave and shared their hearts, emotions and the decorations (by sight).

Now Straf was turning 15 and in three years he would not be able to get presents from Santa anymore as he would turn into an adult by 18. So he thought and thought! During the last wishing year he wished for a gift that would help him nothing more but to celebrate more Christmas than ever. He wished for a thing that would remain a secret and still help him see christmas around the world, actually he wished for something magical. (A magical gift is not usually given to humans by Santa. It is usually reserved for the elves). So when elves got his wish letter they were a bit baffled and did not know what to do because they knew that Straf was the nicest of kids, secondly, he was going to turn 18 and also the only thing that he was wishing was for to see how people celebrated Christmas around the world.

The request was initially denied by the senior elves but since Straf needed no other gift than that and was a very nice boy after much thinking that present was accepted to be made. Since he wanted a present that would be secret, the elves thought that why not give him a magical bed which would remain visible and thus not look suspicious and thus would remain a secret. The elves agreed.

So before he turned 18, that christmas they sent him a huge parcel containing that magical bed kept besides his christmas tree during christmas night. Now when Straf woke up he went near the Christmas tree to see what had Santa send for christmas. When he saw a huge gift he was excited but when he opened its and saw it he was confused. Then he read the letter attached to it. The letter said " it will fulfill your dreams to see Christmas around your heart's gleam." Straf first thought that it was joke but when he read the instruction manual for the bed he soon realized that that bed was a magical bed and that it would take him to places whenever he wanted, during christmas to see how people celebrated Christmas in different parts of the world.

Now this christmas went by in which he finished installing the bed in his room.

Next christmas came and he got excited. He followed the instruction manual and visited different parts of the world during that season. All he did was that he had to turn of the candle light of his room and lay on the bed and say " bed take me to the nicest place this season where there are lights so bright and presents so pleasant that I get christmas right" and the bed used wrap him with its legs then become air afloat and "woo" it used to fly in the sky with 100 times the speed of sound and would reach sometimes a small village in the Alps and sometimes a busy intersection in downtown of a busy city, sometimes he use to reach mountain tops and see the lights of the towns in the valleys which would seem like the stars had descended on earth. He saw the entire world with that bed but soon it was his time to get married and he did.

This secret was not not known to his wife until he took her too for a ride. His wife was impressed when she saw the entire world. Now her wife was a bit cunning and money minded. She told her husband that why don't they sell off the bed and they would earn good money from that which they would use in their business and for their future lad. Straf was going to say no but she at that moment suddenly sat on that bed while giving a jerk to it. The bed instantaneously broke . Straf's wife suffered some injures at the back too but then she realized that "Presents are for more valuable than money and they should not be always used to trap in some honey".

TaLe 104 : hELp oF sOmE mAgiC

Now as everybody may or may not know that during olden times when the trains ran, the train station officers used to be very busy. There were so many people calling to schedule a train ticket, to cancel and sometimes even to know the status of train tickets. Due to this people working at the train station used to get terribly busy and sometimes fed up of their jobs. But they still worked.

Now this is a story of a person who worked at a train station also and therefore used to get terribly busy and sometimes cursed his job but he did not leave it because that was the only job that was paying him enough to run his home even if it was not a handsome pay. This person's name was Jack.

Jack would work intensively during his working hours and when he went home he would rest to the core. He had just become a machine but he was hard working and kept on working. Due to his diligence in his work he got promoted to the station headmaster. After getting promoted he had a girlfriend to whom he got married to and she became her wife.

His wife's name was Betty. Betty was a very nice women who was always kind to other people and loved her husband very dearly.

Let's come back to the station headmaster. Since Jack now had the authority he did few things to make his life comfortable, in fact too comfortable. He hired ten more people to work at the station and attend phone calls including in person visits.

And for him after so much hard work he had decided that he will not ever answer phone calls at work because he was tired of attending phone calls forever and had given much of his time doing his duties. He would only attend customers that had come in person and never take a phone call.

Not attending phone calls was difficult for her wife to digest. She asked his husband many times that why was he not attending phone calls. He simply said that he was busy attending customers that he come in person. Now his wife did not liked that because he should at-least pick up the phone sometimes so that she could at-least talk to him sometime. But this was never going to happen.

Now, when this was happening she talked to a person who was also a magician, a good person and also a very nice friend of Betty. Betty told her the situation. She said that it was me alone at home all day and she wished that she could talk to her husband sometimes, at least once a day. Her friend understood that and said " We can make him do that if you really want that."

Betty knew that his friend was a magician so she immediately told him not to use magic on him. He then promised that he would not use magic on him but then asked that was it possible that he could use magic on the things around him? She thought for a while and then said "Yes he could use magic on the things around him." After getting the affirmation he devised a plan.

He thought that lets bug Jack a little bit by making his table where he keeps the phone come alive.

So next day he went to Jack's office just to meet him. When he went there he met Jack and they had a long chit-chat. While chit-chatting he took out his magic stick which was coloured in a different colour so as not to look like a magic stick and rather a brown pointer. Now while talking he touched the stick to the table and whispered a secret magical word. The table became alive but according to the magical enchantment the table was not to show anybody that it was alive with some exceptions and so it did.

Now the table was alive and the magician went out finishing his meeting with Jack. Jack did not even notice that his friend had done any magic on that table (as was in the magical instructions.) The table was given a joyous nature and was supposed to help and calm Jack during his work. When jack would go outside for a break, the table would run and go to an ice cream both. There he would bend down so as not to be seen and hand over magically created money to the ice-cream seller . Then he would say to the the ice cream seller in a hidden voice that he needed a particular type of ice cream. The person working at the booth would give the person or kid he would think that was asking for ice-cream and the table being lower would not be seen. This table after getting the ice cream then would run back to Jack's office and keep the ice cream over it's top as if somebody kept it on the table for Jack. Jack would be surprised at first and would ask his workers that "Whose it was." His workers would say " that they did not know anything about that ice-cream and that he should eat it. This would happen many times. This ice cream trick would make him feel relaxed.

The next step table took was that whenever the phone rang it would make it move all around the tabletop so as to hover on it showing that the phone was quite important and that it was ringing for a reason. Initially as usual jack would not pick up the phone but later seeing the phone running and hovering all over the table he thought one day to pick up the phone and he did. That phone when he picked up he had a customer online who was very nice to talk to and jack realized that it was his duty to pick up the phone and answer calls. He started getting a sense of responsibility back for his work and would answer calls which were sometimes his wife's too. He was happy with that and starting living his work again. His wife was happy too as she got to talk to his husband from then on and she would not get bored sitting at home.

The table always was there in his office till he and it got retired!

tALe 105 : ThE sToRy Of A tALkiNg tRee

Once near a forest many automobiles started getting a flat tyre. They were not punctured, only the air would leak out of tyres and people started feeling suspicious and spooky about it because nothing like this had ever happened before there. Even according to statistics of flat types this was over the charts. People started to fear that and stopped camping near or in that forest with their RVs or cars or bikes. Thus it was a matter of time that it was very rare that anybody came to that forest.

It so happened that one family was out of that state/province and it did not know about the strange mystery of that forest. While travelling they had decided to camp there that night. The family consisted of 3 members. One was the father - the trying to be head of the family , one was mother - truly the head of family and other was their son named Zaouelf.

Zaouelf had a sleeping problem. He used to get up during nights and roam around until he could sleep a little more.

That night would not be different from the other nights when cars or any other automobiles used to park there.

One of the tyre of that RV was going to get flat again but this time the story would be different.

Zaouelf was in his cabin when he heard some sounds of beats on the ground. Zaouelf did not understand the reason for that, so he crept out of the RV and saw a tree walking and trying to fill a balloon with the air that was in right rear tyre by leaking it through its pressure valve. Some air was passing to the atmosphere and some was filling the balloon. Zaouelf kept on seeing that surprisingly and shockingly hiding behind the darkness and open door of RV which he had used to come out by opening it very slowly and politely.

Although he was standing and hiding he was a bit afraid too seeing that alive tree but and so he did not budge. After the tree had completely filled the balloon according to his satisfaction he saw the tree turning back and trying to run away. Zaouelf caught courage at that time and immediately shouted at the tree saying "Wait, listen and talk to me but the tree whose name was Brandeckiy did not pay heed to child's word and ran. Without much thinking Zaouelf also ran after him. After much panting and

Page 309

grasping and travelling a distance the tree stopped and so did Zaouelf.

The tree turned back, looked at the boy and asked him in a rough voice which banged the air "Who are you and why are you following me?" Zaouelf then said " My name is Zaouelf and I saw you filling air in your balloon from one of the tyres of my family's RV!'
Brandeckiy then said politely "Hi! my name is Brandeckiy and I am sorry for doing that. I didn't mean to steal your air but I had no other option". The boy looked at the tree confused and then after a while asked him the reason.

The tree then said " I don't need to tell you this story but since you have asked me for the reason of stealing air, I will tell you the story behind this.

He said that long time ago when he was a young tree and was very fond of running around and playing with his tree friends, one day, he did a grave mistake. He was walking in the forest jumping from one tree to other like a monkey and there on the ground he saw a shiny piece of an artifact like looking thing which later he came to know that it was jewellery - a very precious thing for humans. But at that time he thought that it was nice and looked beautiful so he thought of keeping it without paying much attention as if to who it was. He took it with him and showed it to his tree beings.

When the trees saw the jewellery being brought there they got really furious and scolded him and thus as a punishment he was given a sentence of life long "No talk motion" to other trees by the tree jury (why this serious thing happened because bringing jewellery there could endanger the very existence of trees and they thought that the humans might get angry finding that out and start chopping them down out of rage and also the trees are really strict about there existence and the laws that they govern.

One mistake broke Brandeckiy's heart. He was very upset on what he had done as it had costed him his life. He apologized to the trees but they did not listen to him even a little bit. (Those trees were somewhat delusional in their thinking but that's how they were).

So Brandeckiy remained silent for many years. He was although allowed to play and have fun otherwise without breaking their laws and bringing more danger to their world until one day he did a second blunder.

Brandeckiy used to root himself near a well. One day a fisherman came near that well and had a fish in one of his basket floating in it (it had water in the basket to keep it fresh). He had kept the basket near the well and had gone to fetch water from well. While he was doing so suddenly, the fish fell out of the bucket as it jumped while wiggling inside and the fisherman who was busy drinking water did not notice that. Although the trees had a strict policy of not speaking to or in front of humans to protect themselves but Brandeckiy couldn't stop himself and said "Your fish has fallen off the bucket".The man who was trying to get water from well freaked out hearing a tree speak and ran away yelling "Trees speak!". Now all the trees came to know about this incident as some were there and some heard about it.

From that day Brandeckiy was an outcast for those trees. He used to cry many times in sharp tones but as you know the trees have a thick skin and don't know if they have a heart or not. So Brandeckiy missed company.

For 10 years nobody came near Brandeckiy or that area until one day after a long time some humans celebrated a birthday party of their new born son an that day around the scenic well in the forest. They had tied balloons around many tress including me and that well and had left it like that when they went away.

" This was unique and exciting for me !" " So this is the same balloon that was tied around me which I have kept and play with. Also I now know that without air it is lifeless so I come and fill air in it from the air in the tyres of cars etc by leaking their tyres ". "The balloon has become my soul and sole friend."

Hearing that Zaouelf shouted in excitement saying "That's great!". He also told him that since he is already outcast he can talk to the birds and other animals in the forest and pass his time and that he does not have to live in solitude or fear from others. Brandeckiy was delighted to hear that thought and thought that Zaouelf was right.

From that day Brandeckiy used the small advise to overcome the vice and treachery of his life and got happy with his life once again.

tALe 106 : tHe kNoWeR oF tHe hEaRt

Once there was a very simple guy whose name was Erick. Erick was too simple of a person and for that a witch liked him very much. Before falling in love with that witch he did not know that the lady with whom he is falling in love with was actually a witch. But after many months of dating that lady - the witch whom he fell deeply in love and who had her name as Endora was a very evil witch which Erick did not know. Endora waited for quite a long time for Erick to ask her for marriage and one day that evil but auspicious moment came.

On their final date before marriage they were sitting in a restaurant and Erick asked Endora for marriage very politely and in a gentleman's way. Endora got excited and felt very happy after hearing that proposal but before she proceeded by saying yes she asked Erick for a gift.

Erick said "Anything for you my love."

Then Endora said "I need a promise from you that you will let me listen to everything your heart says or desire or thinks." Erick after hearing to that wish said happily and without much thinking "Of course my darling whatever you want."

But for the wish to come true the witch had too make him drink pork blood mixed with her magical potion. So she ordered one and mixed a drop of her magic potion which she said was a herb for good health and that they both should drink it to the last drop. They both drank the potion. This made the witch listen to every desire of Erick's heart i.e Erick's heart was connected to Endora's mind.

If both of them remained happy this was a good thing maybe but after some years into their marriage Erick would get frustrated from his job at a store and would yell at his darling Endora. Endora initially would not get mad at him but later as in a family, frictions develop, they got developed amongst them that.

One day in a heated confrontation Endora finally told Erick the truth about her. She told him that she was a witch and literary listens to everything that Erick thinks of. Erick hearing that freaked out and did not know how to get rid of that curse which was now looking very heavy.

Erick started thinking evil about Endora. Sometimes he thought of killing her sometimes strangling her and then giving her death. Endora would come to know about everything that Erick would think about her and so she warned him but he did not stop having evil thoughts about her.

So one day Endora got mad and made Erick a parrot and tied a string around its neck and put him in a cage. After much apologies through Erick within his heart she released him and brought him back to human form.

Few days later Erick started thinking evil for that witch again and then Endora could not stop herself being a witch and made him a mouse and set after him a cat. Erick escaped that tortuous punishment somehow with much apologies and tears.

After few days again he got mad at Endora and uttered really bad words to her. This time Endora thought lets make him a pig and put him in a pigpen where he could be slayed. But this time Erick was ready. He had taken a magical potion from another witch which could not cancel the curse but could give him something so that he could defend himself. That potion he had tied around his neck via a string.

As soon he became a pig and was left unattended for a while in a pigpen he somehow managed to open the small magic potion bottle with his mouth and drank it. As soon as he drank it he became a man. It was night at that time and Endora was sleeping. He went to his house where Endora was lying on bed in her sleep. He took out a knife and plundered her heart thus eliminating that evil witch.

This was tit for tat for that evil witch. Thereafter Erick was very wise to choose a girl who he would date and marry.

tALe 107 : A dUeL bEtWeEn A oNe FoOt DwArF aNd A tHoUsAnD fEeT giAnT

There used to be around 500 dwarves living in a forest called Dwarf-land which was deep inside a jungle. They were about one foot each in their heights. They lived in Dwarf-land around a lake called Dwarf-lake which they loved very much.

This was a very dense forest and therefore nobody entered it for fear of getting hunted by wild animals which were none, except some herbivores there which the Dwarves knew and never told to anybody. It was a secret. In that forest they felt a sense of safety and happiness and enjoyed their life to the fullest. They used to drink home-made beers and hunt herbivores which were plenty as there was no hunter other than them to hunt them. They used to play games and love it there. It was like heaven for them. There never would be any quarrel amongst them because everything was available in plenty amongst them and if anybody loses something or other or it gets taken by and used by their friend dwarf mistakingly they could always make new of the same thing or better. They had no leader as they never needed one for they were never at war and always at peace.

Once, the dwarves were sitting and enjoying their life and thinking how they never have had any trouble at all in their lives ever.

Suddenly they heard ground shaking which was something new for them and they did not knew what to make of it. They thought that the shaking was a ride which was being given to them by the forest land and so they should sit calmly and just enjoy it. But suddenly they saw a huge giant measuring about 1000 feet come. He roared at them and said that he was the strongest person there is and that now he has decided to live on their property which they called the Dwarf-Land and that too near the lake. Thus they would have to vacate to the lake and forest area as it belonged to him now.

The dwarves were shocked to hear this. How could they leave their home and dreamland? They thought that they could move to other part of the forest and live there but the giant who was a threat now to them and their family wanted them to leave the entire forest completely. The Dwarves began to worry and thought where could they go and how would they survive at any other place.

But there was a dwarf named Bravo who was listening to all this and was not intimidated by the threats of the giant. After the giant had finished talking he came forward and asked him that was he really the mightiest of all? The giant replied in a heavy and loud voice and said " Yes ". But he laughed at the giant and told him that that was impossible and told that he was only big in size and not the mightiest. The dwarf then told the giant he instead of him was the mightiest of all and can beat him any time.

Hearing that the thousand feet tall giant laughed to his hearts content. He told him that if he wanted to check who is the mightiest of all he can do it any time wherever he wanted and whenever he wanted.

So Bravo put a bet on it and told him that they will have a duel and whoever wins the duel will live in Dwarf-land and the other-kind will have to go. The giant without thinking much about it said "yes" right away.

Now Bravo told him "Give me 3 days time and I will tell you what kind of duel we'll have and the one who wins all of the duel matches wins and will do as decided.

The giant said "Okay". He said "we'll meet at the end of the forest on its east side at dawn of the third day from now. That day you can tell me what kind of duel he wanted". He also warned him that the dwarf should know that if he loses, he and all the dwarfs living in the Dwarf-land will have to leave the forest forever and could never return there ever". Bravo confirmed it and said " Yes ".

The giant left shaking the earth and dwarfs who were there did not enjoy it this time.

As soon as the giant was out of sight all the dwarfs ran towards Bravo who had challenged the giant and asked " How was he supposed to win over the 1000 feet giant? Bravo told them " I don't know that yet but we can't leave this place so I have to defeat him with all means and might " . But the dwarfs said how is it possible to beat somebody who is 1000 times their height and maybe 10000 times their weight. Bravo told them that he had faith in himself and he will defeat the giant somehow. Then he went near a tree which was besides the lake. After pondering around it he started moving in circles around the lake and the tree simultaneously. He circled the tree and the lake all night and the other elves who were sleeping did not know what the dwarf was doing and therefore slept all night long. (They were sleepy and had nothing else to do) (you know how dwarves are.)

Now while circling around the tree and lake the whole night he devised a plan. The morning when all the dwarves woke up he told them that there is nothing to worry about and they will not have to leave this place and that he/they will win definitely.

Bravo was calm too at that time so the remaining two days he slept too .

The third day came and since he had to reach the East end of forest and the forest was pretty big he started his journey the night before. At dawn of the next day he was at their meeting point and earlier than the giant's arrival time. The giant was a bit late as he was sleeping with no worries and therefore the time he woke up delayed his arrival. So finally, when the giant came the dwarf felt the earth shaking again but he enjoyed it this time.

Now the giant came and in a loud voice asked "what is the challenge?"

Bravo told him that they will have 5 types of matches and the dwarf has to win all of them to stay at his current land and the giant agreed.

The challenges were :

A) RACE : This challenge was simple. In this challenge they had to begin from one point called the starting line and one who was the first to reach the finishing line which was common for both of them would win the first duel.

The giant agreed to it.

B) HURDLE RACE : In this challenge the giant and Bravo had to jump obstacles 1000 feet high without breaking them or making them fall. For this they had to begin from a common starting point and whoever reaches the finish line first after making the least of the hurdles or obstacles fall would be the winner for this race.

The giant agreed to it too.

C) FURTHEST THROW : In this duel the person who throws the ball weighing a kilo farthest will win the duel.

The giant agreed to it without any hesitation again.

D) FASTEST SWIMMER : The fourth of the challenge was a swimming race. So in this also they would begin from a single starting point and whoever reaches the finish line first by swimming would win.

This time also the giant agreed to the challenge.

E) TREE BREAKER : The fifth and last of them was tree breaker. In this challenges whoever breaks 50,000 trees first will win the competition.

The giant liked it and said okay to it too.

Now, the giant asked when to start.

Bravo told him "give me the time of one revolution of Earth and then we will meet at this point again and start our duel".

The Giant said " Won't that be too long?"

Bravo told him that if he was brave and strong why does he worry?

The giant told him " I don't worry but am in a hurry and want to live in the Dwarf-land as soon as I can as I have no place to live ".

Bravo told him that time of one revolution of Earth should be not too long for him".

Then he said in a loud voice " OK".

The dwarf then went back to Dwarf-Land and did not tell anybody anything as he did not wanted the dwarves to worry. Although the dwarves would still sleep quietly during their worry but he was cautious not to cause more despair to them.

Dwarf had already thought about how he will practice for the challenges, when he was circling the tree. So, he practiced as below,

RUNNING PRACTICE : Now the dwarfs are pretty fast, quick and agile creatures but he still had to be more fast than normal.

Why he had though that he could win this challenge was because he had seen that, an ant which is smaller than a human could beat him in walking. Then why can't bravo who is also of similar height comparison to the giant can defeat the rude giant?

So he began his training keeping this in mind.

There was a steep mountain slope near his home and also there was a lake on top of it. What he did was, he went to the top of the mountain and dug a trench from river to the end of the slope of the mountain so that all water that was in the lake falls on the slope and makes the mud on the slope behave as quick sand. He then cut a tree and tied it to the back of his body by means of a rope which he would be dragging along with him on the ground when he moves forward.

Now he put a wrist sun dial on and daily sprinted to the top of mountain on the quicksand like puddle path with a tree tied to his back.

On the first day it was nearly impossible. It was tough, he could barely walk to top of the mountain with the tree being dragged by him but he kept on trying it and doing it as he did not wanted to loose the duel.

During the first days, his feet developed blisters out of excessive workout whilst climbing the slope and dragging a tree behind his back.

But after weeks of dragging and walking daily to the top of mountain his body started becoming used to it and became strong. His running pace started increasing. He monitored it daily on his sun-dial until he became so fast that instead of climbing the slope of mountain once a day he could do it 100 times a day which was satisfying. He then relaxed for a day and went to practice for the next duel.

HURDLES PRACTICE : Now to jump 1000 feet by himself it was nearly impossible for him, So he started working on his plan.

He built big water mills on a river nearby the hurdle race area(just to understand water mills are like wind mills except water mills run by flowing river). Then he choose obstacles, which were 1000 feet tall trees and dug mud in front of them. He then attached blower fans in them and put a soiled wooden grass mesh over them to cover them.

Now by means of shafts and gears he attached the water mills to the blower fans. He also attached a gear system to it. Now, with the help of gear system he was able to run the blower fans faster.

He then turned the system on by releasing a clutch that connected the gears. Then he jumped on the top of the meshes to check. The air blowing through the blower fans threw him high above. He was thrown to a height of more than 1000 feet. This much height was sufficient for him to clear the obstacles.

He was satisfied with the system that he had developed and his speed was already up to the mark. Now he could also clear the obstacles with that speed.

FURTHEST THROW PRACTICE : He already knew that it was impossible to throw further than the giant no matter what he did. So he made a machine to do that. He made a contraption that had a log of wood attached to it which was to function as a bat. The log of wood was attached to a high platform through a system of gears. The system was such that when the platform was lowered the log of wood which was parallel to the ground started moving back and forth at very high speeds. This system was capable of converting up and down motion of platform to high speed back and forth motion of the log of wood which was functioning as a bat.

SWIMMING PRACTICE : As far as swimming was concerned he did not practice much of it. He knew that he was a good swimmer and because he had already developed his speed on ground and had gained strength in his legs which was useful for swimming he was okay with it. Secondly he also had a trick up his sleeve.

TREE FALLING PRACTICE : Now the dwarf knew that making the tree falls faster than that of the giant was impossible howsoever fast he was. So he put his plan into action once again. He brought a big cauldron and put water and many other powerful ingredient to make a very powerful acid. The acid was so powerful that one drop of it was sufficient to soften any tree.

Now to handle the acid he made a steel sprinkler. He kept the acid and the sprinkler besides the area where the trees falling challenge was going to take place.

Now, the duel began.

RACE : The race was 500 km long. They began with the sound of first bird chirp after they had taken position at starting point.

The dwarf was confident for this challenge and ran like nobody has ever run before. Before the giant could complete half of the race the dwarf already finished it.

The giant was surprised to see the dwarf run so fast and beat him but he said to Bravo that this was only the first duel and the dwarf has to win all the duels to stay at Dwarf-land. Dwarf didn't say anything at that moment but stayed strong.

HURDLES : Before the start of hurdle race the dwarf went behind a tree where he had attached the clutch. He released it so that the gears of water mill and blower fans get connected and the blower fans start blowing the air at high speeds which were sufficient to throw the dwarf up 1000 feet but were not good to even support the giant who was too heavy for airflow and only felt cold by the movement of air. Now, this did two things. One was that it threw the dwarf at a very high speed to a height of more than 1000 feet and secondly it acted as an air conditioner for the giant and made him sleepy and slow.

So they began the race. The dwarf was fast to finish the race and also he did not break any hurdles (trees). So he won.

FURTHEST THROW : First turn was the giant's and he was asked to throw the kilo weighing ball. He threw a it to a distance of 5000 metres.

Now it was the dwarfs turn. As explained earlier he had already kept the back and forth moving wood machine which he had built at the site of the challenge.

The Dwarf requested if the giant could jump on the top of the platform with all his might as he wanted to see the performance of a machine while he throws. The giant agreed and jumped on the platform with full might. The platform was strongly made and caused a super high back and forth motion of the log of wood that acted as a bat. The dwarf was standing besides the machine and as soon as he saw that the log of wood has reached its maximum back and forth speed he threw the 1 kg ball towards the log so that it hits it in such a way that is thrown forward. And as he did he saw the ball fly and it crosses 5000m meters mark and landed at 50000 meters and the giant was dumb struck. But the giant said that there ate still more challenges left and the dwarf could not possibly win all of them whatever happens.

SWIMMING : In this challenge they had to swim across a lake 5000km long lake which the giant thought was not a big deal.

Now Bravo requested the giant to carry some food for him because it was a long swim for him and he does not want to starve to death while swimming and the giant asked the dwarf that why he could not carry it himself? The dwarf said that the race is too long and that if he carries food it will be heavy for his body to do swimming and he will drown so the giant foolishly agreed.

Bravo told the giant that whenever he would feel hungry he would call him by shouting and the giant should come and give food (which were all fruits) to him. Giant said okay.

Now the race began and every thousand kilometres Bravo yelled and asked for food. However far the giant was he came back and give him food. Bravo used to eat and then swim. This happened three more times and at fourth time when the giant was about to finish the race he shouted again and the giant came back but this time the dwarf went underwater and did not wait for food and swam for the remaining distance till he reached and crossed the finish line and the giant who had swam back kept on looking for the dwarf but he was nowhere to be found as he had already finished the race.

After the swimming race was over the dwarf went to the giant and told him that he had won this challenge also and the giant was quite upset.

TREE BREAKER : Now before the start of the competition Bravo told the giant to wait one day before they can start making the trees fall.

(To keep a track of 50,000 trees was difficult so to keep on counting them, one set of 50,000 trees were put an orange ribbon and the other set of 50,000 trees were put a purple ribbon. The trees with orange ribbon had to be broken by Bravo and the trees with purple ribbon had to be broken by the giant).

Now, during that one day Bravo picked up the sprinkler. He filled it with acid and sprayed on his set of 50,000 orange ribbon trees.

The other day they started the competition and since the dwarf was a faster runner he travelled distance at a faster pace. Until the giant smashed 50 trees the dwarf already had done breaking 150 because the acid he had sprayed on his portion of trees had taken affect. Bravo just had to pass his axe through them like passing through air and ultimately won.

The giant saw all this and started crying because he wanted to live in the Dwarf-land but could not now because the dwarf - Bravo had won the duel and there was no breaking of the deal.

The dwarf was astonished to see such a big giant cry. Bravo told the giant to stop crying and asked him his name. The giant told him that his name was "Caring".

The dwarf laughed at what was going on and then he thought for a while and told him that if he really wanted he could live in the Dwarf-land with other dwarves. The giant hearing this stopped crying and asked " Really? ". The dwarf said " Yes " and the giant picked up Bravo and hugged him and thereafter
the giant made dwarves, his friends and stayed with them forever who enjoyed the shaking of the ground. The giant loved, cared and protected the dwarves forever and so did the dwarves.

The giant and the dwarves lived happily ever after.

tALe 108 : tHe wAtChMaKeR oF tHe sAnTa'S wOrKsHoP - tHe NoRtH pOLe

Ever wondered how the work in the north pole where Santa Claus and his elves live carried out so precisely? And also ever wondered how Santa delivers presents perfectly on time and at all Christmas times? It's because of the watchmaker of the north pole at Santa's workshop who makes watches for Santa and all the elves living in the north pole. And the name of the elf is Watch-Elf.

His watches are something that have never been seen, heard or made by anyone other than him before, in the entire universe. They are specially made by the watchmaker elf - Watch -Elf with a microscope so powerful that the ratio of magnification is $1:10^{50}$.

He requires a microscope so powerful because he has to make things with so much detail that it looks like that size of the parts he makes are the size of photons of light that touch the Earth. He makes watches in which you can see the world to utmost detail just by moving finger over the watch's dome and tapping on the area you want to see and that keeps on magnifying till the person or thing you want to see is visible in the watch without his/her knowledge that that person is being watched by elves. People wonder how is it possible to see a person live what he/she is doing without the use of satellites .

Well to know how is it possible to see live what a person is doing on earth without use of satellites or spy cameras is because of the science unexplored by mankind at the current time.

Light has photons and it is an electromagnetic wave and everybody knows that an electromagnetic wave can carry data or information. Similarly photons are bound by electromagnetic field of light and they can thus store and transfer data.

So as soon as an elf or Santa starts touching the watch and starts zooming on an area the photons and the watch start sending and receiving signals from the photons where the Santa elves are trying to see into and thus watch starts receiving live imaging of what a person or a kid is doing.

So I warn you kids and everybody reading this don't be naughty this Christmas because Santa is watching. Don't ever think that without modern day technology or without satellites Santa or elves can't know who is naughty and who is nice.

Since now everybody knows that Santa does not need satellites to spy on you. God's light is enough to see you. Even when there is no light there is Dark matter which works on same principal as that of light only thing is that the black photons in it are more fine than Light photons but they have same electromagnetic transference properties as that of regular light photons.

So these watches are worn by Santa and deciding committee of elves who see Live everyday different children and check who is naughty and who is nice. Then finally after analyzing a kids behaviour and confirming that he or she is nice the deciding committee gives approval of their desired presents.

Now this type of watch is also used by Santa to navigate around the globe for distributing presents at Christmas time. He uses his watch to make a map of his route by checking where there is low visibility where there is high visibility amongst the clouds. Then he also uses his watch to see if there is some airspace especially restricted airspace which he can use to get flying faster and without obstacles in the way like wind turbines or other flying aircrafts so that he does not get smashed by them.(Actually there is something more to inform you regarding this later in the story.) now, to understand that watch is one type of watch that Watch-Elf makes.

One of the other type of watch he makes is in which it snows real snow continuously.

But it is to wonder how is that possible. I mean, by way of science.

Now to understand this concept we have to understand that it is already too cold in the north pole i.e. below -40 degree centigrade usually and thus their exists no moisture in the air over there because it has already turned to ice. It is mostly totally dry air over there not a spec of water in that air.

So how can their be snow in the watches of elves that the elf watchmaker makes.(We all know that elves love snow and Santa does too but not while flying because it obscures visibility. Elves can't get enough of it and to keep elves going and making presents, elves including Watch-elf had to have that watch anyhow).

These snow watches are personalized 3 dimensional watches, some have lighted Christmas tree in them some having the exact replica of the house of that watch owner-elf with whatever is happening around their house exhibited in the watch. Some like the polar bears cubs so they keep on seeing the new and old polar bear cubs when they are doing something crazy or cute, some want to see their kids all day long, so some have them being exhibited in their watches. And since these watches are snow watches it keeps on snowing in them while exhibiting the things required by the elves.

There are different kind of personalized watches that elves wear at the north pole and there is no end to its personalization capacity of the watches. And these watches help elves to keep on tinkering and making toys and presents for the children of Earth.

Now let's know the technology behind these snow-fall watches and that how it keeps on snowing forever in them with actual snow and similar way of its fall as that of natural snow?

When the watch elf was asked to make this kind of watch he was the most happiest creature in the universe. Watch-Elf always wanted to invent that kind of watch for himself too but had never got the time for it but when he heard this as a request from Santa he immediately replied "Yes I will make this type of watch for sure". So after careful thinking he told Santa that to make these type of watches function properly the watches have to be worn and not kept aside and then only one can see snowfall in them.

All the Elves agreed happily to it and said "That is what we want and would want forever".

The watch elf was a Genius. He thought that even if there is no water vapour in the air the watches can absorb it from the elves body. So when a warm body like elves body will release water vapours from their bodies as body heat or perspiration then those water vapours can be absorbed by the watch to convert it into snow. He calculated that the breathing rate of the elves is almost the same as humans so pretty descent amount of water vapour should be coming out of them during perspiration. These watches were small and therefore they don't require much water vapour to form snow in them and since it is cold too, the snow that is in the watches can be reused.

So he exclaimed "It will be done"!

To make these watches he made a small gear driven compressor and added the engine to it. Then he calculated the ratio and proportion of gears that will compress the compressor which will further compress the water vapours and along side it. At 0 degree Celsius air will be blown through small turbine and snow flakes will fall inside the watches as snowfall.

It worked perfectly when he made it.

The first one he made was all snow watch i.e. it had nothing but only snow-fall in it which would be remain like that forever. But he kept that one for himself.

These watches had solar sail and therefore ran on it. Solar sails are sails or fins made of a material that can move just through the pressure of falling light. To analyze this is that if they can just move with the pressure of light how much more thrust-fully will they move when they will be propelled through things like sound waves.

Yes these watches used to run on sounds and music. Even the slightest sound including the sound of movement of air or movement of air itself used to turn the sails around crank shaft which used to further rotate the wheels of the engine to which gears were attached and that was used to compress the air in the compressor and then the snow would burst in the watch-clock like it was snowing for real. This rotation of crankshaft was also used to drive small dynamos in that watch which used to create electric current in the watch to perform other functions. Since the sound never stopped, so never did the watches and as said since the elves kept these watches near them there was no shortage of supply of water vapour for the watches. These watches kept on forming snow in them and also kept on ticking forever.

Now some of these watches used to get broken too, because of playfulness of elves. Elves sometimes used to break them, sometimes used to crush them in their break or while working. So Far as elves were concerned it was okay to do little mischievous but only during the break time. They used to throw each other around or hit hammer on the head of other elves. They thought hitting hammer on each others head made them strong but Santa knew that was not true. It was only that the elves used to enjoy doing that so he never told them to stop. It was all forgiven because they worked too much and thus they needed to relax and play little bit to have some fun time and therefore Santa never got mad at them for breaking the watches.

So, these watches also told the time of each place on the earth not just time in different time zones but also the exact longitude time where Santa wanted to go .

Long time ago when people started celebrating Christmas, Santa wanted to do something special for the kids. He wanted to know that what gift each of the kid desired and where he wanted that for Christmas. But he could not figure out how to do that all by himself. So one day he asked this to the watch elf that how he could possibly accomplish that for the Christmas?

Watch-Elf laughed at this problem at told him that it will be solved without any difficulty and Santa trusted the words of Watch-Elf and relaxed a little bit but until that time he did not knew how that problem will be solved. Then Santa reluctantly asked later that how could all this be done. The wise elf told him the same theory as explained before that light or dark matter is everywhere and both contain photons , dark matter (dark matter being of smaller size than light) and both have electromagnetic field around them which can transfer information or data from one photon to other by the speed of light and that data can be extracted by something he told that he will invent called a Knowing-Watch which will understand the information and show it on a screen of the working elves and to you and then one can see what each kid wants and where he lives and when Santa can sneak the gifts in and get any other information that Santa or his elves would want. Santa still asked him "Was it possible"? He said "Yes" and told him to wait for some time and he will make it. Santa rejoiced at it and asked the elf that how much time it would take for that? The elf asked Santa to give him time of one revolution of earth and the watch system including the Knowing-Watch will be ready. Santa was rejoiced to hear this and waited for the one revolution of earth to end and when it did the watch elf had already made it and then showed Santa the Knowing-Watch. Santa was first spooked to see this but when he explained to him how it was working Santa got a bit of relief. And from that day the Knowing-Watch which Santa was given it ran just fine without even a single problem. It still keeps on running and keeps on telling what toy a nice kid is truly requesting. Once the toy is made it is final.

Let me now begin the story of a very naughty boy who never received any present from Santa Claus. It was not Santa's fault but his own naughtiness and wickedness that never got him gifts. He was too naughty to be nice to other people.

Since he never got gifts from Santa he had decided to take his revenge from Santa. Santa is not easy to catch many have tried over from the beginning of Christmas to know and get a hold of the person or thing that gave them presents during Christmas but nobody has till now succeeded.

Now, we talk about elves .

They have eyes that humans don't have. Their power of eyes is greater than any creature on earth or universe and same is true for Santa. Since their eyes are so sharp that can see a bird from at-least a 100 km away flying towards them. The use of their special eyes is used to make gifts for nice kids all over the world. They make highly accurate gifts using their very sharp eyes.

Now how do they remain hidden, uncatchable and away from human eye? Everybody knows they live in north pole and people have tried to go there and get a glimpse of them or a picture of them but everybody has failed. Nobody has ever got any proof that they along with the Santa Claus exist in the north pole. Humans have even used satellites to get a glimpse of them but they have failed. They just can't find the hiding place of the elves. Whatever they did failed. So sometimes people including kids get confused about the fact of existence of elves and Santa Claus, which is ridiculous.

Now to understand how are Santa and elves existent in the north pole.

As I had told, elves have eyes that differ from human beings. They can see more colours than human or animal eye in-fact infinite colours but to them they are finite and because they can see them and know them. So over the ages they have discovered that some colours which their eyes can see can't be seen by any human or animal eye. They have used those colours to make "Transparent colour" clothes. This causes them to remain hidden form humans. But elves can see each other even when they have transparency causing coloured clothes on because those transparency causing colours are only for human or animal eye except Santa's reign deers who can see them because they are special.

Now do you think Santa wears just one red gown when he delivers Christmas presents ? No. He wears a transparency causing coloured gown over the top of red gown to protect him from cold and human eye.

But how does Santa's face remain hidden?

Santa and elves blood, skin and hair contain a pigment that causes them to be transparent when it is cold, and when I mean transparent I mean transparent only to the animal kingdom including human beings. So whenever Santa is on his sleigh delivering presents or elves and their kids if are playing outside in the north pole, they are not spotted . It is wonderful how their body chemistry is and this gives proof that Santa and Elves have been made for a reason. This is one more reason why they live in cold because they are never spotted in cold and that they and their children remain protected and never bothered ever (I believe so!)

Now, let's begin the story of a child. This child was desperate to take revenge from Santa for not giving him presents. One day he said "If Santa never comes to me I'll go to him and get my revenge. I'll go and sit at the house of one of the kids that I bully". That kid always gets the best of the presents. He said " I'll get a hold of Santa there and will beat him to crap and that will teach him a lesson of not delivering presents to me."

He then went to the bullied kids house and told him to tell his parents that he was his friend and had come to spend the night with him for a sleepover, otherwise, he told the kid that he would bully him the rest of his life .

The good little kid got scared and did as he was told. That night the bully sat on the sofa downstairs and told the other kid to go to sleep. The kid did as he was told and slept besides the sofa on the carpet.

Suddenly the bully saw that a spec of a shiny particle came from the chimney and immediately inflated to a present. Seeing that the bully realized that it must be Santa who is delivering the gift. He immediately ran outside the door and saw nothing. Although it was a lonely house with no other houses near him he couldn't see any sleigh or reign deers or Santa and got frustrated. He got very annoyed and said to himself that how can he take revenge from Santa if he can't see him. Getting hold of him is a way beyond thing.

And for days he did not have anything to eat or drink.
He just sat thinking about what happened that day and could not make sense of it .His aunt and uncle told him to eat something. (He lived with his aunt and uncle as he had no parents. His parents had died in a plane crash when he was too small.) He was adamant about it and thus did not eat anything.

He was frustrated because there was nobody he couldn't bully in his life or beat the crap out of, if he wanted. It was only Santa that got away and this he did not like as this was a great set back for him. So frustrated he was that suddenly for once, he prayed to The Almighty and requested Him to let him catch Santa anyhow (And in coming days his wish might get granted in this story). He then waited for the next Christmas to come.

There came the next Christmas.

He did the same thing again and went to the same house where he went last Christmas and told the same kid to act the same way as he did last time and telling parents the same thing about him. The kid did as he was asked to do again. This time the bully thought that let's stay outside this night and be ready to catch Santa. But then he realized its not better to stand in cold until he sees gift coming in form of shiny spec of dust. Then only he will know that Santa has come, so thinking that he got a bit confused so as what to do. He then came up with a plan to sit inside but in front of the chimney and keep the door open so he can rush outside when he sees the gift popping out from the tiny shiny speck of particle. He will know then that Santa has come. The plan which he had devised was that since he cannot see Santa he will shout at him and ask him to come down his sleigh and show himself so that he can see him.

It so happened that day that Santa was in a very happy mood. He had received a new watch from the watch elf and it was the latest one too. So he was pretty joyous that day. In his joyousness he forgot to see the route or any aerial traffic on the watch. He had got busy playing games on it. Suddenly while flying on the sleigh, as he lifted his head to see the view in front of him he saw a flock of birds just approaching to hit him (remember he couldn't be seen but he is not massless or body-less) he steered the sleigh to the right and left but couldn't escape the scratches he got on his outer gown and the paint job on the sleigh in some areas. But he was safe and not that much visible. Little bit red colour was popping out showing his gown's cloth but and he thought it was night and so nobody would be able to see him and also this was his last delivery so he thought what harm it could do. Therefore without any worry he threw a fishing rod string at the back and fiddled it right and left until the last shiny particle got in the small net of fishing hook, Santa felt it and winded the string of the fishing rod and got hold of the present which was shrunk to the size of spec of sand (Standard Procedure at Santa's Workshop of squeezing the gifts into the sleigh otherwise how would he carry the presents.)

Now as it was his last delivery he decided to take a sip of coffee and eat some cookies to increase his appetite for his dinner because the more hungry you are the more you eat and Santa is found of eating.

He then threw the particle into the chimney which went through it got grown into the present and landed on the ground. The bully kid was watching all this while sitting and when he saw that something he got freaked out because that something who was Santa was looking like a freak show with some red popping out and that time he dared not to utter a single word. The bully wondered what if that is not Santa but some elf and thought that his revenge was with Santa first of all. So he decided that he will follow this creature who was delivering presents to wherever it goes. Why he was doing that was because he had sensed that it was Santa as it had gone near the table where it was written "coffee and cookies for Santa only". There, he sipped some coffee and just picked up a cookie ate some of it and kept remaining back which the boy did not understand. And as said the boy really wanted to confirm that it was The Santa Claus himself before he could smash him, he was ready to go to any limit to discover that. He took a blanket which was black and covered himself and jumped into something which looked like a seating place with a cavity - which was the sleigh and hid in it.

The Creature (Santa) came and said Hup! Hup! and up they flew towards the north pole.

Now when Santa was flying back the boy was curious to find out the direction towards which he was flying and to where he was heading because he had to come back too. So he removed the blanket from his face and saw down. He freaked out because all he saw was ground. Since sledge was not scratched from below but from the side so transparent colours below the sledge were in effect. He was afraid that he will soon fall down as there is nothing below that is supporting him as all he saw was ground. He had turned pale out of fear but he dared not to utter a word or squeak or squeal as he had other priorities including fear at that time. He kept mum and did not move throughout the whole journey because he was freaking out and thought if he moved he may fall down.

Suddenly he started feeling cold because they were approaching The North pole which he started getting sure of. Now, sometimes his ears starting popping in and sometimes out as the air pressure was increasing and decreasing as at that time Santa was beginning his descent for landing. When he pulled his face out of his blanket he saw that they were approaching ground and he thought they were about to crash because of he winds and felt really scared. But to assure himself he said within to his heart "If I die here I will become a ghost and haunt Santa in his dreams". But nothing of that sort happened and Santa landed safely except a little jerk. As soon as the boy saw that he was on ground he somehow managed to get off the cavity and saw a tree nearby and hid behind it to see what happened next. He saw the creature going towards a big cave which had a dome like appearance was nothing but covered with snow. The cave which was Santa's workshop was about a 100 square kilometre. The shape of itself made it look so beautiful like he had never seen it before. He was dumbstruck seeing it.

He carefully followed the creature to a wooden door which was 50 feet tall and 50 feet wide that opened when the creature uttered "Merry Christmas, open the door".

The creature went inside and the boy followed him in stealthily. There the boy saw a Christmas tree. He suddenly climbed up the tree and hid in it.

Hiding he saw that the creature that had entered starting becoming alive i.e. he started seeing the skin on the creature and suddenly he saw that the creature was wearing a red gown. He starting seeing the skin and white beard of that person whom he discovered was nobody other than Santa.

He felt bad about himself that he got afraid of his enemy and did not punch him at the house and now, there was no chance at all to even shout at him or get even with him at that place but he waited hiding in the tree. He saw that there were at least 50,000 elves working non stop.

While he was thinking he wandered why he could not see Santa and why where there sometimes elves coming as un-seeable and then all of a sudden became seeable. He thought it was something with there clothes and skin and he was right this time. Once he thought of trying to wear those clothes just by sensing and touching through them himself and become invisible . And as he was about to do that he suddenly heard a quarrel that one of the elf was shouting "You wore my coat" but the other elf who was not so sure said I think you are getting me wrong my transparency causing coat is a bit brighter than yours and you see it is. Then the other elf wondered that the elf was right and wore his coat and went away. The boy got scared seeing this because he realized that they could actually see each other wearing transparency causing colours clothes but he couldn't. So he dared not to touch their clothes even if he wanted to disappear.

So he kept hidden in the tree and observed the workshop.
Once in a while he used to come down between 8pm and 8:30 pm to eat some cookies and drink some pop straight from the bottle so that he remains unnoticed. He then used to go up and hid himself again.(no elf noticed a few missing cookies and empty pop bottles because at north pole food is plenty). This was his routine for some days.

He used to see that at break time elves would play around and throw each other around and their watches used to get smashed. They also used to pick up hammers and hit them on each others head. They thought that it was healthy but Santa knew that they were just hurting themselves. But Santa also knew that they worked a lot and got tired so hurting a little bit shouldn't make them feel tired. He did not mind that at all.

He also used to see a guy who used to come in the afternoon and take away previous shifts broken glasses and bring the new shifts fixed watches. He wondered who he was. That elf had no assistant and nobody other than him ever came to fix the broken watches. He became more curios about that elf and his ways.

Now the boy observed that the elves did not worry much about breaking their watches but there was one big clock which actually they protected . There was a no play zone around 50 feet of it in all directions.

The big clock had a printer attached it which used to print something and was transferred to different elves at the workstations who worked according to its instructions. On the other side of the clock would be elderly elves siting and looking at the clock for hours straight. They used to see the clock and then check their watches and kept on doing it for their whole shifts which he did not understand at all but just observed and one day found out that they were observing all the children on nice and naughty list and were checking the behaviour of kids to make sure that their naughty and nice list was correct. One elf used to observe 500 kids at a time and when he confirmed that they were good he used to click nice against the image of the kid on their watches and a paper printed out of the clock printer which was sent to the elves. The paper actually told that what was the gift that the child had desired which was accepted and sent for building.

Then everyday little by little the bully used to move to another tree when there was chance of shift between 8:00pm and 8:30 pm and at the end of 100th day, he had seen the whole workshop . He found that there was only one big clock known as the Knowing-Watch in the whole workshop which was deeply protected but he still wondered why. He thought that this must be the most important equipment in the whole workshop and wondered what if it got broken? An evil smile crept upon him at that time and when he said this to himself. He then said that "Lets go forward with that plan". But the other day he realized that if the watch fixer could fix small watches then what if he fixes the big watch , his whole plan will go in vain and he would not be able to punch Santa (although not physically) mentally at-least because that was the best option he had at that time.

Then he thought" What if the elf watch fixer gets ill? Then he won't be able to fix Knowing-Watch even if he could."

He waited for the watchmaker to come the next day and to do his routine work.

The watch elf came at afternoon as usual. After he collected the broken watches he started turning back and moving to the exit of Santa's workshop. The boy waited for the door to open and stealthily ran behind him and exited the door. He followed watch elf through the woods and saw that his house was like a cave too and was pretty big and also was not far from Santa's workshop.

The boy followed the watch elf and entered his house cunningly. When the watch elf opened the door he snuck behind him. He was care full not to make a sound. He observed the area and as soon as Watch-Elf turned round he ran towards a table and hid under it. Later he realized that that was his dinning table. He used to hide in there and think about how to make the Watch-Elf fall ill.
One night he was unable to sleep as he heard voices coming from Watch-Elf's mouth that don't give me peanuts or i'll die, I am allergic to peanuts, please help" . And then immediately it came to his mind that Watch-Elf never ate peanuts. When his elf friends used to come he used to offer them peanuts but he never put them in his own mouth and nobody asked why.

This knowledge was a jackpot for him.

During afternoon when Watch-Elf went out of his house to Santa's workshop to get broken watches, the boy quickly came out from under the table and ate some food from the kitchen. Then he went outside and brought a big hammer. He opened the jar of peanuts and took out one peanut and kept it on the table. Then he smashed the peanut a 100 times until he made a powder of it so fine that it could be easily inhaled through nose while normal breathing. The plan was put in action.

After sometime when the watchmaker came he was ready with plan and hid himself under the table again.

Now it was dinner time, after a long time and the elf cooked some food and served himself on the dining table. The boy who was beneath the table opened his fist which had extra fine peanut powder in it slowly and slowly started blowing air over the powder through his mouth so as not to make the elf cautious of the sudden strong pungent smell. All he wanted was that somehow the elf inhales the powder and it goes in his body and he falls ill so that he can have revenge from Santa.

Suddenly watch elf started behaving erratically. He started jumping around and started making sounds of a cuckoo bird and behaving like one.

The boy was happy that his plan had started to work.

Now the second step was to dismantle the big clock at the Santa's workshop for which he had to wait to reach because he was very careful. He did not want the watch elf to see him even if he was behaving like a cuckoo at that time. So he still had to wait under the table until the watch elf got tired of cuckooing and had closed his eyes and got lost in his cuckoo dreams. He waited for a few minutes until he was sure that the cuckoo wasn't going to make any cuckoo sounds or see through his cuckoo eyes at that time.To check, he picked up a watch that was lying on the table and tapped it so that even if it caused sound it will be the watches fault and secondly he would make sure that the cuckoo was fast unconscious. He checked that the cuckoo now was fast asleep and was not getting up. He then hurried to reach Santas workshop because he had to reach there by 8 o' clock as that was the time of the shift change and he would get about half an hour gap between the shift changes when there will be no elf around and he would to able to break the Knowing-Watch. He reached the Santa's workshop at 8:01 pm although one minute late but it was the best time because there were no elves around at that time. He then picked up the hammer that was lying on one of the workstations and smashed the power box of the Knowing-Watch. The broken pieces that fell down were put in a packing box and packed perfectly and beautifully by him so that nothing looked conspicuous. He then wrote on that fake present a fake person's name and kept it in front of the shrinking machine and shrunk it to the size of a dust particle as were other gifts shrunken to that size kept . He then ran and climbed one of the Christmas tree and checked time on one of the smaller clocks and it was 8:29pm. He blew a sigh of relief and was very ecstatic at that time. He was at top of the world. He said to himself " I'll wait there and see the what happens" and for his own enjoyment he waited.

When the shift of the elves started and elderly elves sat on the chairs besides the Knowing-Watch and started there work, the clock-watch failed to respond and gave an error message that it was non functional . The elves freaked out and screamed. The Santa was drinking tea when he heard this. By the scream his tea fell from his mouth on his shirt and gown.

Santa immediately went to the person who screamed and asked what had happened. The Elf told him that the big clock was broken and nobody knew the cause of it. Santa double checked the message and he freaked out too.

The only thing left to do was call the Watch-Elf right away.

By that time the kid who did all this was in utter rejoice. He said to himself " Now my revenge is done". He then went to the hangar where the reign deers and Santa's sleigh was kept and since it was not Christmas time the sleigh wasn't painted completely yet, it still had paint scratches on it. So he could see it and therefore he jumped in the cavity and said Hup! Hup! just like the Santa told when they were about to fly from the kid's house but reign deers didn't budge a bit because it was not Santa who was saying Hup! Hup! and they, only listened to Santa. He freaked out! No matter how much he tried they wouldn't move. He started weeping. But he was a brave boy and said "Lets face it" and then he remembered one thing that his aunt used to say "when in trouble tell the truth" and he said in tears "I already avenged myself now its time that I should surrender and say the truth".

He then jumped from the sleigh and headed back to Santa's workshop.

There he saw that Santa was preparing a pigeon to send a note and deliver it to the Watch elf (wherever he was), for it was an emergency as Santa's work was getting delayed and many nice children might miss their presents and might turn into naughty. It was a Danger zone out there.

The pigeon flew and found that the watch elf was lying on the bed making cuckoo sounds. The pigeon landed on his nose and pecked it but Watch-Elf did not regain consciousness. Standard procedure for pigeon when the person to whom the letter had to be delivered is unable to receive it due to unforeseen circumstances they tear the letter in two diagonally and bring it back to the sender. That's what the pigeon did then.

The pigeon returned to Santa with the diagonally torn letter. Santa was in tears after seeing that. He knew that if Watch-Elf was in a condition to get the letter he would have kept the pigeon and letter and sent another letter through another pigeon stating that he was coming as quickly as he could but he didn't.

The whole elf work force was freaking out by that time as there was nothing anybody could do.

Suddenly from behind one of the Christmas tree in the workshop the boy who did all this came out and said weeping "I did all this and can fix it". Everybody was shocked, first of all to see the human boy and second of all that he did all this!

But Santa calmed down all the elves and asked the boy politely that what was his name? He said it was Paul and Santa said "nice to see you Paul" and asked "could you really fix it?"

He said I can't but I can fix the person who can fix it.

Santa was happy to hear this and asked "What does he need to do that"?

He said that when Watch-Elf was asleep he was uttering through his mouth that how he can fall ill. At that time he also told how he could be cured . He said that to cure him he needs to have sunlight for 30 minutes but at that time there was no sunlight and everybody thought how it was possible?

He then said after a while that instead of sunlight we can use sunlight emitting bulbs.

The elves said "that's correct!" Two elves ran and brought the bulbs from the Santa's workshop and put it besides the watch elf's bed and connected it to power. After 30 minutes had passed nothing had happened so it got a bit more depressing but then suddenly in a scream Watch-Elf woke up and asked what was going on ? Santa told him the whole story and said we better hurry or it will be too late.

Watch-Elf immediately sprung in action and went to his room and picked up two power source machines and went to Santa's workshop. (He already knew that the power source was broken because the boy had told him what he did.)

Watch-Elf did some tinkering and loo the Knowing-Watch started working and flooded the workshop with paper flying out of the printer.

Everybody was rejoiced seeing that and immediately started working .

The boy apologized and said that he had realized his mistakes and would never do it again. The Santa and elves forgave him. He then wished if he could stay at north pole at help Santa forever. Santa nodded happily and said yes.

That was the boys dream come true I hope .

From that day on he worked in the north pole and stayed there forever. As for the presents he just went to the elf markets and got what he wanted .

The only limitation for presents was the space in his house.

tALe 109 : oLymPiCs oF tHe sAnTa'S eLvEs aT tHe nOrTh pOLe

Now how is it possible to play olympics at north pole with all the countries spy satellites over north pole? How do Santa and Elves remain hidden from human and animal eyes (other than reign deers of Santa and elves)?

To explain this let me tell you that Santa and the elves have pigments in their body, blood and hair which when get cold, become invisible to human and animal eye.They can only be felt by touching not other wise.They cause Santa and elves to become transparent and invisible. This does not mean that Santa and elves can pass through objects like ghosts.

Now the question comes don't they wear clothes because clothes are visible.They don't wear clothes only while bathing otherwise yes, they do wear clothes, don't they have to protect themselves and their kids from the severe cold?

Then how do they still remain invisible even after wearing clothes? The Elves are clever, they had learned long time ago that the pigment found in their body can be used to make colours that can be put on clothes and then clothes can be made to become invisible.

What they do is they take a small spec of hair from their body and mix it with boiling water and orange juice which forms a base that can be used to mix with colours to form clothes. The base is so strong that one spoon is enough for one tonne of colour so it is not a big problem.

Now can Santa and Elves see each other? I mean they are invisible you know.

That's true. Santa and elves can see 100 zillion times more colours that normal human eye can see. Their spectrum of eye colours is somewhat different and unique. So the colours that are transparent to human eyes are visible to elves easily and in different colours only known to the elves. Because they like colours they make many different transparent colours.

Now, what is the source of electricity in north pole.

Santa has an engine that is caused by movements of solar sail. (Solar sail is a material that can be caused to move just by the pressure of light on it.)

But in North pole the solar sails are run by sounds and movements in air so the north pole never runs out of electricity because solar sails keep on rotating with any sound or movement of air. They are made into fins and attached to a rotor that rotates a dynamo and electricity is produced. They use this technology to power everything from Santa's Workshop-where elves make toys for kids to their watches and their toys and other things if required.

Now, Let's come to the types of olympic games in the north pole and their names. But before beginning let me tell you that while playing games elves wear clothes and swimwear of transparency causing colours so that they remain invisible to humans and also as told since it is cold outside, their body, skin and hair automatically becomes transparent to humans.

Now, in Santa's north pole olympics any elf could take part in olympics because it was up to an elf, as he/she wouldn't want to get a fun made of him if he is not competent.

Now, there are a total of 10 types of olympic games played in the north pole and all except archery and swimming are played on ice and not snow. Elves have a huge ice stadium i.e. an iced lake where these games are conducted. Why these games are conducted on ice is because elves believe that if you have to be a sports elf you should have a perfect balance of your body even on ice and then you are worthy to be called a sports elf.

Now let's name the games

1. E-oe sleigh
2. E-rchery
3. E-avelin
4. E-urling
5. E-wimming
6. E-pring
7. E-urdles
8. E-kiing
9. E-rint
10. E-hot put

Even though the names sound somewhat similar to human olympic games these games are totally different.

How are these games played?

1. <u>E-oe sleigh</u> : This game is totally different than the regular bob sleigh. Usually a person skiing on a sleigh while sitting in it moves from the top of hill towards the downward direction i.e. towards gravity. But in this sport which is played by the elves the sleigh with the person sitting in it moves from bottom to up, yes against the gravity and towards upwards direction i.e uphill. This uphill movement is caused because of a spring that is attached to the back of the sleigh and is connected all the way to the top of the slide. How it is done lets read further to know.

In this game a 5000 meter long spring - (maximum stretch size of the spring), is attached by a means of a hook on the right or left side, to the back of a sporty sleigh. The upper end of the spring is attached at the top of slide. It is up to the elf playing the sport to decide which side of sleigh should he attach the hook to. Then there is an inclined slide that is 189 meters in height over which the sporty sleigh moves with a single elf in it . The slide is 5000 metres (same as the length of the spring) long with at-least 10 tight turns in it. Each segment of slide i.e turn to turn is of uneven inclination so some are 20 degrees some are 35 degrees some some 10 degrees and so on. An elf actually begins from the bottom of the slide and has to steer through the obstacles on the inclined slide backwards. The obstacles are at the side of the slide called pressure hooks.

A person wonders that lighter an elf is the faster he will go but that is not the case here. There are hooks attached to the inner side of the slide. The faster or the more the pressure with an elf's sleigh hits the hooks on the slides the more they extend out and the more curvier they become. The more curvier the slides inner structure becomes the more the sleighs get stuck. And the slower an elf's sleigh hits the slide's hooks , the less extended and less curvier they become and therefore extend or open up less. So the more fast you travel the more you hit hard the more you get stuck in the hooks and the more delayed you get. And also, not only because of the hooks but the faster you (if you are lighter) are the more difficult it is to steer because of speed also. Also if you steer dangerously or not properly (i.e haphazardly) the spring attached to the hook of the sleigh may get unhooked by itself and you'll fall down the slide. So this was a perfectly designed game for elves .

Now how is the spring stretched so far? The Elves use 500 reign deers to pull the spring down the inclined slide and hook it to the right or left side of the sleigh as demanded.

To win the game is to be the fastest one to reach the top of the slide with the sleigh spring attached to it.

2. E-rchery : E-rchery is played with bow and arrow but it is totally different than normal archery.

In E-rchery a gold fish is made to drink few drops of alcohol and become crazily agile and super rapid (Animals usually become crazy when they get drunk). Then the fish is thrown down one by one into a steep river which has rapids and stones in it. The elf-archer stands on a log of wood which is free to rotate on water, who also starts its journey from the top of the steep river. He has 200 feet of distance to cover on the downslope of river and to hit the eye of the gold fish before he falls into the water fall. So he gets approximately 30 seconds to hit the eye of the gold fish. A total of 5 gold fishes (one by one i.e. when the sent gold fish reaches the bottom of the river then a second gold fish is thrown until total of five fishes have been sent) are sent from the top of the river stream into the river stream and the archer elf floating on the log

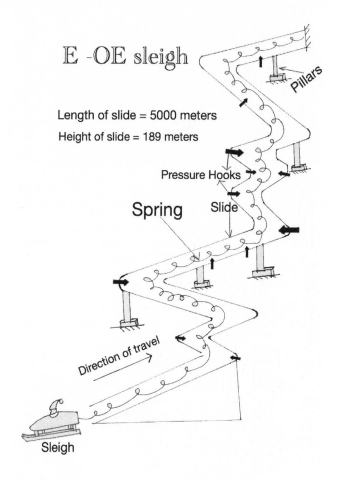

E -OE sleigh

Length of slide = 5000 meters

Height of slide = 189 meters

Pressure Hooks

Spring   Slide

Pillars

Direction of travel →

Sleigh

o   f

wood has to at-least hit one otherwise he gets no points at all. The Elf who hits closest to the eye of the gold fish and the most gold fishes, that elf wins. So its basically decided by judges after seeing the closest eye shots and the more number of fishes you hit.

Deciding points for E-rchery

A) Eye shot - 500 points ,
B) Periphery of eye - 50 points,
C) Outside the eye - on the face - 25 points and
D) On the body of the gold fish - 10 points

E-rchery is a tough game because first of all the elf is floating. Second of all he is floating on a rotatable log of wood which is very slippery because of water on it and he has to get a balance on it otherwise he will fall. And third of all he has to be very quick only then he can hit anywhere near gold fish's eye.

3. E-avelin : The E-avelin is played on frozen ice field frozen where the elves' olympic stadium is.

Now in this game, the E-avelin stick is a very long spear and is not to be thrown just straight in the air like humans do. It has to be thrown in air in such a way that it twists around some obstacles (in air) and falls on the farthest point from start and then the farthest one on the ice field is the winner. And not only this the E-avlin has a motor in it that is run by sound and wind pressure (as explained in technology part of this story). Now this motor has to be started causing the E-avlin to rotate for two things:
1) To cause the rotating arrow to turn for turning in air,
2) To cause a mark on the ice when it falls (Because otherwise the ice is too thick to cause any mark.The drilling action causes a mark on the ice.)

The concept of E-avlin is that an elf should be a master of understanding how different aerofoil shapes effect the flow of object in air and how to create one in case of emergency or not.

4. E-urling : This is a single player game. In human curling the disk that skids on ice is directly touching the ice from below but in here, the disk is kept on the top of 3 equal sized spherical steel balls which are not in any way attached to the disk. Then they have to be pushed through a hockey stick forward and land in the centre of a circle marked with paint and if there is another elves disk there, then the disk should have been pushed in such a way that it should push the already landed disk from back with so much force that the sliding disk gets put in centre.

Now in this game any disk should never ever come off the balls and fall down otherwise the elf gets disqualified.

Now according to laws of physics if we push the disk on the steel balls (which will be sliding a little bit too, above the balls) the disk above it, will fall from the ball very quickly. But in this game their are two wedge supports parallel and on the both side of a path leading straight to a circle centre where the disk should skid to. So the disk is pushed not straight but diagonally and it strikes left and right causing the movement of the disk that has moved in a direction towards a fall to correct itself and keep on being placed on the steel balls and ultimately land at the centre point of the circle.

This game was the favourite of the elves.

5. E-wimming : This game is carried out in cold water and wearing only swimwear .

In this game an elf has to only rotate sideways which will cause movement in the sideways direction and the fastest one to reach the finish line wins.

Now why this game is carried out in only swimwear in cold water is that a sports elf should have so much body power that while rotating he should generate enough heat in its body to counteract the coldness.

Secondly a person can faint doing this but these are elves and elves believe that a sporty elf should have a fit brain and should not faint in any circumstances.

6. E-pring :This Sport is simple. In it an elf has one spring attached to the centre of shoe and which is on both of the shoes and has to run on ice track. The first one to reach the finish line wins.

7. E-urdles : In this game an elf uses the same shoe as that used during E-rint (coming below) and this sport also takes place on ice track.

Now in this game the obstacles are small water ditches and there is a hurdle string attached above them running parallel and horizontal to the water ditches. An elf running E-urdles has to jump over the obstacle and rotate 360+ degrees around the string above it then land on ice forward and keep on running forward until all obstacles like these are cleared. The first one to reach the finish line wins.

8. E-kiing : This is a fun game too because, first of all it is done on ice second of all it is lovable.

In this game there are long blades like that of ice skates attached to the centre of shoe at the bottom and the elf wearing the E-kiis falls from ice covered mountain on the ice path and that too backwards. There are obstacles that look like pillars mounted on the ice. The pillars are arranged in such a way that the skier has to twist and turn to reach below at the finish line otherwise he will fall. The person who reaches at the top speed after clearing the obstacles by turning and twisting wins.

9. E-rint : The E-rint game is also not simple.

In this game an elf runs of-course but on single pin-pointed point of wood attached to the centre of shoe on bottom. So there's again a toughness in this race. The person has first of all learn to balance on a needle and then run on it.

10. E-hot-put : In this last type of game the person has to hold a flat disc with a group of five elves having total weight of 50 pounds standing on it. Then he has to throw the disk straight forward in the air along with elves on it who may fall on the ground . And the person who lands them the most forward wins. The total distance that have been crossed by the landed or fallen elves is added to know the maximum distance for winning.

But the difficulty in it is that elves would be jumping up and down unevenly causing uneven weight distribution at different times which is difficulty to take into account. And also there is no periodicity nor height to which an elf will be jumping.

Let me now begin the story of an elf kid.

There was an elf kid born to elf parents after a long time. His parents wanted a kid for a long time therefore they prayed to god daily for a kid until they finally gave birth to one named Alf meaning alpha elf or top elf.

But as he grew up he had a lot of hard time in his toy making school where all elf kids used to go.

He was the thinnest ones of the whole elf kind. More to know he was actually half of thin of the other thinnest elf around. Thus he used look very weak. But no body used to laugh or mock at him. It was only that he had hard time to understand things and to do them. His parents were worried that he would not make a good worker elf which all elves are. The elf boy new that, but his mom used to tell him not to worry and he will be the shining star of all elves. The boy used to hear this and used to just keep quiet after hearing this. One day he said mom I can't be shinning star because I am weak and thin and I am not strong as other elves. But his mom told him " Son strength is not in muscles of the body but in your inner heart and one who has a strong heart has a strong mind and body." He listened to it and kept it in his mind and continued his daily activities.

Alf was a sports liking person. He used to go to see The North Pole olympics every year. He used to see elves play and win the hearts of people and once he said to himself "I want to be an Elf sports star too". But he never knew how to do it so he used to go in the icy forest sit besides a tree and cry.

Once he was sitting and weeping and saw an ant trying to go beneath his foot. He thought it was trying to climb over him and bite him so he tried to squash it first, but it couldn't be squashed because it kept on changing its direction and moving forward and became very tactical but then he finally aimed to put his feet on top of it and then finally it got squashed. He thought he killed the ant but that was not the case the ant got up and became even faster in moving and tried to go near his foot again but the elf again got scared and tried to squash it again but he missed a couple of times and squashed 2-3 times again but the ant got up and then Alf got scared and jumped moving aside. The ant immediately went into its hole where the elf had kept foot before. The elf was surprised that an ant which was so tiny got squashed many times but got up and reached its destination with all its courage.

That incident changed its life. He thought that if a tiny-miny ant can be squashed by person million times heavier than it and still get up to live why can't I who has everything of an elf be an elf sports star.

He then waited for the next olympics and keenly observed it. He noted down how athletes were doing things and how they won.

After observing them carefully, he devised a plan on how he will train himself for the olympics and he decided to take part not only in one olympic sports but in all 10 of them and win all of them which nobody had ever done before nor thought in his/her wildest dreams .

He said "I will train one hour everyday for each sport until the next olympics comes but it will be meaningful".

A)   <u>E-rchery training machine</u> : To train for E-rchery he said that "It's tough and barely anybody comes close to hitting the eye of the a super agile and fast tagged gold fish , how can I do it".

He then worked on his devised plan.

Instead of water rotatable log he built an Elvish engine consisting of solar sails and attached it to a rotatable log of wood. He then put a mechanism in it that alternatively with no fixed time intervals would rotate sometimes clockwise and sometimes anti-clockwise and also he made arrangement in the mechanism that the more person gets imbalanced and the more noise he creates the solar sails will rotate at a higher speed in either direction which would become almost impossible to balance on machine.

Second thing he built was a flat conductor and devised a mechanism to short circuit it so that it releases only one spark at a time and he had to hit the spark with an arrow from his bow. And how will he know that he hit the spark was that the tip of the arrow will become discoloured (which is only possible when the spark is hot and visible, otherwise his arrow shot will be useless).
He was going to use both the tricks simultaneously to train for shooting.

B) Training machine for E-oe Sleigh : He thought that falling is faster, if fallen from a high altitude. So keeping this thing in mind he made a sleigh similar to that he will use in olympics and attached sharp pins to all exterior sides of it and also attached an air engine run by solar sails. Then he made a catapult to throw the sleigh along with him in air to a height of 50,000 feet. He also made a helium balloon dispensing machine.

Functioning of this training machine was like this : the sleigh was put on the catapult and thrown up as soon as it was thrown up the engine started increasing rpm and increasing the speed of the sleigh until 50,000 feet where air is less and air vibration is less and then it falls.(the elf did not have to wear a mask because they already are used to living in less oxygenated air by living at north pole). Now as soon as the sleigh is thrown upwards the helium balloon dispensing machine which was on the ground starts dispensing balloons and until Alf starts its flight on the sleigh back from that high altitude he has to steer through the balloons floating in the air with help of engine thrust sideways and should not let any balloon get blown by the spikes all around at the exterior of its body .

C) Machine for E-avlin training : To train for E-avlin he had to be a master of understanding aerofoil shapes and know how they behave.

So he put pillars on the ground that could be moved to make different type of obstacle circuits.

Secondly he made a boomerang and decided to change its direction by putting clay on it bending it for desired type of curved flight to understand aerofoil shapes.

Now to understand boomerang. It is a sports or hunting equipment usually made of wood that returns to it sender after throwing it in a particular way in the air because of its aerofoil shape. It used to be a traditional equipment.

D) Training equipment for E-urling : For practicing E-urling he made a 10 times heavier and 10 times lighter disk that will slide on the ball while practicing E-urling.

E) Training equipment for E-wimming : Now to train for E-wimming he made a plastic bag big enough to cover him completely till neck.

The theory was that plastic skids in water and thus requires more thrust to move so he will have to apply more force than normal elf and also since his hands and legs will be in the plastic bag there will be much more power required to do sideways swimming by the elf. While practicing he will match his speed of E-wimming when being covered with a plastic bag with that of the top speed of the fastest elf E-wimmer.

F) Training machine for E-pring : To win in E-pring he attached steel balls to the lower part of the springs which were not only movable in all directions but also reduced the height of the spring to match the regulatory height of the spring shoe from base.

The idea behind it was that the steel balls will be more slippery and hard to manage because when he would try to move forward he will slip and fall head over heels.

So it was real tough to train on them

G) Training equipment for E-urdles and E-rint : So usually it is thought that putting weight on feet while running will make them perform better on the track because putting weight on feet causes resistance when leg moves up but what happens when it comes down. When it comes down it moves with a greater force which further causes rebounds and helps somewhat in moving the leg up and forward. So this training method is not a very efficient one.

What Alf did was he put a jet fan below on the ground while attaching it to the floor and put a grill over it. Secondly he put another jet fan vertically above the ground jet at about a metre and half from his head and added a grill below it (for safety).

Then he made four wooden curved boat like structures. Two pointing upwards and two pointing downwards. He then made two pairs of those structures. Each pair had one "U" shaped structure pointing upward and one "U" shaped structure pointing downwards and attached one pair each to both of his shoes.

The concept involved is that when both the upper and lower jet fans will be throwing air at great speeds he will jog in between the blowing jet fans air wearing the "U" shaped structure attached to the shoes. Doing this will be difficult for him to move upwards and downwards both which will make his E-rinting faster on actual grounds.

H) Training equipment for E-ot-put : So he had to make his arm too strong so that he can win this sport.

For this he built a super high tension spring which he attached to the board on which usually elves are jumping before throwing them forward.

And then he further attached a knocking sledge hammer weighing 75 pounds which will be hitting continually to the disk-board that has to be thrown, to it.

Both the machines will be used together for practice.

So as he will try to do the throwing action with the board attached to the big tension spring whose others side would attached and fixed he will face more and more pressure when he reaches to the top of his hand because springs behave like that (i.e the farther the spring is stretched the more force it requires) and also because of the sledge hammer hitting the board at a very high speed and putting great weight on it.

I) Training equipment for E-kiing : This was simple. He attached jet fans to the ski so that it can go faster than normal and if he can steer backward at faster speeds then he surely can steer at slower speeds.

Alf kept all of his training machines hidden from all elves eyes at a secret location in the forest which only he knew. So if anybody asked he used to say that he is just going to play in the forest which wasn't a lie too.

Except for training with E-avelin all the other training he did were hard which he tried and failed initially but ultimately succeeded and achieved his maximum pace and strength.

Training with E-avelin took him a bit of skill as he had to learn what causes the boomerang to turn around so he tried many aerofoil designs with clay on boomerang and slowly he learnt the art of understanding aerofoil shapes and how do they respond to airflow.

As he had decided he would practice for 1 hour daily on each sport for 365 days and it would be meaningful. So he did it and got skilled in the sports.

Now the olympics begins.

In E-oe sleigh Alf didn't even get hit or stuck by even a single obstacle or the hooks and won the greatest score with greatest speed recorded forever.

In E-rchery Alf hit not only one gold fishes eye but all the five gold fish's eye centre point with his arrows i.e. one arrow in each eye. This was a record never ever broken by any elf ever.

And in the remaining games Alf won with flying colours and made his parents and all the other elves proud.

TaLe 110 : tHe mAgiCaL fReNcH hArP

Summer vacations were about to end and so was the work of this boy. This boy's name was Fin. He had been working at the magician's workshop to help him out with his daily things that did not involve magic or its making. He would only help him out to do things like heat up the water for boiling or cook food and bring stuff including groceries that he needed from the nearby market. The magician was happy with Fin's work. It was now time for the magician to give Fin a reward for all the hard work he had done in the past four months. So at the end of the last day of Fin's work, the magician asked him about the reward that Fin would like to have? Now Fin was a very noble and people caring person. He said that I have a french harp and 5 wooden toy planes. I want you to make my French harp magical which could control my five toy planes when I play it. Thus he also actually wanted to give life to the wooden toy planes. He wanted the toy planes to fly magically when he played his French harp. He also told the magician to make his French harp understandable so that it listens and understands to him and gets aware of what is good and what is wrong in this world. Next he told the magician that when his French harp becomes magically alive it should be caring too. The magician laughed and granted his wish. He uttered the words " L..e..c..k..r..o..c..k..m..i..t.o. " in a loud magical tone and soon Fin's French harp came alive and became magical along with the wooden toy planes that could fly with the playing of his harp and his harp alone.

The magician then asked Fin "what would you do with this magical reward?" Fin replied that he loved taking care of people and that's what he would do with this gift.

Fin in his little life had seen many thefts happening resulting in loss of people's money and other precious things. Although people earned sufficient and there were always many job openings but still some wanted easy cash. Fin wanted to stop all this from happening. So to stop the thefts, at night he would go out at the top of a high mountain, sit there and play his French harp. The French harp he played was in such a tone that all people would fall in a spell. They would sleep wherever they were and that too undisturbed. Then his toy planes would start their propellers, take off from that mountain slope and would become airborne. They would then descend down the mountain and while flying would pick up stolen items from theirs warehouses and would carry them back to their owners. After keeping them safely they would fly away back to Fin were he would pick them and would go down the mountain to his home to sleep.

He kept on doing that every night until the thieves came to know that something was not right and thus they got afraid of that phenomenon and dared not to steal.

Amongst the thieves was a a young thief who would not get under that spell and therefore would not ever fall asleep because of the sound of Fin's French harp. He would only observe what was happening. His name was Finneiy. He would hear the French harp playing and one day got a chance to see the toy planes transferring stolen items from one place to other just after nightfall. He realized that he was helpless against it. Initially he was also afraid of the phenomenon but later after careful observation he came to know what was going on. He then realized and repented his stealing habits. He understood that stealing was bad and therefore quit doing so. He became a hard working man who would only spend the life with the wages he earned. Still he listened to the calm French harp played by the boy and would love the tune and enjoy it at night.

Now after few years when theft had stopped completely because of actions of Fin, Finneiy the young thief would miss the harp's tune.

  Page 349

The only way now that he could listen to that tune again was by buying a harp and playing it himself. So he got a French harp for himself by his earned money and not stealing. After some time of much practicing he could produce the same tune which he used to hear played by Fin and was happy with that. He was also happy that the town was a safe place now as there would not occur thefts anymore.

But one day a tragedy occurred Fin died because of a sudden heart attack and Finneiy got to know about it. Now, Finneiy was a little upset and worried about it as the thieves would start stealing again not because they knew what had happened but because they can't stop their habit when they sense their thief spirit and their intuitions. But Finneiy would not let that happen. He was determined to take whatever steps he could to stop this from happening. So after much thinking he went to steal once again but this time not for himself. He wanted to do it for the society and town where he lived.

He went to Fin's place. He stole his magic harp and magical toy planes. When he got the French harp and the magical toy wooden planes, he reached home and tried to play the harp and see if it worked but the harp was smart as it was magical. As soon as he tried to play the harp it would change its flute columns positioning almost instantaneously while still being attached to the harp and thus any tune produced by blowing air in its flute columns would sound weird. Finneiy at that time did not know what to do. He then tried telling the magical French harp that he was playing the flute for the same purpose as was his previous owner. The flute would not listen to him as his previous master had told him about good and evil in the world and the theory of not talking or obeying to strangers. Finneiy slowly understood the nervousness of harp. He understood that the flute did not wanted to get into wrong hands or do wrong things. So, he got his own French harp and played the same tune that Fin used to play. The magical harp when heard the tune it was surprised to hear the same tune coming from another person's French harp. The magical flute then tried giving Finneiy a chance. It jumped in the air by bouncing off the ground where it was lying and then reached Finneiy's hand. Finneiy seeing the magical French harp do so realized that the harp wanted to get played by him now. So he went to the high mountain carrying also the wooden toy planes with him. The magical French harp watched all that and started to have little bit more trust in Finneiy. He then reached the mountain top and played the same tune again but this time, by using that magical harp. The toy planes responded immediately. They flew and returned the stolen goods to their respective owners while Finneiy kept on playing the harp whole night. The town was back to being a happy and a theft proof place as people knew that there was someone who took care of them.

They knew that there stolen goods were returned to them the other day after a dark night and every night.

TaLe 111 : tHe nAuGhTy pRiNcE

Long time ago, to a family of kings and queen was born a son. He was named as Dewildered. He was born to the king and queen as their last son to be. Dewildered enjoy a beautiful lifestyle as rich princelings do. Even when he was young he would waste a lot of things including money but still he was good at heart in helping others. He would donate a lot as a young princeling and do lot of meetings for charity which made his parents be and be not impressed.

After Dewildered grew up into being a real man i.e. when he got responsibilities over his shoulder he got a bit mismanaged. He once went to a poker club and played poker. Although he lost that game but he started liking it. Even though he did not like the game itself but still he liked the gambling part of it. So he started going to gambling clubs and would gamble a lot there. He was still single when he started doing that but that did not make him stop doing it. He gambled carefree without worrying about his assets getting decreased. Since it would be legal to gamble and he liked it so he could not issue a decree to stop that game and thus he continued playing.

Since there was always more than enough that he always had he did not notice his shrinking assets even after several warnings from his ministers.

One day he was eating food sitting besides his dining table when the cook shouted saying that " the bread is over ". Dewildered got bewildered that how could bread get over for a prince. Then the minister explained to him that before dying his father had passed a legislation seeing the spending habits of his son. The legislation said that the prince would have a fixed asset for his lifetime unless he grows it by fair means and only then he would be able to be called a king and not prince. The money that was collected through taxes would be used only for administration purposes and for running the country. Dewildered was shocked to hear it and asked why he was not told about that earlier or if there could be anything that could be done to change that legislation. But the minister told him that he had tried to tell this to him before but he would not listen as he was too busy gambling and secondly he told him with a sorrowful face that that legislation can't be changed.

Dewildered starting sweating and did not understand what to do. He realized that he had been a real fool and if his dad would not have that legislation in place then he would even have lost the kingdom. From next day he stopped gambling and tried to start changing his life for good. He got determined that he would earn and stand up again as a good prince by doing good and not wasting anything. To do that he would change his dress and try to work at a local shop but since he had always spent life like a king he could not handle the labour involved in that work.

That day he wept. He felt like if he was disabled and had nothing left in his life to do. He then remembered his mom and his mom's words. His mom used to tell him that he was a charming prince and people specially girls loved him which made him have a smile on his face at the spur of thought. Now for few days he had eaten little and was quite upset. But he kept on remembering his mom's words and decided to open a new business under his name. He called it " the Kissing Booth ". It was advertised through out the kingdom that the king would be kissing anyone and everyone at the booth only for a dollar. All girls and women were excited to hear that and the business started.

This business was a great success and he actually started saving some money. Everyday, there would be huge lines of women standing and waiting for a kiss from the prince. He had plans to continue that business but because he had some times in which he had to kiss the older ladies too and sometimes grandmothers too , he started thinking of not doing it forever. Therefore after he had saved quite a bit he stopped that business of kissing and invested that money in a very lucrative business of that time and flourished from there. Thereafter he never had trouble in getting bread for his food, all thanks to the kissing booth. Also, he never assumed the title of a king and tried to remain modest in nature and heart.

tALe 112 : tHe pUp-pEt mAkEr

In a small town called Puppetville there lived a puppet maker. His name was Joy. The puppet maker was a very nice person who loved kids. To show his love for kids he would stage exciting puppet shows at a very reasonable price. The kids who liked seeing puppets in action would come there almost daily to see different type of stories that he would tell showing marionettes and by being a marionettist.

All kids liked Joy very much including the little prince of that town who would come and watch all his shows. All the kids including the little prince had developed a special bond with the puppet maker. They loved him so much that when the puppet maker would be working back sage to prepare puppets they would flock around him and play and sing and make his time go wonderfully.

One day the puppet maker decided to do a special show for the kids which would be free and would involve a special character.

The special character was nothing but a puppet dog. At the end of show he brought the puppet dog and controlled it in such a way that at the end he put some juice at the centre of stage and made it jump in it while controlling it with strings. The puppet dog (marionette) jumped in the juice container and then walked out. When he walked out of the juice container Joy with the help of strings made him wiggle and twist while shaking it's body rapidly. This made the juice that was absorbed by its body cloth (puppet) skin of that puppet dog scorch out of his body and fall on the faces of the kids watching that show. The kids when licked what had fallen on their faces were excited to find out that it was nothing but juice and tasted very tasty at that moment.

Even the kids that did not liked the puppet shows also started liking the puppet show. The dog puppet show got so popular that he had to perform that splashing and the scorching out juice in every show because kids were fan of it and could not go without it. Rich kids could have paid good money for that but he only charged a very reasonable fee which made him get his daily bread and he was satisfied with it.

In matter of time the little prince grew up but never forgot the puppet maker. He would take some time off sometimes from his busy princely work and would meet Joy - the puppet maker. They would spend time talking and passing the time well.

This kept on going for quite a long time until one day the prince got into trouble. The news came that prince had been taken captive by a huge monster whose kid had gotten injured by the prince's arrow when he had gone for hunting. The puppet maker investigated it further. By doing so, he came to know that the prince had mistakingly hit the monster giant's kid while he was shooting a deer. The the monster's kid had come in between. The prince tried to avoid it but could not.

The puppet maker and the grown up prince were good friends and he had decided to save him. The king (father) of prince was ready to attack the monster with full of his army might but he was worried that in amidst of the attack his son - the prince might not get injured so he did not do so.

Now that giant tried curing his son's wound with some herbs but those herbs were not effective enough and the monster's kid would not get cured. The puppet maker knew about that and so he got a special medicine from the king's doctor to cure that injured kid. He then went to see the monster. The monster tried to kill the puppet maker with his club but the puppet maker escaped that and tried to cool him down telling him that he had a medicine for his son's wounds. The giant monster did not trust the medicine that was offered by the puppet maker. So he refused the offer. But then the puppet maker came upon an idea. He introduced himself and said what if he just stays with the monster's kid to entertain him and pass his time. But the monster threatened him by telling him that if he did any harm to his kid then he would be dead even before he knows about it. The puppet maker agreed to the terms

The puppet maker had come with his puppets prepared just in case he needed them. So he did a trick. He did the same dog puppet show that he used to do in his shows but instead of juice alone for the dog puppet to absorb and scorch out he added medicine to the juice. Now the monster kid would enjoy the show and entertainment and would lick the splashing liquid tasting it as if it were juice. Since the medicine was also in the juice the kid started getting cured and the monster was happy seeing that.

After the kid got completely cured Joy told the monster that how he cured his son. The monster got a little mad but hearing that he relaxed too after a while. The puppet maker then requested the monster to remove the prince from captivity and spare his life. The monster was adamant not to do so but the monster's kid said "Papa it's okay, the prince seems to be like a nice person and he has already said that it was a mistake and would never happen again." Hearing the kid's words the monster was calmed and released the prince. Not only that Joy invited the monster's kid to watch the puppet shows whenever he wanted as he liked them very much too.

Later the giant monster like looking creature became friends with the kingdom, the prince and his family.There, then existed a peaceful era of happiness and friendship amongst people and monsters.

tALe 113 : ThE mOuNtAiN AnD hiS sLeEp

Once in a low lying area of a valley, there lived some villagers and that village had a secret. This secret was passed on from generation to generation as it lived until those generations were there. The village was part of the country which surprisingly never came to know the secret of that village.

The secret was the mountain that faced the huge valley was not actually a mountain, it was a sleeping giant. This giant true to its name as denoted by people would always sleep. Not only he slept he had special instructions for the people of the valley too. The two most important instructions of the sleeping giant/mountain were that they can't tell anybody other than who already know that the mountain was a giant, not because he was afraid but because he wanted it that way. Second thing that had to followed was that after sunset nobody could be seen outside their houses for any reason whatsoever. Children and adults alike were stuck in their houses after sunset and thus children could not play and men could not do any other thing other than hiding.

This continued for quite some time until there got born some naughty kids who were too young too know the secret and so were too stubborn to not listen to their parents. There parents would come and try to find them and tell them to come along and stay in their houses but that would not work. 5 days passed and the sleeping mountain started becoming very tired due to not sleeping well at night. Although during the day he half slept properly but that was not enough. He needed lots of sleep because he was a mountain and he liked so, secondly, so that everybody stayed out of trouble.

But after 5 days when the giant got really irritated from the disturbances caused by the mischievous kids in the evening he tried to be humanly friendly and do a thing. He had many magical dragonflies under his control that rested on the sleeping giant. So he ordered them to make few sleep inducing candies and go to the valley village and give it to the naughty playing kids so that they may go to sleep for at least that day. So the dragonflies obeyed the sleeping giant and went to see the kids. Now the kids could have eaten candies otherwise too but the dragonflies were ordered to throw the candies into the kids' mouths so that it was sure they go to sleep and so can the sleeping giant. Now this humanly behaviour continued every night and the kids would thus go to sleep. The giant seemed friendly after all.

Page 355

But one day the king of that country took up a fight of war with his only foe in the world (who was also a king). They had disagreed politically. The king who was the ruler of the country where the sleeping giant lived was always afraid of his foe because of his might but this time he had decided that he would not bend down to his foe as he had gotten too personnel politically this time.

So the war was decided. The king had decided that he would rage war on the enemy in about a year's preparation without letting his foe know. That king whose name was Astelliming ordered the people of his country to make swords and other weapons and work night and day to do so.

This was a pain in the bum of the sleeping giant. All the giant ever wanted was to sleep and this he was not being able to get or do so. The noise of metal hitting metal in the town would not let him sleep at night or in day. Although the giant had its instructions of not disturbing him but the king had his instructions too and they outweighed that of the giant's (as giant was nicer than the king).

Now in sleepless pain and agony of drooling eyes the giant thought of a plan. He made a special candy and looked for the Prime minister of that king though his tiny but huge and long distant monocular. When he found the Prime minister he did his usual trick but with a different medicine. He, this time told the dragonflies to prepare a hypnotizing candy that would hypnotize the Prime minister for at least three days. Then he prepared a puppet that looked like the Prime minister.
The dragonflies were then ordered to force that candy into the mouth of that minister and see that he chews it all. The dragonflies almost did as they were told. They went near the minister. Then, few dragonflies bugged him and one of them threw a candy in his mouth which he swallowed, thus kinda chewed it. As soon as the minister swallowed it he was in control of the giant in fact he was telepathically connected to the dummy that giant had prepared which looked like him. Now the giant would give instructions to the dummy and the real minister since he was hypnotized obeyed them.

Then the giant told the minister of a plan. He told the minister through his dummy to tell the king to go to sleep. It happened according to the instructions. Then the sleeping giant woke up after his long disturbed slumber and went to the king's enemy. The earth shook when the monster walked but he still approached the king's foe fearlessly. On seeing, the foe of the king who was also about to sleep freaked out. The bodyguards had already left the palace where that foe of Astelliming and their master was resting. That foe asked the giant shaking with fear that what was that that the giant wanted? The giant said that "All he wants is peace and that can only be achieved if he stops overpowering or pressurizing Astelliming forever. In fact he waned him to be best friends with Astelliming. Seeing the size and shape and the hearing the voice of the giant that foe obeyed to him obediently.

Next day the foe went to Astelliming and apologized to him for his overpowering nature and gave him few candies of his own. Astelliming got peace in his mind and the war preparations were halted and the giant then could sleep peacefully.

All thanks to the sleep and giant. Sleep is too precious to give away so if you would like to sleep be candy-full.

tALe 114 : ThE sHoEs

Even many centuries ago people walked wearing some thing or the other on their feet. Some wore a set of leaves, some wore leaves tied to a broken branch, some wore shaped stones and some skin obtained from animals which in time turned unknowingly to leather latter due to much organic chemicals being sweated upon the animal skin by live foot skin of those who were wearing them. But few centuries later, ie after many centuries some body invented a real shoe. Why it was a real shoe was because it was made of clothing material and some real knowable leather. This was the most happening thing of all time, and the talk of the town which in actual comprised of the entire earth people. But why? Why it was the talk of people of earth was because the shoes that were invented which they started wearing felt very comfortable. Also they protected people from debris slipping in the shoe and touching their feet. Not only that, they were of many different colours that suited both men and women.

But one day something strange happened. A shoe-maker decided to make shoes that were totally white in colour and so he did by making the shoes. These shoes were quite bright and white . The shoes, seeing all that were quite happy too and liked themselves very much. Those shoes had thought that they would fit on a feet and this would make them feel that they have touched the sky. Everybody knows that shoes are meant for feet and that they love and want to be worn and be praised ?

Many days passed. All the other shoes that the shoe maker had made that were also the white coloured shoes' friends had gotten sold. The white coloured shoes were the only shoes were not getting sold because somehow they were not being liked. This made the white shoes quite upset. But since they were just shoes they could not do anything about it. So they waited and waited for many more days, and months but nothing . No body came to buy those shoes and thus they could not be sold . That made the white shoes quite upset.

Thus one day the shoe maker saw and felt the sadness of the shoes . That day he decided to sell them for free but still people did not wanted to get an ugly thing (which they thought that the shoes were). Sad and frustrated , the shoe maker did not know what to do with the shoes. He although was feeling the sadness of the shoes too but he had no other option other than to throw them away and that he did with a broken heart. Because otherwise they were just utilizing the space of his shop and which was a waste to his showroom's rent. He threw them away and they then landed in a garbage bin .

The shoes started to die ie getting rotten away quite quickly being kept in a garbage bin but some luck arrived. That day an artist was passing by. The artist saw a beggar pick up those white shoes and discard them right away after making a stinky sign by means of his hands! The artist was quite intrigued seeing that a beggar discarding free worn-able stuff . He then walked towards the shoes and picked them up . Then he took them home. The shoes seeing all that, appeared to be a little bit happy. They thought that now they would be worn. But something different was going to happen. The artist did something out of the box. He coloured those shoes in a new way. The artist then thought that he would wear them after the colour dries. But they became exceptionally beautiful after they were washed and coloured. So he thought why dirty such a piece of art by wearing them and therefore he decided to but then in a decorative wall case behind glass walls.

The pitiable thing was that the dream and desire of the shoes still remained unfulfilled even after becoming beautiful. They were never worn so, frustrated one day they decided to do something different themselves. When the wall glass case was slightly open, they wasted no time and ran away never to return.

But where did they go? That's an answer its relative should know. So try asking one of them. They might answer.

To begin with let me first name the witches that are involved in this tale. The female witch's name who is in love with the male witch is Wichon. The male which who is loved by Wichon has a name and that is Wireco. Wireco's stepsister's name is Brenty. Wireco's step mom's name is Aflemmy.

Now, let's begin the story.

This happened at a time when witches were present in great number on earth. So since there were so many witches around, love was around too. But love would only occur between witches or humans and not between witches and humans as this would lead to a dangerous situations "ha ha ha". Now Wichon was a more powerful witch than Wireco but was in love with him. They had gone to the same witch school where she had become fond of him. Wireco liked Wichon too but less than how much Wichon liked him back. Since the childhood they were friends and would do lots of fun together. But as both of them grew up Wireco starting liking chess and got addicted to it. He would play it all by himself. While Wichon would be studying witchcraft and became quite powerful in it. Wireco started neglecting his witchcraft techniques and concentrated in playing chess. Although he knew some witchcraft but his witchcraft had not grown as powerful as his friend, Wichon.

Wichon would ask Wireco many times to come with her and go for some outing but Wichon would not come and would say that he was busy as he would be playing chess. This made Wichon mad and one day when Wireco was busy having a bath in his bathroom when she went and cursed the chess. The curse stated as follows. "Whenever that chess is played and its game is about to get finished the player/players who is playing the chess will suffer the same consequences ie he/she will get finished too. By this she wanted to give death to her love Wireco whom she loved. Before that Wireco would continue game and finish it in five minutes and would keep on playing it as his general routine.

So when Wireco came out of his bath, he wore clothes and started playing chess as that was his addiction. As soon as he started playing and was about to finish it he heard a shout. His stepsister was yelling that she wanted help from her stepbrother. What her stepsister had done was that she had stolen some sheep from some human and wanted to hide them. She wanted to put the sheep inside a room at the top of mountain that she used to use to hide other stolen stuff. But sheep was the first live stock item that she had stolen. She wanted to hide them before its owner came and get her into trouble by complaining to the sheriff-witch.

Brenty told Wireco to think of something so that she can hide the sheep quickly. Wireco wanted to play his chess without wasting time, so in hurry he devised a plan. Since he was sharp minded as he played chess alone he took some wool from the sheep and magically made it into magical bat. Then he told his Brenty to throw the sheep high in the sky one after the other using her magic and then with magic, pinch the sheep to the direction where he was standing with the magical wool bat. Brent did it.

But before that occurred he took some more wool from one of the sheep out and turned it into ball. Then he hit the ball using his magic such that it reached and opened the doors of the room that was on the top of mountain where the sheep had to be sent. One after the other Brenty kept on throwing the sheep towards Wireco. Wireco kept on hitting the sheep with magical bat and the sheep started reaching the top of mountains unhurt and straight in that hiding room. The sheep were not getting hurt because the magical ball he had hit first had already become flat due to so much pressure and had formed a cozy flat bed that acted as a sponge and protected the sheep from getting hurt. It took them about 5 minutes to put all the sheep in the room at the top of the mountain because he was hitting them so quickly from her stepsister's fear who wanted it to be done quickly. Then at the end he took his magical wool bat and threw it directly towards the room which after reaching that place locked it and safeguarded it.

Although it was approximately five minute task but Wireco was quite tired after doing that as it utilized lots of magical energy from his witch body. But he would not stop playing his chess. He went inside to his room and was about to continue make last moves and end his chess play when his mom called.

Aflemmy wanted his Wireco's help to left a 500 pound tomato that had grown under the influence of witchcraft in her backyard and put it in the cold basement. Now, the only way to put that tomato in the cold basement through the door was to make it small or to lift the house and then put it in. Wireco decided that he would rather make the tomato small than lifting the entire house to squeeze it in basement. So he immediately went to the mechanic and bought a very tiny gear. Then he went home and cut a very long vine from that back of his stepmom's garden. He then did some magic on both the things. He somehow inserted the small gear in the centre of tomato after making it enter from the top of leafy part of tomatoes and go straight down to centre. He while doing so had tied the vine to the gear so as to rotate it. The vine since it was magical started turning as he said : "Yes, Turn now, do it now and let me go now." While her stepmom, Aflemmy was doing something else. The tomato magically shrank. But understand it only reduced in size and not weight as mass cannot be destroyed. So he pushed the tomato with his magic and hands and then finally put it in the basement through the house's basement window by letting it slide through a plank until it reached the basement through the window.

He was so tired that he had completely exhausted all his energy and could not even play chess. He went straightaway to his bed and slept.

Next day same thing happened - he could not play chess as he would be busy in some other work forcefully and finished his energy doing that and slept.

Although Wichon had cursed the chess by making it dead zone for the player who played it but her wordings were not perfect. This although made the player finish all his energy when he was approaching the end of chess but did not give him/her death. So, this prevented Wireco from playing chess and later he gave up his addiction.

This sounds like a cruel story but addiction is much more cruel than a curse.

tALe 116 : ThE niCe sErVaNt

Once in a rich family a servant was hired for an expected new born. He was a very nice man and also swore in to take good care of his future master until he was released from duty. The servant meant every word he took in the oath.

The delivery of that child was expected to take place on 4th week from now in the evening. He was expected to be there at the time of delivery so as to start helping the new born right away, funny it may sound but was true.

Before the day of delivery he was supposed to move into the servant quarters. Therefore he got all his required stuff there and happily moved into the huge servant quarters. These servant quarters were actually bigger than his house itself so he was rather happy living in there than his house. He was grateful to his masters (the rich husband and wife who hired him)for that.

The delivery was expected to take place in the room of the mother. The doctor arrived about an hour early than the baby was expected to avoid any delays in getting the child delivered. It was unique that the child got delivered almost at the same time he was expected. The delivery was a normal one and his parents were happy to see their new born baby.

But now as soon as the baby came out he had to be covered in cloth as every child is to protect them from unusual temperature conditions. But, not this child! As soon as they covered the child with a cloth and tried to give him a name he started crying so much that the doctor did not find that sound of crying right. The doctor checked and examined the baby while the parents named him Fryman. When the doctor checked the baby he saw that there were allergic rashes on his body and he had become critical. All were worried. The cloth was made of 100% cotton and still it gave rashes. It surprised the doctor too. The doctor then took off his clothing and realized that the child was allergic to cotton. He immediately gave Fryman some medicine for the allergic rashes.

Cotton was the only material that was used to make clothes those days. The doctor then amazed too, thought of something else. He immediately tried touching leather on Fryman's skin for just a fraction of second so as to know and not cause further harm to the baby. But Fryman was allergic to that too. After treating and after much study they realized that Fryman's skin was only not allergic to metal which one can't wear as a cloth. So everybody was shaken with this discovery and did not know what to do. Even the doctor had no option.

The servant whose name was Joe and who was sworn in to take care of Fryman was standing there and seeing all that felt bad and pitiful for the baby. The baby could only sleep on metal beds, sit on metal things and that's it. This was quite uncomfortable for Fryman or any human being.

Any ways as the baby started to grow up he would roam around the house freely while being naked. He, as he grew a bit more still roamed but could only roam inside his house as he would be naked and wearing clothes caused allergic reactions on him and could kill him. Although the house was quite big but he felt sad that he could not roam outside it as he could not wear clothes and would be naked. After he became 17 years old, God helped him a little bit.

His beard became so long that it reached his feet so that means it covered his front nakedness. But, his butts were still naked. Joe - his servant continued to serve him very dedicatedly. One day he saw Fryman cry real sadly while Joe was cleaning his room. Joe also felt sad and miserable seeing the kid who was trapped forever in his house all because he could not wear clothes. The kid who had all the money in the world could not wear any type of clothes whatsoever was really upsetting.

That day Joe made up his mind to find his master some material that would form his clothes and not hurt him. He came up with idea. He asked his master Fryman if he could shave his body hair as they did not look good on him. Fryman agreed to it and let him shave them. So he started shaving of all the hair from all of the body of his master- Fryman and started storing it. After there were enough hair stored in one of the box in his cabinet he took a month off after request from his master. He stayed in his room all month long. There he took these small hair and then started tying knots to tie them together (he could not use glue to stick them because that would hurt Fryman's skin too). He was quick and meticulously tied a hundred thousand knots and formed a fabric made of Fryman's hair. He had realized that natural hair of Fryman never hurt him or his skin and so that was the way to go. He had stored so much hair in his cabinet's box that after forming fabric of his hair and sewing them together to form clothes he made 5 pairs of pants and shirts of Fryman's current body size.

Then came his day of working. He immediately took those clothes made of his masters body hair and coloured them with paint having different designs on them so that they looked like natural clothes and presented them to his master - Fryman. Fryman saw the clothes and was amazed to see them. He then politely with tears in his eyes said to his servant "you know that this would not work". But Fryman's servant told his master to trust him and try wearing those clothes. Fryman sadly said okay listening to his servants request and tried them on.

Fryman wore them for a minute and then another and then so on.... And to Fryman's surprise the clothes did not cause any pain or rashes on his body. He was surprised to see that. He could not hold his happiness and immediately went running out of his house and saw the streets of his town. Then he gave this surprise to his parents who were even more happy than their son.

After much wondering, wandering and goofing around the town for the first time when Fryman came back home he was happy. The nice servant Joe then told him the secret of his clothes. From that day on there was no problem for Fryman. He would wear clothes made of his body hair and would have whatever design he wanted , coloured on them and would enjoy them. He became happy from that day on. Then Fryman's father parents asked that if there was anything that they could do for Joe. Joe simply said: "Just be my masters and friends forever."

tALe 117 : tHe sOn

Once on a planet similar to earth existed human like creatures including some giants. These giants would devour then as game meal or simply as food.

These human like creatures were called Ticklicks. Ticklicks, since as told were human like creatures were bound by feelings of hearts and therefore felt terrorized by the Act of devilness which was exhibited by those giants. Giants were not only huge in built and height but also had magical powers. But, the magical powers that the giants had were unique to each of the giant and thus no two giants had the same magical powers.

There also was a king of giants and after long time was born a son to the king of the giant. When his son was born his happiness know no bounds. He named his son as Barafelony. As Barafelony grew up he had realized that he had new magical power to call his own. He had the power to minimize and to multiply.

As Barafelony's started going to school his friends would laugh upon him because they would think that since he was a giant's son his power should actually increase the size of things rather than minimize them if and when he required. The giants believe in big and minimizing power was considered to be a curse. But Barafelony could not do anything about it. The other reason why they laughed at him was because Barafelony could not eat meat and was therefore a vegetarian. This biological gift or curse made him not be able to eat ticklicks.

Despite this Barafelony grew up to a giant size and was healthy in all ways. He loved nature and peace. He had always thought about sustaining all forms of life. Now his thoughts would be possible if ticklicks did not get exterminated by ruthless giants. He wanted to save ticklicks anyhow but could not find a way.

One day Barafelony went to see a circus show. There he saw that a trickster clown take out a small ring twice the diameter of his little funny finger's radius. Then he took a straw and tried to adjust it in the ring such that it stays bound with the ring and does not fall. The straw which was too small could not fit the ring perfectly as the ring was too big. It would only pass through it and fall. The trickster clown kept on trying and the straw kept on passing through and falling down on the ground. Then the joker tried cutting the straw in half from its side to make it smaller and lighter so that it could stay in the ring but still he could not achieve

          Page 364

what he wanted.   Giants laughed at that silly clown. Finally his idiotic brain came to pass. He brought multiple straws and fit them into the ring perfectly binding them with it. This put an end to people's laughter and realized that the clown had brains too.

Barafelony kept on thinking about the clown's act. After much thinking he came up with an idea. He had actually gotten an idea to save Ticklicks from the cruel giants including his father.

He went home and gathered some wood. Then he built a wooden house from it. He then put all the resources like water, mud and seeds in the house. He had now wanted to use his power to shrink or minimize a thing. So with all his might he puffed air in his body and drank water that gave all the giants there magical powers. Then he blew air on top of the house running all around it while doing so. Then he used his next power. With all his might he multiplied the house to make it 10,000 in number . Those 10,000 houses were so small that they could fit in the palm of his hand. Then he built a frame around a cardboard and put the houses in them. The houses were so small and also they were arranged in such a way in that frame that they looked like a 2 dimensional thing i.e. looked like a painting of dots in that frame.

It was now time to show his actual giant powers. He multiplied himself to a 100 in number with magic and then all of him puffed in air and drank the water causing magical powers. He then blew the air all over that planet. This magical air and that magic was meant for ticklicks and ticklicks alone. All the ticklocks shrank to a size of dust grain. There were approximately 5000 Ticklicks left during atet time on that planet. They all shrank and then the giant who was 100 in number at that time collected them by going two each of there houses using powerful glass lenses to locate them. He then put them in that cardboard frame with houses which only the Ticklicks could explore and enjoy.

From that day on the Ticklicks and their life was safe . As far as giants were concerned they thought they had eaten all the Ticklicks and never looked for them again.

tALe 118 : tHe LaSt WiSh

Once there lived a person named Peter. Peter had a talking parrot. Peter was a very nice person and loved his talking parrot very much. Peter's talking parrot had gone very old and Peter knew that his parrot did not have much days left to live. So they would spend the last days of Peter's talking parrot quite peacefully while having fun so that the time does not hurt the talking parrot .

Peter's talking parrot loved the plants, greenery, forests, etc very much. The parrot was wise. The parrot's last wish was that when he passes away to meet his ancestors his body should be buried behind in the backyard where all the trees and plants that he and his master had planted grew. Peter's parrot although talkative but was a somewhat wise too. He wanted his body to be used as a complete food for the plants that grew in the backyard of his house and not go to any waste. It was the last and a very sad wish but had to obeyed by his master because he loved his talking parrot very much.

Time passed by and a few months later Peter's talking parrot died. Peter buried him exactly the way he had wished .

Now, since his body was supposed to be used by soil, it meant that grass should have grown there along with some flowers that Peter had planted but nothing had happened there. Peter after a few days seeing no flora being grown there realized that his pet's last wish was not gelling fulfilled. Since Peter loved his pet very much he decided to do something about that situation. After looking for answers to this situation he came to know that sometimes the evil spirits of rituals did not liked the rituals for dead animals or birds to be altered. So if somebody alters the rituals they don't allow the last wishes of animal or bird because of which they were altered to come to a pass. Now the only way to make his parrot's last wish come to fruits was to appease the ghastly spirits. But how to please those spirits? This he found out by consulting some old evil textbooks. According to those books the spirits shall be appeased in his case if he steals an orange berry from a tree high up in the evil snow mountains and plants it where his dad was buried.

Before he started his journey he went to his priest telling him the situation he was in and what he was going to do. The priest told him to take the following two things along with the other things when he goes to get the berry. One was a candle that priest took out from his pocket with some matchsticks lying on his prayer bench and second was a bugle that was played by the priest during his free time. Peter did not understand the reasons for which these were given to him but he happily accepted them and thanked the priest. Then he went home and packed up his bag for journey next day.

Next day he woke up at dawn and started his journey. It was an arduous and a forbidden job to steal anything that grew on the evil snow mountains. But just because he loved his parrot very much he wanted to cast away evil from it's last wishes by challenging evil. It took him 7 days to reach the foothills of that mountain. After reaching the foothills it was another 7 day journey into the mountain to find that orange berry tree. It snowed continuously for seven days and wind showed no mercy in blowing but Peter continued his task and journey. When he reached the location he checked out that in that snowy and wintry zone there was just one tree standing that appeared to have some orange berries on it. He went closer and confirmed that if that was the orange berry tree. Now due to cold, snow and the ruthless wind it was impossible to climb the tree and pluck a berry. But he was determined to get the orange berry even if it costed him his life. It was night that time and due to sever cold Peter started feeling chills and shivered. He took an axe out to chop the tree but as soon as he hit it to chop it down the axe's metal shearing part broke. It was a cursed tree, he realized then. Now his only hope had broken. He took a break and lay with his back resting on the tree, thinking and frustrated. As soon as he sat, in a minutes time he started feeling more cold. He put his hand in the bag he was carrying. He found the candle the priest gave him. So he lit it up with the matchsticks he had. He then tried to feel its warmth which he got and felt a bit cozy. Then finding himself helpless he threw his back on the ground hitting it and wrestling in anger and the bugle felt on the snow covered ground. He saw that and remembered that it was also given to him by the priest. As soon as he lifted the bugle up in rage to throw it away as it looked useless, the air that was blowing, blew through the bugle and created a beautiful tone. This tone was such that the frequency generated through it broke an orange berry which fell on Peter's lap. Peter was surprised to see that he had gotten and actually stolen an orange berry from the tree in the evil snowy mountains. He stood up immediately and picked up his bag ran straight back through the snow and ice travelling non stop back to backyard of his house. There, rejoiced he dug up soil a little bit and planted the berry. Then he poured some water on it and slept for 5 days, tired from the ordeal. To his surprise when he woke he saw a 100 sprouts of a plant with ink blue buds coming out from the ground. Then he was happy that his lovely talking parrot's last wishes were fulfilled. Then he thanked Almighty and gave himself a thumbs up.

tALe 119 : ThE AfFiT

During an old age of this world there once lived an affit. Affits are bold semi human, semi animal beings. This affit was cursed with long life while living among humans. But long life does not mean that his aging would stop. He was the last one left of his kind and was quite old. Being too old his body including his face looked crippled, crooked and wierd. The place where he lived which consisting of humans was not a livable or a lively place for him anymore. The humans where he lived had started hating him due to his weird looking body. He started to look more like a curse to their neighbourhood. The Affit knew about-it and therefore one day he packed his bag and left the village.. He was upset because he had feelings attached to that place but he could not tolerate obscurity towards him by his neighbours are other people living in that village. He packed a bag then tied it to his stick and hung the stick over his shoulder. Then he kept on walking out of the village until he reached a forest.

He relaxed in that forest for a while and then kept on moving trying to go far away from his previous place of living. While he was moving out of the forest he heard that people were talking amongst each other quite amusingly. They were discussing about a princess and laughing and talking about her. The affit found that quite un-understandable. To better know what was going on the affit went to see the princess who was supposed to be standing in the outer garden the palace. When the affit went near the wall of the outer garden he saw that the princess was standing on a chair. She was holding a stick and screaming shoo shoo while freaking out. While she was doing that affit went near the gate of the outer garden of the palace. The guards standing near the gate of the outer garden of the palace immediately saw the affit who got more freaked out seeing the weird looking thing/person. But then after being at peace the affit went near the guards and asked the what was going on? The guards told him that the princess was cursed by a witch and that was what was going on. The affit out of a good heart asked is there no cure for it?

They then told him that the only cure as suggested by the less powerful friendly witch was that, if a person truly and willfully transfers the curse to himself/herself accepting it with his/her heart. Secondly the person accepting the curse should be a true marksman ie he/she should be able to shoot an eye of a flying bird in front of the princess exhibiting that the person was not blind.

Seeing the poor condition of the would be head of the state he told the guards that he is willing to take the curse of the princess upon him. Then happily he was handed a bow and arrow to shoot the eye of a bird in front of the princess and her loved ones.

The affit was so old and experienced that he did not need a bow to shoot an arrow into the right aim. He, then saw few pigeons hovering around a tree in the garden and aimed and struck an eye of a pigeon while throwing the arrow straight through the aim of his hand. Then he prayed standing still for the curse to transfer to him. While in meditation in an instant the curse got transferred to him because the princess stopped spitting out mice.

Now, when the curse got transferred to him he was ready to spit mice and make them his friends. He was ready to get rid of lonely life and start a new life with mice. He had decided that he will make a home and live with all his mice friends in it.

But even though the curse got transferred he never spitted out mice even though he had tried sneezing a little bit due to the effect of cold blowing air. How could he not spit mice? The curse was transferred and to prove that, the princess was free of curse. Everybody was shocked to see it.

Then the princess parents realized the curse remembering it's words. The witch told the princess "You shall spit out what you hate." At first everybody had thought that it was a boon because leaving something that you hate is a good heart's job. But in a second as the witch disappeared they realized that it was a curse as the princess started spitting out rats while sneezing.

Why the affit did not get the curse because he did not hate anything. He was only upset from few things but did not have hatred in him for anything. Thus the affit got rid of curse but wait he actually got rid of his sad life too because he made human friends who kept him with him forever.

Tale 120 : tHe bALLrOoM dAnCe

Once, in olden times rats, mice and other smaller animals like hedgehogs, etc used to go to school together. In one of the grade there studied a mouse named Cleo who was in love with a female hedgehog. The female hedgehog's name was Penny. Penny also loved Cleo very much. As time passed Penny and Cleo grew up. They then also graduating from the same college together.

One day, Cleo proposed Penny for a relationship deeper than any other and that was nothing other than marriage. Penny was waiting for that proposal from Cleo from quite some time. She rejoicingly accepted it. Penny then went home and told her dad about this.

Since Cleo was a mouse her dad got really mad and furious at that wish. He immediately demanded that Cleo should come and meet him at the earliest.

Penny's dad was a politician. When Cleo came to meet Penny's Dad, he mocked at him. He told Cleo that mouse and their community are the least favourable for everybody. He said that mice are known for their destructive nature and values. He further said that even humans hated them and considered them pests that caused the most problem.

But Cleo said that mice were equally honourable if not more. He agreed that humans hated mice but that was not because of their generation. It was because of older mice generations who out of fear and hatred took revenge from humans and were much less civilized. This generation of mice was much more advanced and civilized. He further said that the newer generation of mice were much more wise and did noble work in their community.

Penny's dad got a bit infuriated but calmed down and quickly thinking said "So it's a deal." He said that if mice have grown wiser, they (at least a 100 of them) should be able to dance amongst humans in the same ballroom with humans. He further said that if they could do it then he will happily get her daughter married to him.

Penny's dad knew that that was impossible because humans are afraid of mice. He thought that humans could not withstand sight of a single mouse how could they withstand seeing 100 mouse and that to especially in the ballroom dancing with them.

But Cleo loved Penny very much and so he happily agreed to the almost impossible challenge.

But how would he make it true? Cleo was very upset. But, he was adamant to make this happen. He told his parents about this and also kept on thinking to devise it out. His parents sighed and thought that it was impossible and gave up already. They thought that time would pass and Cleo would heal and would forget about this. But Cleo kept on thinking on how to make it happen.

Christmas was 6 weeks away and then!... Cleo came up with a plan.

He new that there was always a dance in a nearby ballroom during Christmas. The dress code for the shoes of people who came for the dance was "Furry ball shoe tips." This dress code was followed every year including this year. He knew this because he had seen them doing dance during that time of year many a times with the same dress code.

By that time all mice community and his friends knew about the challenge the grumpy or would be father-in-law of Cleo had given to him and his community . They were ready to make it happen any how. It was a matter of their self respect and honour.

Just two days before the Christmas ballroom dance Cleo told all 100 mice from his community to go to the houses of people who would be coming to the ballroom dance. He knew who would be coming to the dance by hiding and listening to calls made by the ballroom owner to his clients and noting their names and addresses down. Instructions were given to mice to chew and remove the fur balls from the shoes of their owners. Then they were told to roll and form a ball themselves and stick on the respective shoes. The mice obeyed and did exactly as they were instructed.

That day Cleo went to Penny's father's house and told him that there will be a   ballroom dance as requested by him. Penny's dad was surprised and did not think it was possible.

So on the invited day he showed up with 100 hedgehogs hiding at different locations within the ballroom on the day of dance. Penny's dad thought it was impossible and to further cause a mockery he had brought a crowd from his community.

So to celebrate Christmas the people came in their positions and started to dance . But there was no sign of the mice at that moment. But as soon as the dance became alive the dancers gazed at each other at their eye levels. At that time the mice became active too. They turned from fur balls to real mice and danced on the tip of the shoes of their respective owners. As the humans danced so did the mice.

Penny's dad was surprised too see that and was thus wonder struck at the wisdom of Cleo. He had no other option now but to marry his daughter to Cleo. And so since nothing more was left to see he ordered all the hedgehogs to appear from hidings and rejoice at the occasion.

By that time humans had started noticing huge animal crowd of mouse and hedgehogs and so some left screaming, some slyly and some following the crowd itself. This all further added to the cracking of the party.

Penny's dad screamed "let's enjoy the food and party." Everybody but the humans ate the food and danced and rejoiced at this blessed occasion.

That day Cleo and Penny got married happily and with a twist. They remained married happily ever after.

tALe 121 : tHe KiNg Vs ThE eLf

Once there lived a very ambitious King. His name was Matchstick. Now Matchstick being very cunningly ambitious wanted to rule the earth. So he talked to many advisors but the answers given to him by the advisors were not very satisfying. So he took his entire army and marched towards a deadly witch. The witch although was deadly and powerful but seeing the enormous army and other magicians in the king's army got intimidated and out of fear told him the secret. She said "Use the flying whales." The king then seeing the witch reveal the secret asked her boastfully " and what would be the key to do that?" The witch then said " I shall answer no more but this last time. To use the flying whales capture their babies and then tame them to fulfill your hearts desire." The king although in rage said "witch you have given me the understanding to rule the earth and as per your wish I shall ask you no more right now. If needed I may summon you but I doubt that now, as I have the answer to rule the world known. Take care."

Matchstick ordered his special soldiers to swim into the oceans at night where flying whales rested after their day flights. He ordered them to steal all the babies of flying whales in a single day so that they don't get more seriously alarmed after the discovery of their missing children during the coming days. He also ordered to remove all the scents of their babies by spraying magical potion created by his magicians so that the babies of flying whales could not be tracked from any part of the world by their parents or any other. The soldiers carried the magical potion and did as they were ordered to do.

They quietly and slyly entered the ocean at night where the whales would sleep. Some whales would sleep just on the shore some just in the shallow waters. They then sprayed a drug that caused deep sleep into the whales. After the whales were dead sleep the soldiers then searched for their babies. After finding the babies, they sprayed the magical potion on them and put them in bags. They then carried them away without the flying whales noticing any of their actions.

These orders were obeyed with utmost secrecy.

(the lifespan of these flying whales was mere 20 years but they were the mightiest and biggest creatures at that time.)

About 1000 eggs were stolen and given to Matchstick.

The whales when woke up in the morning saw that their eggs were missing. They flew around the earth in search but since they could not smell their babies they gave up and stopped searching after many mighty weeks of restless search.

By that time the trainers in Matchsticks army started training the flying whale babies to be very ferocious and obey Matchstick. They used magic and physical torturing to force the baby flying whales who were growing up to do that. The flying whales were completely enslaved with hard obedience towards Matchstick. They now were wearing armor and were ready to attack anybody or anything the king wished.

These tamed flying whales that grew up were now also used to tug the mighty ships of the kings in air or in water over through all lands and waters including attacking enemies ruthlessly.

Using the tamed flying whales the king raged war on all the kings bigger or smaller than his class. He killed them and captured their territory. He even captured the free lands and start to rule them under his tyranny. He captured so much land that all the earth was under the torturous and unexplainable tyranny.

But don't worry things don't always go bad there is always some light that shines to remove darkness just like after every night their is a day.

This was all being seen by the Elf who lived on the moon. He was a bit late in responding to the catastrophes happening because of his mighty slumber. He was although seeing all the cruelty happening in his sleep but was very tired to get up or respond. But one day he finally woke up.

That day he planned. He realized that the age of flying whales was not more than 20 years and so he started stealing the new eggs of the tamed flying whales so as to not let the further new born tamed flying whale babies being forced into Matchstick's weapon.

He would bring those eggs of the tamed flying whales stealthily with him to the moon and as soon as the babies emerged out of them he put them in a deep magical sleep that did not needed breathing because moon lacks oxygen atmosphere.

The tamers of the flying whales started noticing missing eggs and reported to the king about that. The spies then found out that an elf was stealing all the eggs from the whales stables. Matchstick when came to know about this became very furious and decided to trap and give death to the elf who was stealing the flying whales' eggs.

He consulted his generals and magicians. They told him that the elf was very difficult to kill or capture but still obeying the orders of the king they devised 6 traps to trap and kill the elf. Elf had some magic but that was not very powerful for fighting battles but he was courageous and smart.

In the daytime when the tamed flying whales gave more eggs the spies and the soldiers immediately secured those eggs and put them in a place surrounded by non penetrable magical walls and having 6 traps in them. Now to trap the elf they opened a path towards the eggs and let the elf choose his destiny.

Animals know magical beings like that elf but when hypnotized they loose their ability to recognize.

Other powers of the elf were that he could fly but not locally on earth. His flying was only done in no atmosphere or for reaching the moon after huge jump towards the upper atmosphere from a mountain. He although walked and was vulnerable to physical hurting.

1) So in the entrance they built a water body with magically hypnotized hungry sharks. These sharks could not now recognize the elf and were ready to attack anything that entered their territory and quench their hunger.

2) Then there was land with hungry lions who had no empathy for elf as their and their kids stomachs were left hungry too without food and they would rather eat and kill than die.

3) The third trap involved a magical giant being who was ready to kill the elf just for some gold from the Matchstick (but that was not it he was under threat too from all the king's magicians and his army, so he decided to be on king's side.)

4) If the elf managed to escape these three he would then have to face a fire breathing dragon who did not understand magic or well being.

5) The fifth trap involved tiny evil magical grasshoppers . These grasshoppers were so tiny and deadly that if the elf enter the area in which they were kept they would enter the body of the elf from the space between two cells of the prey's body by enlarging it through their tentacles. Then they would bounce into the prey's body wildly which would cause immediate and dead crazy jumping of elf and that would eventually kill him including all his flesh getting apart and destroyed.

6) The last 6th trap was the deadliest. In this trap the magicians had let loose microscopic magical leeches in air of that boundary of magical walls. These leaches if would see anybody near, would enter and drain all the blood out of that person's body. Also there were obnoxious gases in that trap which made the leaches to multiply rapidly on getting food - which was blood of any being excluding them.

After setting these 6 traps the king was satisfied that the elf now was dead meat and nobody could now let him not be the ruler forever.

Elf when came to know about this by seeing from the moon what the king did to trap him, he was not mad or furious but prepared to get the eggs from the traps without himself or the eggs getting hurt and show king who's the boss.

To escape the sharks he went to a blacksmith disguised and bought from him a small steel boat like looking structure in exchange for a wild boar he caught on his way from a forest. The blacksmith thought first, then, agreed and sold him the solid steel structure. Then what, the elf took the boat like structure and cut the high edges of it. He then melted them with high temperatures of burning coal in a small burning chamber and build very strong net like cage all-around it. It was done because if the sharks attack and the steel boat tumbles it will remain afloat and due to its structure would tumble back to being cage on the top i.e. it won't remain capsized for more than a few seconds. This would thus protect the elf from raging sharks.

Now, using the steel caged boat he safely crossed that trap.

Then came the lions. To clear the hungry lion trap he already gotten steel armor wearing miniature puffer fishes that grew enormously big when their defense mechanism was activated. He then put one in each lion's mouth using a slingshot to throw those tiny armored puffer fishes. His aim was immaculate. He aimed from far and in the mouth of the lions when they were roaring in hunger. The fishes as soon as they entered the lions started inflating themselves and became huge sticky non penetrable puff-balls. The lions could neither swallow nor through them out from their mouths. Their jaws and they themselves became trapped and too occupied, thus could not cause any harm to the elf. The elf safely crossed that trap.

Then came the trap where the giant was. To appease the giant the elf had brought a humming bird with him. Then the elf let the loosened humming bird get near the giant. The giant so mad at the humming sound and its constant moving and noisy nature got furious at the bird and started hitting it with his club. But the humming bird being small and fast could not be hit. The giant instead hit himself with the club when trying to hit the humming bird sitting on his nose and made him get unconscious from the hit. The elf safely crossed that trap too.

The dragon was a tricky trap. But the elf was smart and wise. As soon a he entered the trap he took out a special magical powder from his pocket and threw in the dragon's eye. The magical powder caused the dragon to see the dust in the air as bees. The elf also looked like queen bee to him. This scared the dragon away and the elf crossed that trap too.

Now, to handle the grasshoppers before entering their area he hummed a tune and many crows came and gathered there. They ate all the grasshoppers in a flash gobbling 100's of them at a time. The elf crossed that trap too.

Now, to pass through the leech land he brought two stones and put 2 cotton balls in each of his nostril. Then he hid behind the magical wall and threw two stones on the ground. The throw was such that second stone hit the first stone only after the first stone landed on the ground. This produced a spark and an explosion was generated. The highly obnoxious gases that were there being flammable burnt and destroyed all the leeches. He was safe as he hid behind the magical walls.

Thus he entered and took away all the eggs.

Matchstick when came to know this got scared and begged for mercy and forgiveness from the elf because now he was afraid of elf for his life. Matchstick saw his death, if, he did not ask for forgiveness from the elf. So peace returned back to earth. He gave up the tamed and captured flying whales and all the territories and the earth was free and safe now.

Victorious was elf and his goodness for earth.

AniMe fAiRy tALeS

TaLe 1 : tHe fLyiNg pEnS

These were war times and evil monarchs of 5 separate nations
wanted to destroy the only good nation of that time in that world.
This good nation had a very noble monarch who believed in peace
and taking care of people. He really loved his subjects very dearly
and had made his country very beautiful to show so. That was also
the biggest and the most powerful nation of that planet thus it was
very difficult to destroy or defeat that nation.

The 5 nations that had evil monarchs wanted to do whatever they
could to destroy the only good nation of that time and that nation
was called Keleprin. Keleprin in their language meant "never
ending" or "never dying" which looked true always until the war
clouds appeared.

For 20 years the diplomatic ties between the nations were cut off
and no communication took place. Secretly those 5 nations
enhanced their technologies so they could capture Keleprin and its
people and make it their own .

The ruler of Keleprin was noble but not foolish. He knew what was
going on amongst the 5 nations. His country had spies hidden in
those nations who were of elite class. Since all the 5 nations were
developing and enhancing their technologies to throw Keleprin of
the map, Keleprin scientists were also working to keep them
protected and safe.
During those times the problem was that altering messages sent
through radio frequencies had become a child's play. Also fooling
encryption was easy. Because of this, radio messages sent to the
soldiers waiting for orders easily were altered by the enemies and
thus got faulty. Therefore some other method had to be devised to
deliver messages safely and securely.

Keleprin scientists were aware of this and thus had been working on a new system of delivering military orders and messages safely. After 10 years of technological enhancements they came to a very different and a unique solution. Since radio messages could be bugged they devised a new method keeping in mind that radio waves are something that don't have a signature embedded in them so they made pens that had inks derived from the DNA of the generals of Keleprin army. The ink lasted only for 10 minutes after getting exposed to air. Also the new RNA formed by mixing ink and the DNA of superiors had a very short life which was also 10 minutes after getting in contact with air for security purposes.

But to deliver the messages there had to to be some secure way that did not have any loopholes in it. So they made these flying pens. These pens were robotic flying pens that had artificial recognition intelligence embedded in them. They could recognize the message giver and fly at super speeds. These pens flew so fast that they could fly around the whole planet in less than a second without getting caught by eyes or radio waves or sonars etc. They had the capability to get activated to send an order or a message written by superiors/generals and then at the time of delivery they gave the message exactly in the same way, (while moving in air and on paper) with the exact same hand writing style as that of the sending general. These exact orders were received by army men who were waiting for orders. These pens flew at lightning speeds while carrying messages when the secret DNA ink was put in them. After the pens delivered orders by writing them on the paper, the personnel of the forces had special ink with which they checked the genuineness of the message. They had a chemical which when rubbed with or on the ink changed to a unique identifiable colour which confirmed that the message was genuine. This was a landmark in establishing foolproof method of communication between the superiors and the soldiers.

After 20 years of cold war the real war actually started and the technology was on the side of Keleprin people. They had already advanced very much and their spying network had also got very strong. They already knew what the evil countries' army, air Force or navy had plans and where they were about to attack. Also due to well established communication system the forces of Keleprin got genuine orders which informed them about the enemy's plans of attack. The Keleprin armed forces attacked with stealth and might and caused the destruction of armies of evil enemy nations. This caused the evil monarchs to surrender which also marked the end of war.

The people and monarchs of those 5 nations realized their folly and become better people with better understanding for future. Peace prevailed forever thereafter ever-after.

tALe 2 : MeSsAgE tRaNsMiTtErS

Long ago there occurred a war between a very cruel nation and a very good nation. The cruel nation captured many POWs (Prisoners of war) during the war. But that's something that every nation does during war. The evil nation brutally tortured the captured prisoners.

The second problem with that nation was that it did signed agreements for release of prisoners but never released them . The POWs of both the countries were supposed to get released from their Prisons after 15 years in captivity. The good nation released its prisoners but the evil and cruel nation did not. It offended the good nation and its people. The families of the good nations had waited quite long for their loved ones to return home but they did not return. The good nation tried talks with the cruel nations but the cruel nation did not agree, nor listened to the talks of good nation for peace and moderation.

But since the good nation was good so it I was not interested in war but wanted to get its people released from the clutches of that cruel nation. So the ruler of the good nation called a meeting of high ranking officials and its scientists. In the meeting all of them decided that they somehow needed to penetrate the defences and get their people out of that cruel nation.
The most difficult thing was that they did not know where where the cruel nation was keeping POWs. They wanted to have that information so that they could get their prisoners out from their cells with surgical stealthiness.

Many scientist came up with many ideas but that did not look feasible as those ideas required lots of time for them to get matured and put them into action . They needed something that was unique and simple and that they could implement it fast.

After 10 days of brainstorming while sitting in the same meeting chamber they came upon an idea.They thought that they needed eyes for that mission and what could be better than solar cameras. But how could they get solar cameras in the cruel nation.

At that moment some scientist were smoking and seeing the smoke moving in the room one of the scientist came upon an idea. He said that they could put self destructing, micro plastic solar cameras with 360 degrees of view which had almost the same density as that of bubble forming soap solution in a special soap solution. When bubbles are formed through that soap solution they will travel in air and will reach far and wide. Also, they won't burst quickly because they would be made of a strong solution of soap and chemicals (made by them many years ago).

Everybody cheered at this idea and said Bravo! Bravo! to the scientist who came up with this idea. Now the only problem was that how would they make these bubble solution cameras available to the cruel nation?

The best time for that they thought should be the national parade of cruel nations when the cruel nation rained bubbles through the sky blowing them from exhaust air of the fighter jets.

They then thought that they could send some of their men disguised as their people and mix this bubble solution with the bubble solution required for blowing bubbles during the parade and so they did.

The day came when the national parade of the cruel nation was held. The bubbles were produced from the jets all over the cruel nation. The soap solutions from which these bubbles were produced from had the cameras sent by the good nation mixed into them. Those cameras that were in the bubbles sent video messages through set of radio signals at the required secret frequency to the good nation's headquarters. The cruel nation did not come to know about it ever. Wherever the bubbles went the cameras inside them took video footages of the cruel nation's territories and the good nation got to know where the cruel nation had kept the POWs.

They then sent a team of many men disguised as cruel country people and got their people released from their prisons by bribing the men (surgical stealthiness) that worked for the prison. That was a real happy day for the people of good nation as their country people were back to where they belonged in peace, love and safety.

tALe 3 : FiRe pOwEr

After many years from now i.e. in 26th century earth had lost many types of fuels including rocket fuel. The thing to worry about at that time was not the hindering of space exploration but meeting people. There had already been lots of human settlements in space done so they were in dire need of an alternative rocket fuel for travelling through space to meet their loved ones. They were very desperate to do that and could not think a way for it.

So many governments of various countries started announcing millions of dollars in prize money to discover or invent any type of rocket fuel. This was a very noble opportunity for many scientists including retired scientists and other intellectuals to design or discover something that would make a good rocket fuel. Many scientist tried searching for something that was an alternative to previous rocket fuels but they failed except one young man.

There was this one young scientist whose name was Aprikot. He was a very enthusiastic and an intelligent young man who was in his early 30's. When he had heard that the rocket fuel was surely over he felt really bad because many of his loved ones lived on other planets which were in different star systems and thus would be very difficult and nearly impossible to meet them without fuel to propel rockets.

He did not care about the prize money which amounted in million of dollars that was to be given to the rocket fuel discoverer or inventor. The only thing that he wanted was that people should be able to meet each other without any restrictions or boundaries. So from that day he started working on to make a new rocket fuel.

To do that, next day he went to the marketplace to get supplies for his work. While he was walking on the road he saw a boy blowing bubbles in the air. After seeing that he realized that lots of air pressure was needed to make a bubble or bubbles form from the soap solution. But he did not think much about it at that time as he was overwhelmed thinking about the supplies which he had to buy. After buying supplies he reached home and lay a setup and did some experiments, of which all failed. Then he sat on a chair, stressed and thinking about the failures he had that day. While doing that he stretched out his arms and legs and also started thinking about the bubbles that were being blown by the boy on street. He kept on thinking about it for quite sometime and suddenly he became excited and got up the chair and went back to his experiment table.

At that moment he had come up with a brilliant idea that would never stop a man from entering space as long as sun lived.

He had devised the concept of acceleration of rocket through reusable magnetic unbreakable bubbles. According to the method, the rocket would work on solar cells and thus would be a solar powered rocket that would give instantaneous energy to operate a system that would propel the rocket. That system involved use of electric power to push hydraulics which further would be used to push an unbreakable steel bubble out of the rocket such as a gun firing a bullet. Only difference would be that bullet here would be lot heavier and the firing mechanism would be way bigger and would sync with the amount of propulsion required. Also in this method of propulsion, the steel bubble that would be pushed out would get magnetized instantaneously as it gets out and out of contact of rocket and thus would return back to the rocket for further propulsions due to magnetic capturing of that bubble. He also had thought that for bigger rockets more than one bubble could be used to propel rockets forward and in space. Since the bubble or bubbles would be heavy they would provide enough reaction to move or propel the rocket forward according to Newtons laws of motion and laws of conservation of momentum.

Now to prove this concept he made a miniature model of that propulsion system. It took him 8 days to make the model but he made it and it worked very efficiently.

This model was then shown to the scientists and then to the world. The concept was approved immediately for putting it into practicality for propulsion of bigger rockets.

 He was then awarded $500 million for such a wonderful invention but he was only contented when the system worked for bigger rockets and that people knew no boundaries.

TaLe 4 : A mAn'S wOoDeN tOy

Mostly men that are grown up don't buy toys save this man who went shopping for his nephew's birthday and ended up getting something for himself too. He had bought a wooden toy dragon for himself.

The toy dragon was very beautifully designed. It was made from natural light coloured wood. The structure it had was not carved from single piece of wood. In fact it was made up of several pieces of wood shaped into its different parts and then put together. Thus was very detailed.

The man's name who bought that dragon was Fillomia. Fillomia was actually a gear designer. He used to design motors and gears for various things for people of his town.

When Fillomia had seen this toy he was very attracted towards it as it looked extremely special to him. He had something unique in his mind that he wanted to do with that wooden toy. Actually, he wanted to make the dragon fly for real.

He spent lots of nights thinking of a way that could make that possible. He used to closely inspect the dragon's body, its wings etc. while thinking about how to make it fly. He had seen that the dragon's wings were movable and thus could flap up and down. So after days of planning and designing he made a motor system that was geared and which could make the dragon fly. He was very excited at that moment. So putting his drawings aside he went to sleep that night and slept quite well.

Next day, he got up early and started attaching the gears and motors to the wings. After doing that he set up the motor speed which was driven through air pressure derived by flapping of the wings and vice versa, of that toy dragon and connected the entire system together. He also made a binocular vision that ran through a gear system, for that dragon and attached it where the dragon's eyes were. He also made ears for the dragon using the same material that is used for making actual drums and put them besides his head. Now after connecting all of it, the system worked and the dragon could fly autonomously. This made Fillomia happy as he had some special plans for the dragon.

Although Fillomia was a gear mechanic he did not always have enough money to do charity for helping sick kids so, he had thought of making this dragon fly.

This system that was put into the dragon which also caused it to fly was also designed to see that if penny or coin had remain fallen on the ground for more than 2 hours. If yes, and was not picked up by its owner or anybody else the dragon would fly towards the ground and pick up that coin, put it in its pocket on its belly and then fly again towards the clouds like a bird and it would not come to anybody's notice. Although it was a dragon it flapped its wings like a bird and therefore looked like one thus people did not come to know that it was a wooden dragon when it came down to collect a coin or coins or when it flew in air. Also it was the size of a regular eagle.

The dragon was made to fly quite long. It had an almost unlimited hours of endurance. At the end of 24 hours of flight or having filled his belly completely with coins, whichever came sooner, the dragon would fly low and donate all the collected coins to sick kids charity box.

This system worked because first of all it had unlimited amount of flying endurance (as told earlier). Secondly it could keep track of multiple locations where the coins had fallen and could time their stay.

Since the owners of those fallen currency did not care about what they had lost as they did not know or did not come looking for it. It was better that that cash went to a noble cause and thus did a noble deed rather than getting dumped on the ground.

With the help of wooden dragon the gear mechanic fulfilled his dream of helping sick kids. Since the day the dragon flew all the charity boxes used to keep full and thus was a great help for sick kids and a boon for their parents.

tALe 5: ThE mAgiCaL wAtCh

We all know that almost all of the magicians use magical potions to perform magic but where do they come from. Well let me tell you that then. Magical potions are made by magicians themselves. They use a variety of substances and previously made magical potions for making new magical potions. They mix those substances and magical potions under fire, cold, pressure or a catalyst while chanting beautiful magical words which causes different type of magical reactions. These reaction cause creation of wondrous magical potions. Now this all happens when precise timings are followed to mix the substances and magical potions along with timely utterance of magical words. Without proper timings magical potions can't be created. So let's begin the story keeping that in mind.

Once there existed a magician who was in charge of creating magical potions for a small magical shop. But this magician was quite old and he used to fall asleep in any position even when he was working. This caused him to forget the timely addition of substances with timely chanting of spells to create magical potions. He tried using alarm clocks but they did not help. There were two reasons for that.

First of all because the magician used to fall in quite deep sleep so much so that the alarm clocks would not budge him. Secondly, even if he woke up after a while hearing the gruesome alarm clocks he used to get confused. Because although the alarm clocks woke him up somehow by changing their tones and volumes etc. themselves but that or they did not tell him which alarm was ringing for which magical potion(as he would be working on creating many magical potions at once).

One day he was tired of messing up his work and potions. He got irritated working on creating the same potions again and again because of missing timely action so he decided to make a magical watch.

This magical watch that he decided to create would remain his assistant forever. It will not only tell him what magical potion to mix at what time but it will also mix them itself if he falls asleep with also timely chanting of spells by itself. He also decided to give him hands and legs when it got formed.

So in the evening after his messy work he took one of his best watch out of his cupboard. This watch was quite big in size and actually looked like a small wall clock but was wearable on wrist. Then, he kept it on the table and threw a magical powder on it will reciting a very long spell.

In an instant a flash of lightning occurred and the watch came alive. The watch then immediately opened his eyes and stood up on his legs. It then said "Hi" to the magician. The magician felt happy and thrilled seeing the alive watch. He named that watch Haouleiy. Haouleiy meant a wondrous Halo.

Haouleiy helped the magician whom it called "Fil" in all his work. The watch never got tired even though his master did. It was awake even in night and did not like to sleep. As nights passed, it started feeling lonely. He did not know how he could solve this problem.

One day while working with Fil it asked him what do people do when they become lonely? The magician laughed and said, "Nothing! They simply make friends". Then the night came and Haouleiy starting about thinking of making friends. But he needed someone of his own kind to talk to and be friends with. So he woke up Fil who was deep asleep with his special magical ability and asked him that where could he find somebody like him? Fil was quite sleepy and yawning but he still told him that everybody in this world wears watches so it could find it in anybody's house. Fil then slept again.

By that time he decided to go to the house of Fil's neighbour and decided to look for somebody of its own kind. When he went to Fil's neighbour's house he went in, from beneath the door where there is always a gap and saw a shiny thing besides the table where Fil's neighbour was sleeping. That shiny thing was lying on top of a table. There he jumped and went near it.

He saw that it was a wrist watch but it was not responding to its talks or signs. He did not know the reason why it was not doing that but in a few moments he realized that that watch was not alive. He then kept on thinking that what it should do. Suddenly an idea came to his mind. He uttered a big spell and blew air on to the non-talking, non alive watch and suddenly it came to life. (When it came alive it had the same abilities as that of Haouleiy).

As soon as it came alive it looked at itself and yelled "Hey! I am alive!" and looked towards Haouleiy. Haouleiy then told him that it was it that brought him to life. That watch whom Haouleiy named Taouckeiy then thanked it and they became very good friends. Every night they used to meet and have fun playing with the magic they had within them. This continued for quite sometime but then both of them started missing something else.

They realized that they were males and that they needed some female watches to talk to and go out on date with. So then what? They made some female wrist watches to come to life and then started to date them and have fun with them. This made them very happy.

But due to too much magic happening amongst the non living world of watches and also because of the magical aura of watches many other watches around the world started to come to life. Even the watch softwares on phones started to behave weirdly.

For example in meetings at workplaces where many different types of businessmen would be meeting the watches in the smartphones used to get crazy seeing each other. They created holographic hearts and things flying through the space of the rooms so that they could attract the female smartphone watches and vice-versa and be friends with them.

This looked beautiful but wasted times of rich businessmen who at that moment could not use their smartphones for their work or anything else. Secondly if they somehow controlled the smartphone watches by turning the phones off their wrist watches behaved weirdly. The wrist watches would start transforming to different shapes to exhibit their capabilities to other females for attracting them and vice-versa was true too.

This was a huge problem for the working class of people as watches were alive and they had to watched after to keep everything going.

So the politicians passed a new law that banned people from wearing watches until they could be fixed.

But that's just a statement. How could alive watches be fixed?

They can't be. So only one thing could be done to prevent people from going to Stone Age. They made mini atomic watches that could not be transformed to a live watch because of radiations in them and continued life and work.

So when the watches came alive people lost time.

tALe 6 : tHe cHeSt tHaT wAs fOrbiDdEn To tOuCh

Once in the suburbs of an area in Japan there lived a girl who was very nice and polite in nature. She loved all types of animals, plants and insects. For this reason she was sometimes bullied by seniors of her school. She tried to pay no attention to that and continued her daily school activities which were sometimes painful under those circumstances.

One day she was going to the school it was raining. While walking she saw a frog getting drenched in rain. She thought that it needed shelter. So she picked it up and brought it in the classroom to prevent it from getting wet in rain or getting sick from it. All the girls in the school laughed at this and many of the seniors when they came to know about it came and bullied this little girl. This girl whose name was Teardrop felt very sad that day. After finishing school she went straight to her home and promised herself that she will never ever go to school as she was always getting mocked and bullied by seniors of her school. She also told this to her father. Her father whose name was Ribnock was a micro-robotics engineer. Ribnock felt very sad hearing that. He decided to do something about it. He knew that going to school and complaining would not help so he had thought of something special to help her daughter out.

Until the time he made that special happen Teardrop used to cry in her room all day long and used to barely come out of it to eat food or drink some water or juice. Meanwhile, Ribnock used to feel bad seeing all that and so he tried talking to Teardrop out of it. But teardrop was too preciously depressed and would not listen to her dad. She got so depressed that she actually needed anti-depression medicine to overcome her condition of depression which her family doctor prescribed. Ribnock tried giving it to her daughter but SHE WOULD NOT TAKE IT!

Her father did not know what to do at that time so he hurried to complete making of that special thing which he was working on to help her daughter.

After 10 days of her getting diagnosed with depression Ribnock created 4 things.

He created a mini chest which was about 3cm by 1.5cm. Then he created 3 robotic creatures. One was a small robotic kangaroo, second was a small robotic dog and third was a small robotic snake. These 3 robotic animals could easily fit in the small chest that teardrop's father had created.

Ribnock tried gifting this chest to Teardrop but she would not take it as she was under depression.

Ribnock was an educated man. So he talked to his family doctor about it. He advised him to use reverse-psychology on her daughter.

So next day he unwrapped the wrapped gift (which was the mini treasure chest with the 3 robotic animals he had created) and kept it on the table which was in the lobby of their house. Then he told Teardrop not to go near the chest or touch it.

Whenever Teardrop came to the lobby to have some water, juice or food she used to see that chest shine and shake while jumping up and down as if it was excited to see her and was calling her. At first, she did not go near the chest as her father had forbidden her to go near or touch that mini chest? But slowly, the tiny chest started looking beautiful to Teardrop and one day she went near that chest but did not open it. She touched the chest and started playing with it without opening it. She then wanted to see what was inside the chest but it was locked so she could not open it. Secondly her father also had told her not to open that chest so she sticked to the instructions given. That day she realized that she had started feeling better. (Why Teardrop had started feeling better was because the mini robotic kangaroo that was created by Ribnock used to sense the DNA & characteristics of Teardrop. After making sure that it was Teardrop near it, it used to release medicine while jumping and shaking the mini chest. This highly advanced robot used to send anti depressive medicines directly in Teardrops body by redirecting them to air molecules going towards her nostrils while inhaling air.)

She started liking that chest thereafter so much that she took a string and tied the tiny chest to it. Then she put it around her neck.

Next day she decided to go to school and told her father about that. Her father felt happy hearing that. Now he knew that it was happening all because of the chest and the animals that were inside it. He had already seen Teardrop wearing that chest and asked her about it. Teardrop said that it was something that she found when she was playing so her Ribnock said "Okay"and did not ask any more questions.

Ribnock was happy and therefore giggled inside.

When she went to school that day nobody teased her or bullied her which was surprising to her and she was happy about it. One girl tried to come near her and pull her hair but as soon as she came near her she got afraid, screamed and went away. Teardrop felt a little relieved seeing that.

The mini chest as I Told also consisted of a mini robotic dog and mini robotic snake other than mini robotic kangaroo. The purpose of the robotic dog was to sense any danger and calm it down by sending ultrasonic brainwaves to divert a dangerous thought thought by anybody. Secondly the robotic snakes job was to sense an attack and come out of chest and threaten the enemy incase pacifying brain waves (by robotic dog) did not help. This was also the reason that the girl who came near Teardrop threatening her went away screaming. She had seen the robotic snake pop out of the chest which scared her.

Ribnock knew that her daughter was very precious so he made a precious gift for her that would be with her forever even after he dies.

tALe 7 : ThE mAgiCaL pAnTs

Magical pants just don't pop out of anywhere. They have to be magically created.

This is a story of magical pants that got created magically.

Long time ago, during the modern era of magic there existed a magician named Goof. As the name suggests he was a very funny magician but had a short height and was of old age.

During this modern era of magic, people used to go to magicians quite often to cure illnesses or get treatments that were medically impossible to get. For example: to cure black and white or upside down eye vision. Or for example: if somebody wanted to become fat and/or if somebody wanted to be thin without doing much effort.

The eyes problem were curable through direct implementation of magical potions but since it was modern era, to cure fatness or thinness it was altogether a different story.

The person that wanted to have fat and was hereby thin had to bring a person along with him that was thin and wanted to grow or have fat on his body or vice-versa. This happened because magician could not dispose of fat from a person's body directly. He could only transfer it from one body to other all because of law conservation of mass. This is funny but it was true.

It so happened that one day Goof was returning from a party and it was evening that time. He had forgot to put a closed sign on his dispensary that day. Therefore there was a huge line up of people who were waiting to get fixed by Goof. Goof did get puzzled and didn't knew what to do at that time. But he thought for a while a then realized that since he had forgotten to put a close sign on his dispensary, it was his legal and moral obligation to fix people as they had been waiting for quite long. So in a hurry, he went inside the dispensary took off his pants, hung them on his chair and wore a robe. While wearing that robe and keeping his pants hung on that chair he started calling in people for treatments.

That day lots of different magical potions and that too in lots of quantities were used besides the pant that lay on the chair of Goof. So much magic was done that day that it affected those pants drastically that were lying on Goof's chair. This actually made the pants sneeze and come to life. The magician at that time had just finished fixing people and was trying to relax. After he heard the sneeze coming from pants, he knew that he had created the un-creatable even though by mistake. He then went closer to those pants slowly and touched them. The pants saw what was going on and when it got the touch it got scared and immediately jumped off where from where it was already hanging to find a place where it could hide. As it was trying to do so the magician said that it does not need to worry and that it can stop trying to hide and get comfortable around him as they were his pants. The pants heard that, looked at Goof, stopped running and came near him. The pant then shook its right leg with goof's hand and said "Hello!" Goof was happy to see and hear that. Goof then explained to the pants about their purpose in life and that people wear them on their legs. Then, Goof told it that since it had gotten life now it should be named. Goof then immediately named him Goofball. Goofball liked that name and he then said "Thanks!" to Goof.

Now, since the pants had power and magic of their own they helped magician to walk, run and play tirelessly. Both of them used to enjoy that. Those pants also enjoyed eating food and relaxing on a drying wire in Goof's backyard. This continued for quite a while until one day.

During one occasion the king wanted something to be done with his right foot. So he tried asking all the magicians that who was a good magician for that particular type of job. All of them pointed towards Goof.

The king then invited Goof to his palace for a meeting. When goof came, the king told him that he would like to request a procedure from Goof. Goof was willing to help. Then the king told him that he wanted to make his right foot become bigger than left foot while keeping his left foot of the same size. Goof thought about it for a while and looking at the dangerousness of that process he simply said "No" to the king for that procedure. Secondly to increase the size of right foot without decreasing the size of left foot was not possible because of law of conservation of mass and also because of some other scientific norms.

The king became furious after he heard "No" from Goof and sentenced him to death right away.

Goof got upset hearing that and said that he would lovingly accept the death sentence if anybody could beat him in two things. One was in sprinting and the other was, walking on frozen wire. The king laughed at Goof and said "you old man you can't even walk properly and you think that you can win a sprinting race or walk on a frozen wire." The king then said "Okay" to what Goof had asked for.

They then agreed that if Goof wins both the events he would be spared for life and if he losses, he will be given a torturous death.

Then the magician asked for his (magical) pants to be brought from home because those were his favourite pants and he wanted to sprint in them. He was then immediately brought those (magical) pants.

The race began next day. The king had summoned the best sprinter in the kingdom for the race. Since Goof was wearing Goofball he easily defeated the sprinter. The king was amazed to see that. But he said to himself that even though Goof had won the sprinting race, he would not be able to walk on frozen wire or win that competition. But the king would be wrong.

The walking on frozen wire started . The competitor of Goof fell immediately as soon as he kept his first foot on the frozen wire. When Goof's turn came, he had already told Goofball to help him out. Goofball which was a magical pant caused the frozen wire to melt very slightly and then get frozen back immediately it by causing air around it to do that. This lead to the wire becoming sticky over which Goof with support of Goofball walked easily and won the competition.

The king was surprised to see that and realized his folly. He forgave the powerful magician and let him free.

Goofball actually saved the day. Goof then thanked Goofball and then they lived happily forever.

tALe 8 : tHe KiNg tHaT pRoTeCtEd A WhALe

This is mostly a funny, somewhat sad story about a king who utilized quite a lot of its resources to protect a whale. So let's begin with it.

Once there lived a king. He was the king of kings and the lord of lords. In short he was quite a powerful emperor of his time. This king's name was Predy and he was very fond of hunting. It was also his favourite way to pass his somewhat boring time of the day or night.

It was summer and the breeze was quite cool. So this gave an idea to the king to go hunting. He called all his servants to get ready for hunting and prepare his horse for that. The servants did as they were told. They prepared each and everything for Predy including his horse that was required for hunting. After everything was done Predy and his servants went to the hunting grounds of the forest for Predy to hunt. It took them an hour or so to reach the forest where and when Predy decided that he would hunt a deer today. And the deer he wanted to hunt would not be just any deer but a special deer that would not be juvenile and would have lots of fat in his body that would give him enough fat for the steak from it that he will barbecue. For doing that he had decided that he would use his one lucky arrow. This lucky arrow was also used by him for other special purposes like to show off in parade, betting etc.

          Page 393

Why that luck arrow was so was because this was the arrow with which he had bullseye shot when he had just started to learn to use bow and arrow. He never left that arrow attached to the hunted animal or on ground. He picked that arrow up always after the hunting has been done and would put it back in his royal quiver . He never missed with that arrow.

Now, he had only walked a kilometre into the hunting grounds of the deep and dense forest along with his servants when he found the perfect deer that he wanted to hunt. He immediately took out his lucky arrow mounted it on the string of his bow and aimed at the deer. After making the aim steady he released the arrow. But to his shock the arrow missed. This was the first time in his trained life that he had missed the shot which he was trying to get from his lucky arrow. It was unbelievable! He lost his heart and felt it sink but in short span he gathered courage again and ran towards, where that arrow had fallen to try to use it again to shoot. That lucky arrow had flown and fallen on the sea shore which was adjoining the forest. So he went towards the sea to search for it. When he came near the sea shore he picked up the arrow but while doing that he saw a huge dead whale lying and its baby trying to swim towards it from the sandy waters on the shore with the water pushing it from behind.

Predy felt very sad seeing that. He felt really horrified and sorry for the baby whale. Since the baby whale was near its mom on the shore with very less water there for the whale to breathe he was worried that the baby whale might loose its breath. By that time his servants also had reached the shore and were standing behind him.

He then immediately ordered his servants to build a small container out of wood and put the baby whale in it, after adding lots of water in the container. His servants did as they were told to do. In about 15 minutes they built a container of the type requested by their king - Predy. His servants were then lifted the baby whale and put it in that container and took it close to its mom. He then let the baby whale be near its mom for a while. After sometime the whale had completely passed away. This caused Predy to cry a lot. He then told his servants to take the baby whale along with them towards his palace.

Now the king had fallen in love with the cute baby whale and had decided that he will take care of it like its father until it grows old enough to take care of itself.

There was a huge lake near the palace and he thought that he would keep the baby whale there but he was worried that big fishes there might not devour it or kill it. So he made a plan. To protect the baby whale he appointed 600 of his fine sharp soldiers. 100 of those sharp soldiers were to stay afloat and 100 of them were to stay underwater in the lake. 100 were to be with the baby whale swimming all the time surrounding it and protecting it at the instant whenever and wherever. Remaining 300 were those who would coordinate with the previous 300 and change shifts of their jobs accordingly. They were all supposed to fill air in bags and breathe through it if and when they were underwater. Those soldiers had vowed to protect the baby whale with their life and they did.

Slowly the baby whale grew up and turned into a mighty whale. All of the men including the king had fulfilled their vows of taking care and protecting the baby whale.

Now, since the baby whale had grown up it was time for it to explore the oceanic world thus it had to leave for the oceans. But the matter was that it had grown and thus was too heavy to carry. Even though Predy was the king of kings and the lord of lords but he could not carry such a huge mighty whale to ocean.

Predy then made a plan. He decided to dig a huge canal from that lake where its baby whale lived to the nearby ocean and then let the whale to go and enter the ocean itself. The plan worked. After they had built a huge canal from the lake to the ocean the baby whale that had now grown up took some time to realize that and then entered the ocean saying good bye to its protected or as I may say "over-protected" life style.

Those 600 soldiers that were assigned to protect the whale took some days off to rest and the king decided to go on hunting once again looking for another venture.

tALe 9 : tHe wArRiORs oF tHe LaNd oF tHe RiSiNg sUn

Once in Japan existed three mighty warriors and an evil Japanese sorcerer (among other evil sorcerers). These Japanese warriors were elite in their class and had remained undefeated for a very long time. Only people that could defeat them were each other. Nobody else had neither the strength or capability to defeat them.

The evil Japanese sorcerer that I am talking about was one of the most powerful sorcerer of all times in Japan. He had great sorcery powers through which he could launch deadly sorcery towards his foes and make them suffer. The thing that he lacked was defensive powers which made him a sitting duck sometimes from attack of other evil and good sorcerers. He had tried to create defensive magic many times to protect himself but he had failed.

After few years of struggling with the ability or sorcery to create defensive powers this evil sorcerer who was also called Sasha devised a plan. He planned to capture the three mighty warriors of Japan and then use them for his protection. He developed an evil sorcery through which he would trap the three most powerful warriors of Japan and would put them in a jewel. That jewel that he would wear would hang loose from his neck like a necklace and would cover and protect his heart both physically and magically from attacks. (His heart was a weak point that could give give him death if hurt physically or magically).

How this jewel would protect him was that the trapped warriors would be forced to protect him (since the jewel in which they will be trapped would be facing the direction of attacks) or die from attacks of other evil sorcerers themselves. All they had to do would be to defend themselves using swords and other weapons (in which they were highly trained) from the juice of attacks as they usually did like in physical fights. The magical jewel that Sasha would be wearing would then magnify and convert those attacks into magical forces. It would then release those forces from itself that would erode the attack.

To put this plan into action all he had to do was to show the jewel to the warriors anywhere and anytime and he succeeded in doing so. After the warriors saw that jewel they shrinked and got trapped in it one after the other.

The news of disappearance of these warriors spread. It got heard far and wide in Japan. People were surprised to hear that the mighty warriors who could not be defeated by anyone had disappeared all of a sudden. Even the cops were helpless as they had no clue about their disappearance.

After capturing those three warriors Sasha told those warriors that if they love their life and want to live even so in captivity they would have to defend and wade off the evil attacks that come towards him. Otherwise, neither he would live and neither would they. All they had to was to fight with their swords and weapons normally in an elite manner as they would fight for physical fights and the evil forces or juice of forces would be waded off. Rest they should leave to the jewel.

The mighty warriors who had never lost a battle or let even a single scratch come to their body in their trained life had to obey to live their life even though it was a captive life trapped in a jewel.

While being trapped in the jewel they fought many forces but were tired of being trapped in the stone. Staying with Sasha and staying in that jewel for a very long time they came to know some secrets about destroying the jewel and Sasha. The secret on how to kill that sorcerer and get released lied in shattering the jewel and his heart. But the problem was that these warriors had too much power and whatever they did was amplified by the jewel to protect Sasha. They then thought for a while and decided to meditate . This was done so that they could reduce their physical attack capability to only that much that it does not got amplified by the jewel and therefore it is used only for their own protection and not Sasha's. After quite a lot of meditation they were able to reduce their attack capability and capacity to a minimum that could not be magnified and thus would only be used for their protection and not Sasha's when attacked.

They then waited for a day to come when somebody attacked straight towards Sasha's heart. This happened on one fine day when the evil soccer was practicing his sorcery in a river in front of the rising morning sun. What happened was that suddenly another sorcerer came from the hiding of the bushes and sent a magical force straight to Sasha's heart. The warriors were ready but Sasha was not. The warriors used only so much defence that they got protected but Sasha did not. That magical force went straight through the jewel destroying it and heart of Sasha. Sasha died at that instant and since the jewel had broken the warriors grew back to their original size and were let loose and thereby set free.

After the warriors were set free they requested the king of Japan to banish all sorcery from the kingdom and which was immediately done. Sorcerers who did not comply were arrested and send behind bars. Thus later, peace prevailed in Japan.

tALe 10 : GoD oF bALLoOnS

Once there lived a magician and a tiny human like creature together in the same house. But both of them had never met each other. Although the tiny human like creature had seen the magician many times in the house but the magician had never seen the tiny human creature and thus had never known about his whereabouts. The reason for that was that the tiny human like creature lived in the mouse holes of the house and the magician lived in the actual house and its rooms.

Now let's come to their names. The tiny human like creature's name was Brenny and the magicians name was Sprek.

Also let me tell you the characteristics of creatures like Brenny. Brenny was a tiny human like creature who had a life span of about 500 years and currently he was quite young. His parents had died long time back (in terms of human ages and time) in the same house. They had actually died when Brenny was born. The second characteristics of creatures like Brenny was that they could not only walk and run like humans but also could hop and jump like a kangaroo. In fact, he could jump to about 50 times of his own height while hopping, if required. Whatever food or drinks he needed he got them from the supplies of magician who never realized that they got missing.

One night Brenny slept early. At about 1:00 am, just an hour after midnight he started to hear lots of yelling and screaming. This caused him to get up from his bed and see what was going on. When he sneaked out from his mouse hole he saw that magician was upset and sad. He was yelling and saying that "why can't I find an assistant." Then he also said that "If I find an assistant I would do anything for him. I would make his wildest dreams come true."

(As I told you earlier that Brenny could hop like a kangaroo and run like humans but it was not enough for him, he also wanted wings behind his ears that could be concealed whenever required and could also make him fly to his hearts desire whenever he wanted.)

Hearing that Brenny got excited and thought this might be his lucky day as Sprek was a magician. He immediately came out from his hiding and hopped and ran as fast as he could and climbed the table top besides which the magician was sitting. He then immediately went near Sprek's shirt's sleeve end and pulled it. Magician did not release the pull until Brenny pulled it real hard. When magician saw somebody pulling his shirt's sleeve he looked at it and before he could react upon it, Brenny said "Hi!" to him. Sprek surprised to see the human like creature also said "Hi!" to him but after a minute of staring at that tiny human like creature. Brenny then said to the magician, "My name is Brenny!" The magician then also introduced himself saying "My name is Sprek." Brenny then said "I am one of the house owners." Sprek was surprised to hear that and said in a funny tone "But I have never seen you here". Brenny then told him about his whereabouts and told him that he lived in the mouse holes hiding from him. Then the magician had a question. He asked Brenny "Why show yourself today then?"

Brenny then said that he heard loud screams coming out from Sprek and thus as a nice house-mate he came out to see what was going on. Then Sprek said "So you know." Brenny said "Yes" and told him that he was willing to help Sprek and be his assistant if he made his wish come to life. The magician was excited to hear this and said "Yes" to whatever Brenny might want. Brenny then told Sprek that he wanted wings behind his ears which could be easily concealed and could also make him fly whenever he wanted and to wherever he wanted. Magician then said that it should not be any problem at all. Hearing that Brenny happily started working the next day as an assistant to Sprek. But according to the terms and conditions of the contract of service, Brenny would get his wings after completion of 10 years of his job to which he had happily agreed upon.

Brenny worked many years tirelessly for the magician. One day Brenny was off work as he had that day off and was outside the house sight-seeing but magician had to do something so he was working on his own. While magician was working he suddenly felt extreme pain in his heart and fell on the floor. The magician realized that he might not survive that pain. Then somehow he pulled himself up and remembered what Brenny, his faithful assistant had asked for, for being at his service. So he hurried up and made a magical potion for him that would give him flapping concealable wings behind his ears which he always wanted. Then he wrote a small note to Brenny stating that the magical potion that he always requested was in the shinny flask which was marked so on the table where they first met. Then he lay dead on the floor.

The magician had done his part of the job.

When Brenny came and saw he felt very sad seeing that the Sprek had passed away. But then he saw that note lying besides Sprek's hands and read it. It made him a little happy. He then went near that flask and drank the entire potion that was in it. In a fraction of a second small tiny wings popped out from behind both of his ears and started flapping. He then tried controlling them and was able to do so through his body's will. He thanked the magician in his heart as he got what he had dreamt of and wished him good luck in his after-life from within.

Now since his house mate had died he did not feel like living in that house anymore. He flapped the wings behind his ears and flew up near the clouds. He then tried sitting on the clouds but could not as they are not that dense. So he condensed the clouds by pressure of his flapping wings and when they got condensed he sat on them thinking what to do. For a few days he made that cloud his home. He slept on it, he wept on it, he enjoyed on it. He also used to see human kids play outside their houses on the streets from there. This would make him very happy. He kept on being there on the cloud for quite sometime and kept on watching kids play. This was his favourite way to pass time and also used to make him very happy seeing kids play. He started liking kids very much and wanted to do something for them. He realized that why not give them something that looked like a cloud and could be popped out loud or blown into any size which they wished out. So he confirmed that he would give kids this present. But during those time there was no material which could do that or had this kind of properties. But he was determined to find such a thing.

So he flapped the wings behind his ear and entered earth grounds. He looked here and there, checked many things but nothing soft and stretchable as he required and wanted so he went to the waters, he searched for it stealthily in the grocery shops but could not find such a thing. One day he went to a hot forest and was moving from tree to tree in search for that desired material. Suddenly a huge gooey thing fell on him and trapped him. He tried to come out of it by wrestling it with his arms and legs but could not do so. So he remembered that how he had condensed the cloud where he lived. Therefore he immediately started flapping his ear wings real hard. To his surprise he saw that the gooey thing that had trapped him form a huge bubble like thing that looked like an inflated cloud. He then kept on flapping his wings and this kept on increasing the size of the bubble and later it burst. He was set free from the bubble but he had found what he was looking for. He then named it as "Balloon" as it had a bubbly ball shape and could be increased or decreased in size at ones will (signifying "oo" in balloon).

But how would humans come to know about it? He then devised a plan. He used to inflate quite a lot of balloons and when it used to rain he used to send and throw those balloons from the cloud where he used rest and let them enter the houses of kids. The kids use to first be intrigued and intimidated by it but later they started playing with it. Since they were always less in number and kids wanted more and more of them their parents then tried to create them on earth themselves for their kids. They prayed to the gods for a while to help them discover the mysterious material that made balloons. It took them some time and hints (from Brenny) until they found out the material which was nothing but rubber mixed with some other ingredients. After getting to know the material they started to create it on their own on earth exactly as Brenny used to create them for their kids.

Later Brenny passed away, but gave a present to human kids who still enjoy it by popping it on their birthdays to cause candies to fall onto the floor or filling them with water and throwing and splashing them at each other.

So Brenny gave one of the things that kids could enjoy and could give it to their kids in future for enjoyment - Balloons.

tALe 11 : tHe sWoRd ThAt sPLiT

Once there existed an era in time which was mostly magical but somewhat mechanical. In this era there existed a mighty empire that existed because of magic. This empire was the most powerful empire of that time because of its superiority in magic and peacekeeping will. This Empire which was called Samoree had the most powerful defences and most powerful peace keeping forces. Now, Samoyed had a capital named Sinooka. Sinooka lied at the border of the empire and it also bordered a small village named Miclock on its outskirts. Samoree had tried asking people of Miclock that if they would like to seek the protection of Samoree and be a part of their country but people of Miclock had gently refused that offer.

Miclock's people did not believe in magic. They were more of a mechanical type of people and made mechanical things.

But, whatever, Miclock's people were also peace loving people and had never engaged in war.

Now, in Miclock there was a little girl who was a mechanical genius. She used to create many mechanical contraptions to enjoy by playing with them. Not only that she was also the daughter of chief of Miclock. This girl's name was Nelomi. Nelomi had seen many mechanical contraptions being created by her dad and her uncles for security, fishing, hunting, etc purposes. She always wanted to make better than the things that she had seen.

This little girl, Nelomi as she started to grow up she realized that through mechanical might she can create a metal form that looks just like a human and works like it too. So she started working with metal to create a metal-human like machine. It took her 7 years to create that master piece but if she was a genius she could have done it in a year. Let me tell you that she actually had done that in a year itself but was not satisfied with it as it was too small. She wanted to make a metal - human like machine that was sky high. So she asked her father if she could use her dad's machines to manufacture and design parts of her project and to which her father happily agreed to.

So in 7 years she created a metal-human that was 500 feet high and 50 feet wide and was perfect for her fun. She used to sit in it and make it run here and there and cut trees, hunt animals and do fishing with it. It was also a very good security thing.

It so happened that one day a diplomat from Samoree who was also the brother of king of Samoree was passing through Miclock. At the same time Nelomi was hunting some deers and things got bad. While hunting Nelomi did not knew that a diplomat from Samoree was passing through and also since she was sitting quite high in the human - like machine she could not the see the king's brother while she was hunting for deers. The king's brother mistakingly got hit by one of the deer's horn when the human-machine was trying to nab the herd of deers with the its arm, while Nelomi controlling it. The king's brother was hurt bad. The soldiers who were marching behind Samoree's king's brother and were in charge of his security saw the huge human like machine and got really scared seeing that huge creature. They had seen nothing of that kind before and so the soldiers whose moral had already gotten low and were otherwise too low in numbers thought that it was better to help the diplomat and take him to the palace for his soon recovery than to fight the metal giant.

When Sameera's king came to know about his brother getting injured he was really furious about it and in a rage and without much thinking he ordered a group of knights to destroy that giant creature and whomsoever comes in the way.

This creature as you know was Nelomi's favourite machine and she was daughter of the chief of Miclock. She would not let it get destroyed. The knights attacked the giant but they failed in harming it even a little bit as they could not penetrate its armour. All of their swords broke or bended while attacking the metal giant. Many of the knights got injured very badly while fighting with the metal-machine, some of them even got slayed. The remaining knights returned back to the kingdom and told about this to the king.

Now since this king had mighty magic in his kingdom. The king asked its sorcerers to make a blade that could not be destroyed by metal or magic and would help in maintaining peace. The sorcerers used all their powerful spells and magical chemicals to make such a blade in a few days.

This sword was then given to the king to destroy the metal-human thing. This sword was also given strength that it shall not harm innocent to maintain peace and integrity of the kingdom. The king then with his entire army marched towards Miclock to destroy the man-metal.

There was a huge fight between the king, its soldiers and people of Miclock including its man-metal. King's army destroyed many of Miclock's machines using magical might but the huge man-machine was not getting affected by the magic of Samoree's army.

So it was king and it's sword's turn to destroy the metal giant. The king came near the metal giant while flying cunningly and hit its arm with his sword(blade) and everybody was shocked to see a huge cut on the metal-human giant. Nelomi saw that too and she became alarmed. She realized that the sword the king had could definitely kill her favourite toy so as soon as the king tried to fly in the air again using magic and cast another blow through the heart of the metal giant, Nelomi jumped in between the sword and the metal giant. The sword that was meant to pierce the heart of the metal giant split into two equal pieces (lengthwise) and thus could not be used anymore as it could not be held. Everybody was shocked to see that. The king soon realized his folly and stood on ground thinking that what kind of hell he raised just because of his stupid rage.

He then asked for a formal and a moral apology from people of Miclock. He then used the magic of his kingdom to help bind machines of people of Miclock including the huge metal giant that had got completely or almost destroyed in the battle back to their original form.

Peace existed later and Miclock became a powerful ally of Samoree then.

tALe 12 : tHe MaGiCaL pOwDeR

Once there existed a territory in Japan who had its own ruler. That ruler's name was Hucklickoksy and he at that time had ordered seizure of all gold from common man as he believed that gold was prestigious thing and did not belong in the hands of commoners. Many people did not agree to it and tried hiding their gold from his soldiers and keeping it withheld from the king but when the king came to know about it he decided to use force. The king's soldiers entered   people's house and other properties forcefully to check for gold and grab it. This was found very effective and thus all gold was getting seized brutally but surely.

One day the soldiers invaded a witch's house on their routine who had no gold. But as they were checking one of the soldiers found a small hen which had a golden feather attached to its tail . The soldiers were ordered not to live any gold behind so that soldier went and forcefully plucked the golden feather from that hen's short tail. The witch was furious seeing that, so she objected it but that soldier did not listen and simply took that feather away.

Now the soldier was not sure that the feather was of pure gold or not and also did not know that the king would like it or not but still he showed this feather to the king and presented him with that.

The king was amazed to see such a beautiful golden feather and immediately after getting that golden feather he pronounced that soldier not only the general of his army but also the care-taker of that golden feather. The king along with his team of sorcerers checked the golden feather and saw that it had a unique property of "drip and dry" thus it got completely dry is a second. So the king decided to use it for writing i.e. he was to use it as his royal pen.

Now since this feather was only one of its kind it had to be kept safe and secure. The new general along with his team and the king had a meeting. They decided That the best way to keep it secure was to keep it moving when it was not in use. So they trained a small fish for that. This fish that they trained could only recognize the voice of general or the king and obey their commands.

Now the king started using the pen during the day for his royal work and at the end of the day the general took the feather towards the lake where the fish used to swim. He then used to call upon the fish by its name and would tie the feather to it at that time (which was night). The fish who recognized the general's voice would come near the general and get the golden feather tied to its body in such a way that there was no obstruction in her swimming. The fish would then dive back into the huge lake (which was in the king's palace) and thus the golden feather would remain safe until the king called for the fish in the morning to get it back. This was at how the king protected the golden feather.

But the witch who had her hen's golden tail feather stolen was very furious about it and thus decided to take revenge on the king and avenge for her hen and its respect.

By that time everybody knew about the king's golden feather that he used for his royal Pen and that how it was kept safe. The witch thought for days on how to get back her hen's golden feather and one day went in her kitchen and made a unique magical powder. This powder she would use to enchant the general and force him to bring the feather back to her. But this could only occur when the general was deeply and truly intoxicated with it. So she made a plan for that.

The general lived in a huge mansion which had an artificial forest around it. The general used to get up in the morning and would go outside his mansion and would grab a fruit from a tree of his artificial forest and while eating it would take a walk around the mansion. The witch had her evil flying birds spy on him and so she knew about the general's daily routine.

So at dawn the witch sat on her magically created flying pig which was as big as an elephant and flew towards the general's mansion. There she sprayed the magical powder in huge quantities by using the flapping of air by the pig's wings while they were flying in the air. She had made the magical powder so concentrated that 1mg was enough for one tree and she had sprayed about 500 grams of that powder on the trees and its fruits. Now the sun was almost visible and by that time the witch had completed spraying and had returned back to her home after spreading that magical chemical densely.

At that time the general had got up and started following his usual morning routine. As soon as he went out to walk in the forest of his mansion and had a fruit he got a completely enchanted at intoxicated by that magical powder.

Now it was the witch's turn. She was watching the general through her magical glass ball while in her house. And after the general got enchanted with the magical powder he got in control of the witch who from the comfort of her house kept on commanding the general to go right, left or move forward etc like one commands a toy robot but it was done as humanly as possible to reach the place. Before the king could get the feather the general was commanded by the witch to get to the place first where the fish was kept and take out the golden feather from there before the king comes for it and so the general did. The general was so intoxicated that he did not know what he was doing. It was only the general that could pass the security check of the king's soldiers and reach that lake where the fish was kept.

Now, after getting the feather before the king did the general raised his arm in the air holding the golden feather while standing near the lake. The witch after seeing through her magical glass ball that the general had the golden feather in his hands sent her favourite pigeon to grab the golden feather and get it back to her. The pigeon then brought the feather back to the witch's house who then took the feather and hid it in a secret place. The witch was then happy and kind of relaxed that she got her stuff back.

Meanwhile the general who had snatched the feather was punished for treason and put behind bars.

The king then tried making an artificial gold feather for his pen but it did not go well. Later the king died of heart attack. The kingdom was then free of tyranny of the cruel king.

tALe 13 : tHe tHiEf sHaDoWs

God initially made shadows of light i.e. there were no shadows visible although they existed . As mankind or man (Un)kind advanced through ages shadows started shedding light because man started doing bad deeds. They became pit dark and started becoming alive.

But as they started becoming alive they started to feel hungry too. So a truce was made between the leaders of shadows and the shadows themselves that they could eat food like fruits and vegetables (in form of shadows) only when it is completely dark. The shadows obeyed and agreed to it.

But some shadows were evil minded and could not resist themselves. They started eating shadows of food and other things including forbidden ones even during the day. Most of the times there eating went unnoticed. But there was one person that started noticing it. Initially he did not bother himself too much for that but strange things started to happen in the world like there would be light for more than 24 hours and sometimes even more than that (as the evil shadows would eat the moon's shadow leaving no darkness on earth when was meant to be). This caused damage to the crops which further lead men and women and their kids to suffer because of lack of food.

That boy started to feel that shadows were alive and were behind all this.

Now, this boy had a strong name. His name was "Arakruno" which meant destruction of mightiest evil. Arakruno told about this to his parents and friends. He told them that this was all happening because of shadows, may not be all of them. He also told them that they were alive i.e had life in them. His loved ones did not pay heed to him and told him that he was thinking too much. Arakruno did not wanted the world to suffer so he decided to take matters in his own hand.

He had observed that only some shadows ate other shadows and that he thought those must be the evil ones. He devised a plan to trap those though a trap made up of shadows.
He kept some delicious food which included lots of meat and fruits in front of a candle light in a deep dense forest and let its shadow smell propagate there. The shadow of the food was cast inside a cage whose bars looked like branches of a tree so the trap remained unnoticed. He then waited for the evil shadows to sniff the food and come there.

After about 2 hours he saw a huge numbers of shadows attacking the food like piranha attacks its prey. He saw that and shouted in a ghostly voice asking "if there was anybody left" as if he was a friend of shadows. The shadows were busy eating and said without looking upon the person or thing that called upon them. They said "No more of us are left because we hunt together like a pack of wolves and don't leave our sisters hungry."

As Arakruno made sure that there was no other evil shadow left to destroy he trapped them in the shadow of the cage by releasing its door and then put the trees surrounding it on fire.

The intense heat and light killed the shadows in an instant and the world became a much safer place to live.

Later, just to make sure that all evil shadows were dead he set up the traps quite a few times and found that no other evil shadow came to eat the trapped food. Thus he made sure that he had killed all the evil shadows.

The good shadows also understood the importance of not stealing and obeying rules of nature and mankind. Peace then and now exists between mankind and shadows.

tALe 14 : uNaFuRtAnGt

Once when there were no humans on earth and only many gods lived on earth. These although were gods but had many similarities to humans. They used to fight, love, play, cry, be happy and do many other things that humans do. These gods mostly lived on an island called Japan.

To begin with, this story is about two friend gods that were like brothers from their childhood. They had very strong friendship amongst themselves and truly cared a lot about each other. One of those god's name was Unafurtangt. The other god's name was Sintret . As they grew up they became strong gods and met a girl named Betoon which was from another god village on earth.

Betoon loved Unafurtangt very dearly and wanted to marry him. But on the other hand Sintret loved Betoon too and wanted to marry her. Betoon had seen some evil in the eyes of Sintret and so she rejected him and did not like him.

On one fine occasion Unafurtangt told Betoon that he likes her and wants to raise a family with her. Betoon was thrilled to hear that and happily agreed to that proposal. They then got married.

This could not be digested by Sintret who left Japan and went to live on the mainland-earth. There he decided that would take revenge and avenge what had happened to him.
He knew that he was a single god and if he wanted to take revenge from Unafurtangt he would have to fight all the gods living on that island where Unafurtangt lived. That thought did not make the idea of revenge go away in fact it strengthened his god blood. He kept on thinking and tried to figure out a way to beat those gods and Unafurtangt. After much pondering he remembered one day that even though they all were god they still had mortal forms and they could be killed by if something causes their blood to stop absorbing oxygen. This was only possible though the venom from serpents mouth. He put this plan to reality.

First he made a magical armour for himself to protect himself from venom and wore it. Then with his godly powers he captured and trapped many snakes and squashed them to release poison from their mouths. He then collected and stored that poison. After he had collected sufficient amount of poison he did the next step. Then he worked with all his godly powers to quickly build mighty numerous ships for launching attack.These ships were fitted with poisonous arrows. Secondly he loaded clouds with poison and sent them towards Japan. While the clouds were reaching there he sent a message of declaration of war towards all gods and Unafurtangt with his long shot bow. In the message he wrote that he will bring venom through ships and also make it rain through the clouds as they had insulted his love for Betoon.

When Unafurtangt received that letter he was shocked and worried . Other Gods who read the letter of declaration of war got worried and shocked too as they were unprepared for that and did not see it coming.

But even if they were prepared for war or not the war was knocking at their doors. There was no time for them to practice war arts.

By that time the venomous clouds reached Japan and also the ships had surrounded the island of Japan completely but were at a distance from the shores. All the ships were controlled by Sintret. Sintret moved faster than lightning jumping from one ship to another and started shooting arrows that were loaded with venom of deadly snakes. Many gods used shields to defend themselves but the arrows were so venomous that the shields got destroyed. The venom acted as acid that ate the shields.

Unafurtangt had to do something to protect his friends and family.

He then decided that if Sintret wants to die he than shall surely will. The clouds that had venom in them were already surrounding and over the land of rising sun (Japan). With his magic he grew in size so that he goes beyond the altitude of clouds but was shielded against their venom through his magical armour that grew in size with him. He was doing it without breathing so that not a single drop of venom touches its inside of the body and makes him weak. Then he went near the ocean and drank ¾ of the ocean water and spit it in space. This made the ships arrows not reach Japan as they had gone too low thus were far from Japan's gods' habilitations.

Seeing all that Sintret was in fear and had caused the clouds to rain venom. When Unafuratngt saw that he caused tremendous lightning in the clouds with his anger. This set fire to venom that was raining over Japan and thus not a single drop of venom reached/touched the land. Although no venom was reaching Japan's land but it was surely reaching and raining at the ocean-shores and waters near the ships. Lots of venom acid that had already accumulated in the ocean waters by rain also caught fire and burnt the ships that Sintret had brought to destroy Japan. Sintret suffered injuries too as his magical armour was not meant for that much damage. It was although protected for venom but not from its fire.

Later all the gods-jury decided that Sintret would forever be banished from heavens and would to have to find his own space to live. He still says today in a place called hell where people like him go and live after death and is not a good place to live or to stay in.

TaLe 15 : tHe tALon oF A sPy

It is mostly said that spies have a sharp brain but how sharp mostly depends upon the training given to them and their learning skills.

In olden times there was this country that had many of its spies in its neighbouring country. The reason for that was that the neighbouring country's leader had sworn to destroy its neighbouring enemies and Anesia was one of its neighbouring target. On hearing this news and knowing the commitment of evil enemy country named Baminock, Anesia wasted no time in sending its spies to Baminock. Baminock was already cautious of there plan and had placed strong laws against spies of enemy states. They were using all of there resources and techniques to trap spies of enemy nations and they were quite successful. So a state of cold war existed. Anesia was a nation whose people had strong feelings of patriotism and would die to protect their country. For that reason all of its spies recieved training very diligently and through heart.

While spying the spies of Anesia had come to know that Baminock had made a biological bomb. That bomb contained a chemical which when exploded reacted with the moisture in the air to form a chain reaction releasing and making further of that biological chemical multiply to a very indefinite amount which was enough to harm people, plants and animals in about 1000km^2 of an area. This was a lot of area for destruction.

Now the objective of the spies was to anyhow know the chemical composition of that biological bomb and tell it to Anesia. The reason for knowing the composition was to prepare an antidote that would protect people of Anesia and its property and also would warn the leader of Baminock that the bomb they are making would be ineffective as they already have the antidote for that.

In some time one of the spies named Soriack had stolen the access card for biological labs of Baminock. It was a golden opportunity for Anesia to get to know the chemical composition of that biological bomb . He secretly got it and tried to tell it to Anesia's superior commanding officers by sending it through a radio message. But before he could do that the spies of Baminock came to know about Soriack and thus he got arrested. They tortured him and then threw him in a deep dense dark prison where there was very less sunlight.

Now Soriack was a true patriot and a peace lover. He did not want anything happen to people of his country. This could only happen if he gets out of that confinement/prison cell and radios through the radio of that prison to his superiors the chemical formula of that biological bomb. He stayed locked up for a while but kept on thinking and thinking on how he could open the place where he was locked up and radio the composition to his superiors. He knew that there was a radio communication system just next to the area where he was locked up in the prison. After much thinking he made a plan and somehow saw the key that opened the door of his prison and tried to remember it. Then he started growing up his right hand's first finger nail. As the nail grew to an almost perfect length he cut it and started rubbing the nail and thereby shaping and carving it to the exact shape of the key that he remembered. In a few days he had carved the nail to the exact shape of the key that could unlock his prison door.

At night he began his mission and objective. When nobody was around he took his key-nail out and successfully opened his prison's lock. The next objective was to enter radio room and radio the chemical composition. To do that he stealthily entered the radio room and hid behind a pillar. When the radio operator went out to get a break he sat on the stool besides radio and punctured in he exact frequency code to send his message. After doing that he was able to successfully contact and communicate with his superiors and then he gave them the composition of that biological bomb.

After having done that he slowly, stealthily and quickly went back to his prison room and locked himself up without anybody coming to know about it. Since that frequency in which he aired the formula was unmonitored Baminock did not come to know about that communication.

Anesia scientists wasted no time and in about a month made an antidote for that biological bomb.

Then Anesia fired back at Baminock telling them they now know the compostion of the biological bomb that Baminock had made and that they have developed an antidote for that. Baminock had taken years to make that secret bomb but now all their efforts got into vain.

Therefore as a result of the revelation of that compostion the Cold War came to an end and Baminock retreated as it was taken aback. Both the countries then slowly released spies from their prisons to go back to their respective countries. Thus peace was restored thanks to Soriack and his talon.

tALe 16 : tHe dEnTiSt AnD hiS tiNy AsSoCiAtEs

Long time ago there existed a dentist whose name was Bravo. Bravo was an excellent dentist who had done many arduous tasks of fixing people's teeth without having them taken to an emergency room. He was well known and reputed through out the town and the dental society.

It was about 35 years since he had been practicing dentistry but a nervous illness struck him. Due to his age or maybe due to other conditions of his body his hands started to shake while he used to work on the teeth of people. He thought of retiring but he was addicted to practicing dentistry and therefore would not quit his work just because of his health conditions. He tried taking medicines for his illness but that would not work on his nerves and therefore would not make him okay.

One day he was working and he got a message from a very high brass official that wanted his daughter's mouth to have been worked upon to fix her tooth or teeth. This made him a bit nervous which he otherwise would never be. He did not know what to do. He could not say no that high brass official and thus he had to do it. After much thinking he thought why don't I hire an assistant that would obey my instructions and do accordingly.

Next day he went to an advertising office and told them to put an advertisement for a dental assistant on newspapers and other forms of media in a good budget. During the first week he did not got any call because during those times there were not much people who were educated or had dental skills. Secondly many people were afraid to do that because of the consequences that if anything goes wrong while performing their duties.

During the second week he received a call from the advertising office that there were 3 people who wanted to work for the dentist as their assistant and the three of them insisted on meeting together. The dentist did not understand at first because he had asked for one assistant and there were three who wanted to meet him. He thought for a while and then finally decided to meet the three persons who wanted to be assistants of Bravo. He told them to meet him early in the morning at 5 am the next day and they agreed to it.

Next day he was sitting in the office at the appointed time and was waiting for the three persons. Suddenly the door bell rang and he went to open the door of his office. When he opened he saw nobody. He looked here and there but he found nobody, then he looked down to see if somebody had dropped a parcel or mail on his doorsteps. When he looked down he saw three tiny men waiving at him. He was surprised to see those men as he had thought that tiny people did not live in this world anymore. He out of confusion said "Hi!" to them and welcomed them inside his office for an interview after they told them that they were the three men who had asked to come together for that meeting.

Those three men jumped and hopped and finally reached the table of the dentist.

The dentist immediately came to the point. He then asked them what are their skills and capabilities that would make them fit for the job. The leader of the three men whose name was Dret said that the common capability of us three is that we are small and can go to the nook and corner to fix things where human hands have trouble doing things but individually we have other assets also which would help you in performing your daily job.

Then Dret said that I work in the mouse holes as a heavy lifter who picks up giant boulders and removes them from the way when the houses of mice collapse due to earthquakes. So I am a strong man and can help pick up the tooth or put it in the exact spot where you want inside the mouth. Secondly I can help you to inject medicines where and when required.

Then came the turn of second tiny man whose name was Bret. He said that I am a bomb expert and plant the exact amount and required mixture of explosives to remove or crack heavier things when they fall in their masters (which were the mice) ways during too much mice moving through the same holes or when they fight and accumulate large stones at a place. I can help you blow the teeth roots through right amount of explosives that the person would not even know that his tooth has been removed

Third tiny man whose name was Cret said that I work for mice too but I am thin and so I do the cleaning of their houses and clean every nook and corner of their houses. I can help you clean the mouth of the patient perfectly after they have been worked upon.

Bravo was impressed and without much thinking hired them. Then he discussed the pay. They said the pay would be electronic transfer of funds to their bank accounts as they can't hold cash and carry. Bravo agreed to their terms and they handed them their direct deposit slips to their bank accounts.

Before he worked upon that Brass's daughter's mouth he tried testing those men on somebody else. When they all were working on somebody else's mouth everything was going well until Cret went from the mouth while cleaning it and felt into the lungs through the trachea when the patient tired to sneeze sucking Cret into the trachea thus ending him in the alveoli of lungs. This was a dilemma for the dentist. But then he immediately put a chemical in the person's mouth. This forced the person to cough tremendously and this brought Cret out of lungs which relived the doctor and the three men.

Later when the team worked on the brass's daughter's mouth the men tied a string around each of their bodies like they do for mountain climbing so that they don't fall into her mouth or trachea. This was then set as standard while working i.e. they worked while strings were attached to them. The brass's daughter dental work was done perfectly and then she went home happily making the dentist happy and less nervous too.

tALe 17 : tHe dAtE!

 Long time ago in one of the solar systems, just like our's there existed a planet which was just like our earth and a moon that was like ours too. The planets name was Halolit. The people that lived on that planet had similar financial structures like that on earth i.e. they used money to buy goods but like any other economy poverty and richness existed there too.

Now lets begin the story it so happened that once a very rich businessman decided to take his date to the neighbouring moon of that planet so that they can have a peaceful, enjoyable and undisturbed moonlight dinner. So to do that both of them get dressed. They wore highly compressed oxygen cylinders which fitted on their back. Next instead of helmets they turned on a force-field shield on their heads which would not allow the air to escape while eating but would still let your hand put food in your mouth without letting the air around their face and mouth go away. Then they wore transparent pressurized suites over their suit and dress so as to not be devoid of aesthetics . This made them ready to go.

Then they both went to the garage. Zhimayfi which was the name of the rich business man taking her girlfriend Ufisioki
space rolling to the moon, unlocked his car wirelessly through a remote. Then they both sat in the car and Zhymafi turned on the force-field of the car so that the journey was comfortable. He then started the rocket engines of the car and loo they went to the moon to eat, date and enjoy.

Now since Zhymafi was a very rich businessman and had many political contacts he had made some enemies across his planet too. Those enemy included some countries and some very dangerous people.

But lets not disturb the date and come back to the dating scene. Zhymafi and Ufisioki landed on one of the areas of moon which was actually a huge gigantic crater. There Zhymafi turned on the music of the car and came out. That music could be heard in vacuum or area where there was no air too because that music system sent vibrations through an unknown wave to ears which already had air around them due to force field of helmet and thus it could be heard very clearly and neatly. Then Ufisioki got out of car too and sat on that cold ground of the moon and both talked and had their lunch.

But, suddenly while they were doing so Zhymafi saw 5 rocket propelled arrows hit the moon floor around the area where they were eating and enjoying. This shocked Zhymafi and he was taken by surprise. He got raged with anger and thought that how dare his enemies barge on him like that and also when he was using his free time very preciously . He couldn't withstand it. He told Ufisioki to get up and run towards the car and seek shelter in it while he finishes some unfinished business.

Zhymafi was very angry because first of all he was on moon and second of all he was with a date. Since Zhymafi was a very rich person he had many custom tools made specially for him to protect himself and his loved ones if required. He thought of many things to be used to protect himself at that time but the only thing that came into his mind was a chemical that was very dangerous but he had no other option. The chemical was made from the dried blood of 10,000 dead dragons and a chemical called chemical Alpha. Secondly he was going to use it in a very high concentration to protect himself and his girlfriend. He was supposed to take only .01 ml of that chemical but he took 10 ml of it.

That chemical made him grow 30 times the size of that Moon in space and due to increased size his sight capability including other body capabilities also increased. To protect himself and his date he held moon with the palm of his two hands and crushed (which should never be done) it keeping his car and his date safely in his pants right pocket. The moon then was crushed into many small rocks. He then looked through his then sharp eyes and tracked where the arrows were coming from (as they had not stopped and were raining like a meteorite rain).

Then he used his right foot to hit the small moon rocks like a person hits a soccer ball, towards Halolit and destroyed those targeting equipments sending rocket propelled arrows from the specified locations. It rained moon rocks that day on Halolit. All his enemies including the machinery got trashed one by one which was targeting Zhymafi.

After Zhymafi saw that damage was done he brought the moon pieces together and tried to join them again. Thanks to God that due to gravitational force the pieces joined together although not perfectly. Then he put his hand in his right pant pocket and took out the car in which his date was sitting and put it at the same place on the moon. Then he shrank and apologized to Ufisioki. The girl which was scared at first but highly impressed later thanked Zhymafi and they went back to their home in Halolit after finishing their left food.

That was a date night to remember.

TaLe 18 : ThE gOdS oF cLoUdS

As is known in history that although clouds in some places were considered as gods but to know, they did all the work like raining water and thus making crops grow. Even though they were considered to be godly gods and divine and all, they once got tired doing work for the people and did not rain for a very long time.

This had all occurred before the development of canals and where the ground water was scarce to feed the fields.
The truth is that something had happened amongst the cloud gods and in their kingdom. A baby was born to King of cloud gods and every cloud was given a vacation to enjoy and relax. This had happened after a very long time. Now, during vacation, clouds

enjoyed a lot. They travelled and saw many different places and did their thundering and regular chit-chats. This vacation was given for two months and after that they were supposed to return to back to their duty. Now they did return back but not to duty.

They told and asked their king that if they were gods why were they working. They wanted to relax now because all their lives they had worked and now they wanted to enjoy the views of earth without doing anything other than floating and chit-chatting. The king was of cloud gods heard them and realized that they were right. If they were gods why were they working. The king then issued a commandment and said to the clouds that now they could relax indefinitely without ever being disturbed or doing work.

This came known amongst people of those places that entirely depended on rain water for their crops to grow in their fields. Now mortals are helpless against gods I believe so they were and they did not know what to do. The leaders of those places had a meeting. The leaders could not decide anything themselves or understand or decipher a way out of it. Seeing and understanding that they called upon a meeting of wise men that included scientists belonging to their regions to discuss how to cause the clouds to change their mood and rain so as to be godly and let grow food in their fields.

After much discussion a wise man said that the only way to cause them to change their mind would be by luring them into something that these ungodly gods become tamed to and that then they would work more diligently than before.

Hearing that a scientist said that since now we know that clouds want to relax why don't we give them something that makes them really work with re lax. He said that why don't we give them that thing that is available on earth that would teach them a lesson. Everybody wanted to know what did he mean by that? The scientist said that why don't we give them a fiery candy ie. let them taste it which would make them understand that they are not the only gods in the world and that they are not godly . But everybody asked that how was that possible because " the clouds don't come down and we cant go up to them."

The scientist then said that he had a plan. He said that he had consulted his books and knows of a gas that makes things afloat in air which was at that time, hydrogen whic when compressed or hit with a spark would burst teaching clouds a lesson. He then further said that "I know how to make this gas and I can make it in sufficient quantity safely." The leaders agreed on this idea and agreed to support him in his plan. (hydrogen is flammable that is, is a supporter of combustion and thus is dangerous to handle due to its exploding ability) .

The Scientist said "I need some help i.e. I need help from some kids" (because they have small hands and were right people for the task). Due to intensity of food shortage about 5000 kids agreed to help that scientist. It was a dangerous mission but he made sure that it was done in a very safe environment so that he does not cause any harm to the kids .

In a few days he manufactured enough hydrogen to make the candies. He then gave small syringes to the kids to fill in hydrogen and pump it in the specially made candies that would inflate and would not burst even upon getting filled up with the gas. The kids did that and filled the entire warehouse with the floating hydrogen candy.

After sufficient amount of candy was made they let loose the floating candy. The candy bubbles/small balloons then reached the clouds. The clouds felt curios seeing that and tried to crush it with their mouths and some with lightning, some out of anger and some out of rage (because they said how could human make gods). Now when some clouds crushed the candies it initially felt tasty but they bursted when the clouds got squashed. Sometimes the candy dismantled the clouds' teeth and sometimes it dismantled their bodies.

The clouds got afraid from that thing and there was no escaping as humans said that if they did not rain they would cause more retaliation. The clouds then finally made a pact with humans that they would work for them but would get rest times too. The humans agreed and now they work and rest according to their agreements. They don't talk to humans because they are afraid that if they waste time chit chatting they might be dismantled again (which is although the not true but the fear from humans is still their among gods, HA HA HA!)

tALe 19 : tHe FLyiNg cLoThEs

This story is a peaceful but a melancholy story with a happy ending. The story is about a boy and his beautiful nature that made him get a friend in his life. So let me begin telling it.

Long time ago when electricity was not invented or discovered people used to dry their clothes on a wire in their backyard.

                         Page 418

During those times in a small town called Freeheart there existed a beautiful and a huge mansion. Alongside that mansion in that countryside area of that town there was meagre cottage whose backyard although small was adjacent to the backyard of that huge mansion.

The owner of that mansion was a very rich businessman whose name was Robert. Robert had business of manufacturing airships. He lived alone in that mansion with no wife or kids except for some servants who did his chores.

It used to happen so that the owner's servants would dry clothes outside on a wire in the mansions backyard and sometimes due to strong winds the dried washed clothes would fall in the backyard of that meagre cottage where a boy named Joy lived. This boy whenever tried to return the clothes they would not accept it back for some or the other reason. The actual reason why they would not accept clothes was because of strict rules of Mr. Robert who had told his servants not to accept anything from anybody so as that they would have to return favour later. This simple rule made the clothes that flew to Joy's shanty because of the wind non returnable to its owner.

Now Joy was a very modest and a descent guy. Initially when the clothes could not be returned to his neighbour and rightful owner they were kept aside in one of the corner of his shanty. But then due to having low money in his pocket all the time he one day decided that since he could not buy clothes for himself he would wear the clothes that flew towards him from their neighbours backyard even though they were not his and were quite a loose fit.

Joy was a very observant boy. He had seen that the owner of that mansion used to remain upset for some reason or other as had seen tears coming through his eyes sometimes through his window. Robert never wanted to show them and remained very hard skinned on the outside but Joy had seen and knew that.

One day he decided that even though Robert does not talk or let him come to his house, even to give him his clothes back which was in favour for Joy all the time. He decided that he would try to ease the troubled man. So he in the evening when Robert - the owner of the mansion would return from work, he would start playing violin from his home. This violin when heard by Robert made him feel calm and peaceful and would somewhat have a feeling of joy around him. This, Joy knew because he used to see that through the window of his cottage.

Now days went by and due to savings because of buying no or very less clothes for himself from outside as he got them flying from his neighbour he thought of helping more to that man from whose house or whose clothes he wore. He had discovered that Robert was constantly having trouble in his business. Robert owned a company that made airships for people to ride on, enjoy and travel. Due to explosive nature of hydrogen that was used in the airships they sometimes would burst in flames and would cause sufferings to man and property. For this reason Robert would always be stressed out and would remain grumpy. Joy had decided to something to help him because he always felt indebted to him because of his clothes he wore which although were bit loose but covered his body and earned him respect that may be little or more.

With his savings Joy went to a college and took science as his major in it. In a few years he became researcher and researched for something that would not blow up the airships. Firsts he tried finding out a gas that would inhibit the explosions but ultimately he discovered a rare gas which was also found in atmosphere through very accurate and fine distillation of air. That gas was helium and it could be filled in the airships easily, to make it float without causing it to burst. He, after discovering the gas, its features and the process of its extraction got the process for its extraction patented.

Robert had come to know about that gas and also had come to know that it was the same neighbour how discovered the gas that he would not see or let come in. Roberts used to feel very bad thinking that but Joy did not. Actually Joy was waiting for Robert's birthday to make the patent of extraction of helium under Robert's name a s a present of gratitude to him. It was January and his birthday came in April. By that time Robert used to work and in the evening when he returned home would still play violin to calm Robert and make him a little joyful. Robert hearing that would feel sorry for how he was and what he had done with his neighbour.

Never mind, April came and there was a knock at Mr. Robert's door. It was the postman and the servant of Mr. Robert opened the door and got the mail. The mail required signature. This made the servant of that house immediately go and give the mail to Mr. Robert after receiving it.

When Robert received the mail he kept it on the table and opened it after about 2 hours. When he saw what was in the mail his feet would not touch the ground his happiness had no bounds. He could not believe what had happened and was that for real. He was very excited and overjoyed with that piece of mail. According to that document in the mail Mr. Robert was transferred the patent of extraction rights of helium gas onto his name. Robert's joy had no boundaries. He immediately rushed outside his house towards his neighbour's house and knocked at Joy's door. Joy opened the door and Robert asked him " Why, why all this ?" Joy said " just a Thank you in return of your flying clothes." Robert did not understand at first completely what Joy was saying. Then Joy explained him the whole ordeal. Robert then thanked Joy and asked " is there anything he could do to help him?" Joy said "Just be my friend."

tALe 20 : ThE sUpErStiTiOn!

There is nothing more stupid than a superstition and especially when it is in you to the deep. Let me tell you this story which would further clear what I mean to say.

This story begins in a kingdom where a son is born to the royals of that region. As during olden times royals had many enemies near and around them so did they. After the kid was born they took him to a fortune teller as they believed that their kid was their fortune and would help to sustain and grow it further. Now, the fortune teller when studied the kid's future through a magical glass ball including his parent's future, in order to show them that he was a very high fortune teller he told them something strange and stupid. He told them two things.

First thing was that the child should have another door for entrance to their home/palace just along its main door which should just fit him. Also as that child grows the door should grow too i.e every year they should increase the length breadth and height of that door until the child becomes an adult. Thereafter that door shall remain and shall not be broken.

Second thing he told them was that they should not do anything be it administrative, be it drinking water, be it taking out a sword, be it any task in the world except moving themselves without measuring the luminosity of the sun. Only when it is more than 50,000 lux they should start their daily works.

He said otherwise you shall suffer.

When those royals listened to the fortune teller and as they were already superstitious they discussed that amongst each other while they were on there chariot home. Both the parents thought that to listen to that fortune teller would be a good idea as it should not hurt anything but would let them get by without getting hurt themselves.

(The only thing that these things hurt is that they cause great misery among the minds of people and affect their lives deeply. They get attuned in believing superstitious things because believing in one is a stepping stone to believing in all. One gets adhered to it strongly and superstition becomes beliefs which sometimes lead into religious beliefs. So be aware!)

Now they did as they were told.

The child had a separate entrance for the palace and he would only enter through there. Secondly they would always start their day after measuring the luminosity of sun which as they were told should be more than 50,000 lux.

Their life continued being involved in the superstitious beliefs but not their enemies'. Their enemies had heard about that superstition and that those royals believed in it. They also knew that they adhered to it very sharply. So as the time went by the boy grew and his parents grew old but their enemies grew stronger.

Their enemies had started training a snake and a hyena to kill those royals and one day it happened. They knew that those royals including their son did not do anything until they had checked the luminosity of sun was more than 50,000 lux at that time. They sent their wild tamed beasts to kill that family. Now it so happened that when the royals saw those animals attacking them, the son and his father tried taking out the sword but the royal lady told them not to do so as they had not yet measured the sun's luminosity and they tried simply to hide, run and duck. But the animals had got their scent and they were not going to spare them.

For sure they were killed as they were only allowed to move and not do anything else before measuring the sun's luminosity. That superstition killed all those royals. So watch out kids do not let superstition betray you or feed you any trouble.

Bye.

tALe 21 : tHe cLeVeR sCiEnTiSt

Once there existed two scientists. The less clever one always wanted to prove the more clever one inferior but he had always failed to do so.

The scientist that was more clever had his name as Civonee and the scientist who wanted to prove him inferior and was thus less smarter than him had his name as Crapo.

Civonee and Crapo would meet each other in meetings and would always have a smart talk thus Crapo trying to know tricks from Ciavnoo to fool him later. Crapo would then say I did this and I did that that changed the course of history. Actually what he did that had caused to change the course of history was making things in union with other scientists and Civonee would always know that. But, he still would appreciate Crapo for his works. But Crapo knew that the person who used to come in the news and press was Civanoo. He was a distinguished scientist and things that he did were marvellous and people could not keep their eyes or mouth shut seeing the accomplishments and projects that he made.

Crapo was jealous and tired of all the praises that sounded for Civanoo. Civanoo had actually won not one but 5 Nobel prizes during course of his life at that time. Crapo was fed up of this and so one day...

One day he met Civanoo and asked him that what was the most precious thing in his life. Civanoo said " The most precious thing in my life is my home which I built myself to keep me happy. " He also said that even if anybody steals things from my home I would still not feel bad because my house is with my emotions that are tied to it and nobody could ever steal it. Crapo then asked him " what if somebody did something that would not allow you to enter your house? Civanoo said that was not possible and even if somebody did that I would figure a way out to still enter and live in my house because I love my house so much. So he said then its a deal. Civanoo surprisingly asked what deal? He said the same as you said but with a little twist. Civanoo was confused. Crapo then said that I would do something that would not allow you to enter your house forever and if you could possibly enter it then I would stop being trickily smart in front of you. Civanoo thought for a while and said slowly " Ok, as you wish."

Crapo got into work. He thought lets make something that fills his house and also could not be destroyed. He kept on thinking for 5 day and 5 nights and then came up with a plan that he would make a balloon material that would inflate and would never ever get bursted with any sort of prickly or destructible substance.

At those time some of that kind of material existed and so he got into work. He combined fine impure materials like steel, silica, titanium and rubber etc and did a molecular fusion process for them so that they become unbreakable but only extendable. After testing that material several times, he was happy with the results and was ready to make his egoistic desire come true.

The next day he went to Civanoo's house and told him that he needed his house keys to implant the thing that would not allow him to enter his house ever. Civanoo said politely and with a little giggle " Oh so the time has come. " He then put hand in his pocket and gave Crapo the key. Crapo went to his house and implanted the un-inflated balloon made up of unbreakable and indestructible materials and let air pass into its opening so that it fills it and covers the whole house from inside such that there is no space for Civanoo to enter from any part of his house or to stay there. The material worked as had thought of and it surrounded the entire house from inside without leaving any space for Civanoo to enter in his house. After the material of that balloon stretched and filled the house it automatically locked its mouth due to pressure in it.

Crapo then went to Civanoo and brought him to his house. He then told him to check his house. Civanoo went there and figured out that it was true that that material won't crack or break and therefore balloon looked unbreakable and indestructible. Now, Crapo was so confident that he gave Civanoo a time of 5 years to break that balloon and enter his own house. Civanoo who was a wise person and then told   Crapo politely that " Mighty always have a way to fall " and left his house to go to his lab.

Civanoo was a little upset with Crapo's actions but was determined to save his house. He worked in his lab for days and nights and made two capsules. After he was confident, he told Crapo that he was ready to enter his house. Crapo thought that Civanoo was joking but then he said in a arrogant tone " Show me how! "

Ciavnoo went to his house and implanted the two capsules just beneath the balloon near his entrance door. He then poured water on them so as to melt the capsules and the he closed the door. Civanoo had seen the material and was sure that these capsules would work in getting him his home back.

The capsules consisted of two separate things. One capsule consisted of highly compressed steam which had pressure distributed in it in such a way that it could be held easily without dealing the weight of it. Second capsule consisted of 50 gear boxes that had rolling pins attached to it to flatten out things. Those 50 gear boxes further had 100,000 nano gears fitted in each of them.

Now when he poured water on the two capsules which were also made up of a special material and closed the door, the capsules melted. The steam and gear boxes in them worked in such a way that they entangled the balloon with intense pressure and force rolling it through the rolling pins so as to form a Rubik's cube.

After 5 minutes Civanoo open the door of his house and to Crapo's surprise there was no balloon that had surrounded the interior of that house, instead and Rubik's cube of that balloon material was sitting in one of the corners of his house. He picked up the Rubik's cube and said " Here is your indestructible balloon. "

Crapo yelled with his high voice and ran away screaming. He never confronted or even talked to Civanoo ever. Civanoo proved to be the best scientist in his class that day.

tALe 22 : sOmEtiMeS nOt HeLpiNg hELpS tOo

Now, God made the creation which is great but why do mishaps happen. Could not there be only good and good forever without there happening any mishaps ever. Well just to think, this is earth and we together with other things in the universe are mortal beings and things. If mishap was not created then how could feelings in the world exist. There has to be a little down to see the up in this mortal world.

So to manage mishaps God created a department of mishaps which is still managed by mishap beings. Yes, mishap beings! As the name suggests they are not any ordinary mishap creatures. They beings are tiny and invisible mishap creatures that have wings attached to their body and can sometimes travel at one-tenth the speed of light. There whole kingdom exists right under our nose on earth where humans exist but since they are invisible we can't see them. We only experience the mishaps that happen because of them (I suppose). They have a whole kingdom and work orders but there population is quite controlled and that is also the cause of less mishaps but nevertheless they do occur.

Before going further let me tell you one more thing about them. The mishap beings don't need oxygen to survive, they are magical and have the ability to travel through space and for many light years although they don't do such things as they are interested in living with humans and having fun with them which they sometimes think it is.

How they control things is that they have power to overshadow decisions of beings and things thus sometimes leading to blunders. Now blunders lead to disaster by man himself and not by these beings. These beings only sometimes cause you to make a bit mistakes through which you can learn. I mean one should know that they are very small beings and thus according to their size they only have small overshadowing powers and not making you blind minded.

Now, let us begin the story.

Few centuries ago a son was born to the kings of mishap beings. His name was Jolls. Jolls always listened to his dad who had desires for him to become great by actually not doing mishaps. He wanted him to have the power to control mishap mistakes that could be serious by mishap beings. So he always told him to think big.

Now, Jolls begin to grow up and started thinking of things to practice on so that e could be what his dad wanted.

Normal mishap beings practice on rocks or old people (yes that's the way it is) but the son of the king of mishap beings needed something big enough to practice on. He kept on thinking and thinking.

During those days he could not find a dragon nor he could find a giant to practice on. So he looked into the sky and saw a bright thing throwing heat, light and energy on earth which he later came to know that it was sun - a huge ball of fire. He then thought that why not practice on the sun. So he did. Every morning he would fly to the sun which took him approximately 79 minutes and would start practicing his powers to overshadow thinking of molecule and atoms in the sun that would be causing fusion reactions in it. Initially he could not control even a single atom but slowly he started causing fusion reactions of selective atoms according to his wishful magic which he was happy about. But such a small being practicing on sun is no joke. It started making his brain a bit tired and weak. Since he would practice his powers and would come back home there started to be a shift in sun's behaviour due to unnatural obstruction by Jolls and his presence, being what he was. Jolls caused fusion of those molecules or atoms in the sun that would cause a bit of red star formation of the sun. This formation was dangerous. But Jolls was too young too know and he kept on doing this even if he got tired.

One day his dad's astronomer was taking some readings of the distance between the earth and Venus and other astronomical creations. The astronomer confirmed with the king of mishap beings that the planet Venus was moving towards the earth and this could result it in hitting the earth and putting humans to death. The king of mishap beings was alarmed and did not understand why this was happening. According to his charts there was enough fuel in the sun and also according to him nobody was causing disruption in the sun's behaviour that could have caused it.

Jolls how was listening to all this said " Dad, I am sorry I was trying to think big and to do that I was practising on the sun and its atoms ". His dad then understood the whole phenomenon dilemma. He then called a meeting of his entire team. The king of mishaps then told in a powerful speech about the problem they had been facing and that they have to solve it anyhow as it was his son's mistake. He said that he can't do it alone as Venus was already off-track and only way to bring back it on track was causing the sun to behave normally and return back to its natural processing of its atoms (about which they had come to know). He then told that it could only be done by a set of two teams. One team would restore normal functionality of sun's atomic fusions and the other would force Venus to come back on track. Jolls was told not to be in either team as his magical powers were not in his complete control at that moment.

So the mission started and was completed safely and on time. Although Jolls did not help but as his father always wanted him to control mishaps, he did that by not helping the mishap beings and therefore not causing another blunder. Thus sometimes not helping helps too.

TaLe 23 : ThE ArT oF A sCiEnTiSt

In those days of scientific evolution many scientists were studying light. Now, while studying light some experiments revealed and confirmed that that light had dual features or characteristics that it is made up of waves and particles, both. This baffled many scientists but it was a fact and could not be ignored or removed.

One of the scientist whose name was Amanackia was intrigued by this findings and was very much curious to find more about light especially its particle nature. But to know more about the particle nature of light the first thing that was required was to visually inspect light particles and for that there needed to be an image of light particles. It looked impossible during that time to do something to get that but still he decided that he will make it possible and would get an image anyhow. He thought to trap the light somehow and get an image of its particles.

Now it is known that to get an image of a light particle or anything one needed an image capturing device like a camera that can get it. But even if one had that it should have a very strong magnifying lens that could capture the images of light particle. Secondly the camera should have something special in it that allows its capture. That special thing was the camera film's capacity and capability.

So he started working on this project.

He worked to make the lens first. He consulted many scientists and after much intellectual discussions Amanackia found out a way to make a very powerful camera lens that had high optic powers at close distance to capture the light particles (which was sufficient according to him).

Secondly he had to make some sort of camera roll's film that could capture the tiniest particles present in the universe.

Currently the camera roll films that were used and put in camera rolls were made up of a chemical called silver-iodide. Now, when he looked up and confirmed the molecular structure of silver iodide he realized that it was made up of very big molecular elements found in periodic table and thus was difficult to use it to capture smaller molecular compositions even when using a very high powered lens to do so.

Now the task of Amanackia was to find something like maybe a smaller chemical formula that can be used in camera roll's film to capture image of light particles. He kept on struggling to find such a chemical or compound but he could not get any closer to making it. One day he was looking at the periodic table, frustrated, he looked at the noble elements of periodic table. He then thought out of the box and thought that if he could make a compound reacting lithium and helium it might help. But how it would help, for this he had thought about. He thought that if somehow the extra electron in lithium ion which would otherwise waste away while reaction could be used to continually or upon reacting alter the electromagnetic field of lithium and helium (thus altering their shape) in presence of another substance like light to form the shape of substance while being captured on a film, that would be wonderful. He thought that if through use of some insulating material which included chemicals, he could make a stable compound of lithium and helium it would be wonderful. The compound formed would have molecules that could change their shape when light falls on them and thus could take or form the picture and shape of light particles on camera roll's film.

This looked difficult but was not impossible. He used pressure and a ton of catalysts including lots of other chemicals to make such a compound. He was successful in making such a compound which he confirmed after testing and called it helium lithiite. But to take image of light particles, it had to be done in a dust free area so that dust particles don't block their visibility.

For this he made a helium balloon and attached the high powered lens to a special camera with the bendable molecule formula - helium lithiite chemical film in it. Then he added a timer for the camera to take picture. Secondly he added a timed spark that will burst the helium balloon at a given height. He also attached a small parachute to the entire equipment.

The experiment was then carried out. Helium was filled in the balloon and then the helium balloon was let to escape in atmosphere. Things functioned as they were required to and Amanackia waited for the results to check when the balloon came down after capturing pictures. When he checked the film he found that although light particles still were un-capturable but he captured other smaller molecular structures of elements like nitrogen, oxygen, water vapour etc whose molecular images were never captured before. This was still a success but not what Amanackia wanted it was really looking for. But just in a desire to capture light he captured much more than that and was considered an achievement.

Later, the concept of bendable molecules that could alter shape in presence of other electromagnetic and chemical fields became wide known and started to be used in making of different things. The whole concept involved changing of shape through the electron revolving around the atom or molecule when together which changed the shape and adjusted them according to the influence of nearby electromagnetic or other type of fields in nature.

tALe 24 : A sToRy oF a MoUsE wHo LiVeD iN a hOuSe oN a cLoUd

This is actually a story where instead of people i.e men and women and their kids, mice and their family and their kids lived on Earth.

Now before beginning please note down that in this story there is no difference between rats and mice. They will both mean the same.

Now let us begin.

Long time back the earth was hit by a meteorite which actually didn't hurt the earth but made it better.

This meteorite was not a meteorite made of metals but of solid gaseous elements consisting of elements having same composition as that of Earth's atmosphere. This meteorite was a giant meteorite which was 50 times as heavier as that of the earth's atmosphere and as soon as it started falling towards the earth and entering earth's atmosphere it started burning as all meteorites do. It finished burning completely before hitting the surface of Earth. Since it was made of condensed gaseous matter it was easy to get burnt by the earth's atmosphere and even though it was pretty big it was thoroughly burnt.

Ultimately what happened was the gaseous matter that the meteorite was composed of was released in the earth's atmosphere causing it to become 50 times heavier than the previous atmosphere without any oxygen or carbon dioxide or nitrogen and other gases concentration getting altered (just to note that there was not much difficulty in movement of mice and rats except a little, which was never felt and only was a workout for body without stressing the mind and thus they started being fitter and better). Some people may think that it could have been like, movement under water, but that was not true. To understand water is more than 700 times heavier than air, as density of water is 1000 kg/m^3 and that of air is 1.275 kg/m^3 approximately(air is heaviest at sea level). Therefore it did not affect the mice or the plant life on the the earth other than in a new awesome way.

Now 50 times heavier air means that the air will be more buoyant which caused the mice scientists of earth to start playing with helium to make it into a new buoyant material. (It took them some time till they made a super-strong helium material that was dense and strong as a solid metal but soft and light as a cloud.)

To get that material rat Scientists did many experiments but they did not succeed until one day, a group of mouse scientists passed the helium through epoxy glue and dust of carbon fibre at some 400 degree centigrade. What happened then was that a cloud got formed which was 333 times the volume of the reactants and that was incredible. In this cloud there was a molecular composition such that in the centre of it, which was the biggest of all, it was 50 times the volume of material and was vacuum because the so called cloud material formed called "HECK"Cloud(Helium Epoxy Carbon-fibre Kicking a Cloud as it was made of helium epoxy glue and carbon fibre kicking in to form a new cloud like substance but heck of a strong substance) had reached a molecular composition that repelled air and other liquids including water and did not allow any of it to enter inside it. It formed a strong wall of bonds that were similar to that of carbon fibre but were much stronger than it.

Now we come to the outer composition of molecule. It was nothing but a compound made of glue(epoxy), helium and carbon fibre but as soft and foam shaped as a cloud and together with the whole molecule it floated. This cloud was strong enough to support weight on it and float according to normal buoyancy laws applicable in air.

The people who formed Heck of a cloud were given noble prize later.

This discovery or invention took the whole rat civilization by storm. It started a new civilization order and changed the course of life for all the rats and governments of earth.

Just realize that from thin air to thick air a lot of buoyancy will be possible and then there will be lots of possibilities because of that. It changed the entire course of mice history.

Rats stepped into a new era called "Heck of an era"."

The new construction material was HECK because it was cheap to make and thus mice started making HECK and building houses on it which were fixed to it. The whole cloud along with the house attached to it floated in the air in sky at approximate elevation of 7000 feet which was the maximum altitude set according to new government formed from the new Earth.

Rats could have used helium balloons to do that but they are not strong enough and can easily be punctured . Even if helium was filled in steel vessels and caused to float due to increase in buoyancy, the vessels could not have avoided getting collided and broken and leaking helium, resulting in falling down on earth and thus leading to a catastrophe when hit by other floating steel vessel filled with helium in air. But this was not the case with HECK formed clouds or floating things due to its soft but sustainable properties.

Note that, it was a matter of mouse and rat lives at stake.

All the world's political boundaries were removed as clouds float wherever they want to and are never limited by boundaries and HECK was a cloud too where houses and buildings started to be built. Rats and mice started living on HECK in Air which floated and supported the weight of other things on it as well.

All the mouse nations of the Earth joined hands in a common economy and boundary and friendship. This was a new era towards world peace.

They formed one country on earth called "Heck of an Earth".

This was the most peaceful era of all times .

Mice started living in the clouds and in this case on HECKs.

Farms and forests although still existed on the lands of Earth but all other things were on HECK.

Factories, buildings, warehouses etc all floating and were on top of the cloud.

All sports field were made on clouds too.

Now let's come to the explanation that how did it all work? I mean how were mice and rats able to get electricity and water and dump of their sewage and wastes? How did transportation occur? I mean how did they survive by living on clouds?

All houses had installed wind turbines and/or solar cells, so wind turbines caused enough amount of electricity to be produced for the whole year round.

Now, for water, mice did rain water harvesting. During those times science had reached to such advancements that if it had not rained sufficiently they could cause artificial rain as most of the mice used rain water harvesting for supply of bathing and toilet water in their houses. Drinking water could be purchased from market or delivered.

Sewage and waste was stored in the houses in sewage storage. It along with garbage bags which was collected weekly.

Now how did transportation occur?

In this Era due to more buoyancy and making of HECK, airships were built which supported 200 times more weight than before. So before if they could only carry 50kg now they could carry

10,000kg of load which was enough to support daily food requirements of warehouses and big grocery stores of rats.

Also, there were many different type of sports that were played by mice following creation of HECK. They were :

1.   Hockey called HECK of a hockey
2.   Soccer called HECK of a soccer
3.   Rugby called HECK of a rugby
4.   Baseball called HECK of a baseball
5.   Lacrosse called HECK of a lacrosse

1. HECK of a hockey: HECK of a hockey was played in air instead of ground made of HECK floating in air. It had 6 players in each team, with 2 teams playing. The player rat had to put the puck in the opposite players goal post to score a goal and the team that scores most wins,

In this game the mouses had their lower part of shoes and the puck attached to approximately 1 cm^3 of HECK which caused buoyancy and caused them to float and play game. But since different mice have different weight therefore to cause the mice to play on the same level of height from surface, the exact volume of HECK attached to their shoe was somewhat different.

Even if the volume of HECK attached to shoe's sole was altered by the manufacturer of the shoes according to weight of mouse but still the height level of mouses playing hockey was not exact which was the fun part. Mouses could move up and down, do some skidding tricks and play hockey. They could also do jumping tricks and rollover tricks to clear the puck(which also had HECK attached all around it) and put in the floating goal post.

The second fun thing about this game was that goal post was not stationary thereby changing directions so it was fun to do goal and it was a challenge for the goal keeper too which made him a better goal keeper.

So HECK of a hockey was really Heck of a hockey!

It was one of the sought game by rats of the world.

2. HECK of a soccer : HECK of a soccer was also played on air grounds rather than on HECK formed playgrounds. In this game too HECK was attached below the shoes to the sole and adjusted by manufacturer for buoyancy to the appropriate height or altitude.

Now in this game there were 2 teams each with 9 players on each side. You had to hit only a light ball filled with HECK having a diameter of roughly 6 inches by your foot or feet into opposite team's goal post which was 5 meters wide and 5 meters high and was protected by a goal keeper similar to that of soccer game played on ground.

The team who scored most goals won

. Since the level of altitude of soccer player got a little up and down due to altered weight because of change of slight body weight (due to breakfast, lunch or dinner) or because of application of force while playing soccer ball was pretty hard to dribble and make it to goal.

What used to happen while playing this game was that while dribbling, force by leg was applied by player which used to result in a downward force application and the players altitude level went low which made the ball to get out of altitude/control and thus getting in control of the other team player. Secondly even if the player was able to control the ball by maintaining same altitude as that of ball or causing the ball to have same altitude as that of him then it become difficult for other players to even touch the ball because of continued same distance from ground (height/ altitude). So it was a tough game to play and to master it was even tougher.

3. HECK of a rugby : Now HECK of a rugby was a cool one.

This game had 2 teams with 9 players in each of it. The aim of the player rat was to put the soccer shaped ball filled with HECK in the opposite teams goal and there was no goal keeper. But the other team could stop the player who was running holding the ball in his hands to throw it in the opposite team's goal post to score a goal. The opposite team's player could prevent that from happening by dashing into him and constraining the player running with ball with their hands etc.

The team who puts most goals in the opposite teams goal won .

This rugby was better than ground rugby and was a very exciting game as players got hurt less in it as it was played in air. Also, it may seem that if a whole team fell on a player to prevent the player with the ball to throw it in the goal the player might get hurt. But since the player running with ball was in air he never got hurt as it used to sneak from below (as he was playing in air and air is 3D with space all around it including below) and score a goal.

So the players had to hold the player running with the ball from below too so that he does not escape their clutches or score a goal.

It was a very awesome game and thus was called HECK of a rugby.

4. HECK of a baseball : This game had 7 players in each of its two teams. This game was also played on air with shoes having HECK fitted on their soles.

Now the player of one of the team had to throw ball and the other had to hit it with a baseball bat. There was a rat player standing behind the rat player hitting the ball who had to catch the ball if it was missed to hit by the hitter . If the hitter misses the ball five times while the player standing behind the hitter catches it then the hitter was out and then it was next player of the same team's turn until all 7 players were done hitting.

Also, the runs were scored same way as in baseball.

This game was tougher than the normal baseball game because to score run in it was tougher. It was so because as the player aimed at the coming ball to hit and then strikes it, due to force that was used to a hit the ball it would make him go off-track from his hitting position as he was floating in air (as that force causes movement in various directions.)

It was a tricky game and required more practice than usual and was named HECK of a baseball.

5. HECK of a lacrosse : This was way awesome than normal lacrosse . It had 2 teams with 7 players in it and as in regular lacrosse in it too the player scored goals by throwing ball in other teams goal post.
Now it was a tricky game because when the thrower threw the ball to pass to the other player the other player had to be very agile to catch it. Because as explained earlier due to reaction forces the player playing moved up and down or left and right along with his regular running motion causing him difficulty to stabilize physically and also to get his aim for the catch steady.

This was a tougher game than normal lacrosse but was more fun and thus was called HECK of a lacrosse.

Now, let's come to story of a little mouse. In this world of HECK was born a mouse named Rephictreity who was always scared to walk with his shoes on air even if HECK was attached to it.

Rephictreity never played any game in air . Whatever he played was on HECK grounds but not in the air directly.

He tried but he couldn't. He was too afraid. He wanted to play HECK of a soccer but was too afraid to even step on the air.

So this carried on until he was 7 years of age (remember on this earth mouses lived a life span of about 70 years).

During this age what happened was once all of his family members had gone to see HECK of a baseball in a stadium.
He and his grandmother were at home doing their stuff and suddenly his grandmother started having a severe pain in chest she screamed and the Rephictreity heard that. He then tried calling emergency services immediately with his cell phone at house and in his nervousness the phone fell on the floor and got broken and then he did not know what to do. But he loved his grandma too much and wanted to do whatever he could do to help her out.

So he wore his normal shoes (without HECK attached to them) with a backpack of HECK for support and went outside and tried waiting for the taxi but he couldn't get one because of the big game at the stadium. Even the taxi drivers had gone to watch the game.

Now he could not run without HECK shoes because he will fall on the surface of earth. Secondly even after wearing a backpack of HECK to support him in air there will be no friction between his regular shoes (without HECK attached to them) and air to run.

Now, he had never ran on air with HECK shoes before. But even then he was adamant to save his grandmother so he went to the shoe rack of his house and took out his brother's shoes (as he had none of his own HECK shoes) which were a bit longer than his shoe size and wore them. He then went outside and tried running while wearing those shoes towards the hospital which was nearby. (NOTE: HECK shoes provided some if not complete or the required friction to run on air.) When first, he started running since he was not used to or practiced to run wearing HECK shoes he slipped and fell on air but he did not give up. He was sure to do whatever he could to save his grandmother so he did not loose courage and continued his falling and moving forward wearing the HECK shoes . He somehow, after rolling and running reached the hospital. It took him about 15 minutes to reach hospital which was about a kilometre away but he did reach there and immediately informed the emergency services who then reached his home and brought his grandma to hospital and saved her from death as she was in critical condition and about to have a heart attack.

When his parents came to know about the incident they rushed to the hospital immediately and were surprised to hear that Rephictreity saved his grandma all by himself after making himself run on air . They were really proud of him because they knew Rephictreity was always afraid of running on air wearing HECK shoes.

The next day when Rephictreity went to school he was a changed mouse.

He first started observing soccer - which was his dream sport. He saw how the rat players played it and how they dribbled.

He tried playing with rats which were of his same age but was laughed and mocked at because he was new at this game and did not know how to play properly that game with the rats of his age.

He then once sitting on a bench near a lake and decided that he wanted to play soccer and be the best player in that game one day. But since he had never played it before his classmates wouldn't allow him to play with them because he'll waste their time. Then he said to himself that I'll practice by myself and be the best soccer player there is.

So he started doing it. He bought HECK soccer shoes and after school he would go to an air play ground daily and practice there for 5 hours everyday .

He first felt that he should know how to control the ball. So he starting controlling the ball with his feet. So he used to make about 35 km of rounds by just moving the ball forward, hitting it left and right without letting it go away from the centre smoke line of the round air track where he practiced

He used to first loose control of the ball but slowly he started getting a hold of it until he was perfect in it. It took him 1 year to get perfect in it after practicing 5 hours every day

The next step was to move ball forward by making it jump little on shoes only and not letting it fall down in air. Whilst the jumping he had to move it through the centre smoked line of the circular air track he was following.

It was tough at first because when he used to hit the ball he used to go down and then he had to come up so that he can hit the ball up again but he kept on hitting it until he completed the 5 hrs of everyday training.

He would loose hope many times but then he realized that even if he does not become world's best soccer player but still he would learn how to play good soccer so this kept him moving.

One day came and he had mastered the art of moving ball forward by making it jump on his shoes only and in whichever direction he wanted. He was happy about it. That day he was 13 years old.

Now he had to learn how to be quick in the game with his feet work and body. To do that he attached rockets on the soccer ball which were touch responsive i.e. they started when the ball got hit and increased its speed the faster the ball was hit. They then made the ball go faster in up direction and down direction by rotating their positions/directions. Thus it was very difficult and almost impossible to balance the ball on his shoes and to make it move forward.

But this time also he did not give up.

He kept on practicing. Sometimes it was difficult for him to even make it jump on other shoe by hitting it with one shoe but as they say "When the going gets tough the tough gets going".

His game was on and off. Sometimes he used to complete half the round without making it falls but sometimes the ball used to fall away on the first hit itself but he still continued until one day he did 35 km of running with the ball jumping on his feet without it falling down. He then became perfect in it and then the ball never fell out of control from him.

Now to dribble from obstacles was tough so he devised a way for it.

To be the best he piloted his private family plane and flew it to the earth ground to cut some trees and bring them to his air practice ground.

What he did was that he attached some trees with HECK around them and then attached rockets to them. He did this so that some trees could move horizontally straight some could move laterally straight while rotating on a click of a button one after the other and which he could shuffle any time. But for his safety he wore some protection equipment on whole of his body.

He choose trees for hurdle practice because they had greater thickness.

Now what he did was that he let the HECK soccer ball be attached to the rockets that made the ball move up and down faster as earlier and then let the trees come straight to him vertically and horizontally at slow speeds first which he had to dribble with and escape without letting the ball get away from his control.

He did not succeed at all at first but he was not giving up that easy. He kept on trying to dribble from the obstacles and move forward by making the ball jump through toes of his feet also by simply controlling it. Sometimes the tree came vertically straight sometimes laterally and sometimes it was a miss and sometimes it was a hit.

After 7 months of struggling at slow speeds too dodge the tree/ hurdle moving towards him while keeping ball in his feet's control he started beginning to get a hold of dribbling. Only moving left or right was not the case. The trees were rotating also and they had branches and leaves which if hit the ball caused it get out of control of Rephictreity. So it was tough but the best way to learn the best soccer there could ever be. He continued this for two and a half years for five hours daily and then he increased the speed of the trees as he became good in dribbling at slow speeds.

Now it took him another 3 years for practicing at high speeds which finally he had succeeded.

Now by that time he had never played soccer with his friends. And now he was 19 years old.

One day he went to a HECK of a soccer stadium and saw group of mice playing soccer. He asked if he could play with them too.

The mice first said no and then one of their player got injured and then they thought if they could bring in Rephictreity in. Rephictreity was still there and he accepted the call.

Now when Rephictreity started playing he was too fast and he had scored more than five times the goals the whole of other team combined could score and therefore the losing team was dumbstruck seeing that. A rat coach who was sitting and watching, wondered who was that mouse? He went closer to him and asked him straight away that if he would be interested in playing for a local team, Rephictreity was looking forward for this movement and accepted the offer.

As the matches were held there was no stopping for Rephictreity who kept on advancing and until he was 20 he became a world champion in soccer game and there was never any stopping for him. He won soccer game like there was nobody else on the air grounds and was respected by everyone including his old school friends.

tALe 25 : ALL fOr eLvEs aNd eLvEs fOr tHeMsELvEs

As an as mortality became more prominent for elves they started getting injured. Sometimes they would get so much injured that they needed lots of blood to replenish. Mostly the blood was donated by family members.

But there started to be times when family members would be too old and did not have enough blood even to support themselves. So to help rejuvenate elves' lives they needed answers. They wanted to know that what was there blood type and what were the parts of their blood. The elf scientists after removing the plasma from blood discovered that their blood was made up of seven different colours which matched that of rainbow and each blood colour going further had seven different types. Also, the blood was nothing but all different types of sugar.

The total types of elves' blood types was of 49 different types, more than that of humans which was jaw dropping but was true and was nothing but sugar in various forms. The elf scientists then got into work.

Since natural blood supply was less they started searching for artificial sources of sugar that could form their blood. So they looked everywhere and found no such source. Few sources of sugar they found but that could not make that many types of elves blood from it.

One day an elf scientist was studying a meteorite that they had found in the north pole. The meteorite that he was studying had the same composition as that of the moon and its rocks. But while he was doing so he suddenly saw a test mice escape from its cage and started nibbling that rock. He was wonderstruck and asked himself that how could a mice eat a rock. Then, he immediately caught the mice and put it back into the cage. Next, he went to the meteorite and tasted it himself. He found it sugary. He started thinking there and then that what if this meteorite which had composition of moon rock could be made into 49 different types of elf blood? He then immediately called his boss who after testing further called a meeting of various high ranking scientists. They then tried to make 49 different types of blood types for elves and were finally successful.

This brought a revolution amongst the elves. Now they knew that they could make blood from moon rocks or moon itself. So what next. They had to get lots of moon rocks to make blood from so as to keep as reserves and for regular supply. But they knew that moon was quite far away and did not have oxygen to support any kind of activity like drilling or mining without elves dying. They could make some masks but that would be only good for 15 minutes of support and then you know what would happen.

Well for one elf 15 minutes was good enough time to get moon rocks. Scientist were puzzled in thinking that how would that be possible. They knew that they did not have a sling shot huge enough to throw them to moon so how was all that possible. The elf that had thought about that was known as Freck. Freck then explained them the whole deal.

He said that they know that they can climb rainbows and have fun on them so they would use rainbow and their 5 million + elves. They would form elf pyramids by standing on top of each other that would look like a pyramid on top of a rainbow (to have some altitude at start) until they reach the end of breathable atmosphere extremities. Then they would use a huge slingshot to throw something which they called a blaster towards the moon. (That blaster worked without air (oxygen support for combustion) and was previously used by elves to blast mountains to divert water or dig into resources for making toys.) Freck would be standing at the top of elves' pyramid thus at the edge of the atmosphere wearing mask and would sling shot the blaster. The blaster's task would be to blast a part of moon where and when it touches. The smashed moon-rock or the part that would be produced due to blast would then try to get away from the main moon part. This will be the right time to throw a huge rope with a loop towards the moon rock and then let it tie that rock, cowboy-way and bring it home. They would do it as many times as would be required to produce and store sufficient blood for elves going back and forth.

The scientist when heard that said that that was a good idea. But they confirmed with Freck that would he be able to enter and leave extremities of atmosphere in 15 minutes time. Freck said " Affirmative! "

All the elves then started preparing. When it was a summer day at the north pole they waited for some rain to fall and form a rainbow. After 8 days rain fell and a rainbow formed. The elves wasted no time and formed a pyramid of elves by climbing on top of each other on top of the rainbow. Then they did as was planned. Everything went smoothly and Freck got many moon rocks back to earth after blasting them with blasters. It then eventually became

Freck's job to monitor the storage of blood and keep on bringing more moon rocks to form sugar required to make blood of elves.

That is why sometimes we see holes in moon and that too in shape of a smiling face. Because elves always do it for us and we love them for that.

TaLe 26 : A wOrM sToRy

This is a story of a place wherein many trees grew and lived. In the trees, many worms lived. Where these worms lived they lived quite happily.

As time passed slowly but steadily the population of these worms grew and so they became more and more modernized and lazy. Due to more population more and more money started pouring into the government. Since worms are slow moving creatures the government of these worms had made a law according to which food should be delivered straight to their house's door step because only then it was possible for worms to do other work. The "other" Work of most of the worms usually involved art and entertainment and nothing else which they secured by eating all day and playing and creating video games and selling them through internet. This was what worms economy rested on and their government earned a lot by this. There were very few worms that worked outside their houses. This sounds a bit odd but it was true. The main reason behind this concept was that worms are slow and they had gotten real lazy and due to much wealth accumulation and giving to the government they needed luxurious lives.

To do that they had hired one and only pilot in the worm world-wide community whose name was Wormscious. He was was an exceptional pilot who was also fit for this job to fly when nobody flies i. e when no eagle or bird flies i. e during rainy and stormy weather. This type of weather was the only weather which was actually safe from eagles and vultures and also according to the flying regulation this was the only time Wormscious could fly (for safety purposes).

Wormscious job was to make as many trips as possible using a wooden charge dissipating (from lightning strikes, using an umbrella charge dissipitator that dissipitated charge directly back into the air backwards) cargo plane, when the bad weather persisted to deliver loads of oranges, apples, grapes and other food items to the doorsteps of worms without landing. He had to be very acute in delivering the grocery so as one's grocery does not gets messed up or mixed with the other one's and it lands directly in the front of the door steps of worms while escaping the branches and thorns and leaves of plants and trees. Wormscious did his job perfectly and with great detail and honour.

Wormscious always wanted to train other worms to do so but they were not interested in doing so as they thought it was a tough job. But Wormsciuos knew that a bad day will come and so the worms should be ready for it.

One day, Wormscious was feeling quite severely sick but he could not stop working. So he started flying the plane without doing the ground checks for the plane. It was mandatory for him to deliver food so he could not stay at home even if he was sick. When he was flying it so happened that suddenly lightning struck his plane and since Wormscious that day had not done the ground checks he had failed to see that the charge dissipating umbrella was cracked. So the lightning caused his plane to fall and crash. This was a wake-up call for the poor worker and all the worms because the only pilot who was working to help the lazy worms of that era had almost got near death and come back . Life could not be more dangerous than that.

He then called upon the meeting of officials of the worm government and told them that its okay if worms don't like flying but sticking to the internet and not doing anything else could not only be dangerous for them but can also be dangerous for others who help them.

That day the worms realized and a new law was passed which stated that one was responsible for their own food and from then on, no deliveries will be provided. This helped worms reduce their obesity also and overcome many other illnesses because of that.

tALe 27 : The general and his pupil

Once a general of a country was with his soldiers on a field where and when suddenly a mine exploded. This mine when found out looked to be an old war mine and thus there was no need to worry about a war taking place but still, the general was hurt. The general was immediately taken to a hospital. Although all the wounded area of general's body were fixed but one area which was the pupil of general's right eye got hurt really bad and according to king's order that had to be fixed too by all means.

The doctors who were treating the general were faced with a tough decision because during those times they could not get an organic pupil that could replace the general's original pupil of his right eye. So, since everything in their power had to be done according to the king's orders they replaced the general's right eye pupil with a highly advanced plastic pupil of a very high optic power that they thought would make the king and general happy and proud. The only thing wrong or correct with the general's plastic pupil was that it had to be adjusted every time to see properly i.e. it had to be focused manually by general himself using fingers and thumb of his hand or hands as it was protruding out of the actual eye. The plastic pupil had a nook at its edge which when was at the topmost position caused the general to see far distances and when the nook was rotated towards a downward position he could see the near ones in focus.

This became fun and amusement for the kids when they saw him on tv or giving speeches in crowd when he had to twist his plastic protruding pupil to see people and then twist its position again when he would have to read his speeches.

General thought that whatever reputation he had gained all through his career by years of honourable service was going in vain because of the plastic pupil. But the general had to see properly and so he stayed with having that plastic pupil except one day when he woke up. When he woke up his plastic pupil had tilted while he was in sleep (because of him tumbling over his bed while sleeping) to the extreme downwards position causing his eyes to have a very high microscopic vision. This freaked him out because he was seeing germs and microbes all around him when he woke up opening his eyes/eyelids. While he was freaking out his eyes started hurting real bad and then therefore he tried to rub his eyes.

As soon as he touched his right eye with his right hand to rub, he touched the plastic pupil that of his eye and suddenly realized that his right eye had an enhanced manually adjusting pupil. He immediately tried turning the nook of that pupil up with his hand and began to not see the germs or microbes and feel a bit better. Then he had a sigh of relief.

He then got ready to go to his office. After he reached there he then discussed this with his soldiers and scientists. He had at first thought that it was a biological attack but was then calmed down by the scientists who told him the real reason for that which was that his eyes got focused to an extreme powerful microscopic vision while he had tumbled in his sleep. Then he said "Oh! okay," and understood what had happened. This made feel a bit better, maybe.

But since everybody does some tumbling in his sleep and so did the general his pupil would fall to the lowest level everyday due to gravity and therefore when he would get up he would see microbes. One day he was so sick and tired of seeing weird and crooked germs floating in the air he said "I did rather see dead enemy men than microbes floating in air."

So that day he thought that he would rather go blind on right eye than have a funny plastic pupil there and see the freak show everyday. So a decision was made. The doctors were ordered to remove the plastic pupil and have general go blind from the right eye. The surgery was to be done next week as before that he had to take some medicines so that the effect of blindness from one eye does not destroy the other eye. Until that time general tried to relax but its enemy nation who had actually planted the mines which looked like old war mine with only purpose of killing the general came back again with another plan.

It had developed a virus that on contact with people would lead to development of such type of sickness that would not stop until it had killed that organism or person. (Also that virus changed its form when it entered a human body.) It had not only developed the virus but also an antidote to protect themselves that only it had the capacity to use. The virus was then let loose in the enemy's central area and people started dying in that general's country.

Since the virus spread through air and changed its structure after entering a human body it was difficult for microscopes to focus on it therefore the scientists first put protective equipment on themselves and then on the general's body that would make them and general's body remain quarantined from any attack of that virus. They then also ordered people to quarantine themselves.

Then, they came to the point. They requested the general if he could help them out to know that virus through his wonderful pupil that only he could use to focus on that virus. Microscopes could not do that because they need the virus to be lying on a slide to see through which was not possible at that time.

Only the general had now the capability to see the virus and catch it if possible to know its behaviour and help in developing an antidote for that. Since the general was seeing micro organisms everyday he kind a started to recognize the general microbes in air. So he had gotten smart with the microbes. He figured out that the virus that was attacking to kill should look quite weird and different from other microbes and so his army blood called upon him and he and the scientists went near the people who were infected with that virus so that there was a high chance of the virus's visibility . There he started focusing in the air near and around the infected people with his pupil. After much focusing he saw a virus that looked quite weird and strange. So he wasted no time and gave description about it to the scientists who were standing close to him. According to the comparative size and description the scientists figured out that that could be the virus that was killing people as it had an unusual description of its physical structure, behaviour, movement and size. After a short discussion amongst themselves the scientists had confirmed that that was the virus they had been looking for. Then what? The general was given a test-tube who took it and held it in one of his hand and while doing so he blew air over the virus through his mouth. The virus then entered the test-tube due to being floating/submerged in the moving air. Then he placed a cork over the test-tube so as to stop the virus from leaving the test tube.

The scientists then analyzed the virus and developed an antidote in some quick time frame. This antidote was then distributed along with the vaccine that was developed to prohibit the virus spread. Thanks to general and his wonderful plastic pupil the country was saved. He was then again a proclaimed hero and never got his plastic pupil removed which became a second eye for security once again.

tALe 28 : tHe RiDe

This is a true fictitious story.

It is sometimes known that Japanese were the first to have moon rides. But is it true and even if it is how was this possible back in those ages.

Long time ago the emperor of Japan had a beautiful, loving and a caring daughter. In the night she would see the moon and dream of going there. She told her father - the Emperor many times about that wish. But her father whose name was Mighten and as the name suggests was one of the most powerful and a wise ruler of that time even he could not devise a way to travel to the moon but was determined to do so. He gathered many of his wise men in a meeting and asked them that how could he fulfiller her daughter's

Page 446

wish of travelling to the moon. The wise men at that time did not have any answer about that. But there was one monk who did and was present there in the meeting. He thought for a while and told the king that it was possible to bring her daughter's wish to life but only with the help of a dragon. The dragon who could do it was called the Laughing Dragon.

This dragon lived underground and was quite unknown but only quite until that day. The Laughing dragon's laugh was so powerful that it caused the lesser magnitude earthquakes in Japan when he laughed beneath the ground. This dragon was a friend of that monk who was attending the wise men's meeting at the king's palace. He had kept the secret of the dragon hidden to himself for a very long time and never told the king before about that for he protected the dragon by doing so.

But since the monk cared also for the Emperor's royal wishes that included the wishes of his entire royal family he had to tell this to the Emperor. So he told the secret to the Emperor. The Emperor was shocked to hear that a dragon had such powerful laugh. The monk who told the Emperor about that had also asked for promise from emperor that he would not to put harm to the thing that would help her daughter to go to the moon and be back and thus have moon rides. The Emperor had agreed to that and kept his promise after knowing the secret of the dragon and what caused earthquakes in Japan. But it was known that the earthquakes were less and this meant that the dragon was difficult to be made to laugh. But the monk knew all that and he had a plan.

The monk had thought that if it was possible to ask dragon to laugh above the ground and not beneath it so as to use the laughing energy to slingshot capsule carrying a kid to the moon and bring him back. How was that possible? They had calculated that they need lots of pressure to throw the capsule to the moon and bring it back after the kid enjoys moon. They were also prepared for emergencies just in case the environment on moon was different from that of earth. The monk had come up with a plan. He told the king that they needed a long plank the size of the side of dimension of the square shaped city where the king lived.

So it was ordered by the king to build a long plank of the size requested by the monk. It took 500 days to build that size plank. It was tough job but the king's workers built it flawlessly.

It was the next day that king met the dragon. The dragon greeted the king and so did the king. The dragon looked a bit worried that what if he could not laugh when required and the objective fails but the monk told the dragon in front of the king that there was no need to worry.

The capsule that was to be sent to the moon was made and filled with food and other supplies (of importance and of Emperor's daughter's wishes) if required. The monk then whispered something into the dragon's ear. The monk had whispered the plan that how the dragon would not look dumb and would be able to send the king's daughter to go to the moon and be back safely.

The dragon took the plank and put it's centre point on the top of a tip of a mountain. Then he flew back. The king/Emperor's daughter was ready and excited to have a trip around the moon and be back. The dragon then took the Emperor's daughter (who was sitting in the capsule) to the giant teeter totter. He then kept the capsule with the girl in it on the lower side of the seesaw which was touching the ground. Then he flew to the maximum height of the atmosphere and dived back to the high end of he teeter totter and pounced on it with a incredible force. When he hit the higher end of teeter totter the girl bounced high up in the sky and then the dragon was amused to see that. Bing amused he giggled and then laughed seeing the girl go high in the sky in that direction. It was evening at that time and with such pressure while laughing and the great bounce the daughter reached moon. Her capsule touched the moon and bounced . Then the monk who was flying high in the atmosphere while riding the dragon to keep an eye at the safety of the king's daughter and to bring her back took out a feather. He then tickled the dragon who again had a mighty laugh. The laugh send shock waves to the moon which forced the capsule to come back to earth's gravity after it had touched the moon's surface. The laugh which sent shock waves to the moon was just a giggle which the dragon mentioned later had caused the capsule to return back to earth where the dragon caught it in its mouth and brought the emperors daughter home safely.

Emperor's daughter came back unharmed. She enjoyed the ride and it became official for the kids of Japan to travel to he moon and be back all because of the laughs of a dragon. The dragons would then always feel happy and would only laugh above the ground and thus never caused earthquakes.

tALe 29 : tHe CoMb

Once there lived a Japanese scientist named Zuoko. Zuoko was a self made man who had worked for the army and helped in making many secret weapons for his country. Zuoko was so passionate about making secret scientific inventions that in his spare time at home too he stopped at nothing less.

This scientist Zuoko had a daughter. Her name was Kassandra. Zuoko was very fond of Kassandra. He would buy many expensive toys for her to play with and she loved and enjoyed that. One day a bee struck him and he started felling sick. He lay down on his bed and at night passed away suffering extreme pain. But still he left a gift for her daughter. On the wrapped gift paper it was written : "For my crackling daughter - Kassandra." When Kassandra woke up in the morning she realized that her dad was still asleep and after trying to wake him up and he not getting up she immediately called her relatives and a doctor. The doctor pronounced him dead. Kassandra cried a lot seeing her dad pass away. She came near him and sobbed for quite a while. While sobbing she saw that gift wrapped in a gift wrap lying near her dad. On further examining it she saw that it was left for her by her dying father.

After performing the cremation she opened the gift. When she opened it she saw a comb for their cattle in it. She looked a bit confused and did not know what to think of after seeing it. But since it was a gift she decided to use it as it was meant to be, even if it was meant for the cattle.

Actually while course of his scientific evaluations Zuoko had found out that there was an anticipated risk of a tick attack on the cattle and he was trying to make a cure for it. The ticks would be modified ticks sent by their enemy nation to destroy all the food in their country. The ticks would be so powerful that the poison this time would not affect them so something different had to be invented.

As time passed Kassandra continued going to school and continued grooming her cattle with the comb that her father had left her.

Now there was a tick attack and as had been anticipated by Zouko ticks kept on killing cattle and could not be removed by any sort of medicine or poison whatsoever. Kassandra's neighbours were surprised that Kassandra's cattle remained unaffected and not single of her cattle died because of the deadly ticks while the entire nation's cattle was affected and dying.

This news reached the army general who came for an inspection to Kassandra's house. He knew that she was the daughter of Late Zuoko so he asked her some polite questions. While he was asking some questions that would be helpful to the entire country Kassandra took her comb out and started combing the hair of its cattle as this was what she did and liked doing in her free time.

The comb looked quite weird and the general wanted to inspect it. On request Kassandra gave it to the general for a day for inspection.

The general took it to the lab and the scientists started examining it. They found out that comb had built in capacitors and amplifiers with dampening oscillators. The capacitors and amplifiers stored the static energy of the comb when it was used and amplified to release small shock waves killing any ticks. Then the dampening oscillators would produce such a frequency that would stop the flow of blood that if any the ticks had caused to flow from the body of cattle and would also temporarily immunize the cattle's body blood. After studying this they told the general about this. The general was happy that Zuoko before dying had anticipated the attack and had made a cure to defend from it. The scientists were immediately ordered to replicate the comb in thousands and give it to the cattle owners. After quickly replicating the comb it was mass produced and given to the cattle owners. This protected the cattle, their owners and the entire nation from shortage of food, mass hunger and deaths.

Kassandra was forever remembered in the country because of her dad and the gift.

TaLe 30 : tHe mAgiC oF pOrTrAiT

This is a story of a naughty kid. His name was Fred. Fred would do all the mischief in the world and would only stop doing it in front of his grandfather, whom he was afraid of. Why he was afraid of his grandfather was because grand father would scold him in a very penalizing way. Secondly he was the one who bought him the most of gifts including toys and presents that Fred liked. So in order to maintain peace with his desires and family Fred would obey his grandfather. Now it so happened that in a few years Fred's grandfather suffered a serious heart attack and died there and then. Fred was a little upset because who would give him the best presents now. Annoyed and sad, he put up a very rude behaviour that day and got a lot of scoldings but that day he did not mind them at all.

Now the thing that had to happen happened and it could not be undone. So the days after mournings continued and he started going to school but he did not leave his naughty attitude. He actually became so naughty that he had now become a bully in school as days passed. One day the teacher came to know about his rude and bullying behaviour and got very annoyed. She told this to the principal of the school who called up a meeting with his parents. Now his parents were very upset because of what they came to know from the meeting. Previously they used to think that his naughty nature was just a matter of time and that it would go away once he starts growing up. But this was not the case as they came to know from the principal. She told them that Fred would steel candies, chocolates and would force kids to do things that were not reasonably sound.

His parents gave some counselling to him but still he would not behave in school or at home. One day a friend of Fred's grandfather came to visit his long gone friend's grandson and brought him some chocolates. Fred behaved very rudely with his grandfather's friend. He snatched the chocolates from his hands right as he saw them in his hands and ran away without saying thank you or being humble in any way. Fred's grandfather's did not feel nice seeing that and asked his parents that is he same with everybody? Fred's parents sadly said : "yes" confirming his rude and bad behaviour. They also told him that they have been trying to correct their son's behaviour but they can't find a way out. Fred's grandfather's friend said that I have a way out. He said " do you know that Fred was only afraid of his grandfather when he was alive. " They confirmed it by saying " yes ". He then told them that why don't you hang a picture of Fred's grandfather on all the walls of their house. Then he also told that whatever pictures they hang of him those pictures should have the eye balls in the median position of his eyes. Then he explained the reason for that and how it would affect Fred's behaviour. He told them to tell Fred that wherever you go his grandfather is watching through pictures because then he explained that when the picture's eye balls are at median of the eye they appear to be looking at you when you look towards the picture, no matter fro which direction you look it from. He then explained that this would put fear in Fred's heart that grandfather was watching from the other side and could do something bad to him so Fred would hopefully start behaving. His parents tried this out and it worked. Fred would start getting freaked out seeing grandfather's eyes looking at him and thus he started behaving and became good.

tALe 31 : iT's wAr. Oh yEaH!

Long time ago in a very distant planet approximately 5 million light years from the earth's sun there existed a planet called Raphy. On Raphy existed ants, plants and elephants. The unique properties of ants that lived on Raphy was that they inhaled carbon dioxide and exhaled helium which was quite unique and strange. The plants that lived there would inhale helium and exhale carbon dioxide and now coming to the elephants. The elephants inhaled carbon dioxide a but exhaled oxygen. Let's now understand that due to their different habits of inhaling and exhaling gases a unique and a quite effective ecosystem amongst them existed.

But all things always are not perfect. There existed a problem for the ants that lived there. On Raphy, there were lot of plants and trees and the elephants in that world were huge and monster-like. They would come daily to where the ants colonies were and where they lived and would eat the plants there and nearby to the dwelling of the ants. In this process the ants and ant houses would sometimes get squished and thus many ants would die by the blow of their trunks and feet.

This was not tolerated by the ant society So, the ant society called an emergency meeting with the elephants. In the meeting they requested the elephants to not come to their colonies for eating plants. They told the elephants about the places on Raphy where the ants did not live. They requested them to go to those places and eat plants and their food, enjoy there as much as they would like and destroy there as much as they liked. The elephants on that planet were wicked as a fox . They told the ants that they would love to change their eating spots but could not as they were very found of the place and was difficult for them to change their eating spots. They said only if they could be carried to the place where ants were talking about that was away from ants dwellings then they would happily live there and eat only the nearby plants and trees and thus would not destroy ants and their houses .

Now, the ants were less and tiny and thus they could not lift the elephants even if they tried together and no matter how badly they wanted. The wise ants started thinking. One day one of of the wise ants on a tree branch and was out of ideas. So, just to kill time it folded a tiny leaf and tied a knot on it in such a way that it formed a fully enclosed bag. It then tried to blow some air in the bag from its tiny mouth holding its opening together so as it tried to burst it with its mouth's air pressure. Now remember, the air it was blowing or exhaling through its mouth was helium and as soon as it filled the leaf bag, it grew in size and started floating in air and going higher up in it. The ant was surprised seeing that. So out of that idea and anger it decided to blow air in the elephants and blow them away. But how? Then he realized that the ants knew about an ingredient that caused indigestion in elephants and caused it to expand quite a bit ie about 2-5 times their initial size. The ants after being told the idea thought that why don't they pump up so much air the elephants' stomach and blow them away. They wanted to try it out and see if it worked.

So they tried a plan out. At night when all the elephants were sleeping they entered their stomachs through their trunks and put that indigestion causing ingredient which was nothing other than a specially crafted gum by the ants in their stomachs. In matter of few minutes the indigestion occurred in elephants and their stomachs grew in size. As soon as it happened the ants started exhaling helium rapidly by continuing their respiration process.

Due to what was happening the elephants had great pain and further remained passed out by getting unconscious. The ants when realized that the elephants were floating in the air they wasted no time. Some ants came out while some remained inside the elephants (to keep them floating). The ants that had come out took hold of the elephants through their trunks and transferred them to the place where they did not live and could not be hurt. It took them quite so time to do that.

By that time the elephant remained passed out being unconscious. When they woke up they realized the strength of the mighty ants and never dared to enter or destroy their colonies.

tALe 32 : ThE WiT

Long time ago in a far away galaxy there was a planet called Movitony. On Movitony there were two separate land masses or continents with water between them. Both the land mass was forever moving on the planet at a higher rate than the continents on earth. But these land masses never collided because they were of same magnetic field thus there existed a repulsive force between them. These landmasses had a fixed time and a day when they came the closest. That day and time they came so close that if people on that planet acted fast a bridge could be built to join them. Since the land masses were moving so if a bridge was built to join them then they would move together on that planet by becoming due to the linkage by the bridge between the two land masses. So as people on that planet realized this fact. They communicated and tried building a bridge to connect the two land masses at the right day and time and were successful. But to do that the people had used a very strong metal that could not be broken ever. The linkages between the bridge could become loose but the bridge itself was indestructible.

Now, it so happened that generations passed and people of the two land masses did not got well together. The people of the two land masses did not like each other so they kept to themselves and did not cross the bridge for a very long time. Then the disparities turned to huge differences and finally they became sworn enemies.

Due to huge differences the bigger of the two landmasses people became more strong in their militia and wanted to raid the people of the opposite land mass and destroy them. The people of the smaller opposite land mass had never strengthened their armies because they did not knew that they would have to see this day.

Then idea came into their minds. They thought of destroying the bridge to break the physical link between the two landmasses so that they could be saved from the enemy if required. But that could not be easily done. The metal that their ancestors used still was strong and could not be destroyed.

Then the people of the weaker landmass were sent a war notice. According to which they were given 6 months to surrender or be destroyed.

Now the people of weaker landmass got worried and they had to think of a way to stop getting raided by enemy armies. They had to break the bridge anyhow. They knew that the bridge was unbreakable so something else had to be done.

Then the wise men of the weaker landmass devised a material from scratch just like their ancestors would do. The material was an unbreakable rubber. With that rubber they formed huge balloons and at night secretly tied their mouths loosely around the bridge.

There were lots of forests at the side of bridge which had a huge number of trees. So they did a trick. During the night itself they started burning their side of trees and throwing them in the water so as to form lots of steam. This steam started entering the balloons through their loosely opened mouths and started inflating balloons that were tied to the bridge. The balloons became so huge that the bridge although could not be broken but got lifted away and thus the landmasses got free and became as they were before the bridge was built - moving.

Now, the link was broken and the stronger armies of the bigger landmass could not attack or destroy the weaker, all because of the intellect of the people of smaller landmass.

tALe 33 : tHe Not sO AmAziNg CLoUd

Once there lived a scientist and his wife. Both the scientist and his wife were happy but missed the joy of having kid of their own. But after consulting many doctors and much trying the scientist's wife gave birth to a son. They named him - Joy. Both the scientist and his wife were very happy that they had their family complete now.

After much rejoice the family was coming home sitting in a taxi. When they were coming from the hospital, the baby who was sitting in his mom's lap was very much amused by the lightning caused by the cloud. So, the scientist seeing that decided for a gift for Joy.

As soon as they came home the scientist went inside his lab which was in a room in his house and started working in it.

There he worked continuously for 3 days and created an artificial cloud with artificial understanding in it. The cloud could speak and obey. Then, feeling happy and excited he put the cloud in a box and gift wrap wrapped the box. Then he went near his son and gave it to him.

As soon as Joy saw the small box he got more amused and tried to open it. As soon as
opened the box, he saw how the cloud started floating in the air and was always around him.

Now, to understand that since the gift was a cloud it would cause a bit of thunder and some lighting. This was actually one of the job of the cloud which it did without forgetting for some time. This would always cause happiness in Joy who was always excited to be with the cloud.

As time passed Joy and the cloud grew. Joy grew vertically and the cloud grew mostly horizontally with a little bit vertically.

Also as Joy became older in age his dad and mom passed away.

Due to sudden found depression Joy stopped playing with the cloud. The cloud who was artificially intelligent realized that and became sad himself. He too stopped thundering and stopped producing lightning. But the cloud was obedient and liked Joy very much. He would ask Joy from time to time if he liked to play. But "No" was always the answer. The two things living under the same roof were very depressed. Not only depressed, the cloud actually started getting angry and would produce sparks in rage. Once he tried to burn a part of the house.

This drew Joy's attention towards estranged behaviour of his best friend - the cloud. Joy started becoming concerned and tried to calm the cloud down by asking him to do so. He thought it was artificially intelligent cloud and instructing him would turn it better. But, simple instructions could not help. Joy started studying some books about clouds and their behaviours ie he wanted to know how to control them.

So after much studying and getting haunted by books he found a book and it enlightened him.

Then what! He ran to his house immediately and took a small plank of wood and lit it on fire. Then he went near his best friend - the cloud. He told the cloud not to be afraid and stay near him and the fire he lighted up for him. The cloud although scared and angry then, listened to his master and friend. After 5 hours of burning planks of wood the cloud initially felt anger but then it was the happiest thing alive. It shrunk in size and weight and felt much better than before.

Actually the moisture of the cloud was causing him much pain and anger because of getting his body system unwillingly over-loaded with it. The moisture had escaped due to the heat of the fire. It had escaped out of the house as Joy had planned by making arrangements for it. The moment he had lit the fires on the planks he had opened the entire house's windows and doors etc. just to save his friend from moisture which had accumulated in it from years.

The cloud and joy both felt rejuvenated because of each other. Joy was happy and so was the cloud. Both the cloud and his friend Joy lived happily ever after.

tALe 34 : tHe sHoT GuY

He enters the chess board and starts playing by himself just by riding the mechanical chessmen. This game turns into a dangerous match. The chessmen's mechanical mechanism fail's and the fuse in them gets overloaded because he played it for a very long time. This causes the control on chessmen to go haywire because the fuses break overloaded with power. Thus the radio control this guy that was using to control the chessmen goes un-functional. The game goes really killing with the chessman acting crazily malfunctioned. He then could not handle more of craziness and deadliness which became superior in game rather than the game's enjoyment or joy. For his security and safety he quickly uses his reading glasses and refracts and concentrates the sunlight falling on the chess board from the nearby window to a security button which is sensitive to stronger radiations and was also devised as a infrared activated switch when it exceeds certain infra red limits. This causes a latch to be opened. The opened latch releases a mechanical dragon. The dragon is all mechanical with ability of pouring in lots of fire through his mouth. The dragon immediately senses danger for his master - the shot guy and burns down the chessmen with his deadly fire.

This produces lots of burning gases in and around the chessboard. This fire is then collected by the dragon after concentrating it with a mechanical collector device and puts it in a tank that would help in immediate flying of the hot air balloon. (This hot air balloon was built just yesterday for him to take him to his vacation to a nearby country). This country is just 200 miles from his house. He immediately jumps into the basket of the hot air balloon and cuts its ropes that were tied to the ground holding it.

Now his journey begins.

He starts flying amongst the clouds while sitting and controlling his hot air balloon to one of the candy worlds first, which is a town and his first stop for refuelling in 50 miles. He gets some mechanical candy from that town after he lands there. This candy had the capability of running and keeping other candies in control as by not allowing them to have more luring in the mouth of the short guy because then he gets intoxicated with candies and gets a sugar Coma which is not good for his or anybody's health. He can keep himself in control by not thinking of buying them in first place but he can't stop himself from buying them after he see's them. So only way for him to stop himself eating them is keeping the candies he buys in control with the help of the mechanical candy, so that they don't lure him. The mechanical candy runs and uses a mechanical transformation technique that hides the candies by disguising them to look like something else that is of no use to the shot guy but may still be required someday. So the candies stay, are hidden and don't lure the shot guy all because of the mechanical candy.

Then he flew past the chocolate mountains getting a special sucrose from the rivers filled in abundance with it flowing through the mountains that acted as a fuel for his hot air balloon. This fuel did not give burnt smell while burning rather gave different types of magnificent odours that were like the smells of most exotic fragrances that could ever be smelled or inhaled.

Then he descended to the town called the blackhole. There he collected a mechanical black hole. This black hole he used could attract and absorb any type of animal in it by its mechanical ability to sense cold blood and thereby acted as a hunting device for his meal. He had bought this because in his town animals for meal were hard to find.

After that he reached the magical town and country that was waiting for him and for whom he took flight for in his hot air balloon.

Now why he had come here was a secret. He had come there to help the king of that country to bring down a dragon and a witch that had stolen his daughter.

The short guy was a bit unable to understand the scenario that even after having such a gigantic army why could not the king rescue his daughter himself. The king told him the reason. He told him that his army is visible and if either the witch or the giant sees his army they would kill his daughter there and then, even before the army reaches to fight those two.

So he needed somebody like him short and a shot.

He then planned and slyly hiding reached the the cave where the evil witch and the giant dragon were playing card games. He then immediately took out a mechanical rope that he had made in his machine-shop and whispered in it an order of linkage and binding for the cold hearted near him. The rope stretched itself and grew in size. It then split into two and immediately bonded the bodies of witch and the giant dragon with each other in blink of an eye. Then the short guy took out his mechanical wings and ordered them to take the breaths of the giant dragon and witch away. The mechanical wings flapped so fast that they sucked all the breath of the dragon and the witch. This caused sudden death of the two. Then he ordered the mechanical rope to unwind and attach to the mechanical eyes that he had taken out from his pocket. He further told them to get attached to the wings and carefully find the king's daughter and fly her back home comfortably by forming a basket of the mechanical rope to hold the king's daughter in it. The mechanical devices then found the secretly hid daughter of the king and flew her home. She was unconscious and lying on the ground in cave when she was found.

And for him his hot air balloon was waiting for him around the mountain cave which he boarded by a huge jump and then said bye to that country for some time finishing this action adventure story.

Made in the USA
Middletown, DE
21 July 2022